I0784583

Dane Coolidge

Hidden Water
(Western Novel)

OK Publishing 2021

Dane Coolidge

Hidden Water

(Western Novel)

An Exciting Cowboy Adventure Tale Set in Arizona

Published by

Books

- Advanced Digital Solutions & High-Quality book Formatting -

musaicumbooks@okpublishing.info

2021 OK Publishing

ISBN 978-80-272-7591-5

Contents

CHAPTER I
THE MOUSE

After many long, brooding days of sunshine, when the clean-cut mountains gleamed brilliantly against the sky and the grama grass curled slowly on its stem, the rain wind rose up suddenly out of Papaguería and swooped down upon the desolate town of Bender, whirling a cloud of dust before it; and the inhabitants, man and horse, took to cover. New-born clouds, rushing out of the ruck of flying dirt, cast a cold, damp shadow upon the earth and hurried past; white-crested thunder-caps, piling-up above the Four Peaks, swept resolutely down to meet them; and the storm wind, laden with the smell of greasewood and wetted alkali, lashed the gaunt desert bushes mercilessly as it howled across the plain. Striking the town it jumped wickedly against the old Hotel Bender, where most of the male population had taken shelter, buffeting its false front until the glasses tinkled and the bar mirrors swayed dizzily from their moorings. Then with a sudden thunder on the tin roof the flood came down, and Black Tex set up the drinks.

It was a tall cowman just down from the Peaks who ordered the round, and so all-embracing was his good humor that he bid every one in the room drink with him, even a sheepman. Broad-faced and huge, with four months' growth of hair and a thirst of the same duration, he stood at the end of the bar, smiling radiantly, one sun-blackened hand toying with the empty glass.

"Come up, fellers," he said, waving the other in invitation, "and drink to Arizona. With a little more rain and good society she'd be a holy wonder, as the Texas land boomer says down in hell." They came up willingly, cowpunchers and sheepmen, train hands, prospectors, and the saloon bums that Black Tex kept about to blow such ready spenders as he, whenever they came to town. With a practised jolt of the bottle Tex passed down the line, filling each heavy tumbler to the brim; he poured a thin one for himself and beckoned in his roustabout to swell the count —- but still there was an empty glass. There was one man over in the corner who had declined to drink. He sat at a disused card table studiously thumbing over an old magazine, and as he raised his dram the barkeeper glowered at him intolerantly.

"Well," said the big cowboy, reaching for his liquor, "here's how —- and may she rain for a week!" He shoved back his high black sombrero as he spoke, but before he signalled the toast his eye caught the sidelong glance of Black Tex, and he too noticed the little man in the corner.

"What's the matter?" he inquired, leaning over toward Tex and jerking his thumb dubiously at the corner, and as the barkeeper scowled and shrugged his shoulders he set down his glass and stared.

The stranger was a small man, for Arizona, and his delicate hands were almost as white as a woman's; but the lines in his face were graven deep, without effeminacy, and his slender neck was muscled like a wrestler's. In dress he was not unlike the men about him —- Texas boots, a broad sombrero, and a canvas coat to turn the rain, —- but his manner was that of another world, a sombre, scholarly repose such as you would look for in the reference room of the Boston Public Library; and he crouched back in his corner like a shy, retiring mouse. For a moment the cowman regarded him intently, as if seeking for some exculpating infirmity; then, leaving the long line of drinkers to chafe at the delay, he paused to pry into the matter.

"Say, partner," he began, his big mountain voice tamed down to a masterful calm, "won't you come over and have something with us?"

There was a challenge in the words which did not escape the stranger; he glanced up suddenly from his reading and a startled look came into his eyes as he saw the long line of men watching him. They were large clear eyes, almost piercing in their intentness, yet strangely innocent and childlike. For a moment they rested upon the regal form of the big cowboy, no less a man than Jefferson Creede, foreman of the Dos S, and there was in them something of that silent awe and worship which big men love to see, but when they encountered the black looks of the multitude and the leering smile of Black Tex they lit up suddenly with an answering glint of defiance.

"No, thank you," he said, nodding amiably to the cowman, "I don't drink."

An incredulous murmur passed along the line, mingled with sarcastic mutterings, but the cowman did not stir.

"Well, have a cigar, then," he suggested patiently; and the barkeeper, eager to have it over, slapped one down on the bar and raised his glass.

"Thank you just as much," returned the little man politely, "but I don't smoke, either. I shall have to ask you to excuse me."

"Have a glass of milk, then," put in the barkeeper, going off into a guffaw at the familiar jest, but the cowboy shut him up with a look.

"W'y, certainly," he said, nodding civilly to the stranger. "Come on, fellers!" And with a flourish he raised his glass to his lips as if tossing off the liquor at a gulp. Then with another downward flourish he passed the whiskey into a convenient spittoon and drank his chaser pensively, meanwhile shoving a double eagle across the bar. As Black Tex rang it up and counted out the change Creede stuffed it into his pocket, staring absently out the window at the downpour. Then with a muttered word about his horse he strode out into the storm.

Deprived of their best spender, the crowd drifted back to the tables; friendly games of coon-can sprang up; stud poker was resumed; and a crew of railroad men, off duty, looked out at the sluicing waters and idly wondered whether the track would go out —- the usual thing in Arizona. After the first delirium of joy at seeing it rain at all there is an aftermath of misgiving, natural enough in a land where the whole surface of the earth, mountain and desert, has been chopped into ditches by the trailing feet of cattle and sheep, and most of the grass pulled up by the roots. In such a country every gulch becomes a watercourse almost before the dust is laid, the *arroyos* turn to rivers and the rivers to broad floods, drifting with trees and wreckage. But the cattlemen and sheepmen who happened to be in Bender, either to take on hands for the spring round-up or to ship supplies to their shearing camps out on the desert, were not worrying about the railroad. Whether the bridges went out or held, the grass and browse would shoot up like beanstalks in to-morrow's magic sunshine; and even if the Rio Salagua blocked their passage, or the shearers' tents were beaten into the mud, there would still be feed, and feed was everything.

But while the rain was worth a thousand dollars a minute to the country at large, trade languished in the Hotel Bender. In a land where a gentleman cannot take a drink without urging every one within the sound of his voice to join in, the saloon business, while running on an assured basis, is sure to have its dull and idle moments. Having rung up the two dollars and a half which Jefferson Creede paid for his last drink —- the same being equivalent to one day's wages as foreman of the Dos S outfit —- Black Tex, as Mr. Brady of the Bender bar preferred to be called, doused the glasses into a tub, turned them over to his roustabout, and polished the cherrywood moodily. Then he drew his eyebrows down and scowled at the little man in the corner.

In his professional career he had encountered a great many men who did not drink, but most of them smoked, and the others would at least take a cigar home to their friends. But here was a man who refused to come in on a treat at all, and a poor, miserable excuse for a man he was, too, without a word for any one. Mr. Brady's reflections on the perversity of tenderfeet were cut short by a cold blast of air. The door swung open, letting in a smell of wet greasewood, and an old man, his hat dripping, stumbled in and stood swaying against the bar. His aged sombrero, blacksmithed along the ridge with copper rivets, was set far back on a head of long gray hair which hung in heavy strings down his back, like an Indian's; his beard, equally long and tangled, spread out like a chest protector across his greasy shirt, and his fiery eyes roved furtively about the room as he motioned for a drink. Black Tex set out the bottle negligently and stood waiting.

"Is that all?" he inquired pointedly, as the old man slopped out a drink.

"Well, have one yourself," returned the old-timer grudgingly. Then, realizing his breach of etiquette, he suddenly straightened up and included the entire barroom in a comprehensive sweep of the hand.

"Come up hyar, all of yoush," he said drunkenly. "Hev a drink —- everybody —- no, every-body —- come up hyar, I say!" And the graceless saloon bums dropped their cards and came trooping up together. A few of the more self-respecting men slipped quietly out into the card rooms; but the studious stranger, disdaining such puny subterfuges, remained in his place, as impassive and detached as ever.

"Hey, young man," exclaimed the old-timer jauntily, "step up hyar and nominate yer pizen!" He closed his invitation with an imperative gesture, but the young man did not obey.

"No, thank you, Uncle," he replied soberly, "I don't drink."

"Well, hev a cigar, then," returned the old man, finishing out the formula of Western hos-pitality, and once more Black Tex glowered down upon this guest who was always "knocking a shingle off his sign."

"Aw, cut it out, Bill," he sneered, "that young feller don't drink ner smoke, neither one —- and he wouldn't have no truck with you, nohow!"

They drank, and the stranger dropped back into his reading unperturbed. Once more Black Tex scrubbed the bar and scowled at him; then, tapping peremptorily on the board with a whiskey glass, he gave way to his just resentment.

"Hey, young feller," he said, jerking his hand arbitrarily, "come over here. Come over here, I said —- I want to talk with you!"

For a moment the man in the corner looked up in well-bred surprise; then without attempt-ing to argue the point he arose and made his way to the bar.

"What's the matter with you, anyway?" demanded Brady roughly. "Are you too good to drink with the likes of us?"

The stranger lowered his eyes before the domineering gaze of his inquisitor and shifted his feet uneasily.

"I don't drink with anybody," he said at last. "And if you had any other waiting-room in your hotel," he added, "I'd keep away from your barroom altogether. As it is, maybe you wouldn't mind leaving me alone."

At this retort, reflecting as it did upon the management, Black Tex began to breathe heavily and sway upon his feet.

"I asked you," he roared, thumping his fist upon the bar and opening up his eyes, "whether you are too good to drink with the likes of us —- me, f'r instance —- and I want to git an answer!"

He leaned far out over the bar as if listening for the first word before he hit him, but the stranger did not reply immediately. Instead, with simple-minded directness he seemed to be studying on the matter. The broad grin of the card players fell to a wondering stare and every man leaned forward when, raising his sombre eyes from the floor, the little man spoke.

"Why, yes," he said quietly, "I think I am."

"Yes, *what?*" yelled the barkeeper, astounded. "You think you're what?"

"Now, say," protested the younger man. Then, apparently recognizing the uselessness of any further evasion, he met the issue squarely.

"Well, since you crowd me to it," he cried, flaring up, "I *am* too good! I'm too good a man to drink when I don't want to drink —- I'm too good to accept treats when I don't stand treat! And more than that," he added slowly and impressively, "I'm too good to help blow that old man, or any other man, for his money!"

He rose to his utmost height as he spoke, turning to meet the glance of every man in the room, and as he faced them, panting, his deep eyes glowed with a passion of conviction.

"If that is too good for this town," he said, "I'll get out of it, but I won't drink on treats to please anybody."

The gaze of the entire assembly followed him curiously as he went back to his corner, and Black Tex was so taken aback by this unexpected effrontery on the part of his guest that he made no reply whatever. Then, perceiving that his business methods had been questioned, he drew himself up and frowned darkly.

"Hoity-toity!" he sniffed with exaggerated concern. "Who th' hell is this, now? One of them little white-ribbon boys, fresh from the East, I bet ye, travellin' for the W. P. S. Q. T. H'm-m —- tech me not —- oh deah!" He hiked up his shoulders, twisted his head to a pose, and shrilled his final sarcasms in the tones of a finicky old lady; but the stranger stuck resolutely to his reading, whereupon the black barkeeper went sullen and took a drink by himself.

Like many a good mixer, Mr. Brady of the Hotel Bender was often too good a patron of his own bar, and at such times he developed a mean streak, with symptoms of homicidal mania, which so far had kept the town marshal guessing. Under these circumstances, and with the rumor of a killing at Fort Worth to his credit, Black Tex was accustomed to being humored in his moods, and it went hard with him to be called down in the middle of a spectacular play, and by a rank stranger, at that. The chair-warmers of the Hotel Bender bar therefore discreetly ignored the unexpected rebuke of their chief and proceeded noisily with their games, but the old man who had paid for the drinks was no such time-server. After tucking what was left of his money back into his overalls he balanced against the bar railing for a while and then steered straight for the dark corner.

"Young feller," he said, leaning heavily upon the table where the stranger was reading, "I'm old Bill Johnson, of Hell's Hip Pocket, and I wan'er shake hands with you!"

The young man looked up quickly and the card players stopped as suddenly in their play, for Old Man Johnson was a fighter in his cups. But at last the stranger showed signs of friendliness. As the old man finished speaking he rose with the decorum of the drawing-room and extended his white hand cordially.

"I'm very glad to meet you, Mr. Johnson," he said. "Won't you sit down?"

"No," protested the old man, "I do' wanner sit down —- I wanner ask you a question." He reeled, and balanced himself against a chair. "I wanner ask you," he continued, with drunken gravity, "on the squar', now, did you ever drink?"

"Why, yes, Uncle," replied the younger man, smiling at the question, "I used to take a friendly glass, once in a while —- but I don't drink now." He added the last with a finality not to be mistaken, but Mr. Johnson of Hell's Hip Pocket was not there to urge him on.

"No, no," he protested. "You're mistaken, Mister —- er —- Mister —- "

"Hardy," put in the little man.

"Ah yes —- Hardy, eh? And a dam' good name, too. I served under a captain by that name at old Fort Grant, thirty years ago. Waal, Hardy, I like y'r face —- you look honest —- but I wanner ask you 'nuther question —- why don't you drink now, then?"

Hardy laughed indulgently, and his eyes lighted up with good humor, as if entertaining drunken men was his ordinary diversion.

"Well, I'll tell you, Mr. Johnson," he said. "If I should drink whiskey the way you folks down here do, I'd get drunk."

"W'y sure," admitted Old Man Johnson, sinking shamelessly into a chair. "I'm drunk now. But what's the difference?"

Noting the black glances of the barkeeper, Hardy sat down beside him and pitched the conversation in a lower key.

"It may be all right for you, Mr. Johnson," he continued confidentially, "and of course that's none of my business; but if I should get drunk in this town, I'd either get into a fight and get licked, or I'd wake up the next morning broke, and nothing to show for it but a sore head."

"That's me!" exclaimed Old Man Johnson, slamming his battered hat on the table, "that's me, Boy, down to the ground! I came down hyar to buy grub f'r my ranch up in Hell's Hip Pocket, but look at me now, drunk as a sheep-herder, and only six dollars to my name." He shook his shaggy head and fell to muttering gloomily, while Hardy reverted peacefully to his magazine.

After a long pause the old man raised his face from his arms and regarded the young man searchingly.

"Say," he said, "you never told me why you refused to drink with me a while ago."

"Well, I'll tell you," answered Hardy, honestly, "and I'm sure you'll understand how it is with me. I never expect to take another drink as long as I live in this country —- not unless I get snake-bit. One drink of this Arizona whiskey will make me foolish, and two will make me drunk, I'm that light-headed. Now, if I had taken a drink with you a minute ago I'd be considered a cheap sport if I didn't treat back, wouldn't I? And then I'd be drunk. Yes, that's a fact. So I have to cut it out altogether. I like you just as well, you understand, and all these other gentlemen, but I just naturally can't do it."

"Oh, hell," protested the old man, "that's all right. Don't apologize, Boy, whatever you do. D'yer know what I came over hyar fer?" he asked suddenly reaching out a crabbed hand. "Well, I'll tell ye. I've be'n lookin' f'r years f'r a white man that I c'd swear off to. Not one of these pink-gilled preachers but a man that would shake hands with me on the squar' and hold me to it. Now, Boy, I like you —- will you shake hands on that?"

"Sure," responded the young man soberly. "But I tell you, Uncle," he added deprecatingly, "I just came into town to-day and I'm likely to go out again to-morrow. Don't you think you could kind of look after yourself while I'm gone? I've seen a lot of this swearing-off business already, and it don't seem to amount to much anyhow unless the fellow that swears off is willing to do all the hard work himself."

There was still a suggestion of banter in his words, but the old man was too serious to notice it.

"Never mind, boy," he said solemnly, "I can do all the work, but I jist had to have an honest man to swear off to."

He rose heavily to his feet, adjusted his copper-riveted hat laboriously, and drifted slowly out the door. And with another spender gone the Hotel Bender lapsed into a sleepy quietude. The rain hammered fitfully on the roof; the card players droned out their bids and bets; and Black Tex, mechanically polishing his bar, alternated successive jolts of whiskey with ill-favored glances into the retired corner where Mr. Hardy, supposedly of the W. P. S. Q. T., was studiously perusing a straw-colored Eastern magazine. Then, as if to lighten the gloom, the sun flashed out suddenly, and before the shadow of the scudding clouds had dimmed its glory a shrill whistle from down the track announced the belated approach of the west-bound train. Immediately the chairs began to scrape; the stud-poker players cut for the stakes and quit; coon-can was called off, and by the time Number Nine slowed down for the station the entire floating population of Bender was lined up to see her come in.

Rising head and shoulders above the crowd and well in front stood Jefferson Creede, the foreman of the Dos S; and as a portly gentleman in an unseasonable linen duster dropped off the Pullman he advanced, waving his hand largely.

"Hullo, Judge!" he exclaimed, grinning jovially. "I was afraid you'd bogged down into a washout somewhere!"

"Not at all, Jeff, not at all," responded the old gentleman, shaking hands warmly. "Say, this is great, isn't it?" He turned his genial smile upon the clouds and the flooded streets for a moment and then hurried over toward the hotel.

"Well, how are things going up on the range?" he inquired, plunging headlong into business and talking without a stop. "Nicely, nicely, I don't doubt. I tell you, Mr. Creede, that ranch has marvellous possibilities —- marvellous! All it needs is a little patience, a little diplomacy, you understand —- *and holding on*, until we can pass this forestry legislation. Yes, sir, while the present situation may seem a little strained —- and I don't doubt you are having a hard time —- at the same time, if we can only get along with these sheepmen —- appeal to their better nature, you understand —- until we get some protection at law, I am convinced that we can succeed yet. I want to have a long talk with you on this subject, Jeff —- man to man, you understand, and between friends —- but I hope you will reconsider your resolution to resign, because that would just about finish us off. It isn't a matter of money, is it, Jefferson? For while, of course, we are not making a fortune —- "

He paused and glanced up at his foreman's face, which was growing more sullen every minute with restrained impatience.

"Well, speak out, Jeff," he said resignedly. "What is it?"

"You know dam' well what it is," burst out the tall cowboy petulantly. "It's them sheepmen. And I want to tell you right now that no money can hire me to run that ranch another year, not if I've got to smile and be nice to those sons of —- well, you know what kind of sons I mean —- that dog-faced Jasper Swope, for instance."

He spat vehemently at the mention of the name and led the way to a card room in the rear of the barroom.

"Of course I'll work your cattle for you," he conceded, as he entered the booth, "but if you want them sheepmen handled diplomatically you'd better send up a diplomat. I'm that wore out I can't talk to 'em except over the top of a six-shooter."

The deprecating protestations of the judge were drowned by the scuffle of feet as the hangers-on and guests of the hotel tramped in, and in the round of drinks that followed his presence was half forgotten. Not being a drinking man himself, and therefore not given to the generous practice of treating, the arrival of Judge Ware, lately retired from the bench and now absentee owner of the Dos S Ranch, did not create much of a furore in Bender. All Black Tex and the bunch knew was that he was holding a conference with Jefferson Creede, and that if Jeff was pleased with the outcome of the interview he would treat, but if not he would probably retire to the corral and watch his horse eat hay, openly declaring that Bender was the most God-forsaken hell-hole north of the Mexican line —- for Creede was a man of moods.

In the lull which followed the first treat, the ingratiating drummer who had set up the drinks, charging the same to his expense account, leaned against the bar and attempted to engage the barkeeper in conversation, asking leading questions about business in general and Mr. Einstein of the New York Store in particular; but Black Tex, in spite of his position, was uncommunicative. Immediately after the arrival of the train the little man who had called him down had returned to the barroom and immersed himself in those wearisome magazines which a lunger had left about the place, and, far from being impressed with his sinister expression, had ignored his unfriendly glances entirely. More than that, he had deserted his dark corner and seated himself on a bench by the window from which he now looked out upon the storm with a brooding preoccupation as sincere as it was maddening. His large deer eyes were fixed upon the distance, and his manner was that of a man who studies deeply upon some abstruse problem; of a man with a past, perhaps, such as often came to those parts, crossed in love, or hiding out from his folks.

Black Tex dismissed the drummer with an impatient gesture and was pondering solemnly upon his grievances when a big, square-jowled cat rushed out from behind the bar and set up a hoarse, raucous mewing.

"Ah, shet up!" growled Brady, throwing him away with his foot; but as the cat's demands became more and more insistent the barkeeper was at last constrained to take some notice.

"What's bitin' you?" he demanded, peering into the semi-darkness behind the bar; and as the cat, thus encouraged, plunged recklessly in among a lot of empty bottles, he promptly threw him out and fished up a mouse trap, from the cage of which a slender tail was wriggling frantically.

"Aha!" he exclaimed, advancing triumphantly into the middle of the floor. "Look, boys, here's where we have some fun with Tom!" And as the card players turned down their hands to watch the sport, the old cat, scenting his prey, rose up on his hind legs and clutched at the cage, yelling.

Grabbing him roughly by the scruff of the neck Black Tex suddenly threw him away and opened the trap, but the frightened mouse, unaware of his opportunity, remained huddled up in the corner.

"Come out of that," grunted the barkeeper, shaking the cage while with his free hand he grappled the cat, and before he could let go his hold the mouse was halfway across the room, heading for the bench where Hardy sat.

"Ketch 'im!" roared Brady, hurling the eager cat after it, and just as the mouse was darting down a hole Tom pinned it to the floor with his claws.

"What'd I tell ye?" cried the barkeeper, swaggering. "That cat will ketch 'em every time. Look at that now, will you?"

With dainty paws arched playfully, the cat pitched the mouse into the air and sprang upon it like lightning as it darted away. Then mumbling it with a nicely calculated bite, he bore it to the middle of the floor and laid it down, uninjured.

"Ain't he hell, though?" inquired Tex, rolling his eyes upon the spectators. The cat reached out cautiously and stirred it up with his paw; and once more, as his victim dashed for its hole, he caught it in full flight. But now the little mouse, its hair all wet and rumpled, crouched dumbly between the feet of its captor and would not run. Again and again the cat stirred it up, sniffing suspiciously to make sure it was not dead; then in a last effort to tempt it he deliberately lay over on his back and rolled, purring and closing his eyes luxuriously, until, despite its hurts, the mouse once more took to flight. Apparently unheeding, the cat lay inert, following its wobbly course with half-shut eyes —- then, lithe as a panther, he leaped up and took after it. There was a rush and a scramble against the wall, but just as he struck out his barbed claw a hand closed over the mouse and the little man on the bench whisked it dexterously away.

Instantly the black cat leaped into the air, clamoring for his prey, and with a roar like a mountain bull Black Tex rushed out to intercede.

"Put down that mouse, you freak!" he bellowed, charging across the room. "Put 'im down, I say, or I'll break you in two!" He launched his heavy fist as he spoke, but the little man ducked it neatly and, stepping behind a table, stood at bay, still holding the mouse.

"Put 'im *down*, I tell you!" shouted the barkeeper, panting with vexation. "What —- you won't, eh? Well, I'll learn you!" And with a wicked oath he drew his revolver and levelled it across the table.

"Put —- down —- that —- mouse!" he said slowly and distinctly, but Hardy only shook his head. Every man in the room held his breath for the report; the poker players behind fell over tables and chairs to get out of range; and still they stood there, the barkeeper purple, the little man very pale, glaring at one another along the top of the barrel. In the hollow of his hand Hardy held the mouse, which tottered drunkenly; while the cat, still clamoring for his prize, raced about under the table, bewildered.

"Hurry up, now," said the barkeeper warningly, "I'll give you five. One —- come on, now —- two —- "

At the first count the old defiance leaped back into Hardy's eyes and he held the mouse to his bosom as a mother might shield her child; at the second he glanced down at it, a poor crushed thing trembling as with an ague from its wounds; then, smoothing it gently with his hand, he pinched its life out suddenly and dropped it on the floor.

Instantly the cat pounced upon it, nosing the body eagerly, and Black Tex burst into a storm of oaths.

"Well, dam' your heart," he yelled, raising his pistol in the air as if about to throw the muzzle against his breast and fire. "What —- in —- hell —- do you mean?"

Baffled and evaded in every play the evil-eyed barkeeper suddenly sensed a conspiracy to show him up, and instantly the realization of his humiliation made him dangerous.

"Perhaps you figure on makin' a monkey out of me!" he suggested, hissing snakelike through his teeth; but Hardy made no answer whatever.

"Well, *say* something, can't you?" snapped the badman, his overwrought nerves jangled by the delay. "What d'ye mean by interferin' with my cat?"

For a minute the stranger regarded him intently, his sad, far-seeing eyes absolutely devoid of evil intent, yet baffling in their inscrutable reserve —- then he closed his lips again resolutely, as if denying expression to some secret that lay close to his heart, turning it with undue vehemence to the cause of those who suffer and cannot escape.

"Well, f'r Gawd's sake," exclaimed Black Tex at last, lowering his gun in a pet, "don't I git *no* satisfaction —- what's your *i*-dee?"

"There's too much of this cat-and-mouse business going on," answered the little man quietly, "and I don't like it."

"Oh, you don't, eh?" echoed the barkeeper sarcastically; "well, excuse *me*! I didn't know that." And with a bow of exaggerated politeness he retired to his place.

"The drinks are on the house," he announced, jauntily strewing the glasses along the bar. "Won't drink, eh? All right. But lemme tell you, pardner," he added, wagging his head impressively, "you're goin' to git hurt some day."

CHAPTER II
THE MAN FROM CHERRYCOW

After lashing the desert to a frazzle and finding the leaks in the Hotel Bender, the wind from Papaguería went howling out over the mesa, still big with rain for the Four Peaks country, and the sun came out gloriously from behind the clouds. Already the thirsty sands had sucked up the muddy pools of water, and the board walk which extended the length of the street, connecting saloon with saloon and ending with the New York Store, smoked with the steam of drying. Along the edge of the walk, drying out their boots in the sun, the casual residents of the town —- many of them held up there by the storm —- sat in pairs and groups, talking or smoking in friendly silence. A little apart from the rest, for such as he are a long time making friends in Arizona, Rufus Hardy sat leaning against a post, gazing gloomily out across the desert. For a quiet, retiring young man, interested in good literature and bearing malice toward no one, his day in the Bender barroom had been eventful out of all proportion to his deserts and wishes, and he was deep in somber meditation when the door opened and Judge Ware stepped out into the sunshine.

In outward appearance the judge looked more like a large fresh-faced boy in glasses than one of San Francisco's eminent jurists, and the similarity was enhanced by the troubled and deprecating glances with which he regarded his foreman, who towered above him like a mentor. There was a momentary conference between them at the doorway, and then, as Creede stumped away down the board walk, the judge turned and reluctantly approached Hardy.

"I beg your pardon, sir," he began, as the young man in some confusion rose to meet him, "but I should like a few words with you, on a matter of business. I am Mr. Ware, the owner of the Dos S Ranch —- perhaps you may have heard of it —- over in the Four Peaks country. Well —- I hardly know how to begin —- but my foreman, Mr. Creede, was highly impressed with your conduct a short time ago in the —- er —- affray with the barkeeper. I —- er —- really know very little as to the rights of the matter, but you showed a high degree of moral courage, I'm sure. Would you mind telling me what your business is in these parts, Mr. —- er —- "

"Hardy," supplied the young man quietly, "Rufus Hardy. I am —- "

"Er —- *what?*" exclaimed the judge, hastily focussing his glasses. "Hardy —- Hardy —- where have I heard that name before?"

"I suppose from your daughter, Miss Lucy," replied the young man, smiling at his confusion. "Unless," he added hastily, "she has forgotten about me."

"Why, Rufus Hardy!" exclaimed the judge, reaching out his hand. "Why, bless my heart —- to be sure. Why, where have you been for this last year and more? I am sure your father has been quite worried about you."

"Oh, I hope not," answered Hardy, shifting his gaze. "I guess he knows I can take care of myself by this time —- if I do write poetry," he added, with a shade of bitterness.

"Well, well," said the judge, diplomatically changing the subject, "Lucy will be glad to hear of you, at any rate. I believe she —- er —- wrote you once, some time ago, at your Berkeley address, and the letter was returned as uncalled for."

He gazed over the rims of his glasses inquiringly, and with a suggestion of asperity, but the young man was unabashed.

"I hope you will tell Miss Lucy," he said deferentially, "that on account of my unsettled life I have not ordered my mail forwarded for some time." He paused and for the moment seemed to be considering some further explanation; then his manner changed abruptly.

"I believe you mentioned a matter of business," he remarked bluffly, and the judge came back to earth with a start. His mind had wandered back a year or more to the mysterious disappearance of this same self-contained young man from his father's house, not three blocks from his own comfortable home. There had been a servant's rumor that he had sent back a letter or two postmarked "Bowie, Arizona" —- but old Colonel Hardy had said never a word.

"Er — yes," he assented absently, "but — well, I declare," he exclaimed helplessly, "I've quite forgotten what it was about."

"Won't you sit down, then?" suggested Hardy, indicating the edge of the board walk with a courtly sweep of the hand. "This rain will make good feed for you up around the Four Peaks — I believe it was of your ranch there that you wished to speak."

Judge Ware settled down against a convenient post and caught his breath, meanwhile regarding his companion curiously.

"Yes, that's it," he said. "I wanted to talk with you about my ranch, but I swear I'll have to wait till Creede comes back, now."

"Very well," answered Hardy easily; "we can talk about home, then. How is Miss Lucy succeeding with her art — is she still working at the Institute?"

"Yes, indeed!" exclaimed the judge, quite mollified by the inquiry. "Indeed she is, and doing as well as any of them. She had a landscape hung at the last exhibit, that was very highly praised, even by Mathers, and you know how hard he is to please. Tupper Browne won the prize, but I think Lucy's was twice the picture — kind of soft and sunshiny, you know — it made you think of home, just to look at it."

"Well, I'm glad to hear that," said Hardy, looking up the ragged street a little wistfully. "I kind of lose track of things down here, knocking around from place to place." He seated himself wearily on the edge of the sidewalk and drummed with his sinewy white hands against a boot leg. "But it's a great life, sure," he observed, half to himself. "And by the way, Mr. Ware," he continued, "if it's all the same to you I wish you wouldn't say anything to your foreman about my past life. Not that there is anything disgraceful about it, but there isn't much demand for college graduates in this country, you know, and I might want to strike him for a job."

Judge Ware nodded, a little distantly; he did not approve of this careless young man in all his moods. For a man of good family he was hardly presentable, for one thing, and he spoke at times like an ordinary working man. So he awaited the lumbering approach of his foreman in sulky silence, resolved to leave the matter entirely in his hands.

Jefferson Creede bore down upon them slowly, sizing up the situation as he came, or trying to, for everything seemed to be at a standstill.

"Well?" he remarked, looking inquiringly from the judge to Hardy. "How about it?"

There was something big and dominating about him as he loomed above them, and the judge's schoolboy state of mind instantly returned.

"I — I really haven't done anything about the matter, Jefferson," he stammered apologetically. "Perhaps you will explain our circumstances to Mr. Hardy here, so that we can discuss the matter intelligently." He looked away as he spoke, and the tall foreman grunted audibly.

"Well," he drawled, "they ain't much to explain. The sheepmen have been gittin' so free up on our range that I've had a little trouble with 'em — and if I was the boss they'd be more trouble, you can bet your life on that. But the judge here seems to think we can kinder suck the hind teat and baby things along until they git that Forest Reserve act through, and make our winnin' later. He wants to make friends with these sheepmen and git 'em to kinder go around a little and give us half a chanst. Well, maybe it can be done — but not by me. So I told him either to get a superintendent to handle the sheep end of it or rustle up a new foreman, because I see red every time I hear a sheep-blat.

"Then come the question," continued the cowman, throwing out his broad hand as if indicating the kernel of the matter, "of *gittin'* such a man, and while we was talkin' it over you called old Tex down so good and proper that there wasn't any doubt in *my* mind — providin' you want the job, of course."

He paused and fixed his compelling eyes upon Hardy with such a mixture of admiration and good humor that the young man was won over at once, although he made no outward sign. It was Judge Ware who was to pass upon the matter finally, and he waited deferentially for him to speak.

"Well —- er —- Jefferson," began the judge a little weakly, "do you think that Mr. Hardy possesses the other qualities which would be called for in such a man?"

"W'y, sure," responded Creede, waving the matter aside impatiently. "Go ahead and hire him before he changes his mind."

"Very well then, Mr. Hardy," said the judge resignedly, "the first requisite in such a man is that he shall please Mr. Creede. And since he commends you so warmly I hope that you will accept the position. Let me see —- um —- would seventy-five dollars a month seem a reasonable figure? Well, call it seventy-five, then —- that's what I pay Mr. Creede, and I want you to be upon an equality in such matters.

"Now as to your duties. Jefferson will have charge of the cattle, as usual; and I want you, Mr. Hardy, to devote your time and attention to this matter of the sheep. Our ranch house at Hidden Water lies almost directly across the river from one of the principal sheep crossings, and a little hospitality shown to the shepherds in passing might be like bread cast upon the waters which comes back an hundred fold after many days. We cannot hope to get rid of them entirely, but if the sheep owners would kindly respect our rights to the upper range, which Mr. Creede will point out to you, I am sure we should take it very kindly. Now that is your whole problem, Rufus, and I leave the details entirely in your hands. But whatever you do, be friendly and see if you can't appeal to their better nature."

He delivered these last instructions seriously and they were so taken by Hardy, but Creede laughed silently, showing all his white teeth, yet without attracting the unfavorable attention of the judge, who was a little purblind. Then there was a brief discussion of details, an introduction to Mr. Einstein of the New York Store, where Hardy was given *carte blanche* for supplies, and Judge Ware swung up on the west-bound limited and went flying away toward home, leaving his neighbor's son —- now his own superintendent and sheep expert —- standing composedly upon the platform.

"Well," remarked Creede, smiling genially as he turned back to the hotel, "the Old Man's all right, eh, if he does have fits! He's good-hearted —- and that goes a long ways in this country —- but actually, I believe he knows less about the cattle business than any man in Arizona. He can't tell a steer from a stag —- honest! And I can lose him a half-mile from camp any day."

The tall cattleman clumped along in silence for a while, smiling over some untold weakness of his boss —- then he looked down upon Hardy and chuckled to himself.

"I'm glad you're going to be along this trip," he said confidentially. "Of course I'm lonely as a lost dog out there, but that ain't it; the fact is, I need somebody to watch me. W'y, boy, I could beat the old judge out of a thousand dollars' worth of cattle and he'd never know it in a lifetime. Did ye ever live all alone out on a ranch for a month or so? Well, you know how lawless and pisen-mean a man can git, then, associatin' with himself. I'd've had the old man robbed forty times over if he wasn't such a good-hearted old boy, but between fightin' sheepmen and keepin' tab on a passel of brand experts up on the Tonto I'm gittin' so ornery I don't dare trust myself. Have a smoke? Oh, I forgot —- "

He laughed awkwardly and rolled a cigarette.

"Got a match?" he demanded austerely. "Um, much obliged —- be kinder handy to have you along now." He knit his brows fiercely as he fired up, regarding Hardy with a furtive grin.

"Say," he said abruptly, "I've got to make friends with you some way. You *eat*, don't you? All right then, you come along with me over to the Chink's. I'm going to treat you to somethin', if it's only ham 'n' eggs."

They dined largely at Charley's and then drifted out to the feed corral. Creede threw down some hay to a ponderous iron-scarred roan, more like a war horse than a cow pony, and when he came back he found Hardy doing as much for a clean-limbed sorrel, over by the gate.

"Yourn?" he inquired, surveying it with the keen concentrated gaze which stamps every point on a cowboy's memory for life.

"Sure," returned Hardy, patting his pony carefully upon the shoulder.

"Kinder high-headed, ain't he?" ventured Creede, as the sorrel rolled his eyes and snorted.

"That's right," assented Hardy, "he's only been broke about a month. I got him over in the Sulphur Springs Valley."

"I knowed it," said the cowboy sagely, "one of them wire-grass horses —- an' I bet he can travel, too. Did you ride him all the way here?"

"Clean from the Chiricahuas," replied the young man, and Jefferson Creede looked up, startled.

"What did you say you was doin' over there?" he inquired slowly, and Hardy smiled quietly as he answered:

"Riding for the Cherrycow outfit."

"The hell you say!" exclaimed Creede explosively, and for a long time he stood silent, smoking as if in deep meditation.

"Well," he said at last, "I might as well say it —- I took you for a tenderfoot."

CHAPTER III
THE TRAIL OF THE SHEEP

The morning dawned as clear on Bender as if there had never been storm nor clouds, and the waxy green heads of the greasewood, dotting the level plain with the regularity of a vineyard, sparkled with a thousand dewdrops. Ecstatic meadow larks, undismayed by the utter lack of meadows, sang love songs from the tops of the telegraph poles; and the little Mexican ground doves that always go in pairs tracked amiably about together in the wet litter of the corral, picking up the grain which the storm had laid bare. Before the early sun had cleared the top of the eastern mountains Jefferson Creede and Hardy had risen and fed their horses well, and while the air was yet chill they loaded their blankets and supplies upon the ranch wagon, driven by a shivering Mexican, and went out to saddle up.

Since his confession of the evening before Creede had put aside his air of friendly patronage and, lacking another pose, had taken to smoking in silence; for there is many a boastful cowboy in Arizona who has done his riding for the Cherrycow outfit on the chuck wagon, swamping for the cook. At breakfast he jollied the Chinaman into giving him two orders of everything, from coffee to hot cakes, paid for the same at the end, and rose up like a giant refreshed —- but beneath this jovial exterior he masked a divided mind. Although he had come down handsomely, he still had his reservations about the white-handed little man from Cherrycow, and when they entered the corral he saddled his iron-scarred charger by feeling, gazing craftily over his back to see how Hardy would show up in action.

Now, first the little man took a rope, and shaking out the loop dropped it carelessly against his horse's fore-feet —- and that looked well, for the sorrel stood stiffly in his tracks, as if he had been anchored. Then the man from Cherrycow picked up his bridle, rubbed something on the bit, and offered it to the horse, who graciously bowed his head to receive it. This was a new one on Creede and in the excitement of the moment he inadvertently cinched his roan up two holes too tight and got nipped for it, for old Bat Wings had a mind of his own in such matters, and the cold air made him ugly.

"Here, quit that," muttered the cowboy, striking back at him; but when he looked up, the sorrel had already taken his bit, and while he was champing on it Hardy had slipped the headstall over his ears. There was a broad leather blind on the hacamore, which was of the best plaited rawhide with a horsehair tie rope, but the little man did not take advantage of it to subdue his mount. Instead he reached down for his gaudy Navajo saddle blanket, offered it to the sorrel to smell, and then slid it gently upon his back. But when he stooped for his saddle the high-headed horse rebelled. With ears pricked suspiciously forward and eyes protruding he glared at the clattering thing in horror, snorting deep at every breath. But, though he was free-footed, by some obsession of the mind, cunningly inculcated in his breaking, the sorrel pony was afraid to move.

As the saddle was drawn toward him and he saw that he could not escape its hateful embrace he leaned slowly back upon his haunches, grunting as if his fore-feet, wreathed in the loose rope, were stuck in some terrible quicksands from which he tried in vain to extricate them; but with a low murmur of indifferent words his master moved the saddle resolutely toward him, the stirrups carefully snapped up over the horn, and ignoring his loud snorts and frenzied shakings of the head laid it surely down upon his back. This done, he suddenly spoke sharply to him, and with a final groan the beautiful creature rose up and consented to his fate.

Hardy worked quickly now, tightening the cinch, lowering the stirrups, and gathering up the reins. He picked up the rope, coiled it deftly and tied it to the saddle —- and now, relieved of the idea that he was noosed, the pony began to lift his feet and prance, softly, like a swift runner on the mark. At these signs of an early break Creede mounted hurriedly and edged in, to be ready in case the sorrel, like most half-broken broncos, tried to scrape his rider off against the fence; but Hardy needed no wrangler to shunt him out the gate. Standing by his shoulder and facing the rear he patted the sorrel's neck with the hand that held the reins, while with his right hand he twisted the heavy stirrup toward him stealthily, raising his boot to meet it. Then like a flash he clapped in his foot and, catching the horn as his fiery pony shot forward, he snapped up into the saddle like a jumping jack and went flying out the gate.

"Well, the son of a gun!" muttered Creede, as he thundered down the trail after him. "Durned if he can't ride!"

There are men in every cow camp who can rope and shoot, but the man who can ride a wild horse can hold up his head with the best of them. No matter what his race or station if he will crawl a "snake" and stay with him there is always room on the wagon for his blankets; his fame will spread quickly from camp to camp, and the boss will offer to raise him when he shows up for his time. Jefferson Creede's face was all aglow when he finally rode up beside Hardy; he grinned triumphantly upon horse and man as if they had won money for him in a race; and Hardy, roused at last from his reserve, laughed back out of pure joy in his possessions.

"How's that for a horse?" he cried, raising his voice above the thud of hoofs. "I have to turn him loose at first —- 'fraid he'll learn to pitch if I hold him in —- he's never bucked with me yet!"

"You bet —- he's a snake!" yelled Creede, hammering along on his broad-chested roan. "Where'd you git 'im?"

"Tom Fulton's ranch," responded Hardy, reining his horse in and patting him on the neck. "Turned in three months' pay and broke him myself, to boot. I'll let you try him some day, when he's gentled."

"Well, if I wasn't so big 'n' heavy I'd take you up on that," said Creede, "but I'm just as much obliged, all the same. I don't claim to be no bronco-buster now, but I used to ride some myself when I was a kid. But say, the old judge has got some good horses runnin' on the upper range, —- if you want to keep your hand in, —- thirty or forty head of 'em, and wild as hawks. There's some sure-enough wild horses too, over on the Peaks, that belong to any man that can git his rope onto 'em —- how would that strike you? We've been tryin' for years to catch the black stallion that leads 'em."

Try as he would to minimize this exaggerated estimate of his prowess as a horse-tamer Hardy was unable to make his partner admit that he was anything short of a real "buster," and before they had been on the trail an hour Creede had made all the plans for a big gather of wild horses after the round-up.

"I had you spotted for a sport from the start," he said, puffing out his chest at the memory of his acumen, "but, by jingo, I never thought I was drawin' a bronco-twister. Well, now, I saw you crawl that horse this mornin', and I guess I know the real thing by this time. Say," he said, turning confidentially in his saddle, "if it's none of my business you can say so, but what did you do to that bit?"

Hardy smiled, like a juggler detected in his trick. "You must have been watching me," he said, "but I don't mind telling you —- it's simply passing a good thing along. I learned it off of a Yaqui Mayo Indian that had been riding for Bill Greene on the Turkey-track —- I rubbed it with a little salt."

"Well, I'm a son of a gun!" exclaimed Creede incredulously. "Here we've been gittin' our fingers bit off for forty years and never thought of a little thing like that. Got any more tricks?"

"Nope," said Hardy, "I've only been in the Territory a little over a year, this trip, and I'm learning, myself. Funny how much you can pick up from some of these Indians and Mexicans that can't write their own names, isn't it?"

"Umm, may be so," assented Creede doubtfully, "but I'd rather go to a white man myself. Say," he exclaimed, changing the subject abruptly, "what was that name the old man called you by when he was makin' that talk about sheep —- Roofer, or Rough House —- or something like that?"

"Oh, that's my front name —- Rufus. Why? What's the matter with it?"

"Nothin', I reckon," replied Creede absently, "never happened to hear it before, 's all. I was wonderin' how he knowed it," he added, glancing shrewdly sideways. "Thought maybe you might have met him up in California, or somewheres."

"Oh, that's easy," responded Hardy unblinkingly. "The first thing he did was to ask me my full name. I notice he calls you Jefferson," he added, shiftily changing the subject.

"Sure thing," agreed Creede, now quite satisfied, "he calls everybody that way. If your name is Jim you're James, John you're Jonathan, Jeff you're Jefferson Davis —- but say, ain't they any f'r short to your name? We're gittin' too far out of town for this Mister business. My name's Jeff, you know," he suggested.

"Why, sure," exclaimed Hardy, brushing aside any college-bred scruples, "only don't call me Rough House —- they might get the idea that I was on the fight. But you don't need to get scared of Rufus —- it's just another way of saying Red. I had a red-headed ancestor away back there somewhere and they called him Rufus, and then they passed the name down in the family until it got to me, and I'm no more red-headed than you are."

"*No* —- is that straight?" ejaculated the cowboy, with enthusiasm, "same as we call 'em Reddy now, eh? But say, I'd choke if I tried to call you Rufus. Will you stand for Reddy? Aw, that's no good —- what's the matter with Rufe? Well, shake then, pardner, I'm dam' glad I met up with you."

They pulled their horses down to a Spanish trot —- that easy, limping shuffle that eats up its forty miles a day —- and rode on together like brothers, heading for a distant pass in the mountains where the painted cliffs of the Bulldog break away and leave a gap down to the river. To the east rose Superstition Mountain, that huge buttress upon which, since the day that a war party of Pimas disappeared within the shadow of its pinnacles, hot upon the trail of the Apaches, and never returned again, the Indians of the valley have always looked with superstitious dread.

Creede told the story carelessly, smiling at the pride of the Pimas who refused to admit that the Apaches alone, devils and bad medicine barred, could have conquered so many of their warriors. To the west in a long fringe of green loomed the cottonwoods of Moroni, where the hard-working Mormons had turned the Salagua from its course and irrigated the fertile plain, and there on their barren reservation dwelt the remnant of those warlike Pimas, the unrequited friends of the white men, now held by them as of no account.

As he heard the history of its people —- how the Apaches had wiped out the Toltecs, and the white men had killed off the Apaches, and then, after pushing aside the Pimas and the Mexicans, closed in a death struggle for the mastery of the range —- Hardy began to perceive the grim humor of the land. He glanced across at his companion, tall, stalwart, with mighty arms and legs and features rugged as a mountain crag, and his heart leaped up within him at the thought of the battles to come, battles in which sheepmen and cattlemen, defiant of the law, would match their strength and cunning in a fight for the open range.

As they rode along mile after mile toward the north the road mounted gently; hills rose up one by one out of the desert floor, crowned with towering *sahuaros*, and in the dip of the pass ahead a mighty forest of their misshapen stalks was thrust up like giant fingers against the horizon. The trail wound in among them, where they rose like fluted columns above the lesser cactus —- great skin-covered tanks, gorged fat with water too bitter to quench the fieriest thirst, yet guarded jealously by poison-barbed spines. Gilded woodpeckers, with hearts red as blood painted upon their breasts, dipped in uneven flight from *sahuaro* to *sahuaro*, dodged into holes of their own making, dug deep into the solid flesh; sparrow hawks sailed forth from their summits, with quick eyes turned to the earth for lizards; and the brown mocking bird, leaping for joy from the ironwood tree where his mate was nesting, whistled the praise of the desert in the ecstatic notes of love. In all that land which some say God forgot, there was naught but life and happiness, for God had sent the rain.

The sun was high in the heavens when, as they neared the summit of the broad pass, a sudden taint came down the wind, whose only burden had been the fragrance of resinous plants, of wetted earth, and of green things growing. A distant clamor, like the babble of many voices or the surf-beats of a mighty sea, echoed dimly between the *chuck-a-chuck* of their horses' feet, and as Hardy glanced up inquiringly his companion's lip curled and he muttered:

"Sheep!"

They rode on in silence. The ground, which before had been furred with Indian wheat and sprouting six weeks' grass, now showed the imprints of many tiny feet glozed over by the rain, and Hardy noticed vaguely that something was missing —- the grass was gone. Even where a minute before it had covered the level flats in a promise of maturity, rising up in ranker growth beneath the thorny trees and cactus, its place was now swept bare and all the earth trampled into narrow, hard-tamped trail. Then as a brush shed and corrals, with a cook tent and a couple of water wagons in the rear, came into view, the ground went suddenly stone bare, stripped naked and trampled smooth as a floor. Never before had Hardy seen the earth so laid waste and desolate, the very cactus trimmed down to its woody stump and every spear of root grass searched out from the shelter of the spiny *chollas*. He glanced once more at his companion, whose face was sullen and unresponsive; there was a well-defined bristle to his short mustache and he rowelled his horse cruelly when he shied at the blatting horde.

The shearing was in full blast, every man working with such feverish industry that not one of them stopped to look up. From the receiving corral three Mexicans in slouched hats and jumpers drove the sheep into a broad chute, yelling and hurling battered oil cans at the hindmost; by the chute an American punched them vigorously forward with a prod, and yet another thrust them into the pens behind the shearers, who bent to their work with a sullen, back-breaking stoop. Each man held between his knees a sheep, gripped relentlessly, that flinched and kicked at times when the shears clipped off patches of flesh; and there in the clamor of a thousand voices they shuttled their keen blades unceasingly, stripping off a fleece, throwing it aside, and seizing a fresh victim by the foot, toiling and sweating grimly. By another chute a man stood with a paint pot, stamping a fresh brand upon every new-shorn sheep, and in a last corral the naked ones, their white hides spotted with blood from their cuts, blatted frantically for their lambs. These were herded in a small inclosure, some large and browned with the grime of the flock, others white and wobbly, newborn from mothers frightened in the shearing; and always that tremendous wailing chorus —- *Ba-a-a, ba-a-a, ba-a-a* —- and men in greasy clothes wrestling with the wool.

To a man used to the noise and turmoil of the round-up and branding pen and accustomed to the necessary cruelties of stock raising there was nothing in the scene to attract attention. But Hardy was of gentler blood, inured to the hardships of frontier life but not to its unthinking brutality, and as he beheld for the first time the waste, the hurry, the greed of it all, his heart turned sick and his eyes glowed with pity, like a woman's. By his side the sunburned swarthy giant who had taken him willy-nilly for a friend sat unmoved, his lip curled, not at the pity of it, but because they were sheep; and because, among the men who rushed about driving them with clubs and sacks, he saw more than one who had eaten at his table and then sheeped out his upper range. His saturnine mood grew upon him as he waited and, turning to Hardy, he shouted harshly:

"There's some of your friends over yonder," he said, jerking his thumb toward a group of men who were weighing the long sacks of wool. "Want to go over and get acquainted?"

Hardy woke from his dream abruptly and shook his head.

"No, let's not stop," he said, and Creede laughed silently as he reined Bat Wings into the trail. But just as they started to go one of the men by the scales hailed them, motioning with his hand and, still laughing cynically, the foreman of the Dos S turned back again.

"That's Jim Swope," he said, "one of our big sheep men —- nice feller —- you'll like him."

He led the way to the weighing scales, where two sweating Mexicans tumbled the eight-foot bags upon the platform, and a burly man with a Scotch turn to his tongue called off the weights defiantly. At his elbow stood two men, the man who had called them and a wool buyer, —- each keeping tally of the count.

Jim Swope glanced quickly up from his work. He was a man not over forty but bent and haggard, with a face wrinkled deep with hard lines, yet lighted by blue eyes that still held a twinkle of grim humor.

"Hello, Jeff," he said, jotting down a number in his tally book, "goin' by without stoppin', was ye? Better ask the cook for somethin' to eat. Say, you're goin' up the river, ain't ye? Well, tell Pablo Moreno and them Mexicans I lost a cut of two hundred sheep up there somewhere. That son of a —- of a herder of mine was too lazy to make a corral and count 'em, so I don't know where they are lost, but I'll give two bits a head for 'em, delivered here. Tell the old man that, will you?"

He paused to enter another weight in his book, then stepped away from the scales and came out to meet them.

"How's the feed up your way?" he inquired, smiling grimly.

"Dam' pore," replied Creede, carrying on the jest, "and it'll be poorer still if you come in on me, so keep away. Mr. Swope, I'll make you acquainted with Mr. Hardy —- my new boss. Judge Ware has sent him out to be superintendent for the Dos S."

"Glad to meet you, sir," said Swope, offering a greasy hand that smelled of sheep dip. "Nice man, the old judge —- here, *umbre*, put that bag on straight! Three hundred and *fifteen*? Well I know a dam' sight better —- excuse me, boys —- here, put that bag on again, and weigh it right!"

"Well," observed Creede, glancing at his friend as the combat raged unremittingly, "I guess we might as well pull. His busy day, you understand. Nice feller, though —- you'll like 'im." Once more the glint of quiet deviltry came into his eyes, but he finished out the jest soberly. "Comes from a nice Mormon family down in Moroni —- six brothers —- all sheepmen. You'll see the rest of the boys when they come through next month —- but Jim's the best."

There was something in the sardonic smile that accompanied this encomium which set Hardy thinking. Creede must have been thinking too, for he rode past the kitchen without stopping, cocking his head up at the sun as if estimating the length of their journey.

"Oh, did you want to git somethin' to eat?" he inquired innocently. "No? That's good. That sheep smell kinder turns my stomach." And throwing the spurs into Bat Wings he loped rapidly toward the summit, scowling forbiddingly in passing at a small boy who was shepherding the stray herd. For a mile or two he said nothing, swinging his head to scan the sides of the mountains with eyes as keen as an eagle's; then, on the top of the last roll, he halted and threw his hand out grandly at the panorama which lay before them.

"There she lays," he said, as if delivering a funeral oration, "as good a cow country as God ever made —- and now even the jack rabbits have left it. D'ye see that big mesa down there?" he continued, pointing to a broad stretch of level land, dotted here and there with giant cactus, which extended along the river. "I've seen a thousand head of cattle, fat as butter, feedin' where you see them *sahuaros*, and now look at it!"

He threw out his hand again in passionate appeal, and Hardy saw that the mesa was empty.

"There was grass a foot high," cried Creede in a hushed, sustained voice, as if he saw it again, "and flowers. Me and my brothers and sisters used to run out there about now and pick all kinds, big yaller poppies and daisies, and these here little pansies —- and ferget-me-nots. God! I wish I could ferget 'em —- but I've been fightin' these sheep so long and gittin' so mean and ugly them flowers wouldn't mean no more to me now than a bunch of jimson weeds and stink squashes. But hell, what's the use?" He threw out his hands once more, palms up, and dropped them limply.

"That's old Pablo Moreno's place down there," he said, falling back abruptly into his old way. "We'll stop there overnight —- I want to help git that wagon across the river when Rafael comes in bymeby, and we'll go up by trail in the mornin'.'"

Once more he fell into his brooding silence, looking up at the naked hills from habit, for there were no cattle there. And Rufus Hardy, quick to understand, gazed also at the arid slopes, where once the grama had waved like tawny hair in the soft winds and the cattle of Jeff Creede's father had stood knee-high in flowers.

Now at last the secret of Arizona-the-Lawless and Arizona-the-Desert lay before him: the feed was there for those who could take it, and the sheep were taking it all. It was government land, only there was no government; anybody's land, to strip, to lay waste, to desolate, to hog for and fight over forever —- and no law of right; only this, that the best fighter won. Thoughts came up into his mind, as thoughts will in the silence of the desert; memories of other times and places, a word here, a scene there, having no relation to the matter in hand; and then one flashed up like the premonitions of the superstitious —- a verse from the Bible that he had learned at his mother's knee many years before:

"Crying, Peace, Peace, when there is no peace."

But he put it aside lightly, as a man should, for if one followed every vagrant fancy and intuition, taking account of signs and omens, he would slue and waver in his course like a toy boat in a mill pond, which after great labor and adventure comes, in the end, to nothing.

CHAPTER IV
DON PABLO MORENO

On the edge of the barren mesa and looking out over the sandy flats where the Salagua writhed about uneasily in its bed, the *casa* of Don Pablo Moreno stood like a mud fort, barricaded by a palisade of the thorny cactus which the Mexicans call *ocotilla*. Within this fence, which inclosed several acres of standing grain and the miniature of a garden, there were all the signs of prosperity —- a new wagon under its proper shade, a storehouse strongly built where chickens lingered about for grain, a clean-swept *ramada* casting a deep shadow across the open doorway; but outside the inclosure the ground was stamped as level as a threshing floor. As Creede and Hardy drew near, an old man, grave and dignified, came out from the shady veranda and opened the gate, bowing with the most courtly hospitality.

"*Buenos tardes, señores*," he pronounced, touching his hat in a military salute. "*Pasa!* Welcome to my poor house."

In response to these salutations Creede made the conventional replies, and then as the old man stood expectant he said in a hurried aside to Hardy:

"D'ye talk Spanish? He don't understand a word of English."

"Sure," returned Hardy. "I was brought up on it!"

"No!" exclaimed Creede incredulously, and then, addressing the Señor Moreno in his native tongue, he said: "Don Pablo, this is my friend Señor Hardy, who will live with me at Agua Escondida!"

"With great pleasure, señor," said the old gentleman, removing his hat, "I make your acquaintance!"

"The pleasure is mine," replied Hardy, returning the salutation, and at the sound of his own language Don Pablo burst into renewed protestations of delight. Within the cool shadow of his *ramada* he offered his own chair and seated himself in another, neatly fashioned of mesquite wood and strung with thongs of rawhide. Then, turning his venerable head to the doorway which led to the inner court, he shouted in a terrible voice:

"*Muchacho!*"

Instantly from behind the adobe wall, around the corner of which he had been slyly peeping, a black-eyed boy appeared and stood before him, his ragged straw hat held respectfully against his breast.

"*Sus manos!*" roared the old man; and dropping his hat the *muchacho* touched his hands before him in an attitude of prayer.

"Give the gentlemen a drink!" commanded Don Pablo severely, and after Hardy had accepted the gourd of cold water which the boy dipped from a porous *olla*, resting in the three-pronged fork of a trimmed mesquite, the old gentleman called for his tobacco. This the *mozo* brought in an Indian basket wrought by the Apaches who live across the river —- Bull Durham and brown paper. The señor offered these to his guest, while Creede grinned in anticipation of the outcome.

"What?" exclaimed the Señor Moreno, astounded. "You do not smoke? Ah, perhaps it is my poor tobacco! But wait, I have a cigarro which the storekeeper gave me when I —- No? No smoke nothing? Ah, well, well —- no smoke, no Mexicano, as the saying goes." He regarded his guest doubtfully, with a shadow of disfavor. Then, rolling a cigarette, he remarked: "You have a very white skin, Señor Hardy; I think you have not been in Arizona very long."

"Only a year," replied Hardy modestly.

"*Muchacho!*" cried the señor. "Run and tell the señora to hasten the dinner. And where," he inquired, with the shrewd glance of a country lawyer, "and where did you learn, then, this excellent Spanish which you speak?"

"At Old Camp Verde, to the north," replied Hardy categorically, and at the name Creede looked up with sudden interest. "I lived there when I was a boy."

"Indeed!" exclaimed Don Pablo, raising his eyebrows. "And were your parents with you?"

"Oh, yes," answered Hardy, "my father was an officer at the post."

"Ah, *sí, sí, sí,*" nodded the old man vigorously, "now I understand. Your father fought the Apaches and you played with the little Mexican boys, no? But now your skin is white —- you have not lived long under our sun. When the Apaches were conquered your parents moved, of course —- they are in San Francisco now, perhaps, or Nuevo York."

"My father is living near San Francisco," admitted Hardy, "but," and his voice broke a little at the words, "my mother has been dead many years."

"Ah, indeed," exclaimed Don Pablo sympathetically, "I am very sorry. My own *madre* has been many years dead also. But what think you of our country? Is it not beautiful?"

"Yes, indeed," responded Hardy honestly, "and you have a wonderful air here, very sweet and pure."

"*Seguro!*" affirmed the old man, "*seguro que sí!* But alas," he added sadly, "one cannot live on air alone. Ah, *que malo,* how bad these sheep are!"

He sighed, and regarded his guest sadly with eyes that were bloodshot from long searching of the hills for cattle.

"I remember the day when the first sheep came," he said, in the manner of one who begins a set narration. "In the year of '91 the rain came, more, more, more, until the earth was full and the excess made *lagunas* on the plain. That year the Salagua left all bounds and swept my fine fields of standing corn away, but we did not regret it beyond reason for the grass came up on the mesas high as a horse's belly, and my cattle and those of my friend Don Luís, the good father of Jeff, here, spread out across the plains as far as the eye could see, and every cow raised her calf. But look! On the next year no rain came, and the river ran low, yet the plains were still yellow with last year's grass. All would have been well now as before, with grass for all, when down from the north like grasshoppers came the *borregos* —- *baaa, baaa, baaa* —- thousands of them, and they were starving. Never had I seen bands of sheep before in Arizona, nor the father of Don Jeff, but some say they had come from California in '77, when the drought visited there, and had increased in Yavapai and fed out all the north country until, when this second *año seco* came upon them, there was no grass left to eat. And now, *amigo,* I will tell you one thing, and you may believe it, for I am an old man and have dwelt here long: it is not God who sends the dry years, but the sheep!

"*Mira!* I have seen the mowing machine of the Americano cut the tall grass and leave all level —- so the starved sheep of Yavapai swept across our mesa and left it bare. Yet was there feed for all, for our cattle took to the mountains and browsed higher on the bushes, above where the sheep could reach; and the sheep went past and spread out on the southern desert and were lost in it, it was so great.

"That was all, you will say —- but no! In the Spring every ewe had her lamb, and many two, and they grew fat and strong, and when the grass became dry on the desert because the rains had failed again, they came back, seeking their northern range where the weather was cool, for a sheep cannot endure the heat. Then we who had let them pass in pity were requited after the way of the *borregueros* —- we were sheeped out, down to the naked rocks, and the sheepmen went on, laughing insolently. *Ay, que malo los borregueros,* what devils they are; for hunger took the strength from our cows so that they could not suckle their calves, and in giving birth many mothers and their little ones died together. In that year we lost half our cows, Don Luís Creede and I, and those that lived became thin and rough, as they are to this day, from journeying to the high mountains for feed and back to the far river for water.

"Then the father of Jeff became very angry, so that he lost weight and his face became changed, and he took an oath that the first sheep or sheep-herder that crossed his range should be killed, and every one thereafter, as long as he should live. Ah, what a *buen hombre* was Don Luís —- if we had one man like him to-day the sheep would yet go round —- a big man, with a beard, and he had no fear, no not for a hundred men. And when in November the sheep came bleating back, for they had promised so to do as soon as the feed was green, Don Luís met them at the river, and he rode along its bank, night and day, promising all the same fate who should come across —- and, *umbre*, the sheep went round!"

The old man slapped his leg and nodded his head solemnly. Then he looked across at Creede and his voice took on a great tenderness. "My friend has been dead these many years," he said, "but he was a true man."

As Don Pablo finished his story the Señora opened the door of the kitchen where the table was already set with boiled beans, meat stewed with peppers, and thin corn cakes —- the conventional *frijoles, carne con chili,* and *tortillas* of the Mexicans —- and some fried eggs in honor of the company. As the meal progressed the Señora maintained a discreet silence, patting out *tortillas* and listening politely to her husband's stock of stories, for Don Pablo was lord in his own house. The big-eyed *muchacho* sat in the corner, watching the corn cakes cook on the top of the stove and battening on the successive rations which were handed out to him. There were stories, as they ate, of the old times, of the wars and revolutions of Sonora, wherein the Señor Moreno had taken too brave a part, as his wounds and exile showed; strange tales of wonders and miracles wrought by the Indian doctors of Altár; of sacred snakes with the sign of the cross blazoned in gold on their foreheads, worshipped by the Indians with offerings of milk and tender chickens; of primitive life on the *haciendas* of Sonora, where men served their masters for life and were rewarded at the end with a pension of beans and *carne seco.*

Then as the day waned they sat at peace in the *ramada*, Moreno and Creede smoking, and Hardy watching the play of colors as the sun touched the painted crags of the Bulldog and lighted up the square summit of Red Butte across the river, throwing mysterious shadows into the black gorge which split it from crown to base. Between that high cliff and the cleft red butte flowed the Salagua, squirming through its tortuous cañon, and beyond them lay Hidden Water, the unknown, whither a single man was sent to turn back the tide of sheep.

In the silence the tinkle of bells came softly from up the cañon and through the dusk Hardy saw a herd of goats, led by a long-horned ram, trailing slowly down from the mesa. They did not pause, either to rear up on their hind feet for browse or to snoop about the gate, but filed dutifully into their own corral and settled down for the night.

"Your goats are well trained, Don Pablo," said Hardy, by way of conversation. "They come home of their own accord."

"Ah, no," protested Moreno, rising from his chair. "It is not the goats but my goat dogs that are well trained. Come with me while I close the gate and I will show you my flock."

The old gentleman walked leisurely down the trail to the corral, and at their approach Hardy saw two shaggy dogs of no breed suddenly detach themselves from the herd and spring defiantly forward.

"*Quita se, quita se!*" commanded Don Pablo, and at his voice they halted, still growling and baring their fangs at Hardy.

"*Mira,*" exclaimed the old man, "are they not *bravo*? Many times the *borregueros* have tried to steal my bucks to lead their timid sheep across the river, but Tira and Diente fight them like devils. One Summer for a week the *chivas* did not return, having wandered far up into the mountains, but in the end Tira and Diente fetched them safely home. See them now, lying down by the mother goat that suckled them; you would not believe it, but they think they are goats."

He laughed craftily at the idea, and at Hardy's eager questions.

"*Seguro,*" he said, "surely I will tell you about my goat dogs, for you Americans often think the Mexicans are *tonto*, having no good sense, because our ways are different. When I perceived that my cattle were doomed by reason of the sheep trail crossing the river here at my feet I bought me a she-goat with kids, and a ram from another flock. These I herded myself along the brow of the hill, and they soon learned to rear up against the bushes and feed upon the browse which the sheep could not reach. Thus I thought that I might in time conquer the sheep, fighting the devil with fire; but the coyotes lay in wait constantly to snatch the kids, and once when the river was high the *borregueros* of Jeem Swopa stole my buck to lead their sheep across.

"Then I remembered a trick of my own people in Sonora, and I took the blind pups of a dog, living far from here, and placed each of them with a she-goat having one newborn kid; and while the kid was sucking at one teat the mother could not help but let down milk for the puppy at the other, until at last when the dog smell had left him she adopted him for her own. Now as the pups grew up they went out on the hills with their goat mother, and when, they being grown, she would no longer suckle them, they stole milk from the other she-goats; and so they live to-day, on milk and what rabbits they can catch. But whenever they come to the house I beat them and drive them back ——- their nature is changed now, and they love only goats. Eight years ago I raised my first goat dogs, for many of them desert their mothers and become house dogs, and now I have over a hundred goats, which they lead out morning and night."

The old man lashed fast the gate to the corral and turned back toward the house.

"Ah, yes," he said musingly, "the Americanos say continually that we Mexicanos are foolish — - but look at me! Here is my good home, the same as before. I have always plenty beans, plenty meat, plenty flour, plenty coffee. I welcome every one to my house, to eat and sleep ——- yet I have plenty left. I am *muy contento*, Señor Hardy ——- yes, I am always happy. But the Americanos? No! When the sheep come, they fight; when their cattle are gone, they move; fight, fight; move, move; all the time." He sighed and gazed wearily at the barren hills.

"Señor Hardy," he said at last, "you are young, yet you have seen the great world ——- perhaps you will understand. Jeff tells me you come to take charge of the Dos S Rancho, where the sheep come through by thousands, even as they did here when there was grass. I am an old man now; I have lived on this spot twenty-four years and seen much of the sheep; let me advise you.

"When the sheepmen come across the river do not fight, as Don Jeff does continually, but let them pass. They are many and the cowmen are few; they are rich and we are very poor; how then can a few men whip many, and those armed with the best? And look ——- if a sheepman is killed there is the law, you know, and lawyers ——- yes, and money!" He shrugged his shoulders and threw out his hands, peeping ruefully through the fingers to symbolize prison bars.

"Is it not so?" he asked, and for the first time an Americano agreed with him.

"One thing more, then," said Don Pablo, lowering his voice and glancing toward the house, where Creede was conversing with the Señora. "The *papá* of Don Jeff yonder was a good man, but he was a fighting Texano ——- and Jeff is of the same blood. Each year as the sheep come through I have fear for him, lest he should kill some saucy *borreguero* and be sent to prison; for he has angry fits, like his father, and there are many bad men among the sheep-herders, — - escaped criminals from Old Mexico, *ladrones*, and creatures of low blood, fathered by evil Americanos and the nameless women of towns.

"In Sonora we would whip them from our door, but the sheepmen make much of their herders, calling them brothers and *cuñados* and what not, to make them stay, since the work is hard and dangerous. And to every one of them, whether herder or camp rustler, the owners give a rifle with ammunition, and a revolver to carry always. So they are drunk with valor. But our Jeff here has no fear of them, no, nor decent respect. He overrides them when the fit is on him, as if they were unfanged serpents ——- and so far he has escaped."

The old man leaned closer, and lowered his voice to a hoarse whisper, acting out his words dramatically.

"But some day ——- " he clasped his heart, closed his eyes, and seemed to lurch before a bullet. "No?" he inquired, softly. "Ah, well, then, you must watch over him, for he is a good man, doing many friendships, and his father was a *buen hombre*, too, in the days when we all were rich. So look after him ——- for an old man," he added, and trudged wearily back to the house.

CHAPTER V
HIDDEN WATER

The trail to Hidden Water leads up the Salagua, alternately climbing the hard mesa and losing itself in the shifting sand of the river bottom until, a mile or two below the mouth of the box cañon, it swings in to the edge of the water. But the Salagua is no purling brook, dignified by a bigger name; it is not even a succession of mill ponds like the dammed-up streams of the East: in its own name the Salagua is a *Rio*, broad and swift, with a current that clutches treacherously at a horse's legs and roars over the brink of stony reefs in a long, fretful line of rapids. At the head of a broad mill race, where the yellow flood waters boiled sullenly before they took their plunge, Creede pulled up and surveyed the river doubtfully.

"Swim?" he inquired, and when Hardy nodded he shrugged his shoulders and turned his horse into the water. "Keep your head upstream, then," he said, "we'll try it a whirl, anyhow."

Head to tail the two horses plodded heavily across the ford, feeling their way among the submerged bowlders, while twenty feet below them the irresistible onrush of the current slipped smoothly over the rim, sending up a roar like the thunder of breakers. As they struggled up the opposite bank after a final slump into a narrow ditch Creede looked back and laughed merrily at his bedraggled companion.

"How's that for high?" he inquired, slapping his wet legs. "I tell you, the old Salagua is a hell-roarer when she gits started. I wouldn't cross there this afternoon for a hundred dollars. She's away up since we took the wagon over last night, but about to-morrow you'll hear her talk —- snow's meltin' on the mountains. I wish to God she'd *stay* up!" he added fervently, as he poured the water out of his boots.

"Why?" asked Hardy innocently. "Won't it interfere with your bringing in supplies?"

"Sure thing," said Creede, and then he laughed maliciously. "But when you've been up here a while," he observed, "you'll savvy a lot of things that look kinder curious. If the old river would git up on its hind legs and walk, forty feet high, and stay there f'r a month, we cowmen would simply laugh ourselves to death. We don't give a dam' for supplies as long as it keeps the sheep out.

"Begin to see light, eh?" he queried, as he pushed on up the river. "Well, that's the only thing in God's world that wasn't made to order for these sheepmen; the old Salagua cuts right square across the country east and west without consultin' nobody, not even Jim Swope, and the sheep move north and south.

"How'd you like to have the job of crossing a hundred thousand *borregos* and half of 'em with lambs, when the *rio* was on a bender? I've seen some of these sheepmen wadin' around up to their chins for two weeks, tryin' to float twenty-five hundred head across the river —- and there wasn't turkey buzzards enough in the country when they got through.

"Last year they had the sand bars up around Hidden Water lined with carcasses two deep where they'd jest naturally crowded 'em into the river and let 'em sink or swim. Them Chihuahua Mexicans, you savvy. After they'd wore out their shoes and froze their marrow-bones wadin' they got tired and shoved 'em in, regardless. Well, if this warm weather holds we'll be able to git our *rodér* good and started before the sheep come in. That's one reason why I never was able to do much with these sheepmen," he added. "They hit me right square in the middle of the round-up, Spring and Fall, when I'm too busy gatherin' cattle to pay much attention to 'em. I did plan a little surprise party last year —- but that was somethin' special. But now you're on the job, Rufe," he continued reassuringly, "I'm goin' to leave all sheep and sheepmen strictly alone —- you can bank on that. Bein' as we are goin' to try the expeeriment I want to see it done right. I never made a cent fightin' 'em, that's a cinch, and if you can appeal to their better natures, w'y, go to it! I'd help you if I could, but bein' as I can't I'll git out of the road and give you a chanst.

"Now I'll tell you how it'll be," he continued, turning in his saddle and hooking one leg over the horn, "the boys'll come in for the *rodér* to-morrow or next day; we begin to gather on the first, and it takes us about a month. Well, we look for the sheep to come in on us at about the same time —- first of April —- and we ain't been fooled yet. They'll begin to stack up on the other side any time now, and as soon as the water goes down they'll come across with a rush. And if they're feelin' good-natured they'll spread out over The Rolls and drift north, but if they're feelin' bad they'll sneak up onto Bronco Mesa and scatter the cattle forty ways for Sunday, and bust up my *rodér* and raise hell generally. We had a little trouble over that last year," he added parenthetically.

"Well, I'll turn over the house and the grub and the whole business to you this year and camp out with the boys under the mesquite —- and then you can entertain them sheepmen and jolly 'em up no end. They won't have a dam' thing —- horse feed, grub, tobacco, matches, nothin'! Never do have anythin'. I'd rather have a bunch of Apaches camped next to me —- but if you want to be good to 'em there's your chanst. Meanwhile, I'm only a cow-punch pullin' off a round-up, and your name is Mr. —- you're the superintendent of the Dos S. Your job is to protect the upper range, and I begin to think you can do it."

There was a tone of half-hearted enthusiasm about this talk which marked it for a pre-pared "spiel," laboriously devised to speed the new superintendent upon his way; but, not being schooled in social deceit, Creede failed utterly in making it convincing.

"That's good," said Hardy, "but tell me —- what has been your custom in the past? Haven't you been in the habit of feeding them when they came in?"

"Feed 'em?" cried Creede, flaring up suddenly. "Did I feed 'em? Well, I should guess yes —- I never turned one away hungry in my life. W'y, hell, man," he exclaimed, his anger growing on him, "I slep' in the same blanket with 'em —- until I become lousy," he added grimly.

"What!" exclaimed Hardy, aghast. "You don't mean to say —- "

"No," interrupted Creede ironically, "I don't mean to say anythin' —- not from now on. But while we're on the subject and to avoid any future misunderstandin' I might just as well tell you right now that I can't see nothin' good in a sheepman —- *nothin'!* I'm like my cat Tom when he sees a rattlesnake, my hair bushes up clean over my ears and I see hell, damnation, and sudden death!"

He rose up, frowning, on his mighty horse and gazed at Hardy with eyes that burned deep with passion. "If every sheep and sheepman in Arizona should drop dead at this minute," he said, "it would simply give me a laughin' sensation. God damn 'em!" he added passionately, and it sounded like a prayer.

Half an hour later as they passed through the gloomy silence of the box cañon, picking their way over rocks and bowlders and driftwood cast forty feet above the river level in some terrific glut of waters, he began to talk again, evenly and quietly, pointing out indifferent things along the trail, and when at last they mounted the hill and looked down upon Hidden Water his anger was forgotten.

"Well," he remarked, throwing out a hand, "there's home —- how do you like it?"

Hardy paused and looked it over critically —- a broad V-shaped valley half a mile in length, beginning at the mouth of a great dry wash and spreading out through trees and hummocks down to the river. A broken row of cottonwoods and sycamores stretched along the farther side, following the broad, twisting bed of the sand wash where the last flood had ripped its way to the Salagua; and on the opposite side, close up against the base of the cliff, a flash of white walls and the shadow of a *ramada* showed where man had built his puny dwelling high in order to escape its fury. At their feet lay the ranch pasture, a broad elbow of the valley rich with grass and mesquite trees and fenced in with barbed wire that ran from cliff to cliff. Beyond the eastern wall the ground was rough and broken, cut up by innumerable gulches and waterways, and above its ridges there rose the forbidding crags of a black butte whose shoulders ran down to and confined the silvery river. Across the river and to the south the land was even rougher, rising in sheer precipices, above the crests of which towered a mighty needle of rock, standing out against the sky like a cathedral spire, yet of a greater dignity and magnificence —- purple with the regal robes of distance.

"That's Weaver's Needle," volunteered Creede, following his companion's eyes. "Every lost mine for a hundred miles around here is located by sightin' at that peak. The feller it's named after was picked up by the Apaches while he was out lookin' for the Lost Dutchman and there's been a Jonah on the hidden-treasure business ever since, judgin' by the results.

"D'ye see that big butte straight ahead? That's Black Butte. She's so rough that even the mountain sheep git sore-footed, so they say —- we have to go up there on foot and drive our cattle down with rocks. Old Bill Johnson's place is over the other side of that far butte; he's got a fine rich valley over there —- the sheep haven't got in on him yet. You remember that old feller that was drunk down at Bender —- well, that's Bill. Calls his place Hell's Hip Pocket; you wait till you try to git in there some day and you'll know why."

He paused and turned to the north.

"Might as well give you the lay of the land," he said. "I'll be too busy to talk for the next month. There's the Four Peaks, northeast of us, and our cows run clean to the rocks. They's more different brands in that forty miles than you saw in the whole Cherrycow country, I bet ye. I've got five myself on a couple hundred head that the old man left me —- and everybody else the same way. You see, when the sheep come in down on the desert and around Moreno's we kept pushin' what was left of our cattle east and east until we struck the Peaks —- and here we are, in a corner. The old judge has got nigh onto two thousand head, but they's about twenty of us poor devils livin' up here in the rocks that has got enough irons and ear marks to fill a brand book, and not a thousand head among us.

"Well, I started out to show you the country, didn't I? You see that bluff back of the house down there? That runs from here clean to the Four Peaks without a break, and then it swings west in a kind of an ox bow and makes that long ridge up there to the north that we called the Juate. All that high country between our house here and the Peaks —- everythin' east of that long bluff —- is Bronco Mesa. That's the upper range the judge asked me to point out to you. Everythin' west of Bronco Mesa is The Rolls —- all them rollin' hills out there —- and they's feed enough out there to keep all the sheep in the country, twice over —- but no water. Now what makes us cowmen hot is, after we've give 'em that country and welcome, the sheepmen're all the time tryin' to sneak in on our upper range. Our cows can't hardly make a livin' walkin' ten or fifteen miles out on The Rolls every day, and then back again to water; but them dam' sheep can go a week without drinkin', and as much as a month in the winter-time.

"Why can't they give us a chanst, then? We *give* 'em all the good level land and simply ask 'em as a favor to please keep off of the bench up there and leave our cows what little cactus and browse they is. But no —- seems like as soon as you give one of them Chihuahua Mexicans a gun he wants to git a fight out of somebody, and so they come crowdin' in across our dead line, just to see if they can't git some of us goin'."

Once more his eyes were burning, his breath came hard, and his voice became high and sustained. "Well, I give one of 'em all he wanted," he said, "and more. I took his dam' pistol away and beat him over the head with it —- and I *moved* him, too. He was Jasper Swope's pet, and I reckon he had his orders, but I noticed the rest went round."

He stopped abruptly and sat silent, twisting his horse's mane uneasily. Then he looked up, smiling curiously.

"If you hadn't come up this year I would've killed some of them fellers," he said quietly. "I'm gittin' as crazy as old Bill Johnson —- and he hears voices. But now lookee here, Rufe, you don't want to believe a word I say about this trouble. Don't you pay any attention to me; I'm bughouse, and I know it. Jest don't mention sheep to me and I'll be as happy as an Injun on a mescal jag. Come on, I'll run you to the house!"

Throwing his weight forward he jumped his big horse down the rocky trail and went thundering across the flat, whooping and laughing and swinging under mesquite trees as if his whole heart was in the race. Catching the contagion Hardy's sorrel dashed madly after him, and the moment they struck the open he went by like a shot, over-running the goal and dancing around the low adobe house like a circus horse.

"By Joe," exclaimed Creede as he came up, "that *caballo* of yours can run some. I'm goin' to make a little easy money off of Bill Lightfoot when he comes in. He's been blowin' about that gray of his for two years now and I'll match you ag'inst him for a yearlin'. And don't you forgit, boy, we're going after that black stallion up on Bronco Mesa just as soon as the *rodér* is over."

His face was all aglow with friendliness and enthusiasm now, but as they started toward the house, after turning their horses into the corral, he suddenly stopped short in the trail.

"Gee," he said, "I wonder what's keepin' Tom? Here Tom! Heere Tom! Pussy, pussy, pussy!" He listened, and called again. "I hope the coyotes ain't caught him while I was gone," he said at length. "They treed him a few times last year, but he just stayed up there and yelled until I came —- spoiled his voice callin' so long, but you bet he can purr, all right."

He listened once more, long and anxiously, then his face lit up suddenly.

"Hear that?" he asked, motioning toward the bluff, and while Hardy was straining his ears a stunted black cat with a crook in his tail came into view, racing in wildly from the great pile of fallen bowlders that lay at the base of the cliff, and yowling in a hoarse, despairing voice, like a condemned kitten in a sack.

"Hello, Tommy, Tommy, Tommy!" cried Creede, and as the cat stopped abruptly, blinking warily at Hardy, he strode forward and gathered it gently into his arms. "Well, you poor little devil," he exclaimed, stroking its rough coat tenderly, "you're all chawed up again! Did them dam' coyotes try to git you while I was gone?" And with many profane words of endearment he hugged it against his breast, unashamed.

"There's the gamiest cat in Arizona," he said, bringing him over to Hardy with conscious pride. "Whoa, kitten, he won't hurt you. Dogged if he won't tackle a rattlesnake, and kill 'im, too. I used to be afraid to git out of bed at night without puttin' on my boots, but if any old rattler crawls under my cot now it's good-bye, Mr. Snake. Tommy is right there with the goods —- and he ain't been bit yet, neither. He killed three side-winders last Summer —- didn't you, Tom, Old Socks? —- and if any sheep-herder's dog comes snoopin' around the back door he'll mount him in a minute. If a man was as brave as he is, now, he'd —- well, that's the trouble —- he wouldn't last very long in this country. I used to wonder sometimes which'd go first —- me or Tom. The sheepmen was after me, and their dogs was after Tom. But I'm afraid poor Tommy is elected; this is a dam' bad country for cats."

He set him down with a glance of admiring solicitude, such as a Spartan mother might have bestowed upon her fighting offspring, and kicked open the unlocked door.

The Dos S ranch house was a long, low structure of adobe bricks, divided in the middle by the open passageway which the Mexicans always affect to encourage any vagrant breeze. On one side of the *corredor* was a single large room, half storehouse, half bunk room, with a litter of pack saddles, rawhide kyacks and leather in one corner, a heap of baled hay, grain, and provisions in the other, and the rest strewn with the general wreckage of a camp —- cooking utensils, Dutch ovens, canvas pack covers, worn-out saddles, and ropes. On the other side the rooms were more pretentious, one of them even having a board floor. First came the large living-room with a stone chimney and a raised hearth before the fireplace; whereon, each on its separate pile of ashes, reposed two Dutch ovens, a bean kettle, and a frying-pan, with a sawed-off shovel in the corner for scooping up coals. Opening into the living-room were two bedrooms, which, upon exploration, turned out to be marvellously fitted up, with high-headed beds, bureaus and whatnots, besides a solid oak desk.

To these explorations of Hardy's Creede paid but slight attention, he being engaged in cooking a hurried meal and watching Tommy, who had a bad habit of leaping up on the table and stealing; but as Hardy paused by the desk in the front bedroom he looked up from mixing his bread and said:

"That's your room, Rufe, so you can clean it up and move in. I generally sleep outdoors myself—- and I ain't got nothin', nohow. Jest put them guns and traps into the other room, so I can find 'em. Aw, go ahead, you'll need that desk to keep your papers in. You've got to write all the letters and keep the accounts, anyhow. It always did make my back ache to lean over that old desk, and I'm glad to git shent of it.

"Pretty swell rooms, ain't they? Notice them lace curtains? The kangaroo rats have chawed the ends a little, but I tell you, when Susie and Sallie Winship was here this was the finest house for forty miles. That used to be Sallie's room, where you are now. Many's the time in the old days that I've rid up here to make eyes at Sallie, but the old lady wouldn't stand for no sich foolishness. Old Winship married her back in St. Louie and brought her out here to slave around cookin' for *rodér* hands, and she wanted her daughters to live different. Nope, she didn't want no bow-legged cow-punch for a son-in-law, and I don't blame her none, because this ain't no place for a woman; but Sal was a mighty fine girl, all the same."

He shook a little flour over his dough, brushed the cat off the table absently, and began pinching biscuits into the sizzling fat of the Dutch oven, which smoked over its bed of coals on the hearth. Then, hooking the red-hot cover off the fire, he slapped it on and piled a little row of coals along the upturned rim.

"Didn't you never hear about the Winship girls?" he asked, stroking the cat with his floury hands. "No? Well, it was on account of them that the judge took over this ranch. Old man Winship was one of these old-time Indian-fightin', poker-playin' sports that come pretty nigh havin' their own way about everythin'. He had a fine ranch up here —- the old Dos S used to brand a thousand calves and more, every round-up; but when he got old he kinder speculated in mines and loaned money, and got in the hole generally, and about the time the sheep drifted in on him he hauled off and died. I pulled off a big *rodér* for 'em and they sold a lot of cattle tryin' to patch things up the best they could, but jest as everythin' was lovely the drouth struck 'em all in a heap, and when the Widde' Winship got the estate settled up she didn't have nothin' much left but cows and good will. She couldn't sell the cows —- you never can, right after these dry spells —- and as I said, she wouldn't let the girls marry any of us cowmen to kinder be man for the outfit; so what does she do but run the ranch herself!

"Yes, sir —- Susie and Sallie, that was as nice and eddicated girls as you ever see, they jest put on overalls and climbed their horses and worked them cattle themselves. Course they had *rodér* hands to do the dirty work in the corrals —- brandin' and ear-markin' and the like —- but for ridin' the range and drivin' they was as good as the best. Well, sir, you'd think every man in Arizona, when he heard what they was doin', would do everythin' in his power to help 'em along, even to runnin' a Dos S on an *orehanna* once in a while instead of hoggin' it himself; but they's fellers in this world, I'm convinced, that would steal milk from a sick baby!"

The brawny foreman of the Dos S dropped the cat and threw out his hands impressively, and once more the wild glow crept back into his eyes.

"You remember that Jim Swope that I introduced you to down on the desert? Well, he's a good sheepman, but he's on the grab for money like a wolf. He's got it, too —- that's the hell of it."

Creede sighed, and threw a scrap of bacon to Tommy.

"He keeps a big store down at Moroni," he continued, "and the widde', not wantin' to shove her cows onto a fallin' market, runs up an account with him —- somethin' like a thousand dollars —- givin' her note for it, of course. It's about four years ago, now, that she happened to be down in Moroni when court was in session, when she finds out by accident that this same Jim Swope, seein' that cattle was about to go up, is goin' to close her out. He'd 'a' done it, too, like fallin' off a log, if the old judge hadn't happened to be in town lookin' up some lawsuit. When he heard about it he was so durned mad he wrote out a check for a thousand dollars and give it to her; and then, when she told him all her troubles, he up and bought the whole ranch at her own price —- it wasn't much —- and shipped her and the girls back to St. Louie."

Creede brushed the dirt and flour off the table with a greasy rag and dumped the biscuits out of the oven.

"Well," he said, "there's where I lost my last chanst to git a girl. Come on and eat."

CHAPTER VI
THE CROSSING

From lonely ranches along the Salagua and Verde, from the Sunflower and up the Alamo, from all the sheeped-out and desolate Four Peaks country the cowboys drifted in to Hidden Water for the round-up, driving their extra mounts before them. Beneath the brush *ramada* of the ranch house they threw off their canvas-covered beds and turned their pack horses out to roll, strapping bells and hobbles on the bad ones, and in a day the deserted valley of Agua Escondida became alive with great preparations. A posse of men on fresh mounts rode out on Bronco Mesa, following with unerring instinct the trail of the Dos S horses, balking their wild breaks for freedom and rushing them headlong into the fenced pasture across the creek. As the hired hands of the Dos S outfit caught up their mounts and endeavored to put the fear of God into their hearts, the mountain boys got out the keg of horseshoes and began to shoe —- every man his own blacksmith.

It was rough work, all around, whether blinding and topping off the half-wild ponies or throwing them and tacking cold-wrought "cowboy" shoes to their flint-like feet, and more than one enthusiast came away limping or picking the loose skin from a bruised hand. Yet through it all the dominant note of dare-devil hilarity never failed. The solitude of the ranch, long endured, had left its ugly mark on all of them. They were starved for company and excitement; obsessed by strange ideas which they had evolved out of the tumuli of their past experience and clung to with dogged tenacity; warped with egotism; stubborn, boastful, or silent, as their humor took them, but now all eager to break the shell and mingle in the rush of life.

In this riot of individuals Jefferson Creede, the round-up boss, strode about like a king, untrammelled and unafraid. There was not a ridge or valley in all the Four Peaks country that he did not know, yet it was not for this that he was boss; there was not a virtue or weakness in all that crowd that he was not cognizant of, in the back of his scheming brain. The men that could rope, the men that could ride, the quitters, the blowhards, the rattleheads, the lazy, the crooked, the slow-witted —- all were on his map of the country; and as, when he rode the ridges, he memorized each gulch and tree and odd rock, so about camp he tried out his puppets, one by one, to keep his map complete.

As they gathered about the fire that evening it was Bill Lightfoot who engaged his portentous interest. He listened to Bill's boastful remarks critically, cocking his head to one side and smiling whenever he mentioned his horse.

"Yes, sir," asserted Bill belligerently, "I mean it —- that gray of mine can skin anything in the country, for a hundred yards or a mile. I've got money that says so!"

"Aw, bull!" exclaimed Creede scornfully.

"Bull, nothin'," retorted Lightfoot hotly. "I bet ye —- I bet ye a thousand dollars they ain't a horse in Arizona that can keep out of my dust for a quarter!"

"Well, I know you ain't got no thousand dollars —- ner ten," sneered Creede. "Why don't you bet yearlings? If you'd blow some of that hot air through a tube it'd melt rocks, I reckon. But talk cow, man; we can all savvy that!"

"Well, where's the horse that can beat me?" demanded Lightfoot, bristling.

"That little sorrel out in the pasture," answered Creede laconically.

"I'll bet ye!" blustered Lightfoot. "Aw, rats! He ain't even broke yet!"

"He can run, all right. I'll go you for a yearling heifer. Put up or shut up."

And so the race was run. Early in the morning the whole *rodéo* outfit adjourned to the *parada* ground out by the pole corrals, the open spot where they work over the cattle. Hardy danced his sorrel up to the line where the gray was waiting, there was a scamper of feet, a streak of dust, and Bill Lightfoot was out one yearling heifer. A howling mob of cowboys pursued them from the scratch, racing each other to the finish, and then in a yell of laughter at Bill Lightfoot they capered up the cañon and spread out over The Rolls —- the *rodéo* had begun.

As the shadow of the great red butte to the west, around which the wagon road toiled for so many weary miles, reached out and touched the valley, they came back in a body, hustling a bunch of cattle along before them. And such cattle! After his year with the Chiricahua outfit in that blessed eastern valley where no sheep as yet had ever strayed Hardy was startled by their appearance. Gaunt, rough, stunted, with sharp hips and hollow flanks and bellies swollen from eating the unprofitable browse of cactus and bitter shrubs, they nevertheless sprinted along on their wiry legs like mountain bucks; and a peculiar wild, haggard stare, stamped upon the faces of the old cows, showed its replica even in the twos and yearlings. Yet he forbore to ask Creede the question which arose involuntarily to his lips, for he knew the inevitable answer.

Day after day, as they hurriedly combed The Rolls for what few cattle remained on the lower range, the cowmen turned their eyes to the river and to the cañons and towering cliffs beyond, for the sheep; until at last as they sat by the evening fire Creede pointed silently to the lambent flame of a camp fire, glowing like a torch against the southern sky.

"There's your friends, Rufe," he said, and the cowmen glanced at Hardy inquiringly.

"I might as well tell you fellers," Creede continued, "that one reason Rufe come up here was to see if he couldn't do somethin' with these sheepmen."

He paused and looked at the circle of faces with a smile that was almost a sneer.

"You fellers wouldn't back me up when it come to fightin' —- none except Ben Reavis and the Clark boys —- so I told the old judge we might as well lay down, and to send up some smooth *hombre* to try and jockey 'em a little. Well, Hardy's the *hombre*; and bein' as you fellers won't fight, you might as well look pleasant about it. What's that you say, Bill?"

He turned with a sardonic grin to Lightfoot, who had already been reduced to a state of silence by the relentless persecutions of the *rodéo* boss.

"I never said nawthin'," replied Lightfoot sullenly. "But if you'd've gone at 'em the way we wanted to," he blurted out, as the grin broadened, "instead of tryin' to move the whole outfit by daylight, I'd've stayed with you till hell froze over. I don't want to git sent up fer ten years."

"No," said Creede coolly, "ner you never will."

"Well, I don't see what you're pickin' on me fer," bellowed Lightfoot, "the other fellers was there too. Why don't you sass Ensign or Pete a while?"

"For a durned good reason," replied Creede steadily. "They never *was* for fightin', but you, with that yawp of yours, was always a-hollerin' and ribbin' me on to fight, and then, when the time come, you never said 'Boo!' at 'em. Tucked your young cannon into the seat of your pants and flew, dam' ye, and that's all there was to it. But that's all right," he added resignedly. "If you fellers don't want to fight you don't have to. But, dam' it, keep shut about it now, until you mean business."

As to just who this man Hardy was and what he proposed to do with the sheep the members of the Four Peaks round-up were still in ignorance. All they knew was that he could ride, even when it came to drifting his horse over the rocky ridges, and that Jeff Creede took him as a matter of course. But, for a superintendent, he never seemed to have much to say for himself. It was only when he walked up to his sorrel pony in that gentle, precise way he had, and went through the familiar motions of climbing a "bad one" that they sensed, dimly, a past not without experience and excitement. Even in the preoccupation of their own affairs and doings they could not fail to notice a supple strength in his white hands, a military precision in his movements, and above all a look in his eyes when he became excited —- the steady resolute stare with which his militant father had subdued outlaw horses, buck soldiers, and Apaches, even his own son, when all had not gone well. It was this which had inspired Bill Lightfoot to restrain his tongue when he was sore over his defeat; and even though Hardy confessed to being a rider, somehow no one ever thought of sawing off Spike Kennedy's "side winder" on him. The quiet, brooding reserve which came from his soldier life protected him from such familiar jests, and without knowing why, the men of the Four Peaks looked up to him.

Even after his mission was announced, Hardy made no change in his manner of life. He rode out each day on the round-up, conning the lay of the land; at the corral he sat on the fence and kept tally, frankly admitting that he could neither rope nor brand; in camp he did his share of the cooking and said little, listening attentively to the random talk. Only when sheep were mentioned did he show a marked interest, and even then it was noticed that he made no comment, whatever his thoughts were. But if he told no one what he was going to do, it was not entirely due to an overrated reticence, for he did not know himself. Not a man there but had run the gamut of human emotions in trying to protect his ranch; they had driven herders off with guns; they had cut their huddled bands at night and scattered them for the coyotes; they had caught unwary Mexican *borregueros* in forbidden pastures and administered "shap lessons," stretching them over bowlders and spanking them with their leather leggings; they had "talked reason" to the bosses in forceful terms; they had requested them politely to move; they had implored them with tears in their eyes —- and still like a wave of the sea, like a wind, like a scourge of grasshoppers which cannot be withstood, the sheep had come on, always hungry, always fat, always more.

Nor was there any new thing in hospitality. The last bacon and bread had been set upon the table; baled hay and grain, hauled in by day's works from the alfalfa fields of Moroni and the Salagua, had been fed to the famished horses of the very men who had sheeped off the grass; the same blanket had been shared, sometimes, alas, with men who were "crumby." And it was equally true that, in return, the beans and meat of chance herders had been as ravenously devoured, the water casks of patient "camp-rustlers" had been drained midway between the river and camp, and stray wethers had showed up in the round-up fry-pans in the shape of mutton. Ponder as he would upon the problem no solution offered itself to Hardy. He had no policy, even, beyond that of common politeness; and as the menacing clamor of the sheep drifted up to them from the river the diplomat who was to negotiate the great truce began to wonder whether, after all, he was the man of the hour or merely another college graduate gone wrong.

On the opposite side of the river in bands of two and three thousand the cohorts of the sheep gathered to make the crossing —- gathered and waited, for the Salagua was still high. At the foot of the high cliffs, from the cleft cañon of which water flowed forth as if some rod had called it from the rock, the leaders of the sheepmen were sitting in council, gazing at the powerful sweep of the level river, and then at the distant sand bar where their charges must win the shore or be swept into the whirlpool below. Ah, that whirlpool! Many a frightened ewe and weakling lamb in years past had drifted helplessly into its swirl and been sucked down, to come up below the point a water-logged carcass. And for each stinking corpse that littered the lower bar the boss sheep owner subtracted five dollars from the sum of his hard-earned wealth. Already on the flats below them the willows and burro bushes were trembling as eager teeth trimmed them of their leaves —- in a day, or two days, the river bottom would be fed bare; and behind and behind, clear to the broad floor of the desert, band after band was pressing on to the upper crossing of the Salagua.

As Hardy rode up over the rocky point against which the river threw its full strength and then, flung inexorably back, turned upon itself in a sullen whirlpool, he could see the sheep among the willows, the herders standing impassive, leaning upon their guns as more rustic shepherds lean upon their staves, and above, at the head of the crossing, the group of men, sitting within the circle of their horses in anxious conference. If any of them saw him, outlined like a sentinel against the sky, they made no sign; but suddenly a man in a high Texas hat leaped up from the group, sprang astride his mule and spurred him into the cold water. For the first twenty feet the mule waded, shaking his ears; then he slumped off the edge of a submerged bench into deeper water and swam, heading across the stream but drifting diagonally with the current until, striking bottom once more, he struggled out upon the sand spit. The rider looked eagerly about, glanced up casually at the man on the point below, and then plunged back into the water, shouting out hoarse orders to his Mexicans, who were smoking idly in the shade of overhanging rocks. Immediately they scrambled to their feet and scattered along the hillside. The stroke of axes echoed from the crags above, and soon men came staggering down to the river, dragging the thorny limbs of *palo verdes* behind them. With these they quickly constructed a brush fence in the form of a wing, running parallel to the cliff and making a chute which opened into the river.

Then with a great braying and bleating a huddle of sheep moved unwillingly along it, led by bold goats with crooked horns and resolute beards, and pushed forward by that same reckless rider on his black mule, assisted by a horde of shouting Mexicans. But at the touch of the cold water, two days from the snow beds of the White Mountains, even the hardy bucks stepped back and shook their heads defiantly. In vain with showers of rocks and flapping tarpaulins the herders stormed the rear of the press —- every foot was set against them and the sheep only rushed about along the edge of the herd or crowded in close-wedged masses against the bluff. At last a line of men leaped into the enclosure, holding up a long canvas wagon-cover and, encircling the first section of the leaders, shoved them by main force into the river.

Instantly the goats took water, swimming free, and below them the man on the black mule shouted and waved his broad Texas hat, heading them across the stream. But the timid sheep turned back behind him, landing below the fence against all opposition, and the babel of their braying rose higher and higher, as if in protest against their unlucky fate. Again and again the herders, stripped to their underclothes, pushed the unwilling sheep into the current, wading out to their chins to keep them headed across; each time the sodden creatures evaded them and, drifting with the current, landed far below on the same side, whence they rushed back to join their fellows.

Upon the opposite shore the goats stood shivering, watching the struggle with yellow, staring eyes which showed no trace of fear. Like brave generals of a craven band they were alone in their hardihood and, with their feet upon the promised land, were doomed either to proceed alone or return to their companions. So at last they did, plunging in suddenly, while the man on the mule spurred in below in a vain effort to turn them back.

That night by the camp fire Hardy mentioned the man on a black mule.

"My old friend, Jasp Swope," explained Creede suavely, "brother of Jim, the feller I introduced you to. Sure, Jasp and I have had lo-ong talks together —- but he don't like me any more." He twisted his nose and made a face, as if to intimate that it was merely a childish squabble, and Hardy said no more. He was growing wise.

The next morning, and the next, Jasper Swope made other attempts at the crossing; and then, as the snow water from the high mountains slipped by and the warm weather dried up by so much each little stream, he was able at last to ford the diminished river. But first, with that indomitable energy which marked him at every move, he cleared a passage along the base of the cliff to a place where the earth-covered moraine broke off at the edge of the water. Here a broad ledge shot down to the river like a toboggan slide, with a six-foot jump off at the bottom.

Once on this chute, with the strong tug of the canvas wagon-covers behind, there was nothing for the sheep to do but to take the plunge, and as his brawny herders tumbled them head over heels into the deep current Swope and his helpers waded out in a line below, shunting each ewe and wading toward the farther shore. There on the edge of the sand spit they huddled in a bunch, gathering about the hardier bucks and serving as a lure for those that followed. As cut after cut was forced into the stream a long row of bobbing heads stretched clear across the river, each animal striving desperately to gain the opposite bank and landing, spent and puffing, far below. A Mexican boy at intervals drove these strays up the shore to the big bunch and then concealed himself in the bushes lest by his presence he turn some timid swimmer back and the whirlpool increase its toll. So they crossed them in two herds, the wethers first, and then the ewes and lambs —- and all the little lambs that could not stem the stream were floated across in broad pieces of tarpaulin whose edges were held up by wading men.

From Lookout Point it was a majestic spectacle, the high cliffs, the silvery river gliding noiselessly out from its black cañon, the white masses of sheep, clustering on either side of the water —- and as the work went ahead merrily the Mexicans, their naked bodies gleaming like polished bronze in the ardent sun, broke into a wild refrain, a love song, perhaps, or a *cancion* of old Mexico. Working side by side with his men Jasper Swope joined in the song himself, and as they returned empty-handed he seized the tallest and strongest of them and ducked him in the water while his retainers roared with laughter. And Hardy, sitting unnoticed upon his horse, began to understand why these low-browed barbarians from Mexico were willing to fight, and if need be to die, for their masters. The age of feudalism had returned —- the lords of the sheep went forth like barons, sharing every hardship and leading the way in danger, and their men followed with the same unthinking devotion that the Myrmidons showed for noble Achilles or the Crusaders for their white-crossed knights.

Upon this and many other feats Hardy had ample leisure to meditate, for the sheepmen regarded him no more than if he had been a monument placed high upon the point to give witness to their victory. As the sheep crossed they were even allowed to straggle out along the slopes of the forbidden mesa, untended by their shepherds; and if the upper range was the special reserve of the cowmen the sheep owners showed no knowledge of the fact. For two days the grazing herd crept slowly along the mesquite-covered flat toward Lookout Point, and on the third morning they boiled up over the rocks and spewed down into the valley of the Alamo.

"Well," observed Creede, as he watched the slow creeping of the flock, "here's where I have to quit you, Rufe. In a week this ground around here will be as level as a billiard table and they won't be enough horse feed in the valley to keep a burro. The town herd pulls out for Bender this mornin' and the rest of us will move up to Carrizo Creek."

He hurried away to oversee the packing, but when all was ready he waved the boys ahead and returned to the conversation.

"As I was sayin' a while ago, you won't see nothin' but sheep around here now for the next two weeks —- and all I want to say is, keep 'em out of the pasture, and f'r God's sake don't let 'em corral in the brandin' pens! They're dirty enough already, but if you git about six inches of sheep manure in there and then mill a few hundred head of cattle around on top of it, the dust would choke a skunk. Our cows ain't so over-particular about that sheep smell, but if we poor cowboys has got to breathe sheep and eat sheep and spit up sheep every time we brand, it's crowdin' hospitality pretty strong. But if they want grub or clothes or tabac, go to it —- and see if you can't keep 'em off the upper range."

He paused and gazed at Hardy with eyes which suggested a world of advice and warning —- then, leaving it all unsaid, he turned wearily away.

"I look to find you with a sprained wrist," he drawled, "when I come back —- throwin' flap-jacks for them sheepmen!" He made the quick motion of turning a pancake in midair, smiled grimly, and galloped after the long line of horses and packs that was stringing along up the Bronco Mesa trail. And, having a premonition of coming company, Hardy went in by the fireplace and put on a big kettle of beef. He was picking over another mess of beans when he heard the clatter of hoofs outside and the next moment the door was kicked violently open.

It was Jasper Swope who stood on the threshold, his high Texas hat thrust far back upon his head —- and if he felt any surprise at finding the house occupied he gave no expression to it.

"Hello, there!" he exclaimed. "I thought you folks was all gone!"

"Nope," replied Hardy, and continued his work in silence.

"Cookin' for the outfit?" queried Swope, edging in at the door.

"Nope," replied Hardy.

"Well, who the hell air ye cookin' fer then?" demanded Swope, drawing nearer. "'Scuse me if I pry into this matter, but I'm gittin' interested." He paused and showed a jagged set of teeth beneath his bristling red mustache, sneeringly.

"Well, I'll tell you," answered Hardy easily. "I thought some white man might come along later and I'd ask him to dinner." He fixed his eyes upon the sheepman with an instant's disapproval and then resumed his cookery. As for Swope, his gray eyes flashed sudden fire from beneath bushy eyebrows, and then a canny smile crept across his lips.

"I used to be a white man, myself," he said, "before I lost my soap. What's the chance to git a bite of that bymeby?" He threw his hand out toward the pot of beef, which was sending out odors of a rich broth, flavored with onions and chili.

Hardy looked at him again, little shrimp of a man that he was, and still with disapproval.

"D'ye call that a white man's way of entering another man's house?" he inquired pointedly.

"Well," temporized Swope, and then he stopped. "A man in my line of business gits in a hurry once in a while," he said lamely. "But I'm hungry, all right," he remarked, *sotto voce.*

"Yes," said Hardy, "I've noticed it. But here —- sit down and eat."

The sheepman accepted the dish of beef, dipped out a spoonful of beans, broke off a slab of bread, and began his meal forthwith, meanwhile looking at Hardy curiously.

"What's that you say you've noticed?" he inquired, and a quizzical smile lurked beneath his dripping mustache as he reached over and hefted the coffeepot.

"I've noticed," replied Hardy, "that you sheepmen get in a hurry once in a while. You can't stop to knock on a door so you kick it open; can't stop to go around a ranch, so you go through it, and so on."

"Ah," observed Swope slyly, "so that's what's bitin' you, eh? I reckon you must be that new superintendent that Jim was tellin' about."

"That's right," admitted Hardy, "and you're Mr. Swope, of course. Well, I'll say this for you, Mr. Swope, you certainly know how to get sheep across a river. But when it comes to getting along with cowmen," he added, as the sheepman grinned his self-approval, "you don't seem to stack up very high."

"Oh, I don't, hey?" demanded Swope defiantly. "Well, how about the cowmen? Your friend Creede gets along with sheepmen like a house afire, don't he? Him and a bunch of his punchers jumped on one of my herders last Fall and dam' nigh beat him to death. Did you ever hear of a sheepman jumpin' on a cowboy? No, by Gad, and you never will! We carry arms to protect ourselves, but we never make no trouble."

He paused and combed the coffee grounds out of his heavy red mustache with fingers that were hooked like an eagle's talons from clutching at sheep in the cold water.

"I don't doubt, Mr. Superintendent," he said, with sinister directness, "that these cowmen have filled you up about what bad *hombres* we are —- and of course it ain't no use to say nothin' now —- but I jest want to tell you one thing, and I want you to remember it if any trouble should come up; we sheepmen have never gone beyond our legal rights, and we've got the law behind us. The laws of the United States and the statutes of this Territory guarantee us the right to graze our sheep on public lands and to go where we dam' please —- and we'll go, too, you can bank on that."

He added this last with an assurance which left no doubt as to his intentions, and Hardy made no reply. His whole mind seemed centred on a handful of beans from which he was picking out the rocks and little lumps of clay which help to make up full weight.

"Well!" challenged Swope, after waiting for his answer, "ain't that straight?"

"Sure," said Hardy absently.

Swope glared at him for a moment disapprovingly.

"Huh, you're a hell of a cowman," he grunted. "What ye goin' to do about it?"

"About what?" inquired Hardy innocently.

"Aw, you know," replied Swope impatiently. "How about that upper range?" He shoved back his chair as he spoke, and his eyes lit up in anticipation of the battle.

"Well," responded Hardy judicially, "if you've got the legal right to go up there, and if you're goin' where you dam' please, anyhow, it don't look like I could do anything." He paused and smiled patiently at the sheepman.

"You know very well, Mr. Swope," he said, "that if you want to go up on that mesa and sheep off the feed we haven't got any legal means of preventing you. But you know, too, that there isn't more than enough feed for what cows the boys have left. If you want to go up there, that's your privilege —- and if you want to go out over The Rolls, that's all right, too."

"Of course you don't give a dam'!" said Swope satirically.

"I guess you know how I feel, all right," returned Hardy, and then he lapsed into silence, while Swope picked his teeth and thought.

"Where'd you come from?" he said at last, as if, forgetting all that had passed, his mind had come back from a far country, unbiassed by the facts.

"Over the mountains," replied Hardy, jerking his thumb toward the east.

"Don't have no sheep over there, do they?" inquired Swope.

"Nope, nothing but cattle and horses."

"Ump!" grunted the sheepman, and then, as if the matter was settled thereby, he said: "All right, pardner, bein' as you put it that way, I reckon I'll go around."

CHAPTER VII
HELL'S HIP POCKET

In the days of Ahaz, king of Judah, Isaiah the son of Amoz is reported to have seen in a vision a wolf which dwelt with a lamb, while a lion ate straw like an ox, and a weaned child put his hand in the cockatrice's den. Equally beautiful, as a dream, was the peace at Hidden Water, where sheepman and cattleman sat down together in amity; only, when it was all over, the wolf wiped his chops and turned away with a wise smile —- the millennium not having come, as yet, in Arizona.

Hardy's wrist was a little lame, figuratively speaking, from throwing flapjacks for hungry sheep herders, and the pile of grain and baled hay in the storehouse had dwindled materially; but as the sheep came through, band after band, and each turned off to the west, stringing in long bleating columns out across The Rolls, he did not begrudge the hard labor. After Jasper Swope came Jim, and Donald McDonald, as jolly a Scottish shepherd as ever lived, and Bazan, the Mexican, who traced his blood back to that victorious general whom Maximilian sent into Sonora. There were Frenchmen, smelling rank of garlic and mutton tallow; Basques with eyes as blue and vacant as the summer skies; young Mormons working on shares, whose whole fortune was wrapped up in the one huddle of sheep which they corralled and counted so carefully; and then the common herders, fighting Chihuahuanos, with big round heads and staring eyes, low-browed Sonorans, slow and brutal in their ways, men of all bloods and no blood, lumped together in that careless, all-embracing Western term "Mexicans."

But though they were low and primitive in mental processes, nearer to their plodding burros than to the bright-eyed sensitive dogs, they were the best who would consent to wander with the sheep through the wilderness, seeing nothing, doing nothing, knowing nothing, having before them nothing but the vision of a distant pay day, a drunk, the *calabozo*, and the kind boss who would surely bail them out. Ah, that was it —- the one love and loyalty of those simple-minded creatures who, unfit for the hurry and competition of the great world, sold their lives by spans of months for twenty dollars and found; it was always to the boss that they looked for help, and in return they did his will.

When the great procession had drifted past, with its braying clamor, its dogs, its men on muleback and afoot, the herders with their carbines, the camp rustlers with their burros, belled and laden with water casks and kyacks of grub, the sheep owners hustling about with an energy that was almost a mania, Hardy sat beneath the *ramada* of the ranch house with dog-fighting Tommy in his lap and pondered deeply upon the spectacle. A hundred thousand sheep, drifting like the shadows of clouds across the illimitable desert, crossing swift rivers, climbing high mountains, grazing beneath the northern pines; and then turning south again and pouring down through the passes like the resistless front of a cloudburst which leaves the earth bare and wasted in its wake. For this one time he had turned the stream aside and the tall grass still waved upon the upper range; but the next time, or the next —- what then?

Long and seriously he contemplated the matter, dwelling now upon the rough good nature of the sheepmen and this almost miraculous demonstration of their good will; then remembered with vague misgivings their protestations against the unlawful violence which presumed to deny them what was their legal right —- free grazing on all government lands. And in the end he wrote a brief note to Judge Ware, telling him that while the sheepmen had accepted his hospitality in a most friendly spirit and had respected the upper range, it was in his opinion only a question of time until they would take the whole country, unless they were restrained by law. He therefore recommended that the judge look up the status of the bill to set aside the watershed of the Salagua as a National Forest Reserve, and in case the opposition to it indicated any long delay it would be well either to sell out or reduce his stock. This note he sent out by Rafael, the Mexican roustabout, who was still hauling in supplies from Bender, and then with a glad heart he saddled up his horse, left a bait of meat on the floor for Tommy, and struck out over the mesa for Carrizo Creek.

After his long confinement in the pasture the sorrel galloped along the rocky trail with the grace and swiftness of an antelope, the warm dry wind puffed little whirls of dust before them, and once more Hardy felt like a man. If for the best interests of his employer it was desirable that he cook beef and bread for sheepmen, he could do so with good grace, but his spirit was not that of a man who serves. Since he had left home he had taken a great deal from the world, patiently accepting her arrogance while he learned her ways, but his soul had never been humbled and he rode forth now like a king.

Upon that great mesa where the bronco mustangs from the Peaks still defied the impetuosity of men, the giant *sahuaros* towered in a mighty forest as far as the eye could see, yet between each stalk there lay a wide space, studded here and there with niggerheads of bristling spines, and fuzzy *chollas*, white as the backs of sheep and thorny beyond reason. Nor was this all: in the immensity of distance there was room for *sahuaros* and niggerheads and *chollas*, and much besides. In every gulch and sandy draw the *palo verdes*, their yellow flowers gleaming in the sun, stood out like lines of fire; the bottoms of the steep ravines which gashed the mesa were illuminated with the gaudy tassels of mesquite blossoms; gray coffee-berry bushes clumped up against the sides of ridges, and in every sheltered place the long grass waved its last-year's banners, while the fresh green of tender growth matted the open ground like a lawn. Baby rabbits, feeding along their runways in the grass, sat up at his approach or hopped innocently into the shadow of the sheltering cat-claws; jack-rabbits with black-tipped ears galloped madly along before him, imagining themselves pursued, and in every warm sandy place where the lizards took the sun there was a scattering like the flight of arrows as the long-legged swift-jacks rose up on their toes and flew. All nature was in a gala mood and Rufus Hardy no less. Yet as he rode along, gazing at the dreamy beauty of this new world, the old far-away look crept back into his eyes, a sad, brooding look such as one often sees in the faces of little children who have been crossed, and the stern lines at the corners of his mouth were deeper when he drew rein above Carrizo Creek.

Below him lay the panorama of a mountain valley —- the steep and rocky walls; the silvery stream writhing down the middle; the green and yellow of flowers along the lowlands; and in the middle, to give it life, a great herd of cattle on the *parada* ground, weaving and milling before the rushes of yelling horsemen, intent on cutting out every steer in the herd. Beyond lay the corrals of peeled cottonwood, and a square house standing out stark and naked in the supreme ugliness of corrugated iron, yet still oddly homelike in a land where shelter was scarce. As he gazed, a mighty voice rose up to him from the midst of the turmoil, the blatting of calves, the mooing of cows and the hoarse thunder of mountain bulls:

"Hel-lo, Rufe!"

From his place on the edge of the herd Hardy saw Jefferson Creede, almost herculean on his tall horse, waving a large black hat. Instantly he put spurs to his sorrel and leaped down the narrow trail, and at the edge of the herd they shook hands warmly, for friends are scarce, wherever you go.

"Jest in time!" said Creede, grinning his welcome, "we're goin' over into Hell's Hip Pocket to-morrow —- the original hole in the ground —- to bring out Bill Johnson's beef critters, and I sure wanted you to make the trip. How'd you git along with Jasp?"

"All right," responded Hardy, "he didn't make me any trouble. But I'm glad to get away from that sheep smell, all the same."

The big cowboy fixed his eyes upon him eagerly.

"Did they go around?" he asked incredulously. "Jasp and all?"

"Sure," said Hardy. "Why?"

For a long minute Creede was silent, wrinkling his brows as he pondered upon the miracle.

"Well, that's what *I* want to know," he answered ambiguously. "But say, you've got a fresh horse; jest take my place here while me and Uncle Bill over there show them ignorant punchers how to cut cattle."

He circled rapidly about the herd and, riding out into the runway where the cattle were sifted, the beef steers being jumped across the open into the hold-up herd and the cows and calves turned back, he held up his hand for the work to stop. Then by signals he sent the galloping horsemen back to the edge of the herd and beckoned for old Bill Johnson.

For a few minutes he sat quietly on his horse, waiting for the harassed cattle to stop their milling. Then breaking into a song such as cowboys sing at night he rode slowly in among them, threading about at random, while old Bill Johnson on his ancient mare did likewise, his tangled beard swaying idly in the breeze. On the border of the herd they edged in as if by accident upon a fat steer and walked him amiably forth into the open. Another followed out of natural perversity, and when both were nicely started toward the beef cut the two men drifted back once more into the herd. There was no running, no shouting, no gallant show of horsemanship, but somehow the right steers wandered over into the beef cut and stayed there. As if by magic spell the outlaws and "snakes" became good, and with no breaks for the hills the labor of an afternoon was accomplished in the space of two dull and uneventful hours.

"That's the way to cut cattle!" announced Creede, as they turned the discard toward the hills. "Ain't it, Bill?"

He turned to Johnson who, sitting astride a flea-bitten gray mare that seemed to be in a perpetual doze, looked more like an Apache squaw than a boss cowboy. The old man's clothes were even more ragged than when Hardy had seen him at Bender, his copper-riveted hat was further reinforced by a buckskin thong around the rim, and his knees were short-stirruped almost up to his elbows by the puny little boy's saddle that he rode, but his fiery eyes were as quick and piercing as ever.

"Shore thing," he said, straightening up jauntily in his saddle, "that's my way! Be'n doin' it fer years, while you boys was killin' horses, but it takes Jeff hyar to see the p'int. Be gentle, boys, be gentle with um —- you don't gain nawthin' fer all yer hard ridin'."

He cut off a chew of tobacco and tucked it carefully away in his cheek.

"Jeff hyar," he continued, as the bunch of cowboys began to josh and laugh among themselves, "he comes by his savvy right —- his paw was a smart man before him, and mighty clever to his friends, to boot. Many's the time I hev took little Jeffie down the river and learned him tracks and beaver signs when he wasn't knee-high to a grasshopper —- hain't I, Jeff? And when I tell him to be gentle with them cows he knows I'm right. I jest want you boys to take notice when you go down into the Pocket to-morrer what kin be done by kindness; and the first man that hollers or puts a rope on my gentle stock, I'll sure make him hard to ketch.

"You hear me, naow," he cried, turning sharply upon Bill Lightfoot, who was getting off something about "Little Jeffie," and then for the first time he saw the face of the new cowboy who had ridden in that afternoon. Not since the day he was drunk at Bender had Bill Johnson set eyes upon the little man to whom he had sworn off, but he recognized him instantly.

"Hello thar, pardner!" he exclaimed, reining his mare in abruptly. "Whar'd you drop down from?"

"Why howdy do, Mr. Johnson!" answered Hardy, shaking hands, "I'm glad to see you again. Jeff told me he was going down to your ranch to-morrow and I looked to see you then."

Bill Johnson allowed this polite speech to pass over his shoulder without response. Then, drawing Hardy aside, he began to talk confidentially; expounding to the full his system of gentling cattle; launching forth his invective, which was of the pioneer variety, upon the head of all sheepmen; and finally coming around with a jerk to the subject that was uppermost in his mind.

"Say," he said, "I want to ask you a question —- are you any relation to the Captain Hardy that I served with over at Fort Apache? Seems's if you look like 'im, only smaller."

His stature was a sore point with Hardy, and especially in connection with his father, but making allowance for Mr. Johnson's ways he modestly admitted his ancestry.

"His son, eh!" echoed the old man. "Waal —- now! I tell you, boy, I *knowed* you —- I knowed you the minute you called down that dog-robber of a barkeep —- and I was half drunk, too. And so you're the new superintendent down at the Dos S, eh? Waal, all I can say is: God help them pore sheepmen if you ever git on their trail. I used to chase Apaches with yore paw, boy!"

It was Bill Johnson's turn to talk that evening and like most solitaries who have not "gone into the silence," he availed himself of a listener with enthusiasm.

Stories of lion hunts and "b'ar fights" fell as trippingly from his lips as the words of a professional monologist, and when he had finished his account of the exploits of Captain Samuel Barrows Hardy, even the envious Lightfoot regarded Rufus with a new respect, for there is no higher honor in Arizona than to be the son of an Indian fighter. And when the last man had crawled wearily into his blankets the old hermit still sat by the dying fire poking the charred ends into the flames and holding forth to the young superintendent upon the courage of his sire.

Hardly had the son of his father crept under the edge of Creede's blankets and dropped to sleep before that huge mountain of energy rose up and gave the long yell. The morning was at its blackest, that murky four A. M. darkness which precedes the first glimmer of light; but the day's work had to be done. The shivering horse-wrangler stamped on his boots and struck out down the cañon after the *remuda*, two or three cooks got busy about the fire which roared higher and higher as they piled on the ironwood to make coals, and before the sun had more than mounted the southern shoulder of the Four Peaks the long line of horsemen was well on the trail to Hell's Hip Pocket.

The frontier imagination had in no wise overleaped itself in naming this abyss. Even the tribute which Facilis Descensus Vergil paid to the local Roman hell could hardly be said of the Pocket —- it is not even easy to get into it. From the top of the divide it looks like a valley submerged in a smoky haze through which the peaks and pinnacles of the lower parks rise up like cathedral spires, pointing solemnly to heaven. As the trail descends through washed-out gulches and "stone-patches," now skating along the backbone of a ridge and now dropping as abruptly into some hollow waterway, the cliffs and pinnacles begin to loom up against the sky; then they seem to close in and block the way, and just as the cañon boxes in to nothing the trail slips into a gash in the face of the cliff where the soft sandstone has crumbled away between two harder strata, and climbs precariously along through the sombre gloom of the gorge to the bright light of the fair valley beyond.

It is a kind of fairy land, that hidden pocket in the hills, always covered by a mystic haze, for which the Mexicans give it the name *Humada*. Its steep cañon comes down from the breast of the most easterly of the Four Peaks, impassable except by the one trail; it passes through the box and there widens out into a beautiful valley, where the grass lies along the hillsides like the tawny mane of a lion, and tender flowers stand untrampled in the rich bottoms. For three miles or more it spreads out between striated cliffs where hawks and eagles make their nests; then once more it closes in, the creek plunges down a narrow gorge and disappears, writhing tortuously on its way to the Salagua whose fire-blasted walls rise in huge bulwarks against the south, dwarfing the near-by cliffs into nothingness by their majestic height.

In the presence of this unearthly beauty and grandeur old Bill Johnson —- ex-trapper, ex-soldier, ex-prospector, ex-everything —- had dwelt for twenty years, dating from the days when his house was his fortress, and his one desire was to stand off the Apaches until he could find the Lost Dutchman.

Where the valley narrowed down for its final plunge into the gorge the old trapper had built his cabin, its walls laid "square with the world" by sighting on the North Star. When the sun entered the threshold of the western door it was noon, and his watch never ran down. The cabin was built of shaly rocks, squared and laid in mud, like bricks; a tremendous stone chimney stood against the north end and a corral for his burros at the south. Three hounds with bleared eyes and flapping ears, their foreheads wrinkled with age and the anxieties of the hunt, bayed forth a welcome as the cavalcade strung in across the valley; and mild-eyed cattle, standing on the ridges to catch the wind, stared down at them in surprise. Never, even at San Carlos, where the Chiricahua cattle fatten on the best feed in Arizona, had Hardy seen such mountains of beef. Old steers with six and seven rings on their horns hung about the salting places, as if there were no such things as beef drives and slaughter houses in this cruel world, and even when the cowboys spread out like a fan and brought them all in to the cutting grounds there was hardly a calf that bawled.

As the three or four hundred head that made up his entire earthly possession drifted obediently in, the old man rode up to Creede and Hardy and waved his hand expansively.

"Thar, boys," he said, "thar's the results of peace and kindness. Nary a critter thar that I heven't scratched between the horns since the day his maw brought him down to the salt lick. I even git Jeff and the boys to brand and earmark 'em fer me, so they won't hev no hard feelin' fer the Old Man. D'ye see that big white-faced steer?" he asked, pointing with pride to the monarch of the herd. "Waal, how much ye think he'll weigh?" he demanded, turning to Creede. "Fifteen hundred?"

"Um, more 'n that," responded Creede, squinting his eyes down judicially. "Them Herefords are awful solid when they git big. I reckon he'll run nigh onto seventeen hundred, Bill." He paused and winked furtively at Hardy. "I kin git fifty dollars fer that old boy, jest the way he stands," he said, "and bein' as he can't carry no more weight nohow, I'll jest cut him into the town herd right now, and —- "

"Hyar!" shouted Johnson, grabbing the cowboy's bridle, "who's doin' this, anyhow?"

"W'y *you*, Bill," answered Creede innocently, "but —- "

"That's all right, then," said the old man shortly, "you leave that steer alone. I'll jest cut this herd to suit myself."

Over at the branding pen the irons were on the fire and the marking was progressing rapidly, but out in the open Mr. Bill Johnson was making slow work of his cut.

"He gets stuck on them cows, like an Irishman with his pig," observed Creede, as the old man turned back a prime four-year-old. "He'd rather be barbecued by the Apaches than part with that big white-faced boy. If I owned 'em I'd send down a lot of them big fat brutes and buy doggies; but Bill spends all the money he gits fer booze anyhow, so I reckon it's all right. He generally sends out about twenty runts and roughs, and lets it go at that. Say! You'll have to git a move on, Bill," he shouted, "we want to send that beef cut on ahead!"

The old man reined in his mare and surveyed the big herd critically.

"Waal," he drawled, "I reckon that'll do fer this trip, then. Take 'em along. And the fust one of you punchers that hits one of them critters over the tail with his hondu," he shouted, as the eager horsemen trotted over to start them, "will hev me to lick!"

He placed an order for provisions with Creede, asked him to keep the supplies at Hidden Water until he came over for them with the burros, and turned away contentedly as the cowboys went upon their way.

Down by the branding pen the mother cows licked the blood from their offsprings' mangled ears and mooed resentfully, but the big white-faced steer stood in brutish content on the salting grounds and gazed after the town herd thoughtfully.

A bunch of burros gathered about the doorway of the cabin, snooping for bacon rinds; the hounds leaned their heavy jowls upon his knees and gazed up worshipfully into their master's face; and as the sun dipped down toward the rim of the mighty cliffs that shut him in, the lord of Hell's Hip Pocket broke into the chorus of an ancient song:

> "Oh, *o*-ver the prairies, and *o*-ver the mountains,
> And *o*-ver the prairies, and *o*-ver the mountains,
> And *o*-ver the prairies, and *o*-ver the mountains,
> I'll go till I find me a home."

CHAPTER VIII
A YEAR'S MAIL

The beef herd was safely delivered at Bender, the feeders disposed of at Moroni, and the checks sent on to the absentee owner, who did not know a steer from a stag; the *rodéo* hands were paid off and successfully launched upon their big drunk; bills were paid and the Summer's supplies ordered in, and then at last the superintendent and *rodéo* boss settled down to a little domesticity.

Since the day that Hardy had declined to drink with him Creede had quietly taken to water, and he planted a bag of his accumulated wages in a corner of the mud floor, to see, as he facetiously expressed it, if it would grow. Mr. Bill Johnson had also saved his "cow money" from Black Tex and banked it with Hardy, who had a little cache of his own, as well. With their finances thus nicely disposed of the two partners swept the floor, cleaned up the cooking dishes, farmed out their laundry to a squaw, and set their house in order generally. They were just greasing up their *reatas* for a run after the wild horses of Bronco Mesa when Rafael pulled in with a wagon-load of supplies and destroyed their peaceful life.

It was late when the grinding and hammering of wheels upon the boulders of the creek-bed announced his near approach and Creede went out to help unload the provisions. A few minutes later he stepped into the room where Hardy was busily cooking and stood across the table from him with his hands behind his back, grinning mischievously.

"Rufe," he said, "you've got a girl."

Hardy looked up quickly and caught the significance of his pose, but he did not smile. He did not even show an interest in the play.

"How do you figure that out?" he asked, indifferently.

"Oh, I know," drawled Creede. "Got a letter from her."

A single hawk-like glance was the only answer to this sally.

"She says: 'Why the hell don't you write!'" volunteered the cowboy.

"'S that so!" commented Hardy, and then he went on with his cooking.

For a minute Creede stood watching him, his eyes keen to detect the slightest quaver, but the little man seemed suddenly to have forgotten him; he moved about absently, mechanically, dropping nothing, burning nothing, yet far away, as in a dream.

"Huh!" exclaimed Creede, disgusted with his own make-believe, "you don't seem to care whether school keeps or not. I'll excuse you from any further work this evenin' —- here's your mail."

He drew a bundle of letters from behind his back and dropped it heavily upon the table, but even then Hardy did not rise.

"Guess the Old Man must've forwarded my mail," he remarked, smiling at the size of the pack. "I've been knocking around so, I haven't received a letter in a year. Chuck 'em on my desk, will ye?"

"Sure," responded Creede, and stepping across the broad living-room he threw the bundle carelessly on the bed.

"You're like me," he remarked, drawing his chair up sociably to supper, "I ain't got a letter fer so long I never go near the dam' post office."

He sighed, and filled his plate with beans.

"Ever been in St. Louis?" he inquired casually. "No? They say it's a fine burg. Think I'll save up my *dinero* and try it a whirl some day."

The supper table was cleared and Creede had lit his second cigarette before Hardy reverted to the matter of his mail.

"Well," he said, "I might as well look over those letters —- may be a thousand-dollar check amongst them."

Then, stepping into his room, he picked up the package, examined it curiously, and cut the cords with his knife.

A sheaf of twenty or more letters spilled out and, sitting on the edge of the bed, he shuffled them over in the uncertain light of the fire, noting each inscription with a quick glance; and as he gathered up the last he quietly tucked three of them beneath the folds of his blankets —- two in the same hand, bold and dashing yet stamped with a certain feminine delicacy and grace, and each envelope of a pale blue; the third also feminine, but inscribed in black and white, a crooked little hand that strayed across the page, yet modestly shrank from trespassing on the stamp.

With the remainder of his mail Hardy blundered over to the table, dumping the loose handful in a great pile before the weak glimmer of the lamp.

"There," he said, as Creede blinked at the heap, "I reckon that's mail enough for both of us. You can read the advertisements and I'll see what the judge has to say for himself. Pitch in, now." He waved his hand towards a lot of business envelopes, but Creede shook his head and continued to smoke dreamily.

"Nope," he said briefly, "don't interest me."

He reached out and thumbed the letters over dumbly, spelling out a long word here and there or scrutinizing some obscure handwriting curiously, as if it were Chinese, or an Indian sign on a rock. Then, shoving back his chair, he watched Hardy's face as he skimmed rapidly through the first letter.

"Good news in the first part of it and bad in the last," he remarked, as Hardy put it down.

"That's right," admitted Hardy, "but how'd you know?"

He gazed up at his complacent partner with a look of innocent wonder, and Creede laughed.

"W'y, hell boy," he said, "I can read you like a book. Your face tells the whole story as you go along. After you've been down here in Arizona a few seasons and got them big eyes of yourn squinched down a little —- well, I may have to ast you a few questions, then."

He waved his hand in a large gesture and blew out a cloud of smoke, while a twinkle of amusement crept into Hardy's unsquinched eyes.

"Maybe I'm smoother than I look," he suggested dryly. "You big, fat fellows get so self-satisfied sometimes that you let lots of things go by you."

"Well, I'll take my chances on you," answered Creede placidly. "What did the old judge say?"

"He says you did fine with the cattle," said Hardy, "and sold 'em just in time —- the market fell off within a week after we shipped."

"Um-huh," grunted Creede. "And what's the bad bunch of news at the end?"

The bad bunch of news was really of a personal nature, stirring up unpleasant memories, but Hardy passed it off by a little benevolent dissimulation.

"He says he's mighty glad I steered the sheep away, but there is something funny going on back in Washington; some combine of the sheep and lumber interests has got in and blocked the whole Forest Reserve business and there won't be any Salagua Forest Reserve this year. So I guess my job of sheep-wrangler is going to hold; at least the judge asked me to stay with it until Fall."

"Well, you stay then, Rufe," said Creede earnestly, "because I've kinder got stuck on you —- I like your style," he added half apologetically.

"All right, Jeff," said Hardy. "Here's another letter —- from my father. See if you can guess what it is like."

He set his face rigidly and read the short letter through without a quaver.

"You and the Old Man have had a fallin'-out," observed Creede, with a shrewd grin, "and he says when you git good and tired of bein' a dam' fool you might as well come home."

"Well, that's about the size of it," admitted Hardy. "I never told you much about my father, did I?"

"Never knew you had one," said Creede, "until Bill Johnson began to blow about what an Injun-fighter he was. I reckon that's where you git your sportin' blood, ain't it?"

"Well, I'll tell you," began Hardy. "The Old Man and I never did get along together. He's used to commanding soldiers and all that, and I'm kind of quiet, but he always took a sneaking pride in me when I was a boy, I guess. Anyway, every time I'd get into a fight around the post and lick two or three Mexican kids, or do some good work riding or shooting, he'd say I'd be a man before my mother, or something like that —- but that was as far as he got. And all the time, on the quiet, he was educating me for the Army. His father was a captain, and he's a colonel, and I can see now he was lotting on my doing as well or better —- but hell, that only made matters worse."

He slid down in his chair and gazed into the fire gloomily. It was the first time Creede had heard his partner use even the mildest of the range expletives, for in that particular he was still a tenderfoot, and the word suddenly conveyed to him the depths of the little man's abandonment and despair.

"Why —- what was the matter?" he inquired sympathetically. "Couldn't you git no appoint-ment?"

"Huh!" growled Hardy. "I guess you know, all right. Look at me!" he exclaimed, in a sudden gust of passion and resentment. "Why, damn it, man, I'm an inch too short!"

"Well —- I'll —- be —- dogged!" breathed Creede. "I never thought of that!"

"No," rejoined Hardy bitterly, "nor the Old Man, either —- not until I stopped growing! Well, he hasn't had a bit of use for me since. That's the size of it. And he didn't take any pains to conceal the fact —- most army men don't. There's only one man in the world to them, and that's a soldier; and if you're not a soldier, you're nothing."

He waved a hand as if dismissing himself from the universe, and sank moodily into his seat, while Creede looked him over in silence.

"Rufe," he said quietly, "d'ye remember that time when I picked you to be boss sheep-wran-gler, down at Bender? Well, I might as well tell you about that now —- 't won't do no harm. The old judge couldn't figure out what it was I see in you to recommend you for the job. Like's not you don't know yourself. *He* thought I was pickin' you because you was a peaceful guy, and wouldn't fight Black Tex; but that's where he got fooled, and fooled bad! I picked you because I knew dam' well you *would* fight!"

He leaned far over across the table and his eyes glowed with a fierce light.

"D'ye think I want some little suckin' mamma's-joy of a diplomat on my hands when it comes to a show-down with them sheepmen?" he cried. "No, by God, I want a *man*, and you're the boy, Rufe; so shake!"

He rose and held out his hand. Hardy took it.

"I wouldn't have sprung this on you, pardner," he continued apologetically, "if I didn't see you so kinder down in the mouth about your old man. But I jest want you to know that they's one man that appreciates you for a plain scrapper. And I'll tell you another thing; when the time comes you'll look jest as big over the top of a six-shooter as I do, and stand only half the chanst to git hit. W'y, shucks!" he exclaimed magnanimously, "my size is agin' me at every turn; my horse can't hardly pack me, I eat such a hell of a lot, and, well, I never can git a pair of pants to fit me. What's this here letter?"

He picked one up at random, and Hardy ascertained that his tailor some six months previ-ously had moved to a new and more central location, where he would be pleased to welcome all his old customers. But the subject of diminutive size was effectually dismissed and, having cheered up his little friend as best he could, Creede seized the occasion to retire. Lying upon his broad back in his blankets, with Tommy purring comfortably in the hollow of his arm, he smoked out his cigarette in speculative silence, gazing up at the familiar stars whose wheelings mark off the cowboy's night, and then dropped quietly to sleep, leaving his partner to brood over his letters alone.

For a long time he sat there, opening them one by one —- the vague and indifferent letters which drift in while one is gone; and at last he stole silently across the dirt floor and brought out the three letters from his bed. There in a moment, if he had been present, Creede might have read him like a book; his lips drawn tight, his eyes big and staring, as he tore open one of the pale blue envelopes with trembling hands. The fragments of a violet, shattered by the long journey, fell before him as he plucked out the note, and its delicate fragrance rose up like

52

incense as he read. He hurried through the missive, as if seeking something which was not there, then his hungry eyes left the unprofitable page and wandered about the empty room, only to come back to those last words: "Always your Friend, Kitty Bonnair."

"Always your friend," he repeated bitterly —- "always your friend. Ah, God!" He sighed wearily and shook his head. For a moment he lapsed into dreams; then, reaching out, he picked up the second letter, postmarked over a year before, and examined it idly. The very hour of its collection was recorded —- "Ferry Sta. 1.30 A. M." —- and the date he could never forget. Written on that very same day, and yet its message had never reached him!

He could see as in a vision the shrouded form of Kitty Bonnair slipping from her door at midnight to fling a final word after him, not knowing how far he would flee; he could see the lonely mail collector, half obscured in the San Francisco fog, as he scooped the letter from the box with many others and boarded the car for the ferry. It was a last retort, and likely bitter, for he had spoken in anger himself, and Kitty was not a woman to be denied. There was an exaggerated quirk to the square corners of her letters, a brusque shading of the down strokes —- undoubtedly Kitty was angry. But for once he had disarmed her —- it was a year after, now, and he had read her forgiveness first! Yet it was with a strange sinking of the heart that he opened the blue envelope and stared at the scribbled words:

> DEAR FRIEND THAT WAS: My heart is very sore to-night —- I had trusted you so —- I had depended upon you so —- and now you have deliberately broken all your faith and promises. Rufus, I had thought you different from other men —- more gentle, more considerate, more capable of a true friendship which I fondly hoped would last forever —- but now, oh, I can never forgive you! Just when life was heaviest with disappointments, just when I was leaning upon you most as a true friend and comrade —- then you must needs spoil it all. And after I had told you I could never love any one! Have you forgotten all that I told you in the balcony? Have you forgotten all that I have risked for the friendship I held so dear? And then to spoil it all! Oh, I hate you —- I hate you!

He stopped and stiffened in his chair, and his eyes turned wild with horror; then he gathered his letters together blindly and crept away to bed. In the morning he arose and went about his work with mouse-like quietness, performing all things thoroughly and well, talking, even laughing, yet with a droop like that of a wounded creature that seeks only to hide and escape.

Creede watched him furtively, hung around the house for a while, then strode out to the pasture and caught up his horse.

"Be back this aft," he said, and rode majestically away up the cañon, where he would be out of the way. For men, too, have their instincts and intuitions, and they are even willing to leave alone that which they cannot remedy and do not understand.

As Creede galloped off, leaving the ranch of a sudden lonely and quiet, Tommy poked his head anxiously out through a slit in the canvas bottom of the screen door and began to cry —- his poor cracked voice, all broken from calling for help from the coyotes, quavering dismally. In his most raucous tones he continued this lament for his master until at last Hardy gathered him up and held him to his breast.

"Ah, Kitty, Kitty," he said, and at the caressing note in his voice the black cat began to purr hoarsely, raising his scrawny head in the ecstasy of being loved. Thief and reprobate though he was, and sadly given to leaping upon the table and flying spitefully at dogs, even that rough creature felt the need of love; how much more the sensitive and high-bred man, once poet and scholar, now cowboy and sheep-wrangler, but always the unhappy slave of Kitty Bonnair.

The two letters lay charred to ashes among the glowing coals, but their words, even the kindest meant, were seared deep in his heart, fresh hurts upon older scars, and as he sat staring at the gaunt *sahuaros* on the hilltops he meditated gloomily upon his reply. Then, depositing Tommy on the bed, he sat down at his desk before the iron-barred window and began to write.

DEAR FRIEND THAT WAS: Your two letters came together —- the one that you have just sent, and the one written on that same night, which I hope I may some day forget. It was not a very kind letter —- I am sorry that I should ever have offended you, but it was not gently done. No friend could ever speak so to another, I am sure. As for the cause, I am a human being, a man like other men, and I am not ashamed. Yet that I should so fail to read your mind I am ashamed. Perhaps it was my egotism, which made me over-bold, thinking that any woman could love me. But if what I offered was nothing to you, if even for a moment you hated me, it is enough. Now for all this talk of friendship —- I am not your friend and never will be; and if, after what has passed, you are my friend, I ask but one thing —- let me forget. For I will never come back, I will never write, I will never submit. Surely, with all that life offers you, you can spare me the humiliation of being angry with you.

I am now engaged in work which, out of consideration for Judge Ware, I cannot leave; otherwise I would not ask you not to write to me.

Trusting that you will remember me kindly to your mother, I remain, sincerely,

RUFUS HARDY.

He signed his name at the bottom, folded the sheet carefully, and thrust the sealed envelope into an inner pocket. Then for the first time, he drew out the third letter and spread its pages before him —- a long letter, full of news, yet asking no questions. The tense lines about his lips relaxed as he read, he smiled whimsically as he heard of the queer doings of his old-time friends; how these two had run away and got married in order to escape a church wedding, how Tupper Browne had painted a likeness of Mather in Hades — after the "Dante" of Doré —- and had been detected in the act; and then this little note, cued in casually near the end:

Kitty Bonnair has given up art for the present on account of her eyes, and has gone in for physical culture and riding lessons in the park. She dropped in at the last meeting of The Circle, and I told her how curiously father had encountered you at Bender. We all miss you very much at The Circle —- in fact, it is not doing so well of late. Kitty has not attended a meeting in months, and I often wonder where we may look for another Poet, Philosopher, and Friend —- unless you will come back! Father did not tell me where you had been or what you intended to do, but I hope you have not given up the Muse. To encourage you I will send down a book, now and then, and you may send me a poem. Is it a bargain? Then good-bye.

With best wishes,

LUCY WARE.

P. S. —- I met your father on the street the other day, and he seemed very much pleased to hear how well you were getting along.

Hardy put the letter down and sighed.

"Now there's a thoroughly nice girl," he said. "I wonder why she doesn't get married." Then, reaching for a fresh sheet of paper, he began to write, describing the beauty of the country; the noble qualities of his horse, Chapuli, the Grasshopper; the march of the vast army of sheep; Creede, Tommy, and whatnot, with all the pent-up enthusiasm of a year's loneliness. When it was ended he looked at the letter with a smile, wondering whether to send it by freight or express. Six cents in stamps was the final solution of the problem, and as his pocketbook contained only four he stuck them on and awaited his partner's return.

"Say, Jeff," he called, as Creede came in from the pasture, "have you got any stamps?"

"Any which?" inquired Creede suspiciously.

"Any postage stamps —- to put on letters."

"Huh!" exclaimed Creede. "You must think I've got a girl —- or important business in the States. No, I'll tell you. The only stamp I've got is in a glass frame, hung up on the wall —- picture of George Washington, you know. Haven't you never seen it? W'y, it's right there in the parler —- jest above the pianney —- and a jim-dandy piece of steel engraving she is, too." He grinned broadly as he concluded this running fire of jest, but his partner remained serious to the end.

"Well," he said, "I guess I'll go down to Moroni in the morning, then."

"What ye goin' down there for?" demanded Creede incredulously.

"Why, to buy a stamp, of course," replied Hardy, "it's only forty miles, isn't it?" And early in the morning, true to his word, he saddled up Chapuli and struck out down the river.

From the doorway Creede watched him curiously, his lips parted in a dubious smile.

"There's something funny goin' on here, ladies," he observed sagely, "something funny —- and I'm dogged if I savvy what it is." He stooped and scooped up Tommy in one giant paw. "Well, Tom, Old Socks," he said, holding him up where he could sniff delicately at the rafters, "you've got a pretty good nose, how about it, now —- can you smell a rat?" But even Tommy could not explain why a man should ride forty miles in order to buy a stamp.

The Mormon settlement of Moroni proved to belong to that large class of Western "cities" known as "string-towns" —- a long line of stores on either side of a main street, brick where fires have swept away the shacks, and wood with false fronts where dynamite or a change of wind has checked the conflagration; a miscellaneous conglomeration of saloons, restaurants, general stores, and livery stables, all very satisfying to the material wants of man, but in the ensemble not over-pleasing to the eye.

At first glance, Moroni might have been Reno, Nevada; or Gilroy, California; or Deming, New Mexico; or even Bender —- except for the railroad. A second glance, however, disclosed a smaller number of disconsolate cow ponies standing in front of the saloons and a larger number of family rigs tied to the horse rack in front of Swope's Store; there was also a tithing house with many doors, a brick church, and women and children galore. And for twenty miles around there was nothing but flowing canals and irrigated fields waving with wheat and alfalfa, all so green and prosperous that a stranger from the back country was likely to develop a strong leaning toward the faith before he reached town and noticed the tithing house.

As for Hardy, his eyes, so long accustomed to the green lawns and trees of Berkeley, turned almost wistful as he gazed away across the rich fields, dotted with cocks of hay or resounding to the whirr of the mower; but for the sweating Latter Day Saints who labored in the fields, he had nothing but the pitying contempt of the cowboy. It was a fine large country, to be sure, and produced a lot of very necessary horse feed, but Chapuli shied when his feet struck the freshly sprinkled street, and somehow his master felt equally ill at ease.

Having purchased his stamp and eaten supper, he was wandering aimlessly up and down the street —- that being the only pleasure and recourse of an Arizona town outside the doors of a saloon —- when in the medley of heterogeneous sounds he heard a familiar voice boom out and as abruptly stop. It was evening and the stores were closed, but various citizens still sat along the edge of the sidewalk, smoking and talking in the semi-darkness. Hardy paused and listened a moment. The voice which he had heard was that of no ordinary man; it was deep and resonant, with a rough, overbearing note almost military in its brusqueness; but it had ceased and another voice, low and protesting, had taken its place. In the gloom he could just make out the forms of the two men, sitting on their heels against the wall and engaged in a one-sided argument. The man with the Southern drawl was doing all the talking, but as Hardy passed by, the other cut in on him again.

"Well," he demanded in masterful tones, "what ye goin' to do about it?" Then, without waiting for an answer, he exclaimed:

"Hello, there, Mr. Hardy!"

"Hello," responded Hardy. "Who is this, anyway?"

"Jim Swope," replied the voice, with dignified directness. "What're you doing in these parts?"

"Came down to buy a postage stamp," replied Hardy, following a habit he had of telling the truth in details.

"Huh!" grunted Swope. "It's a wonder you wouldn't go to Bender for it —- that Jew over there might make you a rate!"

"Nope," responded Hardy, ignoring the too-evident desire of the Moroni storekeeper to draw him into an argument. "He couldn't do it —- they say the Government loses money every time it sells one. Nice town you've got down here," he remarked, by way of a parting compliment; but Swope was not satisfied to let him escape so easily.

"Hold on, there!" he exclaimed, rousing up from his place. "What's your bloody hurry? Come on back here and shake hands with Mr. Thomas —- Mr. Thomas is my boss herder up in Apache County. Thinking of bringing him down here next Fall," he added laconically, and by the subtle change in his voice Hardy realized intuitively that that move had been the subject of their interrupted argument. More than that, he felt vaguely that he himself was somehow involved in the discussion, the more so as Mr. Thomas balked absolutely at shaking hands with him.

"I hope Mr. Thomas will find it convenient to stop at the ranch," he murmured pleasantly, "but don't let me interfere with your business."

"Well, I guess that's all to-night, Shep," remarked Swope, taking charge of the situation. "I jest wanted you to meet Hardy while you was together. This is the Mr. Hardy, of the Dos S outfit, you understand," he continued, "and a white cowman! If you have to go across his range, go quick —- and tell your men the same. I want them dam' tail-twisters up in that Four Peaks country to know that it pays to be decent to a sheepman, and I'm goin' to show some of 'em, too, before I git through! But any time my sheep happen to git on your range, Mr. Hardy," he added reassuringly, "you jest order 'em off, and Mr. Thomas here will see to it that they go!"

He turned upon his boss herder with a menacing gesture, as if charging him with silence, and Thomas, whose sole contribution to the conversation had been a grunt at the end, swung about and ambled sullenly off up the street.

"Feelin' kinder bad to-night," explained Swope, as his *mayordomo* butted into the swinging doors of a saloon and disappeared, "but you remember what I said about them sheep. How do things look up your way?" he inquired. "Feed pretty good?"

"It's getting awfully dry," replied Hardy noncommittally. "I suppose your sheep are up on the Black Mesa by this time."

"Ump!" responded the sheepman, and then there was a long pause. "Sit down," he said at last, squatting upon the edge of the sidewalk, "I want to talk business with you."

He lit a short black pipe and leaned back comfortably against a post.

"You seem to be a pretty smooth young feller," he remarked, patronizingly. "How long have you been in these parts? Two months, eh? How'd Judge Ware come to get a-hold of you?"

"Just picked me up down at Bender," replied Hardy.

"Oh, jest picked you up, hey? I thought mebby you was some kin to him. Ain't interested in the cattle, are you? Well, I jest thought you might be, being put in over Jeff that way, you know. Nice boy, that, but hot-headed as a goat. He'll be making hair bridles down in Yuma some day, I reckon. His old man was the same way. So you ain't no kin to the judge and've got no int'rest in the cattle, either, eh? H'm, how long do you figure on holding down that job?"

"Don't know," replied Hardy; "might quit to-day or get fired to-morrow. It's a good place, though."

"Not the only one, though," suggested the sheepman shrewdly, "not by a dam' sight! Ever investigate the sheep business? No? Then you've overlooked something! I've lived in this country for nigh onto twenty years, and followed most every line of business, but I didn't make my pile punching cows, nor running a store, neither —- I made it *raising sheep*. Started in with nothing at the time of the big drought in '92, herding on shares. Sheep did well in them good years that followed, and first thing I knew I was a sheepman. Now I've got forty thousand head, and I'm making a hundred per cent on my investment every year. Of course, if there comes a drought I'll lose half of 'em, but did you ever sit down and figure out a hundred per cent a year? Well, five thousand this year is ten next year, and ten is twenty the next year, and the twenty looks like forty thousand dollars at the end of three years. That's quite a jag of money, eh? I won't say what it would be in three years more, but here's the point. You're a young man and out to make a stake, I suppose, like the rest of 'em. What's the use of wasting your time and energy trying to hold that bunch of half-starved cows together? What's the use of going into a *poor* business, man, when there's a *better* business; and I'll tell you right now, the sheep business is the coming industry of Arizona. The sheepmen are going to own this country, from Flag to the Mexican line, and you might as well git on the boat, boy, before it's too late."

He paused, as if waiting for his points to sink home; then he reached out and tapped his listener confidentially on the knee.

"Hardy," he said, "I like your style. You've got a head, and you know how to keep your mouth shut. More'n that, you don't drink. A man like you could git to be a boss sheep-herder in six months; you could make a small fortune in three years and never know you was workin'. You don't need to work, boy; I kin git a hundred men to work —- what I want is a man that can *think*. Now, say, I'm goin' to need a man pretty soon —- come around and see me some time."

"All right," said Hardy, reluctantly, "but I might as well tell you now that I'm satisfied where I am."

"Satisfied!" ripped out Swope, with an oath. "Satisfied! Why, man alive, you're jest hanging on by your eyebrows up there at Hidden Water! *You* haven't got nothin'; you don't even own the house you live in. I could go up there to-morrow and file on that land and you couldn't do a dam' thing. Judge Ware thought he was pretty smooth when he euchred me out of that place, but I want to tell you, boy —- and you can tell him, if you want to —- that Old Man Winship never held no title to that place, and it's public land to-day. That's all public land up there; there ain't a foot of land in the Four Peaks country that I can't run my sheep over if I want to, and keep within my legal rights. So that's where you're at, Mr. Hardy, if you want to know!"

He stopped and rammed a cut of tobacco into his pipe, while Hardy tapped his boot meditatively. "Well," he said at last, "if that's the way things are, I'm much obliged to you for not sheeping us out this Spring. Of course, I haven't been in the country long, and I don't know much about these matters, but I tried to accommodate you all I could, thinking —- "

"That ain't the point," broke in Swope, smoking fiercely, "I ain't threatening ye, and I appreciate your hospitality —- but here's the point. What's the use of your monkeying along up there on a job that is sure to play out, when you can go into a better business? Answer me that, now!"

But Hardy only meditated in silence. It was beyond contemplation that he should hire himself out as a sheep-herder, but if he said so frankly it might call down the wrath of Jim Swope upon both him and the Dos S. So he stood pat and began to fish for information.

"Maybe you just think my job is going to play out," he suggested, diplomatically. "If I'd go to a cowman, now, or ask Judge Ware, they might tell me I had it cinched for life."

Swope puffed smoke for a minute in a fulminating, dangerous silence.

"Huh!" he said. "I can dead easy answer for that. Your job, Mr. Hardy, lasts jest as long as I want it to —- and no longer. Now, you can figure that out for yourself. But I'd jest like to ask you a question, since you're so smart; how come all us sheepmen kept off your upper range this year?"

"Why," said Hardy innocently, "I tried to be friendly and treated you as white as I could, and I suppose —- "

"Yes, you suppose," sneered Swope grimly, "but I'll jest tell you; we wanted you to hold your job."

"That's very kind of you, I'm sure," murmured Hardy.

"Yes," replied the sheepman sardonically, "it is —- dam' kind of us. But now the question is: What ye goin' to do about it?"

"Why, in what way?"

"Well, now," began Swope, patiently feeling his way, "suppose, jest for instance, that some fool Mexican herder should accidentally get in on your upper range —- would you feel it your duty to put him off?"

"Well," said Hardy, hedging, "I really hadn't considered the matter seriously. Of course, if Judge Ware —- "

"The judge is in San Francisco," put in Swope curtly. "Now, suppose that *all* of us sheepmen should decide that we wanted some of that good feed up on Bronco Mesa, and, suppose, furthermore, that we should all go up there, as we have a perfect legal right to do, what would you do?"

"I don't know," replied Hardy politely.

"Well, supposen I dropped a stick of dynamite under you," burst out Swope hoarsely, "would you jump? Speak up, man, you know what I'm talking about. You don't think you can stand off the whole Sheepmen's Protective Association, do you? Well, then, will ye abide by the law and give us our legal rights or will ye fight like a dam' fool and git sent to Yuma for your pains? That's what I want to know, and when you talk to me you talk to the whole Sheepmen's

Association, with money enough in its treasury to send up every cowman in the Four Peaks country! What I want to know is this —- will you fight?"

"I might," answered Hardy quietly.

"Oh, you might, hey?" jeered the sheepman, tapping his pipe ominously on the sidewalk. "You might, he-ey? Well, look at Jeff Creede —- *he* fought —- and what's he got to show for it? Look at his old man —- *he* fought —- and where is he now? Tell me that!

"But, say, now," he exclaimed, changing his tone abruptly, "this ain't what I started to talk about. I want to speak with you, Mr. Hardy, on a matter of business. You jest think them things over until I see you again —- and, of course, all this is on the q. t. But now let's talk business. When you want to buy a postage stamp you come down here to Moroni, don't you? And why? Why, because it's near, sure! But when you want a wagon-load of grub —- and there ain't no one sells provisions cheaper than I do, beans four-fifty, bacon sixteen cents, flour a dollar-ninety, everything as reasonable —- you haul it clean across the desert from Bender. That easy adds a cent a pound on every ton you pull, to say nothin' of the time. Well, what I want to know is this: Does Einstein sell you grub that much cheaper? Take flour, for instance —- what does that cost you?"

"I don't know," answered Hardy, whose anger was rising under this unwarranted commercial badgering. "Same as with you, I suppose —- dollar-ninety."

"Ah!" exclaimed Swope triumphantly, "and the extra freight on a sack would be fifty cents, wouldn't it —- a cent a pound, and a fifty-pound sack! Well, now say, Hardy, we're good friends, you know, and all that —- and Jasp and me steered all them sheep around you, you recollect —- what's the matter with your buying your summer supplies off of me? I'll guarantee to meet any price that Bender Sheeny can make —- and, of course, I'll do what's right by you —- but, by Joe, I think you owe it to me!"

He paused and waited impatiently for his answer, but once more Hardy balked him.

"I don't doubt there's a good deal in what you say, Mr. Swope," he said, not without a certain weariness, "but you'll have to take that matter up with Judge Ware."

"Don't you have the ordering of the supplies?" demanded Swope sharply.

"Yes, but he pays for them. All I do is to order what I want and O. K. the bills. My credit is good with Einstein, and the rate lies between him and Judge Ware."

"Well, your credit is good here, too," replied Swope acidly, "but I see you'd rather trade with a Jew than stand in with your friends, any day."

"I tell you I haven't got a thing to do with it," replied Hardy warmly. "I take my orders from Judge Ware, and if he tells me to trade here I'll be glad to do so —- it'll save me two days' freighting —- but I'm not the boss by any means."

"No, nor you ain't much of a supe, neither," growled Swope morosely. "In fact, I consider you a dam' bum supe. Some people, now, after they had been accommodated, would take a little trouble, but I notice you ain't breaking your back for me. Hell, no, you don't care if I *never* make a deal. But that's all right, Mr. Hardy, I'll try and do as much for you about that job of yourn."

"Well, you must think I'm stuck on that job," cried Hardy hotly, "the way you talk about it! You seem to have an idea that if I get let out it'll make some difference to me, but I might as well tell you right now, Mr. Swope, that it won't. I've got a good horse and I've got money to travel on, and I'm just holding this job to accommodate Judge Ware. So if you have any idea of taking it out on him you can just say the word and I'll quit!"

"Um-m!" muttered the sheepman, taken aback by this sudden burst of temper, "you're a hot-headed boy, ain't you?" He surveyed him critically in the half light, as if appraising his value as a fighter, and then proceeded in a more conciliatory manner. "But you mustn't let your temper git away with you like that," he said. "You're likely to say something you'll be sorry for later."

"Oh, I don't know," retorted Hardy. "It might relieve my mind some. I've only been in this country a few months, but if a sheepman is the only man that has any legal or moral rights I'd like to know about it. You talk about coming in on our upper range, having a right to the whole country, and all that. Now I'd like to ask you whether in your opinion a cowman has got a right to live?"

"Oh, tut, tut, now," protested Swope, "you're gettin' excited."

"Well, of course I'm getting excited," replied Hardy, with feeling. "You start in by telling me the sheepmen are going to take the whole country, from Flag to the line; then you ask me what I'd do if a Mexican came in on us; then you say you can sheep us out any time you want to, and what am I going to do about it! Is that the way you talk to a man who has done his best to be your friend?"

"I never said we was going to sheep you out," retorted the sheepman sullenly. "And if I'd 'a' thought for a minute you would take on like this about it I'd've let you go bust for your postage stamps."

"I know you didn't *say* it," said Hardy, "but you hinted it good and strong, all right. And when a man comes as near to it as you have I think I've got a right to ask him straight out what his intentions are. Now how about it —- are you going to sheep us out next Fall or are you going to give us a chance?"

"Oh hell!" burst out Swope, in a mock fury, "I'm never going to talk to *you* any more! You're crazy, man! *I* never said I was going to sheep you out!"

"No," retorted Hardy dryly, "and you never said you wasn't, either."

"Yes, I did, too," spat back Swope, seizing at a straw. "Didn't I introduce you to my boss herder and tell him to keep off your range?"

"Oh, I don't know," said Hardy coldly. "Did you?"

For a moment the sheepman sat rigid in the darkness. Then he rose to his feet, cursing.

"Well, you can jest politely go to hell," he said, with venomous deliberation, and racked off down the street.

CHAPTER X
"FEED MY SHEEP"

The slow, monotonous days of Summer crept listlessly by like dreams which, having neither beginning nor end, pass away into nothingness, leaving only a dim memory of restlessness and mystery.

In the relentless heat of noon-day the earth seemed to shimmer and swim in a radiance of its own; at evening the sun set in a glory incomparable; and at dawn it returned to its own. Then in the long breathless hours the cows sought out the scanty shadow of the cañon wall, sprawling uneasily in the sand; the lizards crept far back into the crevices of the rocks; the birds lingered about the water holes, throttling their tongues, and all the world took on a silence that was almost akin to death. As the Summer rose to its climax a hot wind breathed in from the desert, clean and pure, but withering in its intensity; the great bowlders, superheated in the glare of day, irradiated the stored-up energy of the sun by night until even the rattlesnakes, their tough hides scorched through by the burning sands, sought out their winter dens to wait for a touch of frost. There was only one creature in all that heat-smitten land that defied the sway of the Sun-God and went his way unheeding —- man, the indomitable, the conqueror of mountains and desert and sea.

When the sun was hottest, then was the best time to pursue the black stallion of Bronco Mesa, chasing him by circuitous ways to the river where he and his band could drink. But though more than one fine mare and suckling, heavy with water, fell victim, the black stallion, having thought and intelligence like a man, plunged through the water, leaving his thirst unquenched, refusing with a continency and steadfastness rare even among men to sell his liberty at any price. In the round corral at Hidden Water there was roping and riding as Creede and Hardy gentled their prizes; in the cool evenings they rode forth along the Alamo, counting the cows as they came down to water or doctoring any that were sick; and at night they lay on their cots beneath the *ramada* telling long stories till they fell asleep.

At intervals of a month or more Hardy rode down to Moroni and each time he brought back some book of poems, or a novel, or a bundle of magazines; but if he received any letters he never mentioned it. Sometimes he read in the shade, his face sobered to a scholarly repose, and when the mood came and he was alone he wrote verses —- crude, feverish, unfinished —- and destroyed them, furtively.

He bore his full share of the rough work, whether riding or horse-breaking or building brush corrals, but while he responded to every mood of his changeable companion he hid the whirl of emotion which possessed him, guarding the secret of his heart even when writing to Lucy Ware; and slowly, as the months crept by, the wound healed over and left him whole.

At last the days grew shorter, the chill came back into the morning air, and the great thundercaps which all Summer had mantled the Peaks, scattering precarious and insufficient showers across the parching lowlands, faded away before the fresh breeze from the coast. Autumn had come, and, though the feed was scant, Creede started his round-up early, to finish ahead of the sheep. Out on The Rolls the wild and runty cows were hiding their newborn calves; the spring twos were grown to the raw-boned dignity of steers; and all must be gathered quickly, before the dust arose in the north and the sheep mowed down the summer grass. Once more from their distant ranches the mountain men trailed in behind their horses; the *rodéo* hands dropped in from nowhere, mysteriously, talking loudly of high adventures but with the indisputable marks of Mormon hay-forks on their thumbs.

Before their restless energy The Rolls were swept bare of market stock, and the upper end of the mesa as well, before the first sheep dust showed against the hills. The *rodéo* outfit left Carrizo and came down to Hidden Water, driving their herd before them, and still no sheep appeared. So long had they strained their eyes for nothing that the cowmen from the north became uneasy, dropping out one by one to return to their ranches for fear that the sheep had crept in and laid waste their pastures and corrals. Yet the round-up ended without a band in sight, where before The Rolls had been ploughed into channels by their multitude of feet.

In a slow fever of apprehension Hardy rode ceaselessly along the rim of Bronco Mesa, without finding so much as a track. Throughout that long month of watching and waiting the memory of his conversation with Jim Swope had haunted him, and with a sinister boding of impending evil he had ridden far afield, even to the lower crossing at Pablo Moreno's, where a few Mexicans and Basques were fording the shallow river. Not one of those veiled threats and intimations had he confided to Creede, for the orders from Judge Ware had been for peace and Jeff was hot-headed and hasty; but in his own mind Hardy pictured a solid phalanx of sheep, led by Jasp Swope and his gun-fighting Chihuahuanos, drifting relentlessly in over the unravaged mesa. Even that he could endure, trusting to some appeal or protest to save him from the ultimate disaster, but the strain of this ominous waiting was more than Hardy's nerves could stand.

As the town herd was put on the long trail for Bender and the round-up hands began to spit dry for their first drink, the premonition of evil conquered him and he beckoned Creede back out of the rout.

"I've got a hunch," he said, "that these sheepmen are hanging back until you boys are gone, in order to raid the upper range. I don't *know* anything, you understand, but I'm looking for trouble. How does it look to you?"

"Well," answered Creede sombrely, "I don't mind tellin' you that this is a new one on me. It's the first fall gather that I can remember when I didn't have a round-up with a sheepman or two. They're willin' enough to give us the go-by in the Spring, when there's grass everywhere, but when they come back over The Rolls in the Fall and see what they've done to the feed —- well, it's like fightin' crows out of a watermelon patch to protect that upper range.

"The only thing I can think of is they may be held back by this dry weather. But, I tell you, Rufe," he added, "it's jest as well I'm goin' —- one man can tell 'em to he'p themselves as good as two, and I might get excited. You know your orders —- and I reckon the sheepmen do, too, 's fer 's that goes. They're not so slow, if they do git lousy. But my God, boy, it hurts my feelin's to think of you all alone up here, tryin' to appeal to Jasp Swope's better nature." He twisted his lips, and shrugged his huge shoulders contemptuously. Then without enthusiasm he said: "Well, good luck," and rode away after his cattle.

Creede's scorn for this new policy of peace had never been hidden, although even in his worst cursing spells he had never quite named the boss. But those same orders, if they ever became known, would call in the rapacious sheepmen like vultures to a feast, and the bones of his cattle —- that last sorry remnant of his father's herds —- would bleach on Bronco Mesa with the rest, a mute tribute to the triumph of sheep.

All that day Hardy rode up the Alamo until he stood upon the summit of the Juate and looked over the divide to the north, and still there were no sheep. Not a smoke, not a dust streak, although the chill of Autumn was in the air. In the distant Sierra Blancas the snow was already on the peaks and the frosts lay heavy upon the black mesa of the Mogollons. Where then could the sheep be, the tender, gently nurtured sheep, which could stand neither heat in Summer nor cold in Winter, but must always travel, travel, feeding upon the freshest of green grass and leaving a desert in their wake? The slow-witted Mexicans and Basques, who did not follow the lead of the Swopes, had returned on their fall migration with the regularity of animals, but all those cheery herders for whom he had cooked and slaved —- Bazan, McDonald, the Swopes and their kin, who used the upper ford —- were lost as if the earth had swallowed them up.

The stars were shining when Hardy came in sight of the ranch at the end of that unprofitable day, and he was tired. The low roof of the house rose up gloomily before him, but while he was riding in a hound suddenly raised his challenge in the darkness. Instantly his yell was answered by a chorus, and as Chapuli swerved from the rush of the pack the door was thrown open and the tall, gaunt form of Bill Johnson stood outlined against the light.

"Yea, Ribs; hey, Rock; down, Ring!" he hollered. "Hey, boys; hey, Suke!" And in a mighty chorus of bayings the long-eared hounds circled about and returned to the feet of their master, wagging their tails but not abating their barking one whit. Standing bareheaded in the doorway with his hair and beard bushed out like a lion's mane Johnson strove by kicks and curses to quiet their uproar, shouting again and again some words which Hardy could not catch.

At last, grabbing old Suke, the leader of the pack, by an ear, he slapped her until her yelpings silenced the rest; then, stepping out into the opening, he exclaimed:

"My God, Hardy, is that you?"

"Sure," replied Hardy impatiently. "Why, what's the matter?"

"Sheep!" shouted Johnson, throwing out his hands wildly, "thousands of 'em, millions of 'em!"

"Sheep —- where?" demanded Hardy. "Where are they?"

"They're on your upper range, boy, and more comin'!"

"What?" cried Hardy incredulously. "Why, how did they get up there? I just rode the whole rim to-day!"

"They come over the top of the Four Peaks," shouted the old man, shaking with excitement. "Yes, sir, over the top of the Four Peaks! My hounds took after a lion last night, and this mornin' I trailed 'em clean over into the middle fork where they had 'im treed. He jumped down and run when I come up and jist as we was hotfoot after him we run spang into three thousand head of sheep, drifting down from the pass, and six greasers and a white man in the rear with carbeens. The whole dam' outfit is comin' in on us. But we can turn 'em yet! Whar's Jeff and the boys?"

"They've gone to town with the cattle."

"Well, you're dished then," said the old man grimly. "Might as well put up your horse and eat —- I'm goin' home and see that they don't none of 'em git in on me!"

"Whose sheep were they?" inquired Hardy, as he sat down to a hasty meal.

"Don't ask me, boy," replied Johnson. "I never had time to find out. One of them Mexicans took a shot at Rye and I pulled my gun on him, and then the boss herder he jumped in, and there we had it, back and forth. He claimed I was tryin' to stompede his sheep, but I *knowed* his greaser had tried to shoot my dog, and I told him so! And I told him furthermore that the first sheep or sheepman that p'inted his head down the Pocket trail would stop lead; and every one tharafter, as long as I could draw a bead. And by Gawd, I mean it!" He struck his gnarled fist upon the table till every tin plate jumped, and his fiery eyes burned savagely as he paced about the room.

At first peep of dawn Bill Johnson was in the saddle, his long-barrelled revolver thrust pugnaciously into his boot, his 30-30 carbine across his arm, and his hounds slouching dutifully along in the rear. Close behind followed Hardy, bound for the Peaks, but though the morning was cold he had stripped off his coat and shaps, and everything which might conceal a weapon, leaving even his polished Colt's in his blankets. If the sheep were to be turned now it could never be by arms. The sheepmen had stolen a march, Creede and his cowboys were far away, and his only hope was the olive branch of peace. Yet as he spurred up the Carrizo trail he felt helpless and abused, like a tried soldier who is sent out unarmed by a humanitarian commander. Only one weapon was left to him —- the one which even Jim Swope had noticed —- his head; and as he worked along up the hogback which led down from the shoulder of the Four Peaks he schooled himself to a Spartan patience and fortitude.

At last from a high cliff which overshadowed the broad cañon of the middle fork, he looked down and saw the sheep, like a huge, dirty-brown blot, pouring in a hundred diverging lines down the valley and feeding as they came. Higher and higher up the sides the old ewes fought their way, plucking at the long spears of grass which grew among the rocks; and the advance guard, hurrying forward, nipped eagerly at the browse and foliage as they passed, until, at last, some tempting bush detained them too long and they were swallowed up in the ruck. Little paths appeared in the leaders' wake, winding in and out among the bowlders; and like soldiers the sheep fell into line, moving forward with the orderly precision of an army. A herder with his dogs trailed nonchalantly along the flank, the sun glinting from his carbine as he clambered over rocks, and in the rear another silent shepherd followed up the drag. So far it was a peaceful pastoral scene, but behind the herd where the camp rustler and his burros should have been there was a posse of men, and each man carried a gun.

Hardly had Chapuli mounted the ridge before every head was raised; the swarthy Mexicans unslung their guns with a flourish, and held them at a ready. Yet for half an hour the lone horseman sat there like a statue, and if he resented their coming or saw the dust of other bands behind, he made no sign. Even when the guard of men passed beneath him, craning their necks uneasily, he still remained silent and immobile, like a man who has councils of his own or leads a force behind.

The leader of the vanguard of the sheep was a white man, and not unversed in the principles of war, for after trailing safely through the box of the cañon —- where a single rock displaced would kill a score of sheep, and where the lone horseman had he so willed could have potted half of the invaders from the heights —- he turned his herd up a side cañon to the west and hastily pitched his camp on a ridge. As the heat of the day came on, the other bands up the cañon stopped also, and when the faint smoke showed Hardy that the camp rustlers were cooking dinner, he turned and rode for the leader's camp.

Dinner was already served —- beans, fried mutton, and bread, spread upon a greasy canvas —- and the hungry herders were shovelling it down with knives in their own primitive way when Hardy rode up the slope. As he came into camp the Chihuahuanos dropped their plates, reached for their guns, and stood in awkward postures of defence, some wagging their big heads in a braggartly defiance, others, their courage waning, grinning in the natural shame of the peasant. In Hardy they recognized a gentleman of *categoría* —- and he never so much as glanced at them as he reined in his spirited horse. His eyes were fixed upon the lone white man, their commander, who stood by the fire regarding him with cold suspicion, and to whom he bowed distantly.

"Good-morning," he said, by way of introduction, and the sheepman blinked his eyes in reply.

"Whose sheep are those?" continued Hardy, coming to the point with masterful directness, and once more the boss sheepman surveyed him with suspicion.

"Mine," he said, and Hardy returned his stare with a glance which, while decorously veiled, indicated that he knew he lied. The man was a stranger to him, rather tall and slender, with drawn lips and an eye that never wavered. His voice was tense with excitement and he kept his right thumb hooked carelessly into the corner of his pocket, not far from the grip of a revolver. As soon as he spoke Hardy knew him.

"You are Mr. Thomas, aren't you?" he inquired, as if he had no thought of trouble. "I believe I met you once, down in Moroni."

"Ump!" grunted Mr. Thomas unsociably, and at that moment one of the Mexicans, out of awkwardness, dropped his gun. As he stooped to pick it up a slow smile crept over the cowman's lips, a smile which expressed polite amusement along with a measured contempt —- and the boss herder was stung with a nameless shame at the false play.

"Put up them guns, you dam' gawky fools!" he yelled in a frenzy of rage. "Put 'em up, I say. This man ain't goin' to eat ye!" And though the poor browbeaten Chihuahuanos understood not a word of English they felt somehow that they had been overzealous and shuffled back to their blankets, like watchdogs that had been rebuked.

"Now," said the sheepman, taking his hand from his gun, "what can I do for you, Mr. Hardy?"

"Well," responded Hardy, "of course there are several things you *might* do to accommodate me, but maybe you wouldn't mind telling me how you got in here, just for instance?"

"Always glad to 'commodate —- where I can, of course," returned the sheepman grimly. "I came in over the top of them Four Peaks yonder."

"Um," said Hardy, glancing up at the rocky walls. "Then you must've had hooks on your eyebrows, for sure. I suppose the rest of the family is coming, too! And, by the way, how is my friend, Mr. Swope?"

He appended this last with an artless smile, quite lacking in bitterness, but somehow the boss herder felt himself discredited by the inquiry, as if he were consorting with thieves. It was the old shame of the sheepman, the shame which comes to the social outcast, and burns upon the cheek of the dishonored bastard, but which is seared deepest into the heart of the friendless herder, the Ishmaelite of the cow-country, whose hand is against every man and every man's against him. Hunger and thirst he can endure, and the weariness of life, but to have all men turn away from him, to answer him grudgingly, to feed him at their table, but refuse themselves to eat, this it is which turns his heart to bitterness and makes him a man to be feared. As Thomas had looked at this trim young cowboy, smooth-shaven and erect, sitting astride a blooded horse which snorted and pawed the ground delicately, and then had glanced at the low and brutal Mexicans with whom his lot was cast, a blind fury had swept over him, wreaking its force upon his own retainers; and now, when by implication he was classed with Jim Swope, he resented it still more bitterly.

"Dam'fino," he answered sullenly. "Haven't seen 'im for a month."

"Oh, isn't he with you this trip?" asked Hardy, in surprise. "I had hoped that I might find him up here." There was a suggestion of irony in his words which was not lost upon the *mayordomo*, but Thomas let the remark pass in silence.

"Perhaps his brother Jasper is along," ventured Hardy. "No? Well, that's Jim's earmark on those sheep, and I know it. What's the matter?"

"Matter with what?" growled Thomas morosely.

"Why, with Jim, of course. I thought after the pleasant times we had together last Spring he'd be sure to come around. In fact," he added meaningly, "I've been looking for him."

At this naive statement, the sheepman could not restrain a smile.

"You don't know Jim as well as I do," he said, and there was a suggestion of bitterness in his voice which Hardy was not slow to note.

"Well, perhaps not," he allowed; "but you know, and I know, that this is no pleasure trip you're on —- in fact, it's dangerous, and I never thought that Jim Swope would send a man where he was afraid to go himself. Now I've got nothing against you, Mr. Thomas, and of course you're working for him; but I ask you, as a man, don't you think, after what I've done for him, that Jim Swope ought to come along himself if he wants to sheep me out?

"I've fed him, and I've fed all his herders and all his friends; I've grained his horses when they were ga'nted down to a shadow because his own sheep had cleaned up the feed; I've made him welcome to my house and done everything I could for him; and all I asked in return was that he would respect this upper range. He knows very well that if his sheep go through here this Fall our cattle will die in the Winter, and he knows that there is plenty of feed out on The Rolls where our cows can't go, and yet he sends you in where he's scared to go himself, just to hog our last piece of good feed and to put us out of business. I asked him down in Moroni if he thought a cowman had a right to live, and he dodged the question as if he was afraid he'd say something."

He stopped abruptly and looked out over the country toward Hidden Water, while the Mexicans watched him furtively from beneath their slouched hats.

"Expecting some friends?" inquired Thomas, with a saturnine grin.

Hardy shook his head. "No. I came out here alone, and I left my gun in camp. I haven't got a friend within forty miles, if that's what you mean. I suppose you've got your orders, Mr. Thomas, but I just want to talk this matter over with you."

"All right," said the sheepman, suddenly thawing out at the good news. "I don't have so much company as to make me refuse, even if it is a warm subject. But mebby you'd like a bite to eat before we git down to business?" He waved a deprecating hand at the greasy canvas, and Hardy swung quickly down from his saddle.

"Thanks. But don't let me keep you from your dinner. Here's where I break even with Jim Swope for all that grub I cooked last Spring," he remarked, as he filled his plate. "But if it was him that asked me," he added, "I'd starve to death before I'd eat it."

He sat on his heels by the canvas, with the boss sheepman on the other side, and the Mexicans who had been so cocky took their plates and retired like Apaches to the edge of the brush, where they would not obtrude upon their betters.

"They say it's bad for the digestion," observed Hardy, after the first silence, "to talk about things that make you mad; so if you don't mind, Mr. Thomas, we'll forget about Jim Swope. What kind of a country is it up there in Apache County, where you keep your sheep all Summer?"

"A fine country," rejoined Thomas, "and I wish to God I was back to it," he added.

"Why, what's the matter with this country? It looks pretty good to me."

"Ye-es," admitted the sheepman grudgingly, "it looks good enough, but —- well, I lived up there a long time and I got to like it. I had one of the nicest little ranches in the White Mountains; there was good huntin' and fishin' and —- well, I felt like a white man up there —- never had no trouble, you understand —- and I was makin' good money, too."

His voice, which before had been harsh and strident, softened down as he dwelt upon the natural beauty of the mountains which had been his home, but there was a tone of sadness in his talk which told Hardy that ultimately he had suffered some great misfortune there. His occupation alone suggested that —- for there are few white men working as sheep-herders who lack a hard luck story, if any one will listen to it. But this Shep Thomas was still young and unbroken, with none of the black marks of dissipation upon his face, and his eyes were as keen and steady as any hunter's. He was indeed the very type of fighter that Swope had sought, hardy and fearless, and at the same time careful. As they sat together Hardy looked him over and was glad that he had come out unarmed, yet though his host seemed a man of just and reasonable mind there was a set, dogged look in his eyes which warned the cowman not to interfere, but let him talk his fill. And the boss herder, poor lonely man, was carried away in spite of himself by the temptation of a listener; after many days of strife and turmoil, cutting trails, standing off cowmen, cursing Mexicans, at last to meet a white man who would just sit silent and let him talk! His stories were of hunting and fishing, of prospecting, and restless adventures among the Indians, and every time the conversation worked around towards sheep he led it resolutely away. And for his part, never for a moment did Hardy try to crowd him, but let the talk lead where it would, until of his own volition the sheepman told his story.

"I suppose you wonder what I'm doing down here," he said at last, "if I was so stuck on the Concho country? Well, I bet you wouldn't guess in a thousand years —- and you ought to be a pretty good guesser, too," he added, with a gruff laugh. "Now, what do you think it was that put me on the bum?"

"Poker game?" queried Hardy politely.

"Nope," replied the sheepman, showing his teeth, "I'm winners on poker."

"You don't look like a drinking man."

"Naw —- nor it wasn't women, either. It's something unusual, I tell you. I stood and looked at it for ten years, and never turned a hair. But here, I've been holdin' out on you a little —- I never told you what it was I raised on my ranch. Well, it was sheep."

"Sheep?" echoed Hardy, "did you keep 'em there all Winter?"

"W'y sure, man. There's lots of sheep in Apache County that was never ten miles from home."

"Then why does Jim Swope bring his bands south every Fall? I hear he loses five per cent of them, at the least, coming and going."

"Ah, you don't understand Jim as well as I do. I was tryin' to make a livin'; he's tryin' to git rich. He's doin' it, too."

Once more the note of bitterness came into his voice, and Hardy saw that the time had come.

"How's that?" he inquired quietly, and the sheepman plunged into his story.

"Well, it was this way. I kept a few thousand sheep up there in my valley. In the Summer we went up the mountain, followin' the grass, and in the Winter we fed down below, where the ground was bare. It never got very cold, and my sheep was used to it, anyhow. The Navajos don't move their sheep south, do they? Well, they're away north of where I was. We jest give 'em a little shelter, and looked after 'em, and, as I says, I was doin' fine —- up to last year."

He paused again, with his secret on his lips, and once more Hardy supplied the helping word.

"And what happened then?" he asked.

"What happened then?" cried Thomas, his eyes burning. "Well, *you* ought to know —- I was sheeped out."

"Sheeped out? Why, how could that happen? You were a sheepman yourself!"

The boss herder contemplated him with an amused and cynical smile. "You ask Jim Swope," he suggested.

For a minute Hardy sat staring at him, bewildered. "Well," he said, "*I* can't figure it out —- maybe you wouldn't mind telling me how it happened."

"Why hell, man," burst out the sheepman, "it's as plain as the nose on your face —- I didn't belong to the Association. All these big sheepmen that drive north and south belong to the Sheepmen's Protective Association, and they stand in with each other, but we little fellows up in 'Pache County was nobody. It's about ten years ago now that the Swope outfit first came in through our country; and, bein' in the sheep business ourselves, we was always friendly, and never made no trouble, and naturally supposed that they'd respect our range. And so they did, until I found one of Jim's herders in on my ranch last Summer.

"Well, I thought there was some misunderstandin', but when I told him and his *compadres* to move it was a bad case of 'No savvy' from the start; and while I was monkeyin' around with them a couple of more bands sneaked in behind, and first thing I knew my whole lower range was skinned clean. Well, sir, I worked over one of them *paisanos* until he was a total wreck, and I took a shot at another *hombre*, too —- the one that couldn't savvy; but there was no use cavin' round about it —- I was jest naturally sheeped out.

"It looked like I was busted, but I wouldn't admit it, and while I was studyin' on the matter along comes Jim himself and offers me five thousand dollars for my sheep. They was worth ten if they was worth a cent, all fine and fat; but my winter feed was gone and of course I was up against it. I see somethin' would have to be done, and dam' quick, too; so I chased down to St. John and tried to git a higher bid. But these sheepmen stand in with each other on a proposition like that, and I couldn't git nawthin'.

"'All right,' I says to Jim, 'take 'em, and be dam'ed to you.'

"'The price has gone down,' says Jim. 'I'll give you four thousand.'

"'*What!*' I says.

"'Three thousand,' says Jim.

"'You'll give me *five* thousand,' says I, crowdin' my gun against his short ribs, 'or I'll let the light in on you,' and after that Jim and me understood each other perfectly. In fact, we got stuck on each other. Yes, sir, after I got over bein' excited and could listen to reason, he put it to me straight —- and he was right.

"'What's the use of bein' the yaller dog?' he says. 'You can't buck the whole Association. But we've got room for you,' he says, 'so git on and ride.' And here I am, by Joe, leadin' the procession."

The sheepman paused and gazed at the band of sheep as they stood in a solid mass, their heads tucked under each other's bellies to escape the sun.

"Some of them sheep used to be mine," he observed, and laughed slyly. "That's the only thing between me and the boss. He's begged and implored, and cursed and said his prayers, tryin' to git me interested in the sheep business again; but like the pore, dam' fool I am I keep that five thousand dollars in the bank." His shoulders heaved for a moment with silent laughter, and then his face turned grave.

"Well, Mr. Hardy," he said, "business is business, and I've got to be movin' along pretty soon. I believe you said you'd like to talk matters over for a minute."

"Yes," answered Hardy promptly, "I'd like to make arrangements to have you turn out through that pass yonder and leave us a little feed for next Winter."

The sheepman cocked his head to one side and shut one eye knowingly.

"Oh, you would, would you? And what word shall I take back to the boss, then?"

"I expect I'll see him before you do," said Hardy, "but if you get ahead of me you can just say that I asked you to move, and so you followed out your orders."

"Yes," responded Thomas, smiling satirically, "that'd be lovely. But how long since I've been takin' orders off of you?"

"Oh, I'm not trying to give you any orders," protested Hardy. "Those come straight from Jim Swope."

"How's that?" inquired the sheepman, with sudden interest.

"Why, don't you remember what he said when he introduced me to you, down in Moroni? 'This is Mr. Hardy,' he said, 'a white cowman. If you have to go across his range, go quick, and tell your men the same.' You may have forgotten, but it made a great impression on me. And then, to show there was no mistake about it, he told me if I found any of his sheep on my range to order them off, and you would see that they went. Isn't that straight?"

He leaned over and looked the sheepman in the eye but Thomas met his glance with a sardonic smile. "Sure, it's right. But I've received other orders since then. You know Jim claims to be religious —- he's one of the elders in the church down there —- and he likes to keep his word good. After you was gone he come around to me and said: 'That's all right, Shep, about what I said to that cowman, but there's one thing I want you always to remember —- feed my sheep!' Well, them's my orders."

"Well," commented Hardy, "that may be good Scripture, but what about my cows? There's plenty of feed out on The Rolls for Jim's sheep, but my cows have got to drink. We cowmen have been sheeped out of all the lower country down there, and here we are, crowded clear up against the rocks. You've stolen a march on us and of course you're entitled to some feed, but give us a chance. You've been sheeped out yourself, and you know what it feels like. Now all I ask of you is that you turn out through this pass and go down onto The Rolls. If you'll do that I can turn all the rest of the sheep and keep my cows from starving, but if you go through me they'll all go through me, and I'm done for. I don't make any threats and I can't offer any inducements, but I just ask you, as a white man, to go around."

As he ended his appeal he stood with his hands thrown out, and the sheepman looked at him, smiling curiously.

"Well," he said, at last, "you're a new kind of cowman on me, pardner, but I'll go you, if Jim throws a fit."

He advanced, and held out his hand, and Hardy took it.

"If all sheepmen were like you," he said, "life would be worth living in these parts." And so, in a friendship unparalleled in the history of the Four Peaks country, a sheepman and a cowman parted in amity —- and the sheep went around.

CHAPTER XI
JUMPED

Winter, the wonted season of torrential rains, six weeks' grass, and budding flowers, when the desert is green and the sky washed clean and blue, followed close in the wake of the sheep, which went drifting past Hidden Water like an army without banners. But alas for Hidden Water and the army of sheep! —- in this barren Winter the torrential rains did not fall, the grass did not sprout, and the flowers did not bloom. A bleak north wind came down from the mountains, cold and dry and crackling with electricity, and when it had blown its stint it died down in a freezing, dusty silence.

Then the mighty south —- the rain —- wind that blows up out of Papaguería, rose up, big with promise, and whirled its dust clouds a thousand feet high against the horizon. But, after much labor, the keen, steely, north wind rushed suddenly down upon the black clouds, from whose edges the first spatter of rain had already spilled, and swept them from the horizon, howling mournfully the while and wrestling with the gaunt trees at night. In shaded places the icicles from slow-seeping waters clung for days unmelted, and the migrant ducks, down from the Arctic, rose up from the half-frozen sloughs and winged silently away to the far south. Yet through it all the Dos S cattle came out unscathed, feeding on what dry grass and browse the sheep had left on Bronco Mesa; and in the Spring, when all hope seemed past, it rained.

Only those who have been through a drought know what music there is hidden in rain. It puts a wild joy into the heart of every creature, the birds sing, the rabbits leap and caper, and all the cattle and wild horses take to roaming and wandering out of pure excess of spirits. It was early in March when the first showers came, and as soon as the new feed was up Creede began his preparations for the spring *rodéo*. The Winter had been a hard one, and not without its worries. In an interview, which tended on both sides to become heated and personal, Jim Swope had denounced Hardy for misrepresenting his orders to his *mayordomo*, and had stated in no uncertain terms his firm intention of breaking even in the Spring, if there was a blade of grass left on the upper range.

The season had been a bad one for his sheep, windy and cold, with sand storms which buried the desert in a pall and drove many flocks to the hills; and as the feed became shorter and shorter vagrant bands began to drift in along the Salagua. In the battle for the range that followed herders and punchers greeted each other with angry snarls which grew more wolfish every day, and old Pablo Moreno, shaking his white head over their quarrels, uttered gloomy prophecies of greater evils to come. Sheep would die, he said, cattle would die —- it was only a question now of how many, and of which. It was a coming *año seco*; nay, the whole country was drying up. In Hermosillo, so they said, the women stood by the public well all night, waiting to fill their *ollas*; not for nine years had the rains fallen there, and now the drought was spreading north. Arizona, California, Nevada, all were doomed, yet *paciencia*, perhaps —- and then came the rain. Yes, it was a good rain but —- and then it rained again. *Que bueno*, who would not be made a liar for rain? But *cuidado* —- behold, the ground was still dry; it drank up the water as it fell and was thirsty again; the river fell lower and lower and the water was clear; a bad sign, a very bad sign!

But if the young should wait upon the advice of the old there would be no more miracles. Creede and Hardy passed up the weather, strapped on their six-shooters, and began to patrol the range, "talking reason" to the stray Mexicans who thought that, because their sheep were getting poor, they ought to move them to better feed.

The time for friendship and diplomacy was past, as Hardy politely informed his employer by letter —- after which he told Rafael to keep away from the post office and not bring him any more *corréo*, if he valued his job. But though he had made his note to Judge Ware brief, it had said too much. He had suggested that if the judge did not like his change of policy he had better come down and see the actual conditions for himself —- and the old judge came.

It was midafternoon of that fateful day when Creede and Hardy, riding in from up the river, saw Rafael's wagon in front of the house. This was not surprising in itself as he had been down to Bender for round-up supplies, but as the two partners approached the house Creede suddenly grabbed Hardy's rein and drew back as if he were on top of a rattlesnake.

"For God's sake," he said, "what's that? Listen!"

He jerked a thumb toward the house, and in the tense silence Hardy could clearly discern the sound of women's voices. Now you could ride the Four Peaks country far and wide and never hear the music of such voices, never see calico on the line, or a lace curtain across the window. There were no women in that godless land, not since the Widow Winship took Sallie and Susie and left precipitately for St. Louis, none save the Señora Moreno and certain strapping Apache squaws who wore buckskin *téwas* and carried butcher knives in their belts. Even the heart of Rufus Hardy went pit-a-pat and stopped, at the sound of that happy chatter.

"They're rustlin' the whole dam' house," exclaimed Creede, all nerves and excitement. "Didn't you hear that pan go 'bamp'? Say, I believe they're cleanin' house! Rufe," he whispered, "I bet you money we're jumped!"

The possibility of having their ranch preëmpted during their absence had been spoken of in a general way, since Jim Swope had gone on the warpath, but in his secret soul Rufus Hardy had a presentiment which made claim-jumping look tame. There was a chastened gayety in the voices, a silvery ripple in the laughter, which told him what Creede with all his cunning could never guess; they were voices from another world, a world where Hardy had had trouble and sorrow enough, and which he had left forever. There was soldier blood in his veins and in two eventful years he had never weakened; but the suddenness of this assault stampeded him.

"You better go first, Jeff," he said, turning his horse away, "they might —- "

But Creede was quick to intercept him.

"None o' that, now, pardner," he said, catching his rein. "You're parlor-broke —- go on ahead!"

There was a wild, uneasy stare in his eye, which nevertheless meant business, and Hardy accepted the rebuke meekly. Perhaps his conscience was already beginning to get action for the subterfuge and deceit which he had practised during their year together. He sat still for a moment, listening to the voices and smiling strangely.

"All right, brother," he said, in his old quiet way, and then, whirling Chapuli about, he galloped up to the house, sitting him as straight and resolute as any soldier. But Creede jogged along more slowly, tucking in his shirt, patting down his hair, and wiping the sweat from his brow.

At the thud of hoofs a woman's face appeared at the doorway —- a face sweet and innocent, with a broad brow from which the fair hair was brushed evenly back, and eyes which looked wonderingly out at the world through polished glasses. It was Lucy Ware, and when Hardy saw her he leaped lightly from his horse and advanced with hat in hand —- smiling, yet looking beyond her.

"I'm so glad to see you, Miss Lucy," he said, as he took her hand, "and if we had only known you were coming —- "

"Why, Rufus Hardy!" exclaimed the young lady, "do you mean to say you never received *any* of my letters?"

At this Creede stared, and in that self-same moment Hardy realized how the low-down strategy which he had perpetrated upon his employer had fallen upon his own head a thousandfold. But before he could stammer his apologies, Kitty Bonnair stood before him —- the same Kitty, and smiling as he had often seen her in his dreams.

She was attired in a stunning outing suit of officer's cloth, tailored for service, yet bringing out the graceful lines of her figure; and as Hardy mumbled out his greetings the eyes of Jefferson Creede, so long denied of womankind, dwelt eagerly upon her beauty. Her dainty feet, encased in tan high boots, held him in rapt astonishment; her hands fascinated him with their movements like the subtle turns of a mesmerist; and the witchery of her supple body, the mischief in the dark eyes, and the teasing sweetness of her voice smote him to the heart before he was so much as noticed.

No less absolute, for all his strivings, was the conquest of Rufus Hardy, the frozen bulwarks of whose heart burst suddenly and went out like spring ice in the radiance of her first smile.

"I knew you'd be glad to see me, too," she said, holding out her hand to him; and forgetful of all his bitterness he grasped it warmly. Then, tardily conscious of his duty, he turned to Jeff.

"Miss Kitty," he said, "this is my friend, Jefferson Creede —- Miss Bonnair."

"I'm glad to meet you, Mr. Creede," said Kitty, bestowing her hand upon the embarrassed cowboy. "Of course you know Miss Ware!"

"Howdy do, Miss," responded Creede, fumbling for his hat, and as Miss Lucy took his hand the man who had put the fear of God into the hearts of so many sheep-herders became dumb and tongue-tied with bashfulness. There was not a man in the Four Peaks country that could best him, in anger or in jest, when it called for the ready word; but Kitty Bonnair had so stolen his wits that he could only stand and sweat like a trick-broken horse. As for Hardy he saw rainbows and his heart had gone out of business, but still he was "parlor-broke."

"I am afraid you didn't find the house very orderly," he observed, as Creede backed off and the conversation sagged; and the two girls glanced at each other guiltily. "Of course you're just as welcome," he added hastily, "and I suppose you couldn't help cleaning house a bit; but you gave us both a bad scare, all the same. Didn't you notice how pale we looked?" he asked, to mask his embarrassment. "But you were right, Jeff," he continued enigmatically.

"Does he always defer to you that way, Mr. Creede?" inquired Kitty Bonnair, with an engaging smile. "*We* used to find him rather perverse." She glanced roguishly at Hardy as she gave this veiled rebuke. "But what was it that you were right about? —- I'm just dying to ask you questions!"

She confessed this with a naive frankness which quite won the big cowboy's heart, and, his nerve coming back, he grinned broadly at his former suspicions.

"Well," he said, "I might as well come through with it —- I told him I bet we'd been jumped."

"Jumped?" repeated Miss Kitty, mystified. "Oh, is that one of your cowboy words? Tell me what it means!"

"W'y, it means," drawled Creede, "that two young fellers like me and Rufe goes out to ride the range and when we come back some other outfit has moved into our happy home and we're orphans. We've been havin' a little trouble with the sheep lately, and when I heard them pots and kittles rattlin' around in here I thought for sure some Mormon sheepman had got the jump on us and located the ranch."

"And what would you have done if he had?" continued Kitty eagerly. "Would you have shot him with that big pistol?" She pointed to the heavy Colt's which Creede had slung on his hip.

But this was getting too romantic and Western, even for Jeff. "No, ma'am," he said modestly. "We just carry that to balance us in the saddle."

"Oh!" exclaimed Kitty, disappointed, "and didn't you ever shoot *anybody*?"

Creede blushed for her, in spite of himself. "Well," he replied evasively, "I don't know how it would be up where you come from, but that's kind of a leadin' question, ain't it?"

"Oh, you have, then!" exclaimed Kitty Bonnair ecstatically. "Oh, I'm so glad to see a really, truly cowboy!" She paused, and gazed up at him soulfully. "Won't you let me have it for a minute?" she pleaded, and with a sheepish grin Creede handed over his gun.

But if there had been another cowboy within a mile he would have hesitated, infatuated as he was. Every land has its symbolism and though the language of flowers has not struck root in the cow country —- nor yet the amorous Mexican system of "playing the bear" —- to give up one's pistol to a lady is the sign and token of surrender. However, though it brought the sweat to his brow, the byplay was pulled off unnoticed, Hardy and Lucy Ware being likewise deep in confidences.

"How strange you look, Rufus!" exclaimed Lucy, as Kitty Bonnair began her assault upon the happiness of Jefferson Creede. "What have you been doing to yourself in these two years?"

"Why, nothing," protested Hardy, a little wan from his encounter with Kitty. "Perhaps you have forgotten how I used to look —- our hair gets pretty long up here," he added apologetically, "but —- "

"No," said Lucy firmly. "It isn't a matter of hair, although I will admit I hardly knew you. It's in your eyes; and you have some stern, hard lines about your mouth, too. Father says you spend all your time trying to keep the sheep out —- and he's very much displeased with you for disobeying his directions, too. He gave up some important business to come down here and see you, and I hope he scolds you well. Have you been writing any lately?" she asked accusingly.

"No!" answered Hardy absently, "we don't have to *fight* them —- "

"But, Rufus," protested Lucy Ware, laying her hand on his arm, "do take your mind from those dreadful sheep. I asked you if you have been doing any *writing* lately —- you promised to send me some poems, don't you remember? And I haven't received a thing!"

"Oh!" said Hardy, blushing at his mistake. "Well, I acknowledge that I haven't done right —- and you have been very kind, too, Miss Lucy," he added gently. "But somehow I never finish anything down here —- and the sheep have been pretty bad lately. I have to do my work first, you know. I'll tell you, though," he said, lowering his voice confidentially, "if I can see you when no one is around I'll give you what little I've written —- at least, some of the best. A poet at his worst, you know," he added, smiling, "is the poorest man in the world. He's like a woman who tells everything —- no one could respect him. But if we can take our finer moods, and kind of sublimate them, you know, well —- every man is a poet some time."

He hesitated, ended lamely, and fell suddenly into a settled silence. The hard lines about his lips deepened; his eyes, cast to the ground, glowed dully; and in every feature Lucy read the despair that was gnawing at his heart. And with it there was something more —- a tacit rebuke to her for having brought Kitty there to meet him.

"We have missed you very much," she began softly, as if reading his thoughts, "and your letters were so interesting! Ever since I showed Kitty the first one she has been crazy to come down here. Yes, she has been reading 'The Virginian' and O. Henry and 'Wolfville' until it is simply awful to hear her talk. And ride —- she has been taking lessons for a year! Her saddle is out there now in the wagon, and if she could have caught one of those wild horses out in that inclosed field I really believe she would have mounted him and taken to the hills like an Indian. I had to come down to take care of father, you know, and —- aren't you glad to see us, Rufus?"

She gazed up at him anxiously, and her eyes became misty as she spoke; but Hardy was far away and he did not see.

"Yes," he said absently, "but —- I shall be very busy. Oh, where is your father?"

A light went suddenly from Lucy's eyes and her lips quivered, but her voice was as steady as ever.

"He has gone down to the river," she said patiently. "Would you like to see him?"

"Yes," he replied, still impersonally; and with his head down, he walked out to where Chapuli was standing. Then, as if some memory of her voice had come to him, he dropped the bridle lash and stepped back quickly into the house.

"You mustn't notice my rudeness, Miss Lucy," he began abjectly. "Of course I am glad to see you; but I am a little confused, and —- well, you understand." He smiled wanly as he spoke, and held out his hand. "Is it all right?" he asked. "Good-bye, then." And as he stepped quietly out the light came back into Lucy's eyes.

"I am going to hunt up the judge," he said, as he swung up on his horse; and, despite the protests of Jeff and Kitty Bonnair, who were still deep in an animated conversation, he rode off down the river.

It was not exactly like a draught of Nepenthe to go out and face the righteous indignation of Judge Ware, but Hardy's brain was in such a whirl that he welcomed the chance to escape. Never for a moment had he contemplated the idea of Kitty's coming to him, or of his seeing her again until his heart was whole. He had felt safe and secure forever within the walled valley of Hidden Water —- but now from a cloudless sky the lightning had fallen and blinded him.

Before he could raise a hand or even turn and flee she had come upon him and exacted his forgiveness. Nay, more —- she had won back his love and enslaved him as before. Could it mean —- what else could it mean? Nothing but that she loved him; or if not love, then she cared for him above the others. And Kitty was proud, too! Those who became her slaves must respect her whims; she would acknowledge no fault and brook no opposition; whatever she did was right. Yes, it had always been the same with her: the Queen could do no wrong —- yet now she had put aside her regal prerogatives and come to him!

He hugged the thought to his bosom like a man infatuated, and then a chill misgiving came upon him. Perhaps after all it was but another of those childish whims which made her seem so lovable —- always eager, always active, always striving for the forbidden and unusual, yet so dear with her laughing eyes and dancing feet that all the world gave way before her. He bowed his head in thought, following the judge's tracks mechanically as he cantered down the trail, and when he came to the hill above the whirlpool and looked down at the empty landscape he was still wrestling with his pride. Never in the two years of his exile had he so much as mentioned her name to any one; it was a thing too sacred for confidences, this love which had changed the deep current of his life, a secret for his own soul and God —- and yet, Lucy Ware might help him!

And where in all the world would he find a more faithful friend than Lucy Ware? A secret shared with her would be as safe as if still locked in his own breast —- and Lucy could understand. Perhaps she understood already; perhaps —- his heart stopped, and pounded against his side —- perhaps Kitty had told Lucy her story already and asked her to intercede! He dwelt upon the thought again as he gazed dumbly about for his employer; and then suddenly the outer world —- the plain, rough, rocks-and-cactus world that he had lived in before they came —- flashed up before him in all its uncompromising clearness; the judge was nowhere in sight!

A sudden memory of Creede's saying that he could lose his boss any time within half a mile of camp startled Hardy out of his dreams and he rode swiftly forward upon the trail. At the foot of the hill the tracks of Judge Ware's broad shoes with their nice new hob-nails stood out like a bas-relief, pointing up the river. Not to take any chances, Hardy followed them slavishly through the fine sand until they turned abruptly up onto a ridge which broke off at the edge of the river bottom. Along the summit of this they showed again, plainly, heading north; then as the ravine swung to the west they scrambled across it and began to zigzag, working off to the east where Black Butte loomed up above the maze of brushy ridges like a guiding sentinel. At first Hardy only smiled at the circuitous and aimless trail which he was following, expecting to encounter the judge at every turn; but as the tracks led steadily on he suddenly put spurs to his horse and plunged recklessly up and down the sides of the brushy hogbacks in a desperate pursuit, for the sun was sinking low. The trail grew fresher and fresher now; dark spots where drops of sweat had fallen showed in the dry sand of the washes; and at last, half an hour before sundown, Hardy caught sight of his wandering employer, zealously ascending a particularly rocky butte.

"Hello there, Judge!" he called, and then, as Judge Ware whirled about, he inquired, with well-feigned surprise: "Where'd you drop down from?"

This was to let the old gentleman down easy —- lost people having a way of waxing indignant at their rescuers —- and the judge was not slow to take advantage of it.

"Why, howdy do, Rufus!" he exclaimed, sinking down upon a rock. "I was just taking a little short cut to camp. My, my, but this is a rough country. Out looking for cattle?"

"Well —- yes," responded Hardy. "I was taking a little ride. But say, it's about my supper time. You better give up that short-cut idea and come along home with me."

"We-ell," said the judge, reluctantly descending the butte, "I guess I will. How far is it?"

"About two miles, by trail."

"Two miles!" exclaimed Judge Ware, aghast. "Why, it's just over that little hill, there. Why don't you take a short cut?"

"The trail is the shortest cut I know," replied Hardy, concealing a smile. "That's the way the cattle go, and they seem to know their business. How does the country look to you?"

But the old judge was not to be led aside by persiflage —- he was interested in the matter of trails.

"Cattle trails!" he exclaimed. "Do you mean to say that you do all your travelling on these crooked cow paths? Why, it is a matter of scientific observation that even on the open prairie a cow path loses nearly a quarter of its headway by constant winding in and out, merely to avoid frail bushes and infinitesimal stones. Now if you and Jeff would spend a little of your leisure in cutting trails, as they do in forestry, you would more than save yourselves the time and labor involved, I'm sure."

"Yes?" said Hardy coldly. There was a subtle tone of fault-finding in his employer's voice which already augured ill for their debate on the sheep question, and his nerves responded instinctively to the jab. Fate had not been so kind to him that day, that he was prepared to take very much from any man, and so he remained quiet and let the judge go the whole length.

"Why, yes, if you would stay about the ranch a little closer instead of going off on these armed forays against sheep —- now just for example, how much would it cost to clear a passable trail over that ridge to the ranch?"

He pointed at the hill which in his misguided enthusiasm he had been mounting, and Hardy's eyes glittered wickedly as he launched his barbed jest.

"About a billion dollars, I guess," he answered, after mature consideration.

"A billion dollars!" repeated the judge. "A billion dollars! Now here, Rufus," he cried, choking with exasperation, "I am in earnest about this matter! I don't altogether approve of the way you and Jeff have been conducting my affairs down here, anyway, and I intend to take a hand myself, if you don't mind. I may not know as much as you about the minor details of the cattle business, but I have been looking into forestry quite extensively, and I fail to see anything unreasonable in my suggestion of a trail. How far is it, now, over that hill to the ranch?"

"About twenty-five thousand miles," replied Hardy blandly.

"Twenty-five thousand! Why —- "

"At least, so I am informed," explained Hardy. "Geographers agree, I believe, that that is the approximate distance around the world. The ranch is over here, you know."

He pointed with one small, sinewy hand in a direction diametrically opposite to the one his boss had indicated, and struck out down a cow trail. It was a harsh blow to the old judge, and rankled in his bosom for some time; but after making sure that his superintendent was correct he followed meekly behind him into camp. On the way, as an afterthought, he decided not to put down his foot in the matter of the sheep until he was quite sure of the material facts.

They found Creede in the last throes of agony as he blundered through the motions of cooking supper. Half an hour of house-cleaning had done more to disarrange his kitchen than the services of two charming assistants could possibly repair. His Dutch oven was dropped into the wood box; his bread pan had been used to soak dirty dishes in; the water bucket was empty, and they had thrown his grease swab into the fire. As for the dish-rag, after long and faithful service it had been ruthlessly destroyed, and he had to make another one out of a flour sack. Add to this a hunger which had endured since early morning and a series of rapid-fire questions, and you have the true recipe for bad bread, at least.

Kitty Bonnair had taken a course in sanitation and domestic science in her college days, since which time the world had been full of microbes and every unpleasant bacillus, of which she discoursed at some length. But Jefferson Creede held steadily to his fixed ideas, and in the end he turned out some baking-powder biscuits that would have won honors in a cooking school. There was nothing else to cook, his kettle of beans having been unceremoniously dumped because the pot was black; but Kitty had the table spotlessly clean, there was an assortment of potted meats and picnic knicknacks in the middle of it, and Lucy had faithfully scoured the dishes; so supper was served with frills.

If the ladies had taken hold a little strong in the first spasms of house-cleaning, Jeff and Rufus were far too polite to mention it; and while the dishes were being washed they quietly gathered up their belongings, and moved them into the storeroom. Their beds being already spread beneath the *ramada*, it was not difficult to persuade the girls to accept Hardy's room, which for a man's, was clean, and the judge fell heir to Jeff's well-littered den. All being quickly arranged and the beds made, Creede threw an armful of ironwood upon the fire and they sat down to watch it burn.

Three hours before, Hidden Water had been the hangout of two sheep-harrying barbarians, bushy-headed and short of speech; now it was as bright and cheerful as any home and the barbarians were changed to lovers. Yet, as they basked in the warmth of the fireside there was one absent from his accustomed place —- a creature so fierce and shy that his wild spirit could never become reconciled to the change. At the first sound of women's voices little Tommy had dashed through his cat-hole and fled to the bowlder pile at the foot of the cliff, from whose dank recesses he peered forth with blank and staring eyes.

But now, as the strange voices grew quiet and night settled down over the valley, he crept forth and skulked back to the house, sniffing about the barred windows, peeking in through his hole in the door; and at last, drawing well away into the darkness, he raised his voice in an appealing cry for Jeff.

As the first awful, raucous outburst broke the outer silence Kitty Bonnair jumped, and Lucy and her father turned pale.

"What's that?" cried Kitty, in a hushed voice, "a mountain lion?"

"Not yet," answered Creede enigmatically. "He will be though, if he grows. Aw, say, that's just my cat. Here, pussy, pussy, pussy! D'ye hear that, now? Sure, he knows me! Wait a minute and I'll try an' ketch 'im."

He returned a few minutes later, with Tommy held firmly against his breast, blacker, wilder, and scrawnier than ever, but purring and working his claws.

"How's this for a mountain lion?" said Creede, stopping just inside the door and soothing down his pet. "D'ye see that hook?" he inquired, holding up the end of Tommy's crooked tail and laughing at Kitty's dismay. "He uses that to climb cliffs with. That's right —- he's a new kind of cat. Sure, they used to be lots of 'em around here, but the coyotes got all the rest. Tom is the only one left. Want to pet him? Well —- whoa, pussy, —- come up careful, then; he's never —- ouch!"

At the first whisk of skirts, Tommy's yellow eyes turned green and he sank every available hook and claw into his master's arm; but when Kitty reached out a hand he exploded in a storm of spits and hisses and dashed out through the door.

"Well, look at that, now," said Creede, grinning and rubbing his arm. "D'ye know what's the matter with him? You're the first woman he ever saw in his life. W'y, sure! They ain't no women around here. I got him off a cowman over on the Verde. He had a whole litter of 'em —- used to pinch Tom's tail to make him fight —- so when I come away I jest quietly slipped Mr. Tommy into my shaps."

"Oh, the poor little thing," said Kitty; and then she added, puckering up her lips, "but I don't like cats."

"Oh, I do!" exclaimed Lucy Ware quickly, as Creede's face changed, and for a moment the big cowboy stood looking at them gravely.

"That's good," he said, smiling approvingly at Lucy; and then, turning to Kitty Bonnair, he said: "You want to learn, then."

But Kitty was not amenable to the suggestion.

"No!" she cried, stamping her foot. "I don't! They're such stealthy, treacherous creatures —- and they never have any affection for people."

"Ump-um!" denied Creede, shaking his head slowly. "You don't know cats —- jest think you do, maybe. W'y, Tommy was the only friend I had here for two years. D'ye think he could fool me all that time? Rufe here will tell you how he follows after me for miles —- and cryin', too —- when the coyotes might git 'im anytime. And he sleeps with me every night," he added, lowering his voice.

"Well, you can have him," said Kitty lightly. "Do they have any real mountain lions here?"

"Huh?" inquired Creede, still big-eyed with his emotions. "Oh, yes; Bill Johnson over in Hell's Hip Pocket makes a business of huntin' 'em. Twenty dollars bounty, you know."

"Oh, oh!" cried Kitty. "Will he take me with him? Tell me all about it!"

Jefferson Creede moved over toward the door with a far-away look in his eyes.

"That's all," he said indifferently. "He runs 'em with hounds. Well, I'll have to bid you good-night."

He ducked his head, and stepped majestically out the door; and Hardy, who was listening, could hear him softly calling to his cat.

"Oh, Rufus!" cried Kitty appealingly, as he rose to follow, "*do* stop and tell me about Bill Johnson, and, yes —- Hell's Hip Pocket!"

"Why, Kitty!" exclaimed Lucy Ware innocently, and while they were discussing the morals of geographical swearing Hardy made his bow, and passed out into the night.

The bitter-sweet of love was upon him again, making the stars more beautiful, the night more mysterious and dreamy; but as he crept into his blankets he sighed. In the adjoining cot he could hear Jeff stripping slivers from a length of jerked beef, and Tommy mewing for his share.

"Want some jerky, Rufe?" asked Creede, and then, commenting upon their late supper, he remarked:

"A picnic dinner is all right for canary birds, but it takes good hard grub to feed a man. I'm goin' to start the *rodér* camp in the mornin' and cook me up some beans." He lay for a while in silence, industriously feeding himself on the dry meat, and gazing at the sky.

"Say, Rufe," he said, at last, "ain't you been holdin' out on me a little?"

"Um-huh," assented Hardy.

"Been gettin' letters from Miss Lucy all the time, eh?"

"Sure."

"Well," remarked Creede, "you're a hell of a feller! But I reckon I learned somethin'," he added philosophically, "and when I want somebody to tell my troubles to, I'll know where to go. Say, she's all right, ain't she?"

"Yeah."

"Who're you talkin' about?"

"Who're you?"

"Oh, you know, all right, all right —- but, say!"

"Well?"

"It's a pity she don't like cats."

CHAPTER XII
THE GARDEN IN THE DESERT

The sun was well up over the cañon rim when the tired visitors awoke from their dreams. Kitty Bonnair was the first to open her eyes and peep forth upon the fairy world which promised so much of mystery and delight. The iron bars of their window, deep set in the adobe walls, suggested the dungeon of some strong prison where Spanish maidens languished for sight of their lovers; a rifle in the corner, overlooked in the hurried moving, spoke eloquently of the armed brutality of the times; the hewn logs which supported the lintels completed the picture of primitive life; and a soft breeze, breathing in through the unglazed sills, whispered of dark cañons and the wild, free out-of-doors.

As she lay there drinking it all in a murmur of voices came to her ears; and, peering out, she saw Creede and Rufus Hardy squatting by a fire out by the giant mesquite tree which stood near the bank of the creek. Creede was stirring the contents of a frying-pan with a huge iron spoon, and Rufus was cooking strips of meat on a stick which he turned above a bed of coals. There was no sign of hurry or anxiety about their preparations; they seemed to be conversing amiably of other things. Presently Hardy picked up a hooked stick, lifted the cover from the Dutch oven, and dumped a pile of white biscuits upon a greasy cloth. Then, still deep in their talk, they filled their plates from the fry-pan, helped themselves to meat, wrapped the rest of the bread in the cloth, and sat comfortably back on their heels, eating with their fingers and knives.

It was all very simple and natural, but somehow she had never thought of men in that light before. They were so free, so untrammelled and self-sufficient; yes, and so barbarous, too. Rufus Hardy, the poet, she had known —- quiet, soft-spoken, gentle, with dreamy eyes and a doglike eagerness to please —- but, lo! here was another Rufus, still gentle, but with a stern look in his eyes which left her almost afraid —- and those two lost years lay between. How he must have changed in all that time! The early morning was Kitty's time for meditation and good resolutions, and she resolved then and there to be nice to Rufus, for he was a man and could not understand.

As the sound of voices came from the house Jefferson Creede rose up from his place and stalked across the open, rolling and swaying in his high-heeled boots like a huge, woolly bear.

"Well, Judge," he said, after throwing a mountain of wood on the fire as a preliminary to cooking breakfast for his guests, "I suppose now you're here you'd like to ride around a little and take stock of what you've got. The boys will begin comin' in for the *rodér* to-day, and after to-morrow I'll be pretty busy; but if you say so I'll jest ketch up a gentle horse, and show you the upper range before the work begins."

"Oh, won't you take me, too?" cried Kitty, skipping in eagerly. "I've got the nicest saddle —- and I bet I can ride any horse you've got."

She assumed a cowboy-like strut as she made this assertion, shaking her head in a bronco gesture which dashed the dark hair from her eyes and made her look like an unbroken thoroughbred. Never in all his life, even in the magazine pictures of stage beauties which form a conspicuous mural decoration in those parts, had Creede seen a woman half so charming, but even in his love blindness he was modest.

"We'll have to leave that to the judge," he said deferentially, "but they's horses for everybody." He glanced inquiringly at Lucy, who was busily unpacking her sketching kit; but she only smiled, and shook her head.

"The home is going to be my sphere for some time," she remarked, glancing about at the half-cleaned room, "and then," she added, with decision, "I'm going to make some of the loveliest water colors in the world. I think that big giant cactus standing on that red-and-gray cliff over there is simply wonderful."

"Um, pretty good," observed Creede judicially. "But you jest ought to see 'em in the gorge where Hidden Water comes out! Are ye goin' along, Rufe?" he inquired, bending his eyes upon Hardy with a knowing twinkle. "No? Well, *you* can show her where it is! Didn't you never hear why they call this Hidden Water?" he asked, gazing benignly upon the young ladies. "Well, listen.

"They's a big spring of water right up here, not half a mile. It's an old landmark —- the Mexicans call it Agua Escondida —- but I bet neither one of you can find it and I'll take you right by the gulch where it comes out. They can't nobody find it, unless they're wise enough to follow cow tracks —- and of course, we don't expect that of strangers. But if you ever git lost and you're within ten miles of home jest take the first cow trail you see and follow it downhill and you'll go into one end or the other of Hidden Water cañon. Sure, it's what you might call the Hello-Central of the whole Four Peaks country, with cow paths instead of wires. The only thing lackin' is the girls, to talk back, and call you down for your ungentlemanly language, and —- well, this country is comin' up every day!"

He grinned broadly, wiping his floury hands on his overalls in defiance of Miss Kitty's most rudimentary principles; and yet even she, for all her hygiene, was compelled to laugh. There was something about Creede that invited confidence and feminine badgering, he was so like a big, good-natured boy. The entire meal was enlivened by her efforts, in the person of a hello girl, to expurgate his language, and she ended by trying to get him to swear —- politely.

But in this the noble cowboy was inexorable. "No, ma'am," he said, with an excess of moral conviction. "I never swear except for cause —- and then I always regret it. But if you want to git some of the real thing to put in your phonygraft jest come down to the pasture to-morrow when the boys are breakin' horses. Your hair's kind of wavy, I notice, but it will put crimps in it to hear Bill Lightfoot or some of them Sunflower stiffs when they git bucked onto a rock pile. And say, if you call yourself a rider I can give you a snake for to-day."

"Oh, thank you, Mr. Creede," answered Miss Kitty, bowing low as she left the table. "Its tail, if it chanced to be a rattler, would be most acceptable, I am sure, and I might make a belt out of its skin. But for riding purposes I prefer a real, gentle little horse. Now hurry up, and I'll be dressed in half an hour."

Ten minutes later Creede rode up to the house, leading a sober gray for the judge, but for Kitty Bonnair he had the prettiest little calico-horse in the bunch, a pony painted up with red and yellow and white until he looked like a three-color chromo. Even his eye was variegated, being of a mild, pet-rabbit blue, with a white circle around the orbit; and his name, of course, was Pinto. To be sure, his face was a little dished in and he showed other signs of his scrub Indian blood, but after Creede had cinched on the new stamped-leather saddle and adjusted the ornate hackamore and martingale, Pinto was the sportiest-looking horse outside of a Wild West show.

There was a long wait then, while Diana completed her preparations for the hunt; but when Kitty Bonnair, fully apparelled, finally stepped through the door Creede reeled in the saddle, and even Rufus Hardy gasped. There was nothing immodest about her garb —- in fact, it was very correct and proper —- but not since the Winship girls rode forth in overalls had Hidden Water seen its like. Looking very trim and boyish in her khaki riding breeches, Kitty strode forth unabashed, rejoicing in her freedom. A little scream of delight escaped her as she caught sight of the calico-pony; she patted his nose a moment, inquired his name, and then, scorning all assistance, swung lightly up into the saddle. No prettier picture had ever been offered to the eye; so young, so supple and strong, with such a wealth of dark, wavy hair, and, withal, so modest and honestly happy. But, somehow, Jefferson Creede took the lead and rode with his eyes cast down, lest they should be dazzled by the vision. Besides, Jeff had been raised old-fashioned, and Golden Gate Park is a long, long ways, chronologically, from Hidden Water.

As the procession passed away up the cañon, with Creede in sober converse with the judge and Kitty scampering about like an Indian on her pinto horse, Hardy and Lucy Ware glanced at each other, and laughed.

"Did you ever see any one like her?" exclaimed Lucy, and Hardy admitted with a sigh that he never had.

"And I am afraid," observed Miss Lucy frankly, "you were not altogether pleased to see her —- at first. But really, Rufus, what can any one hope to do with Kitty? When she has set her heart on anything she *will have it*, and from the very moment she read your first letter she was determined to come down here. Of course father thinks he came down to look into this matter of the sheep, and *I* think that I came down to look after him, but in reality I have no doubt we are both here because Kitty Bonnair so wills it."

"Very likely," replied Hardy, with a doubtful smile. "But since you are in her counsels perhaps you can tell what her intentions are toward me. I used to be one of her gentlemen-in-waiting, you know, and this visit looks rather ominous for me."

"Well, just exactly what are you talking about, Rufus?"

"I guess you know, all right," replied Hardy. "Have I got to ride a bucking bronco, or kill a sheep-herder or two —- or is it just another case of 'move on'?"

He paused and smiled bitterly to himself, but Lucy was not in a mood to humor him in his misanthropy.

"I must confess," she said, "that you may be called upon to do a few chivalrous feats of horsemanship, but as for the sheep-herder part of it, I hope you will try to please me by leaving them alone. It worries me, Rufus," she continued soberly, "to see you becoming so strong-willed and silent. There was a whole year, when none of us heard a word from you —- and then it was quite by accident. And father thinks you stopped writing to him with the deliberate intention of driving the sheep away by violence."

"Well, I'm glad he understands so well," replied Hardy naively. "Of course I wouldn't embarrass him by asking for orders, but —- "

"Oh, Rufus!" exclaimed Miss Lucy impatiently, "do try to be natural again and take your mind off those sheep. Do you know what I am thinking of doing?" she demanded seriously. "I am thinking of asking father to give me this ranch —- he said he would if I wanted it —- and then I'll discharge you! You shall not be such a brutal, ugly man! But come, now, I want you to help clear the table, and then we will go up to Hidden Water and read your poems. But tell me, have you had any trouble with the sheepmen?"

"Why, no!" answered Hardy innocently. "What made you ask?"

"Well, you wrote father you expected trouble —- and —- and you had that big, long pistol when you came in yesterday. Now you can't deny that!"

"I'm afraid you've had some Western ideas implanted in your bosom by Kitty, Miss Lucy," protested Hardy. "We never shoot each other down here. I carry that pistol for the moral effect —- and it's necessary, too, to protect these sheepmen against their own baser natures. You see they're all armed, and if I should ride into their camp without a gun and ask them to move they might be tempted to do something overt. But as it is now, when Jeff and I begin to talk reason with them they understand. No, *we're* all right; it's the sheep-herders that have all the trouble."

"Rufus Hardy," cried Miss Lucy indignantly, "if you mention those sheep again until you are asked about them, I'll have you attended to. Do you realize how far I have come to see your poems and hear you talk the way you used to talk? And then to hear you go on in this way! I thought at first that Mr. Creede was a nice man, but I am beginning to change my opinion of him. But you have just got to be nice to me and Kitty while we are here. I had so many things to tell you about your father, and Tupper Browne, and The Circle, but you just sit around so kind of close-mouthed and silent and never ask a question! Wouldn't you like to know how your father is?" she asked.

"Why, yes," responded Hardy meekly. "Have you seen him lately?"

"I saw him just before we came away. He is dreadfully lonely, I know, but he wouldn't send any message. He never says *anything* when I tell him what you are doing, just sits and twists his mustache and listens; but I could tell by the way he said good-bye that he was glad I was coming. I am sorry you can't agree —- isn't there something you could do to make him happier?"

Hardy looked up from his dish-washing with a slow smile.

"Which do you think is more important?" he asked, "for a man to please his father or his best friend?"

Lucy suspected a trap and she made no reply.

"Did you ever quote any of my poetry to father?" inquired Hardy casually. "No? Then please don't. But I'll bet if you told him I was catching wild horses, or talking reason to these Mexican herders, you'd have the old man coming. He's a fighter, my father, and if you want to make him happy when you go back, tell him his son has just about given up literature and is the champion bronco-twister of the Four Peaks range."

"But Rufus —- would that be the truth?"

Hardy laughed. "Well, pretty near it —- but I'm trying to please my best friend now."

"Oh," said Lucy, blushing. "Will —- will that make much difference?" she asked.

"All the difference in the world," declared Hardy warmly. "You want me to become a poet —- he wants me to become a fighter. Well now, since I haven't been able to please him, I'm going to try to please you for a while."

"Oh, Rufus," cried Lucy, "am I really —- your best friend?"

"Why sure! Didn't you know that?" He spoke the words with a bluff good-fellowship which pleased her, in a way, but at the same time left her silent. And he, too, realized that there was a false note, a rift such as often creeps in between friends and if not perceived and checked widens into a breach.

"You know," he said, quietly making his amends, "when I was a boy my father always told me I talked too much; and after mother died I —- well, I didn't talk so much. I was intended for a soldier, you know, and good officers have to keep their own counsel. But —- well, I guess the habit struck in —- so if I don't always thank you, or tell you things, you will understand, won't you? I wasn't raised to please folks, you know, but just to fight Indians, and all that. How would you like to be a soldier's wife?"

"Not very well, I am afraid," she said. "All the fear and anxiety, and —- well, I'm afraid I couldn't love my husband if he killed anybody." She paused and glanced up at him, but he was deep in thought.

"My mother was a soldier's wife," he said, at last; and Lucy, seeing where his thoughts had strayed, respected his silence. It was something she had learned long before, for while Rufus would sometimes mention his mother he would never talk about her, even to Lucy Ware. So they finished their housework, deep in their own thoughts. But when at last they stepped out into the sunshine Lucy touched him on the arm.

"Wouldn't you like to bring your poems with you?" she suggested. "We can read them when we have found the spring. Is it very beautiful up there?"

"Yes," answered Hardy, "I often go there to write, when nobody is around. You know Jeff and all these cowboys around here don't know that I write verse. They just think I'm a little fellow from somewhere up in California that can ride horses pretty good. But if I had handed it out to them that I was a poet, or even a college man, they would have gone to tucking snakes into my blankets and dropping *chili bravos* into my beans until they got a rise out of me, sure. I learned that much before I ever came up here. But I've got a little place I call my garden —- up in the cañon, above Hidden Water —- and sometimes I sneak off up there, and write. Would you like to see a poem I wrote up there? All right, you can have the rest some other time." He stepped into the storeroom, extracted a little bundle from his war bag, and then they passed on up the valley together.

The cañon of the Alamo is like most Arizona stream beds, a strait-jacket of rocky walls, opening out at intervals into pocket-like valleys, such as the broad and fertile flat which lay below Hidden Water. On either side of the stream the banks rise in benches, each a little higher and broader and more heavily covered: the first pure sand, laid on by the last freshet; the next grown over with grass and weeds; the next bushed up with baby willows and arrow weed; and then, the high bench, studded with mesquite and *palo verdes*; and at the base of the solid rim perhaps a higher level, strewn with the rocks which time and the elements have hurled down from the cliff, and crested with ancient trees. Upon such a high bench stood the Dos S ranch house, with trails leading off up and down the flat or plunging down the bank, the striated cliff behind it and the water-torn valley below.

Up the cañon a deep-worn path led along the base of the bluff; and as the two best friends followed along its windings Hardy pointed out the mysteries of the land: strange trees and shrubs, bristling with thorns; cactus in its myriad forms; the birds which flashed past them or sang in the wild gladness of springtime; lizards, slipping about in the sands or pouring from cracks in the rocks —- all the curious things which his eyes had seen and his mind taken note of in the long days of solitary riding, and which his poet's soul now interpreted into a higher meaning for the woman who could understand. So intent were they upon the wonders of that great display that Lucy hardly noticed where they were, until the trail swung abruptly in toward the cliff and they seemed to be entering a cleft in the solid rock.

"Where do we go now?" she asked, and Hardy laughed at her confusion.

"This is the gate to Hidden Water," he said, lowering his voice to its old-time poetic cadence. "And strait is the way thereof," he added, as he led her through the narrow pass, "but within are tall trees and running water, and the eagle nests undisturbed among the crags."

"What *are* you quoting?" exclaimed Miss Lucy, and for an answer Rufus beckoned her in and pointed with his hand. Before them stood the tall trees with running water at their feet, and a great nest of sticks among the crags.

"Hidden Water!" he said, and smiled again mysteriously.

Then he led the way along the side of the stream, which slipped softly over the water-worn bowlders, dimpling in pool after pool, until at the very gate of the valley it sank into the sand and was lost. Higher and higher mounted the path; and then, at the foot of a smooth ledge which rose like a bulwark across the gorge, it ended suddenly by the side of a cattle-tracked pool.

"This is the wall to my garden," said Hardy, pointing to the huge granite dyke, "beyond which only the elect may pass." He paused, and glanced over at her quizzically. "The path was not made for ladies, I am afraid," he added, pointing to a series of foot holes which ran up the face of the ledge. "Do you think you can climb it?"

Lucy Ware studied his face for a moment; then, turning to the Indian stairway, she measured it with a practised eye.

"You go up first," she suggested, and when he had scaled the slippery height and turned he found her close behind, following carefully in his steps.

"Well, you *are* a climber!" he cried admiringly. "Here, give me your hand." And when he had helped her up he still held it —- or perhaps she clung to his.

Before them lay a little glade, shut in by painted rocks, upon whose black sides were engraved many curious pictures, the mystic symbols of the Indians; and as they stood gazing at it an eagle with pointed wings wheeled slowly above them, gazing with clear eyes down into the sunlit vale. From her round nest in the crotch of a sycamore a great horned owl plunged out at their approach and glided noiselessly away; and in the stillness the zooning of bees among the rocks came to their ears like distant music. Beneath their feet the grass grew long and matted, shot here and there with the blue and gold of flowers, like the rich meadows of the East; and clustering along the hillsides, great bunches of grama grass waved their plumes proudly, the last remnant of all that world of feed which had clothed the land like a garment before the days of the sheep. For here, at least, there came no nibbling wethers, nor starving cattle; and the mountain sheep which had browsed there in the old days were now hiding on the topmost crags of the Superstitions to escape the rifles of the destroyers. All the world without was laid waste and trampled by hurrying feet, but the garden of Hidden Water was still kept inviolate, a secret shrine consecrated to Nature and Nature's God.

As she stood in the presence of all its beauty a mist came into Lucy's eyes and she turned away.

"Oh, Rufus," she cried, "why don't you live up here always instead of wasting your life in that awful struggle with the sheep? You could —- why, you could do anything up here!"

"Yes," assented Hardy, "it is a beautiful spot —- I often come up here when I am weary with it all —- but a man must do a man's work, you know; and my work is with the sheep. When I first came to Hidden Water I knew nothing of the sheep. I thought the little lambs were pretty; the ewes were mothers, the herders human beings. I tried to be friends with them, to keep the peace and abide by the law; but now that I've come to know them I agree with Jeff, who has been fighting them for twenty years. There is something about the smell of sheep which robs men of their humanity; they become greedy and avaricious; the more they make the more they want. Of all the sheepmen that I know there isn't one who would go around me out of friendship or pity —- and I have done favors for them all. But they're no friends of mine now," he added ominously. "I have to respect my friends, and I can't respect a man who is all hog. There's no pretence on either side now, though —- they're trying to sheep us out and we are trying to fight them off, and if it ever comes to a show-down —- well —- "

He paused, and his eyes glowed with a strange light.

"You know I haven't very much to live for, Miss Lucy," he said earnestly, "but if I had all that God could give me I'd stand by Jeff against the sheep. It's all right to be a poet or an artist, a lover of truth and beauty, and all that, but if a man won't stand up for his friends when they're in trouble he's a kind of closet philosopher that shrinks from all the realities of life —- a poor, puny creature, at the best."

He stood up very straight as he poured out this torrent of words, gazing at her intently, but with his eyes set, as if he beheld some vision. Yet whether it was of himself and Jeff, fighting their hopeless battle against the sheep, or of his life as it might have been if Kitty had been as gentle with him as this woman by his side, there was no telling. His old habit of reticence fell back upon him as suddenly as it had been cast aside, and he led the way up the little stream in silence. As he walked, the ardor of his passion cooled, and he began to point out things with his eloquent hands —- the minnows, wheeling around in the middle of a glassy pool; a striped bullfrog, squatting within the spray of a waterfall; huge combs of honey, hanging from shelving caverns along the cliff where the wild bees had stored their plunder for years. At last, as they stood before a drooping elder whose creamy blossoms swayed beneath the weight of bees, he halted and motioned to a shady seat against the cañon wall.

"There are gardens in every desert," he said, as she sank down upon the grassy bank, "but this is ours."

They sat for a while, gazing contentedly at the clusters of elder blossoms which hung above them, filling the air with a rich fragrance which was spiced by the tang of sage. A ruby-throated humming-bird flashed suddenly past them and was gone; a red-shafted woodpecker, still more gorgeous in his scarlet plumage, descended in uneven flights from the *sahuaros* that clung against the cliff and, fastening upon a hollow tree, set up a mysterious rapping.

"He is hunting for grubs," explained Hardy. "Does that inspire you?"

"Why, no," answered Lucy, puzzled.

"The Mexicans call him *pajaro corazon* —- *páh-hah-ro cor-ah-sóne*," continued the poet. "Does that appeal to your soul?"

"Why, no. What does it mean —- woodpecker?"

Hardy smiled. "No," he said, "a woodpecker with them is called *carpintero* —- carpenter, you understand —- because he hammers on trees; but my friend up on the stump yonder is *Pajaro Corazon* —- bird of the heart. I have a poem dedicated to him." Then, as if to excuse himself from the reading, he hastened on: "Of course, no true poet would commit such a breach —- he would write a sonnet to his lady's eyebrow, a poem in memory of a broken dream, or some sad lament for Love, which has died simultaneously with his own blasted hopes. But a sense of my own unimportance has saved me —- or the world, at any rate —- from such laments. *Pajaro Corazon* and *Chupa Rosa*, a little humming-bird who lives in that elder tree, have been my only friends and companions in the muse, until you came. I wouldn't abuse *Chupa Rosa's* confidence by reading my poem to her. Her lover has turned out a worthless fellow and left her —- that was him you saw flying past just now, going up the cañon to sport around with the other hummers —- but here is my poem to *Pajaro Corazon*."

He drew forth his bundle of papers and in a shamefaced way handed one of them to Lucy. It was a slip of yellow note paper, checked along the margin with groups of rhyming words and scansion marks, and in the middle this single verse.

> "Pajaro Corazon! Bird of the Heart!
> Some knight of honor in those bygone days
> Of dreams and gold and quests through desert lands,
> Seeing thy blood-red heart flash in the rays
> Of setting sun —- which lured him far from Spain —-
> Lifted his face and, reading there a sign
> From his dear lady, crossed himself and spake
> Then first, the name which still is thine."

Lucy folded the paper and gazed across at him rapturously.

"Oh, Rufus," she cried, "why didn't you send it to me?"

"Is it good?" asked Hardy, forgetting his pose; and when she nodded solemnly he said:

"There is another verse —- look on the other side."

Lucy turned the paper over quickly and read again:

> "Pajaro Corazon! Bird of the Heart!
> Some Padre, wayworn, stooping towards his grave,
> Whom God by devious ways had sent so far,
> So far from Spain —- still pressing on to save
> The souls He loved, now, raising up his eyes
> And seeing on thy breast the bleeding heart
> Of Jesus, cast his robes aside and spake
> Thy name —- and set that place apart."

As she followed the lines Hardy watched her face with eyes that grew strangely soft and gentle. It was Lucy Ware of all the world who understood him. Others laughed, or pitied, or overdid it, or remained unmoved, but Lucy with her trusting blue eyes and broad poet's brow —- a brow which always made him think of Mrs. Browning who was a poet indeed, she always read his heart, in her he could safely trust. And now, when those dear eyes filled up with tears he could have taken her hand, yes, he could have kissed her —- if he had not been afraid.

"Rufus," she said at last, "you are a poet." And then she dried her eyes and smiled.

"Let me read some more," she pleaded; but Hardy held the bundle resolutely away.

"No," he said gently, "it is enough to have pleased you once. You know poetry is like music; it is an expression of thoughts which are more than thoughts. They come up out of the great sea of our inner soul like the breath of flowers from a hidden garden, like the sound of breakers from the ocean cliffs; but not every one can scent their fragrance, and some ears are too dull to hear music in the rush of waters. And when one has caught the music of another's song then it is best to stop before —- before some discord comes. Lucy," he began, as his soul within him rose up and clamored for it knew not what, "Lucy —- "

He paused, and the woman hung upon his lips to catch the words.

"Yes?" she said, but the thought had suddenly left him. It was a great longing —- that he knew —- a great desire, unsensed because unknown —- but deep, deep.

"Yes —- Rufus?" she breathed, leaning over; but the light had gone out of his eyes and he gazed at her strangely.

"It is nothing," he murmured, "nothing. I —- I have forgotten what I was going to say." He sighed, and looked moodily at his feet. "The thoughts of a would-be poet," he mused, cynically. "How valuable they are —- how the world must long for them —- when he even forgets them himself! I guess I'd better keep still and let you talk a while," he ended, absently. But Lucy Ware sat gazing before her in silence.

"Isn't it time we returned?" she asked, after a while. "You know I have a great deal to do."

"Oh, that's all right," said Hardy, easily, "I'll help you. What do you want to do —- clean house?"

Lucy could have cried at her hero's sudden lapse —- from Parnassus to the scullery, from love to the commonplaces of living; but she had schooled herself to bear with him, since patience is a woman's part. Yet her honest blue eyes were not adapted to concealment and, furtively taking note of her distress, Hardy fell into the role of a penitent.

"Is my garden such a poor place," he inquired gravely, "that you must leave it the moment we have come? You have not even seen *Chupa Rosa*."

"Well, show me *Chupa Rosa* —- and then we will go."

She spoke the words reluctantly, rising slowly to her feet; and Hardy knew that in some hidden way he had hurt her, yet in what regard he could not tell. A vague uneasiness came over him and he tried awkwardly to make amends for his fault, but good intentions never yet crossed a river or healed a breach.

"Here is her nest," he said, "almost above our seat. Look, Lucy, it is made out of willow down and spider webs, bound round and round the twig. Don't you want to see the eggs? Look!" He bent the limb until the dainty white treasures, half buried in the fluffy down, were revealed —- but still she did not smile.

"Oh, stop, Rufus!" she cried, "what will the mother-bird think? She might be frightened at us and leave her nest. Come, let's hurry away before she sees us!"

She turned and walked quickly down the valley, never pausing to look back, even when Rufus stopped to pluck a flower from among the rocks.

"Here," he said, after he had helped her down the Indian stairway; and when she held up her hand, passively, he dropped a forget-me-not into it.

"Oh!" she cried, carried away for a moment, "do they grow down here?"

"Yes," he said, soberly, "even here. And they —- sometimes you find them where you wouldn't expect —- in rough places, you know, and among the stones. I —- I hope you will keep it," he said, simply. And Lucy divined what was in his heart, better perhaps than he himself; but when at last she was alone she buried her face in the pillow, and for a long time the house was very still.

CHAPTER XIII
A SNOW-SCENE

There was a big fire out under the mesquite that night and a band of cowboys, in all the bravery of spurs, shaps, and pistols, romped around it in a stage-struck exuberance of spirits. The night was hardly cold enough to call for fringed leather *chaparejos*, and their guns should have been left in their blankets; nor are long-shanked Texas spurs quite the proper thing about camp, having a dirty way of catching and tripping their wearers; but the *rodéo* outfit felt that it was on dress parade and was trying its best to look the cowboy part. Bill Lightfoot even had a red silk handkerchief draped about his neck, with the slack in front, like a German napkin; and his cartridge belt was slung so low that it threatened every moment to drop his huge Colt's revolver into the dirt —- but who could say a word?

The news of Judge Ware's visit had passed through the Four Peaks country like the rumor of an Indian uprising and every man rode into Hidden Water with an eye out for calico, some with a foolish grin, some downcast and reserved, some swaggering in the natural pride of the lady's man. But a becoming modesty had kept Lucy Ware indoors, and Kitty had limited herself to a furtive survey of the scene from behind what was left of Sallie Winship's lace curtains. With the subtle wisdom of a *rodéo* boss Jefferson Creede had excused himself to the ladies at the first sound of jangling horse-bells, and now he kept resolutely away from the house, busying himself with the manifold duties of his position. To the leading questions of Bill Lightfoot and the "fly bunch" which followed his lead he turned a deaf ear or replied in unsatisfying monosyllables; and at last, as the fire lit up the trees and flickered upon their guns and silver-mounted trappings and no fair maids sallied forth to admire them, the overwrought emotions of the cowboys sought expression in song.

"Oh my little girl she lives in the town,"

chanted Lightfoot, and the fly bunch, catching the contagion, joined promptly in on the refrain:

"A toodle link, a toodle link, a too —- oo-dle a day!"

At this sudden and suggestive outbreak Jeff Creede surveyed Bill Lightfoot coldly and puffed on his cigarette. Bill was always trying to make trouble.

"And every time I see 'er, she asts me f'r a gown,"

carolled the leading cowboy; and the bunch, not to seem faint-hearted, chimed in again:

"Reladin to reladin, and reladin to relate!"

Now they were verging toward the sensational part of the ballad, the place where a real gentleman would quit, but Lightfoot only tossed his head defiantly.

"O-Oh —- " he began, and then he stopped with his mouth open. The *rodéo* boss had suddenly risen to an upright position and fixed him with his eye.

"I like to see you boys enjoyin' yourselves," he observed, quietly, "but please don't discuss *politics* or *religion* while them ladies is over at the house. You better switch off onto 'My Bonnie Lies over the Ocean,' Bill." And Bill switched.

"What's the matter?" he demanded aggrieved, "ain't anybody but you got any rights and privileges around here? You go sportin' around and havin' a good time all day, but as soon as one of us punchers opens his mouth you want to jump down his throat. What do *we* know about ladies —- *I* ain't seen none!"

The discussion of the moral code which followed was becoming acrimonious and personal to a degree when a peal of girlish laughter echoed from the ranch house and the cowboys beheld Judge Ware and Hardy, accompanied by Miss Lucy and Kitty Bonnair, coming towards their fire. A less tactful man might have taken advantage of the hush to utter a final word of warning to his rebellious subjects, but Creede knew Kitty Bonnair and the human heart too well. As the party came into camp he rose quietly and introduced the judge and the ladies to every man present, without deviation and without exception, and then, having offered Miss Ware his cracker box, he moved over a man or two and sat down.

In the bulk of his mighty frame, the rugged power of his countenance, and the unconscious authority of his words he was easily master of them all; but though he had the voice of Mars and a head like Olympian Zeus he must needs abase his proud spirit to the demands of the occasion, for the jealousy of mortal man is a proverb. Where the punchers that he hired for thirty dollars a month were decked out in shaps and handkerchiefs he sat in his shirt-sleeves and overalls, with only his high-heeled boots and the enormous black sombrero which he always wore, to mark him for their king. And the first merry question which Miss Kitty asked he allowed to pass unnoticed, until Bill Lightfoot —- to save the credit of the bunch —- answered it himself.

"Yes, ma'am," he replied politely. "That was a genuwine cowboy song we was singin' —- we sing 'em to keep the cattle awake at night."

"Oh, how interesting!" exclaimed Kitty, leaning forward in her eagerness. "But why do you try to keep them awake? I should think they would be so tired, after travelling all day."

"Yes, ma'am," responded Bill, twisting his silk handkerchief nervously, "but if they go to sleep and anything wakes 'em up quick they stompede —- so we ride through 'em and sing songs."

"Just think of that, Lucy!" cried Miss Kitty enthusiastically. "And it was such a pretty tune, too! Won't you sing it again, Mr. Lightfoot? I'd just love to hear it!"

Here was a facer for Mr. Lightfoot, and Jefferson Creede, to whom all eyes were turned in the crisis, smiled maliciously and let him sweat.

"Bill ain't in very good voice to-night," he observed at last, as the suspense became unbearable, "and we're kinder bashful about singin' to company, anyway. But if you want to hear somethin' good, you want to git Bill goin' about Coloraydo. Sure, Mr. Lightfoot is our best story-teller; and he's had some mighty excitin' times up there in them parts, hain't you, Bill?"

Bill cast a baleful glance at his rival and thrust out his chin insolently. His Coloraydo experiences were a matter of jest with Jeff Creede, but with the ladies it might be different. His courage rose before the flattering solicitude of Kitty Bonnair and he resolved then and there to fool Mr. Creede or know the reason why.

"Well," he replied, stoutly, "they may look kinder tame alongside of your Arizona lies, but —-"

"Oh, Mr. Lightfoot, *do* tell me all about it!" broke in Kitty, with an alluring smile. "Colorado is an awfully wild country, isn't it? And did you ever have any adventures with bears?"

"Bears!" exclaimed Bill contemptuously. "Bears! Huh, we don't take no more account of ordinary bears up in Coloraydo than they do of coons down here. But them big silver-tips —- ump-um —- excuse *me!*" He paused and swaggered a little on the precarious support of his cracker box. "And yet, Miss Bunnair," he said, lowering his voice to a confidential key, "I slept a whole night with one of them big fellers and never turned a hair. I could've killed him the next day, too, but I was so grateful to him I spared his life."

This was the regular "come-on" for Lightfoot's snow-storm story, and Creede showed his white teeth scornfully as Bill leaned back and began the yarn.

"You see, Miss Bunnair," began the Colorado cowboy, rolling his eyes about the circle to quell any tendency to give him away, "Coloraydo is an altogether different country from this here. The mountains is mighty steep and brushy, with snow on the peaks, and the cactus ain't more 'n a inch high out on the perairie. But they's plenty of feed and water —- you betcher life I wisht I was back there now instead of fightin' sheep down here! The only thing aginst that country up there is the blizzards. Them storms is very destructive to life. Yes, ma'am. They's never any notice given but suddenly the wind will begin to blow and the cattle will begin to drift, and then about the time your horse is give out and your ears frozen it'll begin to snow!

"Well, this time I'm tellin' about I was up on the Canadian River west of the Medicine Bow Mountains and she came on to snow —- and snow, I thought it would bury me alive! I was lost in a big park —- a kind of plain or perairie among the mountains. Yes'm, they have'm there —- big level places —- and it was thirty miles across this here level perairie. The wind was blowin' something awful and the snow just piled up on my hat like somebody was shovellin' it off a roof, but I kept strugglin' on and tryin' to git to the other side, or maybe find some sheltered place, until it was like walkin' in your sleep. And that light fluffy snow jest closed in over me until I was covered up ten feet deep. Of course my horse had give out long ago, and I was jest beginnin' to despair when I come across one of them big piles of rocks they have up there, scattered around promiscus-like on the face of nature; and I begin crawlin' in and crawlin' in, hopin' to find some cave or somethin', and jest as I was despairin' my feet fell into a kind of trail, kinder smooth and worn, but old, you know, and stomped hard under the snow. Well, I follers along this path with my feet until it come to a hole in the rocks; and when I come to that hole I went right in, fer I was desprit; and I crawled in and crawled in until I come to a big nest of leaves, and then I begin to burrow down into them leaves. And as soon as I had made a hole I pulled them leaves over me and fell to sleep, I was that exhausted.

"But after a while I had some awful bad dreams, and when I woke up I felt somethin' kickin' under me. Yes 'm, that's right; I felt somethin' kinder movin' around and squirmin', and when I begin to investergate I found I was layin' down right square on top of a tremenjous big grizzly bear! Well, you fellers can laugh, but I was, all the same. What do you know about it, you woolies, punchin' cows down here in the rocks and cactus?

"How's that, Miss Bunnair? W'y sure, he was hibernatin'! They all hibernate up in them cold countries. Well, the funny part of this was that Old Brin had gone to sleep suckin' his off fore foot, jest like a little baby, and when I had piled in on top of him I had knocked his paw out of his mouth and he was tryin' to git it back. But he was all quilled up with himself under them leaves, and his claws was so long he couldn't git that foot back into his mouth nohow. He snooped and grabbed and fumbled, and every minute he was gittin' madder and madder, a-suckin' and slobberin' like a calf tryin' to draw milk out of the hired man's thumb, and a-gruntin' and groanin' somethin' awful.

"Well, I see my finish in about a minute if he ever got good an' woke up, so I resolved to do somethin' desprit. I jest naturally grabbed onto that foot and twisted it around and stuck it into his mouth myself! Afraid? Ump-um, not me —- the only thing I was afraid of was that he'd git my hand and go to suckin' it by mistake. But when I steered his paw around in front of him he jest grabbed onto that big black pad on the bottom of his foot like it was m'lasses candy, and went off to sleep again as peaceful as a kitten."

The man from Coloraydo ended his tale abruptly, with an air of suspense, and Kitty Bonnair took the cue.

"What did I do then?" demanded Lightfoot, with a reminiscent smile. "Well, it was a ground-hog case with me —- if I moved I'd freeze to death and if I knocked his paw out'n his mouth again he'd mash my face in with it —- so I jest snuggled down against him, tucked my head under his chin, and went to sleep, holdin' that paw in his mouth with both hands."

"Oh, Mr. Lightfoot," exclaimed Kitty, "how could you? Why, that's the most remarkable experience I ever heard of! Lucy, I'm going to put that story in my book when I get home, and —- but what *are* you laughing at, Mr. Creede?"

"Who? Me?" inquired Jeff, who had been rocking about as if helpless with laughter. "W'y, *I* ain't laughin'!"

"Yes, you are too!" accused Miss Kitty. "And I want you to tell me what it is. Don't you think Mr. Lightfoot's story is true?"

"True?" echoed Creede, soberly. "W'y, sure it's true. I ain't never been up in those parts; but if Bill says so, that settles it. I never knew a feller from Coloraydo yet that could tell a lie. No, I was jest laughin' to think of that old bear suckin' his paw that way."

He added this last with such an air of subterfuge and evasion that Kitty was not deceived for a moment.

"No, you're *not*, Mr. Creede," she cried, "you're just making fun of me —- so there!"

She stamped her foot and pouted prettily, and the big cowboy's face took on a look of great concern.

"Oh, no, ma'am," he protested, "but since it's gone so far I reckon I'll have to come through now in order to square myself. Of course I never had no real adventures, you know, —- nothin' that you would care to write down or put in a book, like Bill's, —- but jest hearin' him tell that story of gittin' snowed in reminded me of a little experience I had up north here in Coconino County. You know Arizona ain't all sand and cactus —- not by no means. Them San Francisco Mountains up above Flag are sure snow-crested and covered with tall timber and it gits so cold up there in the winter-time that it breaks rocks. No, that's straight! Them prospectors up there when they run short of powder jest drill a line of holes in a rock and when one of them awful cold snaps comes on they run out and fill the holes up with hot water out of the tea-kittle. Well, sir, when that water freezes, which it does in about a minute, it jest naturally busts them rocks wide open —- but that ain't what I started to tell you about."

He paused and contemplated his hearers with impressive dignity.

"Cold ain't nothin'," he continued gravely, "after you git used to it; but once in a while, ladies, she snows up there. And when I say 'snows' I don't refer to such phenominer as Bill was tellin' about up in Coloraydo, but the real genuwine Arizona article —- the kind that gits started and can't stop, no more 'n a cloudburst. Well, one time I was knockin' around up there in Coconino when I ought to've been at home, and I come to a big plain or perairie that was *seventy miles across*, and I got lost on that big plain, right in the dead of winter. They was an awful cold wind blowin' at the time, but I could see the mountains on the other side and so I struck out for 'em. But jest as I got in the middle of that great plain or perairie, she come on to snow. At first she come straight down, kinder soft and fluffy; then she began to beat in from the sides, and the flakes began to git bigger and bigger, until I felt like the Chinaman that walked down Main Street when they had that snow-storm in Tucson. Yes, sir, it was jest like havin' every old whiskey bum in town soakin' you with snow-balls —- and all the kids thrown in.

"My horse he began to puff and blow and the snow began to bank up higher and higher in front of us and on top of us until, bymeby, he couldn't stand no more, and he jest laid down and died. Well, of course that put me afoot and I was almost despairin'. The snow was stacked up on top of me about ten feet deep and I was desprit, but I kept surgin' right ahead, punchin' a hole through that fluffy stuff, until she was twenty foot deep. But I wasn't afraid none —- ump-um, not me —- I jest kept a-crawlin' and a-crawlin', hopin' to find some rocks or shelter, until she stacked up on top of me thirty foot deep. *Thirty foot* —- and slumped down on top o' me until I felt like a horny-toad under a haystack. Well, I was gittin' powerful weak and puny, but jest as I was despairin' I come across a big rock, right out there in the middle of that great plain or perairie. I tried to crawl around that old rock but the snow was pushin' down so heavy on top o' me I couldn't do nothin', and so when she was *fif-ty-two foot deep* by actual measurement I jest give out an' laid down to die."

He paused and fixed a speculative eye on Bill Lightfoot.

"I reckon that would be considered pretty deep up in Coloraydo," he suggested, and then he began to roll a cigarette. Sitting in rigid postures before the fire the punchers surveyed his face with slow and suspicious glances; and for once Kitty Bonnair was silent, watching his deliberate motions with a troubled frown. Balanced rakishly upon his cracker box Bill Lightfoot regarded his rival with a sneering smile, a retort trembling on his lips, but Creede only leaned forward and picked a smoking brand from the fire —- he was waiting for the "come-on."

Now to ask the expected question at the end of such a story was to take a big chance. Having been bitten a time or two all around, the *rodéo* hands were wary of Jeff Creede and his barbed jests; the visitors, being ignorant, were still gaping expectantly; it was up to Bill Lightfoot to spring the mine. For a moment he hesitated, and then his red-hot impetuosity, which had often got him into trouble before, carried him away.

"W'y, sure it would be deep for Coloraydo," he answered, guardedly.

Jefferson Creede glanced up at him, smoking luxuriously, holding the cigarette to his lips with his hand as if concealing a smile.

"Aw, rats," snapped out Lightfoot at last, "why don't you finish up and quit? What happened then?"

"Then?" drawled Creede, with a slow smile. "W'y, nothin', Bill —- *I died!*"

"Ah-hah-hah!" yelled the punchers, throwing up handfuls of dirt in the extravagance of their delight, and before Bill could realize the enormity of the sell one of his own partisans rose up and kicked the cracker box out from under him in token of utter defeat. For an hour after their precipitate retreat the visitors could hear the whoops and gibes of the cowboys, the loud-mouthed and indignant retorts of Lightfoot, and the soothing remonstrances of Jefferson Creede —- and from the house Kitty the irrepressible, added to their merriment a shriek of silvery laughter. But after it was all over and he had won, the round-up boss swore soberly at himself and sighed, for he discerned on the morrow's horizon the Indian signs of trouble.

CHAPTER XIV
FOREBODINGS

To the Eastern eye, blinded by local color, the Four Peaks country looked like a large and pleasantly variegated cactus garden, sparsely populated with rollicking, fun-loving cowboys who wore their interesting six-shooters solely to keep their balance in the saddle. The new grass stood untrampled beneath the bushes on Bronco Mesa, there were buds and flowers everywhere, and the wind was as sweet and untainted as if it drew out of Eden. But somewhere, somewhere in that great wilderness of peaks which lay to the south and through which only the dogged sheepmen could fight their way, stealthily hidden, yet watching, lay Jasper Swope and his sheep. And not only Jasper with his pet man-killing Chihuahuano and all those low-browed *compadres* whom he called by circumlocution "brothers," but Jim, sore with his defeat, and many others —- and every man armed.

After the first rain they had disappeared from the desert absolutely, their tracks pointing toward the east. The drought had hit them hard, and the cold of Winter; yet the ewes had lambed in the springtime, and as if by magic the tender grass shot up to feed their little ones. Surely, God was good to the sheep. They were ranging far, now that the shearing was over, but though they fed to the topmost peaks of the Superstitions, driving the crooked-horned mountain sheep from their pastures, their destiny lay to the north, in the cool valleys of the Sierra Blancas; and there in the end they would go, though they left havoc in their wake. Once before the sheep had vanished in this same way, mysteriously; and at last, travelling circuitous ways and dealing misery to many Tonto cowmen, they had poured over the very summit of the Four Peaks and down upon Bronco Mesa. And now, though they were hidden, every man on the round-up felt their presence and knew that the upper range was in jeopardy.

After amusing the ladies with inconsequential tales, the *rodéo* outfit therefore rose up and was gone before the light, raking the exposed lowland for its toll of half-fed steers; and even Rufus Hardy, the parlor-broke friend and lover, slipped away before any of them were stirring and rode far up along the river. What a river it was now, this unbridled Salagua which had been their moat and rampart for so many years! Its waters flowed thin and impotent over the rapids, lying in clear pools against the base of the black cliffs, and the current that had uprooted trees like feathers was turned aside by a snag. Where before the sheep had hung upon its flank hoping at last to swim at Hidden Water, the old ewes now strayed along its sandy bed, browsing upon the willows. From the towering black buttes that walled in Hell's Hip Pocket to the Rio Verde it was passable for a spring lamb, and though the thin grass stood up fresh and green on the mesas the river showed nothing but drought. Drought and the sheep, those were the twin evils of the Four Peaks country; they lowered the price of cattle and set men to riding the range restlessly. For the drought is a visitation of God, to be accepted and endured, but sheep may be turned back.

As he rode rapidly along the river trail, halting on each ridge to search the landscape for sheep, Hardy's conscience smote him for the single day he had spent in camp, dallying within sight of Kitty or talking with Lucy Ware. One such day, if the sheepmen were prepared, and Bronco Mesa would be a desert. Threats, violence, strategy, would be of no avail, once the evil was done; the sheep must be turned back at the river or they would swarm in upon the whole upper range. One man could turn them there, for it was the dead line; but once across they would scatter like quail before a hawk, crouching and hiding in the gulches, refusing to move, yet creeping with brutish stubbornness toward the north and leaving a clean swath behind. There were four passes that cut their way down from the southern mountains to the banks of the river, old trails of Apaches and wild game, and to quiet his mind Hardy looked for tracks at every crossing before he turned Chapuli's head toward camp.

The smoke was drifting from the chimney when, late in the afternoon, he rode past the door and saw Lucy Ware inside, struggling with an iron kettle before the fireplace. Poor Lucy, she had undertaken a hard problem, for there is as much difference between camp cooking and home cooking as there is between a Dutch oven and a steel range, and a cooking-school graduate has to forget a whole lot before she can catch the knack of the open fire. For the second time that day Rufus Hardy's conscience, so lately exercised over his neglect of the sheep, rose up and rebuked him. Throwing Chapuli into the corral he kicked off his spurs and shaps and gave Lucy her first lesson in frontier cookery; taught her by the force of his example how to waste her wood and save her back; and at the end of the short demonstration he sat down without ceremony, and fell to eating.

"Excuse me," he said, "if I seem to be greedy, but I had my breakfast before sun-up. Where's your father, and Kitty?"

"Oh, they had the Mexican boy catch their horses for them and have ridden up the valley to watch for the cattle. I stayed behind to make my first water color, and then —- I thought you would be coming back soon, so I tried to cook supper instead. I'm a pretty good housekeeper — at home," she said apologetically.

Hardy watched her as she experimented painstakingly with the fire, scooping out shovelfuls of coal from beneath the glowing logs and planting her pots and kettles upon them with a hooked stick, according to instructions.

"You look like a picture of one of our sainted Puritan ancestors," he observed, at last, "and that's just exactly the way they cooked, too —- over an open fire. How does it feel to be Priscilla?"

"Well, if Priscilla's hands looked like mine," exclaimed Lucy despairingly, "John Alden must have been madly in love with her. How *do* you keep yours clean?"

"That's a secret," replied Hardy, "but I'll tell you. I never touch the outside of a pot —- and I scour them with sandsoap. But I wish you'd stop cooking, Lucy; it makes me feel conscience-stricken. You are my guests, remember, even if I do go off and neglect you for a whole day; and when you go back to Berkeley I want you to have something more interesting than housekeeping to talk about. Didn't I see two ladies' saddles out in the wagon?"

Miss Lucy's eyes lighted up with pleasure as, anticipating his drift, she nodded her head.

"Well then," said Hardy, with finality, "if you'll get up early in the morning, I'll catch you a little pony that I gentled myself, and we can ride up the river together. How does that strike you?"

"Fine!" exclaimed Lucy, with sudden enthusiasm.

"Oh, Rufus," she cried impulsively, "if you only knew how weak and helpless a thing it is to be a woman —- and how glad we are to be noticed! Why, I was just thinking before you came in that about the only really helpful thing a woman could do in this world was just to stay around home and cook the meals."

"Well, you just let me cook those meals for a while," said Rufus, with brotherly authority, "and come out and be a man for a change. Can you ride pretty well?"

Lucy glanced at him questioningly, and thought she read what was in his mind.

"Yes," she said, "I can ride, but —- but I just couldn't bring myself to dress like Kitty!" she burst out. "I know it's foolish, but I can't bear to have people notice me so. But I'll be a man in everything else, if you'll only give me a chance." She stood before him, radiant, eager, her eyes sparkling like a child's, and suddenly Hardy realized how much she lost by being always with Kitty. Seen by herself she was as lithe and graceful as a fairy, with a steady gaze very rare in women, and eyes which changed like the shadows in a pool, answering every mood in wind and sky, yet always with their own true light. Her cheeks glowed with the fresh color which her father's still retained, and she had inherited his generous nature, too; but in mind and stature she took after her dainty mother, whose exquisite grace and beauty had made her one of the elect. Perhaps it was this quality of the petite in her which appealed to him —- for a little man cannot endure to be laughed at for his size, even in secret —- or perhaps it was only the intuitive response to a something which in his prepossession he only vaguely sensed, but Rufus Hardy felt his heart go out to her in a moment and his voice sank once more to the caressing fulness which she most loved to hear.

"Ah, Lucy," he said, "you need never try to be a man in order to ride with me. It would be hard luck if a woman like you had to ask twice for anything. Will you go out with me every day? No? Then I shall ask you every day, and you shall go whenever you please! But you know how it is. The sheepmen are hiding along the river waiting for a chance to sneak across, and if I should stay in camp for a single day they might make a break —- and then we would have a war. Your father doesn't understand that, but I do; and I know that Jeff will never submit to being sheeped out without a fight. Can't you see how it is? I should like to stay here and entertain you, and yet I must protect your father's cattle, and I must protect Jeff. But if you will ride out with me when it is not too hot, I —- it —- well, you'll go to-morrow, won't you?"

He rose and took her hand impulsively, and then as quickly dropped it and turned away. The muffled *chuck, chuck,* of a horse's feet stepping past the door smote upon his ear, and a moment later a clear voice hailed them.

"What *are* you children chattering about in there?" cried Kitty Bonnair, and Hardy, after a guilty silence, replied:

"The ways of the weary world. Won't you come in and have the last word?"

He stepped out and held Pinto by the head, and Kitty dropped off and sank wearily into a rawhide chair.

"Oh, I'm too tired to talk, riding around trying to find those cattle —- and just as I was tired out we saw them coming, away out on The Rolls. Lucy, do put on your riding habit and go back on Pinto —- you haven't been out of the house to-day!"

As half an hour later Lucy Ware trotted obediently away, riding up the cañon toward the distant bawling of cattle, Kitty turned suddenly upon Hardy with half-closed, accusing eyes.

"You seem to be very happy with Lucy," she said, with an aggrieved smile. "But why," she continued, with quickening animus, "why should you seek to avoid me? Isn't it enough that I should come clear down here to see you? But when I want to have a word with you after our long silence I have to scheme and manage like a gypsy!"

She paused, and flicked her booted leg with the lash of a horsehair quirt, glancing at him furtively with eyes that drooped with an appealing sadness.

"If I had known how hard-hearted you could be," she said, after a silence, "I should never have spoken as I did, if the words choked me. But now that I have come part way and offered my poor friendship again, you might —- oh Rufus, how could you be so inconsiderate! No one can ever know what I suffered when you left that way. Every one knew we were the best of friends, and several people even knew that you had been to see me. And then, without a word, without a sign, with no explanation, to leave and be gone for years —- think what they must have thought! Oh, it was too humiliating!"

She paused again, and to Hardy's apprehensive eyes she seemed on the verge of tears. So he spoke, blindly and without consideration, filled with a man's anxiety to stave off this final catastrophe.

"I'm sorry," he began, though he had never meant to say it, "but —- but there was nothing else to do! You —- you told me to go. You said you never wanted to see me again, and —- you were not very kind to me, then." He paused, and at the memory of those last words of hers, uttered long ago, the flush of shame mantled his cheeks.

"Every man has his limit," he said bluntly, "and I am no dog, to be scolded and punished and sent away. I have been ashamed many times for what I did, but I had to keep my own respect —- and so I left. Is it too much for a man to go away when he is told?"

Kitty Bonnair fixed him with her dark eyes and shook her head sadly.

"Ah, Rufus," she sighed, "when will you ever learn that a woman does not always mean all she says? When you had made me so happy by your tender consideration —- for you could be considerate when you chose —- I said that I loved you; and I did, but not in the way you thought. I did mean it at the moment, from my heart, but not for life —- it was no surrender, no promise —- I just loved you for being so good and kind. But when, taking advantage of what I said in a moment of weakness, you tried to claim that which I had never given, I —- I said more than I meant again. Don't you understand? I was hurt, and disappointed, and I spoke without thinking, but you must not hold that against me forever! And after I have come clear down here —- to avoid me —- to always go out with Lucy and leave me alone —- to force me to arrange a meeting —- "

She stopped, and Hardy shifted uneasily in his seat. In his heart of hearts he had realized from the first his inequality in this losing battle. He was like a man who goes into a contest conquered already by his ineptitude at arms —- and Kitty would have her way! Never but once had he defied her power, and that had been more a flight than a victory. There was fighting blood in his veins, but it turned to water before her. He despised himself for it; but all the while, in a shifting, browbeaten way, he was seeking for an excuse to capitulate.

"But, Kitty," he pleaded, "be reasonable. I have my duties down here —- the sheep are trying to come in on us —- I have to patrol the river. This morning before you were awake I was in the saddle, and now I have just returned. To-morrow I shall be off again, so how can I arrange a meeting?"

He held out his hands to her appealingly, carried away by the force of his own logic.

"You might at least invite me to go with you," she said. "Unless you expect me to spend all my time getting lost with Judge Ware," she added, with a plaintive break in her voice.

"Why, yes —- yes," began Hardy haltingly. "I —- I have asked Lucy to go with me to-morrow, but —- "

"Oh, thank you —- thank you!" burst out Kitty mockingly. "But what?"

"Why, I thought you might like to come along too," suggested Hardy awkwardly.

"What? And rob her of all her pleasure?" Kitty smiled bitterly as she turned upon him. "Why, Rufus Hardy," she exclaimed, indignantly, "and she just dotes on every word you say! Yes, she does —- any one can see that she simply adores you. I declare, Rufus, your lack of perception would make an angel weep —- especially if it was a lady angel. But you may as well understand once and for all that I will never deprive dear, patient, long-suffering Lucy of anything she sets her heart on. No, I will *not* go with you the next day. If you haven't consideration enough to invite me first, I have sense enough to stay away. It was only yesterday that you took Lucy up to Hidden Water, and to-day I find you with her again; and to-morrow —- well, I perceive that I must amuse myself down here. But —- oh, look, look! There's a cowboy —- up on that high cliff!"

She started up, pointing at a horseman who was spurring furiously along the side of the cañon after a runaway steer.

"Oh, look!" she cried again, as Hardy surveyed him indifferently. "He is whirling his lasso. Oh! He has thrown it over that big cow's horns! Goodness me, where is my horse? No, I am going on foot, then! Oh, Lucy —- Lucy dear," she screamed, waving her hand wildly, "do let me have Pinto, just for a moment! All right —- and Lucy —- wasn't that Mr. Creede?" She lingered on the ground long enough to give her an ecstatic kiss and then swung up into the saddle. "Yes, I knew it —- and isn't he just perfectly grand on that big horse? Oh, I've been wanting to see this all my life —- and I owe it all to you!"

With a smile and a gay salutation, she leaned forward and galloped out into the riot and confusion of the *rodéo*, skirting the edge of the bellowing herd until she disappeared in the dust. And somehow, even by the childlike obliviousness with which she scampered away, she managed to convey a pang to her errant lover which clutched at his heart for days.

And what days those were for Jefferson Creede! Deep and devious as was his knowledge of men in the rough, the ways of a woman in love were as cryptic to him as the poems of Browning. The first day that Miss Kitty rode forth to be a cowboy it was the *rodéo* boss, indulgent, but aware of the tenderfoot's ability to make trouble, who soberly assigned his fair disciple to guard a pass over which no cow could possibly come. And Kitty, sensing the deceit, had as soberly amused herself by gathering flowers among the rocks. But the next day, having learned her first lesson, she struck for a job to ride, and it was the giddy-headed lover who permitted her to accompany him —- although not from any obvious or selfish motives.

Miss Bonnair was the guest of the ranch, her life and welfare being placed for the time in the keeping of the boss. What kind of a foreman would it be who would turn her over to a hireling or intrust her innocent mind to a depraved individual like Bill Lightfoot? And all the decent cowmen were scared of her, so who was naturally indicated and elected but Jefferson D. Creede?

There wasn't any branding at the round corral that night. The gather was a fizzle, for some reason, though Miss Kitty rode Pinto to a finish and killed a rattlesnake with Creede's own gun. Well, they never did catch many cattle the first few days, —- after they had picked up the tame bunch that hung around the water, —- and the dry weather seemed to have driven the cows in from The Rolls. But when they came in the second afternoon, with only a half of their gather, Creede rode out from the hold-up herd to meet them, looking pretty black.

It is the duty of a *rodéo* boss to know what is going on, if he has to ride a horse to death to find out; and the next day, after sending every man down his ridge, Jeff left Kitty Bonnair talking lion hunt with old Bill Johnson who had ridden clear over from Hell's Hip Pocket to gaze upon this horse-riding Diana, and disappeared. As a result, Bat Wings was lathered to a fine dirt-color and there was one man in particular that the boss wanted to see.

"Jim," he said, riding up to where one of the Clark boys was sullenly lashing the drag with his *reata*, "what in the hell do you mean by lettin' all them cattle get away? Yes, you did too. I saw you tryin' to turn 'em back, so don't try to hand me anything like that. I used to think you was a good puncher, Jim, but a man that can't keep a herd of cows from goin' through a box pass ought to be smokin' cigarettes on the day herd. You bet ye! All you had to do was be there —- and that's jest exactly where you wasn't! I was up on top of that rocky butte, and I know. You was half a mile up the cañon mousin' around in them cliffs, that's where you was, and the only question I want to ask is, Did you find the Lost Dutchman? No? Then what in hell was you doin'?"

The *rodéo* boss crowded his horse in close and thrust his face forward until he could look him squarely in the eye, and Clark jerked back his head resentfully.

"What is it to you?" he demanded belligerently.

"Oh, nawthin'," returned the boss lightly, "jest wanted to know."

"Uhr!" grunted the cowboy contemptuously. "Well, I was killin' snakes, then! What ye goin' to do about it?"

"Snakes!" cried Creede incredulously. "Killin' snakes! Since when did you call a feud on them?"

"Since thet young lady come," replied Clark, glancing around to see if any one had the nerve to laugh. "I heerd her say she was collectin' rattles; an' I thought, while I was waitin', I might as well rustle up a few. Oh, you don't need to look pop-eyed —- they's others!"

He rolled his eyes significantly at the group of assembled cowboys, and Creede took it all in at a flash. There *were* others —- he himself had a set of rattles in his shap pocket that were not two hours from the stump. The situation called for diplomacy.

"Well," he drawled, scratching his bushy head to cover his confusion, "this reflects great credit on your bringin' up, Jim, and I'm sure Miss Bonnair will appreciate what you've done for her, especially as I happened to notice a couple o' head of your own cows in that bunch, but it's a mighty expensive way to collect snake-tails. We ain't gittin' the cattle, boys; that's the size of it, and they're as much yours as they are mine. Now I suggest that we run these few we've got down to the corral and brand 'em quick —- and then the whole shootin'-match goes over to the big white cliff and rounds up every rattlesnake in the rock pile! Is it a go?"

"Sure!" yelled the bunch impetuously, and as they charged down upon the herd Creede quietly fished out his snake-tail and dropped it in the dirt.

If he lacked a virtue he could feign it, anyhow —- but there was no doubt about it, Miss Kitty was putting his *rodéo* on the bum. There had never been so many men to feed and so few calves to brand in the history of Hidden Water. Even old Bill Johnson had got the fever from hearing the boys talk and was hanging around the fire. But then, what were a few head of cows compared to —- well, what was it, anyway? The only man who could stay away was Rufe, and he was in good company.

Yet Creede was not satisfied with this explanation. Miss Kitty was always asking questions about Rufe —- they had known each other well in Berkeley —- and at the same time the little partner with whom he had been so friendly never came around any more. He was always very polite, and she called him by his first name —- and then one of them rode up the river and the other followed the round-up.

The night after the big snake-killing Jefferson Creede picked up his blankets and moved quietly back to the *ramada* with Hardy.

"Them locoed punchers have been skinnin' rattlers and stretchin' their hides," he said, "until the camp stinks like a buzzard roost. I'm due to have some bad dreams to-night anyhow, on the strength of this snake-killin', but it'd give me the jumpin' jimjams if I had to sleep next to them remains. Didn't git back in time to join in, did ye? Well, no great loss. I always did intend to clean out that snake hole over'n the cliff, and the boys was stoppin' every time they heard one sing, anyhow, in order to git the rattles for Miss Bonnair, so I thought we might as well git it off our minds before somethin' worse turned up. See any sheep tracks?"

He kicked off his boots, poked his six-shooter under his pillow, and settled down comfortably for the night.

"Nary one, eh?" he repeated musingly. "Well, when you see one you'll see a million —- that's been my experience. But say, Rufe, why don't you come and ride with the boys once in a while? The *rodéo* has been goin' rotten this year —- we ain't gittin' half of 'em —- and you'd come in mighty handy. Besides, I've been braggin' you up to Miss Bonnair."

He dropped this last as a bait, but Hardy did not respond.

"I told her you was the best bronco-buster in the Four Peaks country," continued Creede deliberately, "and that you could drift Chapuli over the rocks like a sand lizard; but I'm too heavy for anything like that now, and Bill Lightfoot has been puttin' up the fancy work, so far. You know how I like Bill."

Once more he waited for an answer, but Hardy was wrestling with those elementary passions which have been making trouble since Helen of Troy left home, and he received the remark in silence.

"I'll tell you, Rufe," said Creede, lowering his voice confidentially. "Of course I see how it is with you and Miss Ware, and I'm glad of it; but things ain't goin' so lovely for me. It ain't my fault if Miss Bonnair happens to like my company, but Bill and some of the other boys have got their backs up over it, and they've practically gone on a strike. Leastwise we ain't gittin' the cattle, and God knows the range won't more 'n carry what's left. I've got to git out and do some ridin', and at the same time I want to do the right thing by Miss Bonnair, so if you could jest kindly come along with us to-morrow I'll be much obliged."

The elemental passions —- man-love, jealousy, the lust for possession —- are ugly things at best, even when locked in the bosom of a poet. In their simplest terms they make for treachery and stealth; but when complicated with the higher call of friendship and duty they gall a man like the chains of Prometheus and send the dragon-clawed eagles of Jove to tear at his vitals. Never until this naive confession had Hardy suspected the sanity of his friend nor the constancy of Kitty Bonnair. That she was capable of such an adventure he had never dreamed —- and yet —- and yet —- where was there a more masterful man than Jeff? Anything can happen in love; and who was there more capable of winning a romantic woman's regard than good-natured, impulsive, domineering Jeff?

The thoughts flashed through his brain with the rapidity of lightning, and only his instinct of reserve protected him from his blundering tongue.

"I —- I was —- " he began, and stopped short. The idea of loyalty had ruled his mind so long that it had become a habit, ill suited to the cause of a jealous lover; and Jeff had confided to him as a child might run to its mother. Should a man take advantage of his friend's innocence to deprive him of that for which they both strove? Hardy fought the devil away and spoke again, quietly.

"I was going up the river to-morrow, Jeff," he said. "Seemed to me I saw a kind of smoke, or dust, over south of Hell's Hip Pocket this afternoon —- and we can't take any chances now. That would take all day, you know."

He lay still after that, his brain whirling with contending emotions. Each evening as he listened to the music of her laughter he had resolved to quit his lonely watch and snatch from life the pleasure of a single day with Kitty, such days as they used to have when he was her unacknowledged lover and all the world was young. Then he could always please her. He could bend to her moods like a willow, braving the storms of her displeasure, which only drew them closer in the end, secure in the hope of her ultimate yielding. But now the two barren years lay between; years which had stiffened his jaw and left him rough in his ways; years which had wrought some change in her, he knew not what. A single day might solve the crux —- nay, it might bring the great happiness of which he dreamed. But each morning as he woke with the dawn he saw that mighty army without banners, the sheep, marching upon their stronghold, the broad mesa which fed the last of Jeff's cows, and Judge Ware's, and Lucy's —- and sprang from his blankets. And when the sun rose and Kitty came forth he was far away. But now —-

He was awakened from his dreams by the voice of Creede, low, vibrant, full of brotherly love.

"Rufe," he was saying, "Miss Bonnair has told me a lot about you —- a lot I didn't know. She likes you, boy, and she's a good woman. I never knowed but one like her, and that was Sallie Winship. You mustn't let anything that's happened stand between you. Of course she never said anything —- never said a word —- but I'm wise that way; I can tell by their voice, and all that. You want to let them dam' sheep go for a day or two and git this thing patched up."

He paused, and Hardy's mind whirled backward, upsetting his fears, unmaking his conclusions. It was Jeff the friend who spoke, Jeff the peacemaker, who had stampeded him by the equivocation of his words. But now the voice broke in again, apologetic, solicitous, self-seeking.

"Besides, that son-of-a-gun, Bill Lightfoot, has been tryin' to cut me out."

God! There it hit him hard. Kitty, the immaculate, the exquisite, the friend of poets and artists, the woman he had loved and cherished in his dreams —- striven for by Jeff and Bill, revelling in the homage of Mexicans and hard-drinking round-up hands, whose natural language was astench with uncleanliness. It was like beholding a dainty flower in the grime and brutality of the branding pen.

"I'm sorry, Jeff," he said, in a far-away voice. "I —- I'd do anything I could for you —- but I'm afraid of those sheep."

He dragged miserably through the remnant of their conversation and then lay staring at the stars while his hulk of a partner, this great bear who in his awkward good nature had trampled upon holy ground, slept peacefully by his side. The Pleiades fled away before Orion, the Scorpion rose up in the south and sank again, the Morning Star blinked and blazed like a distant fire, such as shepherds kindle upon the ridges, and still Hardy lay in his blankets, fighting with himself. The great blackness which precedes the first glow of dawn found him haggard and weary of the struggle. He rose and threw wood on the coals of last night's fire, cooked and ate in silence, and rode away. There was a great burden upon his soul, a great fire and anger in his heart, and he questioned the verities of life. He rode up the river gloomily, searching the southern wilderness with frowning, bloodshot eyes, and once more, far to the east where the jagged cliffs of the Superstitions sweep down to the gorge of the Salagua and Hell's Hip Pocket bars the river's sweep, he saw that vague, impalpable haze —- a smoke, a dust, a veil of the lightest skein, stirred idly by some wandering wind, perhaps, or marking the trail of sheep. And as he looked upon it his melancholy gaze changed to a staring, hawk-like intentness; he leaned forward in the saddle and Chapuli stepped eagerly down the slope, head up, as if he sniffed the battle.

CHAPTER XV
THE CATASTROPHE

A demon of unrest, twin devil to that which had so clutched and torn at the sensitive spirit of Rufus Hardy, seemed to rise up with the dawn of that ill-omened day and seize upon the camp at Hidden Water. It was like a touch of the north wind, which rumples the cat's back, sets the horses to fighting in the corrals, and makes men mean and generally contrary. Bill Johnson's hounds were the first to feel the madness. They left before sun-up, heading for the wooded heights of the Juate, and led him a weary chase. At the last moment Creede abandoned the unprofitable working of The Rolls and ordered the *rodéo* up onto Bronco Mesa; and Kitty Bonnair, taking advantage of his preoccupation, quietly gave him the slip at the end of their long eastern detour, and turned her pinto's head toward the river.

As for Kitty, her will was the wind's will, which changes with the times and seasons but is accountable to no universal law. Never in her life had she met a man who could quarrel like Rufus Hardy. Beneath her eye he was as clay in the hands of the potter; every glance spoke love, and for her alone. And yet it was something more than a smouldering resentment which made him avoid her, riding out before the dawn; more than the tremulous bashfulness which had stayed his hand when at times he might have taken hers. There was something deep, hidden, mysterious, lurking in those fawnlike eyes, and it made him insurgent against her will. It was a secret, hidden from all the world, which he must yield to her. And then she would forgive him for all the unhappiness he had caused her and teach him what a thing it is for a woman to love and be misunderstood. But first —- first she must see him alone; she must burst upon him suddenly, taking his heart by storm as she had on that first day, and leave the rest to fate. So she lingered to gather some flowers which nodded among the rocks, the shy and dainty forget-me-nots which they had picked together at home; and when Creede was over the first ridge she struck out boldly up a side cañon, tucking the miniature bouquet into the shadows of her hair.

The southern flank of Bronco Mesa breaks off sharply above the Salagua, rising slowly by slopes and terraced benches to the heights, and giving way before the river in a succession of broken ridges. Along these summits run winding trails, led high to escape the rougher ground. Urged on by the slashings of her quirt, Pinto galloped recklessly through this maze of cow paths until as if by magic the great valley lay before them. There in its deep cañon was the river and the river trail —- and a man, mounted upon a sorrel horse, savagely intent upon his way. For a minute Kitty studied him curiously as he hustled along, favoring his horse up the hills but swinging to the stirrup as he dodged bushes across the flats; then she flung out her hand impulsively, and called his name. In a flash he was up in his saddle, looking. Chapuli tossed his head and in the act caught a glimpse of the other horse —- then they both stood rigid, gazing in astonishment at the living statue against the sky. At sight of that witching figure, beckoning him from the mountain top, Hardy's heart leaped within him and stopped. Once more the little hand was thrown out against the sky and a merry voice floated down to him from the sun-touched heights.

"Hello, Rufus!" it called teasingly, and still he sat gazing up at her. All the untamed passions of his being surged up and choked his voice —- he could not answer. His head turned and he gazed furtively over his shoulder to the east, where his duty lay. Then of his own accord Chapuli stepped from the trail and began to pick his way soberly up the hill.

From the high summit of the butte all the world lay spread out like a panorama, —- the slopes and cañons of Bronco Mesa, picketed with giant *sahuaros*; the silvery course of the river flowing below; the unpeopled peaks and cliffs of the Superstitions; and a faint haze-like zephyr, floating upon the eastern horizon. And there at last the eyes of Rufus Hardy and Kitty Bonnair met, questioning each other, and the world below them took on a soft, dreamy veil of beauty.

"Why, how did you come here?" he asked, looking down upon her wonderingly. "Were you lost?"

And Kitty smiled wistfully as she answered:

"Yes —- till I found you."

"Oh!" said Hardy, and he studied her face warily, as if doubtful of her intent.

"But how could you be lost," he asked again, "and travel so far? This is a rough country, and you got here before I did."

He swung down from his horse and stood beside her, but Kitty only laughed mischievously and shook her head —- at which, by some lover's magic, the dainty forget-me-nots fell from her hair in a shower of snowy blossoms.

"I was lost," she reiterated, smiling into his eyes, and in her gaze Hardy could read —- "without you."

For a moment the stern sorrow of the night withheld him. His eyes narrowed, and he opened his lips to speak. Then, bowing his head, he knelt and gathered up the flowers.

"Yes," he said gently, "I understand. I —- I have been lost, too."

They smiled and sat down together in the shadow of a great rock, gazing out over the peaks and pinnacles of the mountains which wall in Hidden Water and talking placidly of the old days —- until at last, when the spell of the past was on him, Kitty fell silent, waiting for him to speak his heart.

But instantly the spell of her laughter was broken an uneasy thought came upon Hardy, and he glanced up at the soaring sun.

"Jeff will be worried about you," he said at last. "He will think you are lost and give up the *rodéo* to hunt for you. We must not stay here so long."

He turned his head instinctively as he spoke, and Kitty knew he was thinking of the sheep.

"Cattle and sheep —- cattle and sheep," she repeated slowly. "Is there nothing else that counts, Rufus, in all this broad land? Must friendship, love, companionship, all go down before cattle and sheep? I never knew before what a poor creature a woman was until I came to Arizona."

She glanced at him from beneath her drooping lashes, and saw his jaws set tense.

"And yet only yesterday," he said, with a sombre smile, "you had twenty men risking their lives to give you some snake-tails for playthings."

"But my old friend Rufus was not among them," rejoined Kitty quietly; and once more she watched the venom working in his blood.

"No," he replied, "he refuses to compete with Bill Lightfoot at any price."

"Oh, Rufus," cried Kitty, turning upon him angrily, "aren't you ashamed? I want you to stop being jealous of all my friends. It is the meanest and most contemptible thing a man can do. I —- I won't stand it!"

He glanced at her again with the same set look of disapproval still upon his face.

"Kitty," he said, "if you knew what lives some of those men lead —- the thoughts they think, the language they speak —- you —- you would not —- " He stopped, for the sudden tears were in her eyes. Kitty was crying.

"Oh, Rufus," she sobbed, "if —- if you only knew! Who else could I go with —- how —- how else —- Oh, I cannot bear to be scolded and —- I only did it to make you jealous!" She bowed her head against her knees and Hardy gazed at her in awe, shame and compassion sweeping over him as he realized what she had done.

"Kitty —- dear," he stammered, striving to unlock the twisted fingers, "I —- I didn't understand. Look, here are your flowers and —- I love you, Kitty, if I am a brute." He took one hand and held it, stroking the little fingers which he had so often longed to caress. But with a sudden wilfulness she turned her face away.

"Don't you love me, Kitty?" he pleaded. "Couldn't you, if I should try to be good and kind? I —- I don't understand women —- I know I have hurt you —- but I loved you all the time. Can't you forgive me, Kitty?"

But Kitty only shook her head. "The man I love must be my master," she said, in a far-away voice, not looking at him. "He must value me above all the world."

"But, Kitty," protested Hardy, "I do —- "

"No," said Kitty, "you do *not* love me."

There was a lash to the words that cut him —- a scorn half-spoken, half-expressed by the slant of her eye. As he hesitated he felt the hot blood burn at his brow.

"Rufus," she cried, turning upon him quickly, "*do* you love me? Then take me in your arms and kiss me!" She spoke the words fiercely, almost as a command, and Hardy started back as if he had been shot.

"Take me in your arms and kiss me!" she repeated evenly, a flash of scorn in her eyes. But the man who had said he loved her faltered and looked away.

"Kitty," he said gently, "you know I love you. But —- "

"But what?" she demanded sharply.

"I —- I have never —- "

"Well," said Kitty briefly, "it's all over —- you don't have to! I just wanted to show you —- " She paused, and her lip curled as she gazed at him from a distance. "Look at my horse," she exclaimed suddenly, pointing to where Pinto was pawing and jerking at his bridle rein. When Hardy leapt up to free his foot she frowned again, for that is not the way of lovers.

He came back slowly, leading the horse, his face very pale, his eyes set.

"You were right," he said. "Shall we go?"

There was no apology in his voice, no appeal. It had grown suddenly firm and resonant, and he fixed her with his great honest eyes steadfastly. Something in the man seemed to rise up suddenly and rebuke her —- nay, to declare her unworthy of him. The thought of those two years —- two years without a word —- came upon Kitty and left her sober, filled with misgivings for the future. She cast about for some excuse, some reason for delay, and still those masterful eyes were fixed upon her —- sad, wistful, yet steadfast; and like a child she obeyed them.

It was a long ride to camp, long for both of them. When he had turned her horse into the corral Hardy wheeled and rode off up the cañon, where the hold-up herd was bellowing and there was a man's work to do. There was wild riding that day, such as Judge Ware and Lucy had never seen before, and more than one outlaw, loping for the hills, was roped and thrown, and then lashed back to his place in the herd. The sensitive spirit of Chapuli responded like a twin being to the sudden madness of his master, and the lagging *rodéo* hands were galvanized into action by his impetuous ardor. And at the end, when the roping and branding were over, Hardy rode down to the pasture for a fresh mount, his eyes still burning with a feverish light and his lips close-drawn and silent.

The outfit was huddled about the fire eating greedily after the long day, when Creede, furtively watching his partner, saw his eyes fixed curiously upon some object in the outer darkness. He followed the glance and beheld a hound —- gaunt, lame, beseeching —- limping about among the mesquite trees which lined the edge of the flat.

"There's one of Bill's dogs," he remarked sociably, speaking to the crowd in general. "Must've got sore-footed and come back. Here, Rock! Here, Rye! Here, Ring!" he called, trying the most likely names. "Here, puppy —- come on, boy!" And he scraped a plate in that inviting way which is supposed to suggest feed to a dog. But Hardy rose up quietly from his place and went out to the dog. A moment later he called to Jeff and, after a hurried conference, the two of them brought the wanderer up to the fire.

"Hey!" called Bill Lightfoot, "that ain't one of Bill's pack —- that's old Turco, his home dog."

"Don't you think I know Bill's dogs yet?" inquired Creede scathingly. "Now if you'll jest kindly keep your face shet a minute, I'll see what's the matter with this leg."

He clamped Turco between his knees and picked up his fore leg, while the old dog whined and licked his hands anxiously. There was a stain of blood from the shoulder down, and above it, cut neatly through the muscles, a gaping wound.

"That was a thirty-thirty," said Creede grimly, and every man looked up. Thirty-thirty was a sinister number on the range —- it was the calibre of a sheep-herder's carbine.

"Aw, go on," scoffed Bill Lightfoot, rushing over to examine the wound. "Who could have shot him —- away over in Hell's Hip Pocket?"

"Um —- that's it," observed Creede significantly. "What you goin' to do, Rufe?"

"I'm going over there," answered Hardy, throwing the saddle on his horse. He looked over his shoulder as he heaved on the cinch. "That's where that dust was," he said, and as the outfit stood gaping he swung up and was off into the darkness.

"Hey, take my gun!" yelled Jeff, but the clatter of hoofs never faltered —- he was going it blind and unarmed. Late that night another horseman on a flea-bitten gray dashed madly after him over the Pocket trail. It was Old Bill Johnson, crazed with apprehension; and behind him straggled his hounds, worn from their long chase after the lion, but following dutifully on their master's scent. The rest of the outfit rode over in the morning —- the punchers with their pistols thrust into the legs of their shaps; Creede black and staring with anger; the judge asking a thousand unanswered questions and protesting against any resort to violence; the women tagging along helplessly, simply because they could not be left alone. And there, pouring forth from the mouth of Hell's Hip Pocket, came the sheep, a solid phalanx, urged on by plunging herders and spreading out over the broad mesa like an invading army. Upon the peaks and ridges round about stood groups of men, like skirmishers —- camp rustlers with their packs and burros; herders, whose sheep had already passed through —- every man with his gun in his hand. The solid earth of the trail was worn down and stamped to dust beneath the myriad feet, rising in a cloud above them as they scrambled through the pass; and above all other sounds there rose the high, sustained tremolo of the sheep:

Blay-ay-ay-ay! Blay-ay-ay-ay! Blay-ay-ay-ay!"

To the ears of the herders it was music, like the thunder of stamps to a miner or the rumble of a waterfall to a lonely fisher; the old, unlistened music of their calling, above which the clamor of the world must fight its way. But to the cowmen it was like all hell broken loose, a confusion, a madness, a babel which roused every passion in their being and filled them with a lust to kill.

Without looking to the right or to the left, Jefferson Creede fixed his eyes upon one man in that riot of workers and rode for him as a corral hand marks down a steer. It was Jasper Swope, hustling the last of a herd through the narrow defile, and as his Chihuahuanos caught sight of the burly figure bearing down upon the *padron* they abandoned their work to help him. From the hill above, Jim Swope, his face set like iron for the conflict, rode in to back up his brother; and from far down the cañon Rufus Hardy came spurring like the wind to take his place by Creede.

In the elemental clangor of the sheep they faced each other, Creede towering on his horse, his face furious with rage; Swope gray with the dust of his driving but undaunted by the assault.

"Stop where you are!" shouted Swope, holding out a warning hand as the cowman showed no sign of halting. But Creede came straight on, never flinching, until he had almost ridden him down.

"You low-lived, sheep-eatin' hound," he hissed, piling in the wickedest of his range epithets, "you and me have had it comin' fer quite a while, and now I've got you. I've never yet seen a sheepman that would fight in the open, but you've got to or take *that!*" He leaned over suddenly and slapped him with his open hand, laughing recklessly at the Mexicans as they brandished their guns and shouted.

"*Quite se, cabrones,*" he jeered, sorting out the worst of his fighting Spanish for their benefit, "you are all gutter pups —- you are afraid to shoot!"

"Here," rasped out Jim Swope, spurring his horse in between them, "what are you fellers tryin' to do? Git out of here, *umbre* —- go on now! Never mind, Jasp, I'll do the talkin'. You go on away, will ye! Now what's the matter with you, Mr. Creede, and what can I do for you?"

Jasper Swope had whirled back from the blow as a rattler throws his coils. His gray eyes gleamed and he showed all his broken teeth as he spat back hate and defiance at Creede; but Jim was his elder brother and had bested him more than once since the days of their boyish quarrels. Slowly and grudgingly he made way, backing sullenly off with his Mexicans; and Jim stood alone, opposing his cold resolution to the white-hot wrath of Creede.

"You can turn back them sheep and git off my range!" yelled Creede. "Turn 'em back, I say, or I'll leave my mark on some of you!"

"How can I turn 'em back?" argued Swope, throwing out his hands. "They's ninety thousand more behind me, and all headin' through this pass."

"You know very well that this is a put-up job," retorted Creede hotly. "You sheepmen have been crawlin' around on your bellies for a month to get a chanst to sheep us out, and now you say you can't help yourself! You're the crookedest, lyingest sheep-puller in the bunch, Jim Swope. You'd rob a graveyard and show up for prayers the next mornin'. I can lick you, you big Mormon-faced stiff, with one hand tied behind me, and what's more —- "

"Here now —- here no-ow —- " protested Swope, holding out his hand for peace, "they ain't no call for no such talk. Mebbe you can lick me, and mebbe you can't, but it won't do you any good to try. My sheep is here, and here they'll stay, until I git good and ready to move 'em. This is a free range and a free country, and the man ain't born that can make me stop."

He paused, and fixed his keen eyes upon Creede, searching him to the heart; and before that cold, remorseless gaze the fighting frenzy in his brain died away. Meanwhile Hardy had come up from where he had been turning back sheep, and as he rode in Jeff instinctively made way for him.

"No," replied Hardy, fastening his stern eyes upon the iron visage of the sheepman, "not if the lives of a thousand cattle and the last possessions of a dozen men lay in your way. You and your legal rights! It is men like you who make the law worse than nothing and turn honest cowmen into criminals. If there is anything in it you will lie to the assessor or rob a poor man's cabin with the best of them, but when it comes to your legal right to sheep us out you are all for law and order. Sure, you will uphold the statutes with your life! Look at those renegade Mexicans, every man armed by you with a rifle and a revolver! Is that the way to come onto another man's range? If you are going to sheep us out, you can try it on; but for God's sake cut it out about your sacred rights!"

He rose up in his saddle, haranguing the assembly as he spoke, and once more Jim Swope felt his cause being weakened by the attacks of this vehement little cowman.

"Well, what kin I do about it?" he cried, throwing out his hands in virtuous appeal. "My sheep has got to eat, hain't they?"

"Sure," assented Hardy, "and so have our cattle. But I tell you what you can do —- you can go out through that pass yonder!"

He pointed at the cañon down which the sheep had come in the Fall, the great middle fork which led up over the Four Peaks; but the sheepman's only reply was a snarl of refusal.

"Not if I know myself," he muttered spitefully. "How'd do, Judge!" He fixed his eyes eagerly upon Judge Ware, who was hastening to join in the struggle. "You're just the man I want to see," he continued, advancing briskly to meet him, "and I want to ask you, here and now before these witnesses, do you claim any right to the exclusive use of this land?"

"Why, certainly not, certainly not," answered the judge warmly, "but at the same time I do claim an equity which rises from prior and undisputed possession, and which has always and ought now to protect my range from any outside invasion."

"Very likely, very likely," remarked Swope dryly. "And now, Judge, I want to ask you another question before these witnesses. Did you or did you not authorize your superintendent and foreman to threaten and intimidate my men and me, with the idea of driving us off this public land?"

"I did not," replied the judge, his mind suddenly filled with visions of criminal proceedings. "On the contrary, I have repeatedly warned them against any such action."

"At the same time," echoed Swope, quick to follow up his advantage, "these men, who are your agents and employees, have systematically moved my herders off this range by armed violence, and your foreman has just now struck my brother, besides threatening to kill some of us if we don't turn back. I want to tell you right now, Mr. Ware, that I have consulted the best lawyers in this Territory as to my rights on public lands, and you will be held personally responsible for any acts of violence on the part of your employees. Now I want to ask you one more question: Do you deny my right to pass through this range on my way to the Sierra Blancas? You don't? Well then, call off these men!"

He paused and jerked his thumb toward Creede and Hardy, grinning evilly, and as he spoke Creede crowded forward, his brow black as a thunder cloud.

"I don't take orders from nobody," he cried vehemently, "not now, and never will. I've got a few hundred head of cows on this range myself and I intend to protect 'em if I have to kill somebody. You'll have to git another foreman, Judge, —- I've quit."

He shot a glance of pitying contempt at the man who had so stupidly marred their fortunes, then he turned and fixed his burning eyes upon his archenemy.

"Jim," he said, speaking quietly at last, "my father had ten thousand head of cattle on this range before you sheepmen came —- and that's all I've got left. If you think you can sheep me out, go to it!"

He turned his horse's head toward Hidden Water, never looking back at the sheep; and the cowmen fell in behind him, glad of an excuse to retreat. What were a bunch of cowboys, armed with six-shooters, to half a hundred sheepmen armed with repeating rifles and automatic revolvers? No, it was better to let the sheep come, let them spread out and scatter, and then jump the herders at night, if it came to that. But what, reasoned the cautious ones, were a few hundred head of cows anyhow, in a losing fight against the law itself? What was a petty revenge upon some low-browed Mexican to the years of imprisonment in Yuma which might follow? There were some among that little band of cowmen who yelled for action, others who were disgusted enough to quit, and others yet who said nothing, riding by themselves or exchanging furtive glances with Creede. The Clark boys, Ben Reavis, and Juan Ortega —- these were the men whom the *rodéo* boss knew he could trust, and none of them spoke a word.

Worn and haggard from his night's riding, Rufus Hardy rode along with Judge Ware and the ladies, explaining the situation to them. The sheep had come in from the far east, crossing where sheep had never crossed before, at the junction of Hell's Hip Pocket Creek and the drought-shrunk Salagua. They had poured into the Pocket in solid columns, sheeping it to the rocks, and had taken the pass before either he or Bill Johnson could get to it. All through the night the sheepmen had been crowding their flocks through the defile until there were already twenty or thirty thousand on Bronco Mesa, with fifty thousand to follow. Bill Johnson had shot his way through the jam and disappeared into the Pocket, but he could do nothing now —- his little valley was ruined. There would not be a spear of grass left for his cattle, and his burros had already come out with the pack animals of the sheepmen. No one knew what had happened when he reached his home, but the Mexican herders seemed to be badly scared, and Johnson had probably tried to drive them out of the valley.

All this Hardy explained in a perfectly matter-of-fact way, free from apprehension or excitement; he listened in respectful silence to Judge Ware's protests against violence and threats of instant departure; and even humored Kitty's curiosity by admitting that Mr. Johnson, who was apparently out of his head when he shot the sheep, had probably taken a shot or two at the herders, as well. But Lucy Ware was not deceived by his repose; she saw the cold light in his eyes, the careful avoidance of any allusion to his own actions, and the studied concealment of his future intent. But even then she was not prepared when, after supper, her father came into the ranch house and told her that Mr. Hardy had just resigned.

"I can't imagine why he should leave me at this time," exclaimed the judge, mopping the sweat from his brow, and groaning with vexation, "but a man who will desert his own father in the way he has done is capable of anything, I suppose. Just because he doesn't approve of my policies in regard to these sheep he coolly says he won't embarrass me further by staying in my employ! I declare, Lucy, I'm afraid I'm going to lose everything I have down here if both he and Creede desert me. Don't you think you could persuade Rufus to stay? Go out and see him and tell him I will consent to anything —- except this *unlawful harrying* of the sheep."

The old judge, still perspiring with excitement, sank wearily down into a chair and Lucy came over and sat upon his knee.

"Father," she said, "do you remember that you once told me you would give me this ranch if I wanted it? Well, I want it now, and perhaps if you give it to me Rufus will consent to stay."

"But, daughter —- " protested the judge, and then he sat quiet, pondering upon the matter.

"Perhaps you are right," he said at last. "But tell me one thing —- there is nothing between you and Rufus, is there?"

He turned her face so that he could look into her honest eyes, but Lucy twisted her head away, blushing.

"No," she said faintly. "He —- he is in love with Kitty."

"With Kitty!" cried Judge Ware, outraged at the idea. "Why, he —- but never mind, never mind, darling. I am glad at least that it is not with you. We must be going home soon now, anyway, and that will break off this —- er —- But I don't remember having seen them together much!"

"No," said Lucy demurely, "he has been very discreet. But you haven't answered my question, father. Will you give me the ranch if I get Rufus to stay? Oh, you're a dear! Now you just leave everything in my hands and see what a good business woman I am!"

She skipped lightly out the door and hurried over to where Hardy and Jefferson Creede were sitting under a tree, talking gravely together. They stopped as she approached and Hardy looked up a little sullenly from where he sat. Then he rose, and took off his hat.

"May I have a few words with you on a matter of business, Rufus?" she asked, with her friendliest smile. "No, don't go, Mr. Creede; you are interested in this, too. In fact," she added mysteriously, "I need your assistance."

A slow smile crept into the rough cowboy's eyes as he sat watching her.

"What can I do for you?" he inquired guardedly.

"Well," answered Lucy, "the situation is like this —- and I'm not trying to rope you in on anything, as you say, so you needn't look suspicious. My father has become so discouraged with the way things are going that he has given the entire Dos S Ranch to me —- if I can manage it. Now I know that you both have quit because you don't approve of my father's orders about the sheep. I don't know what your plans are but I want to get a new superintendent, and that's where I need your assistance, Mr. Creede."

She paused long enough to bestow a confiding smile upon the *rodéo* boss, and then hurried on to explain her position.

"Of course you understand how it is with father. He has been a judge, and it wouldn't do for a man in his position to break the laws. But I want you two men to tell me before you go just what you think I ought to do to save my cattle, and you can say whatever you please. Mr. Creede, if you were a woman and owned the Dos S outfit, what would you do about the sheep?"

For a minute Creede sat silent, surveying the little lady from beneath his shaggy hair.

"Well," he said judicially, "I think I'd do one of two things: I'd either marry some nice kind man whose judgment I could trust, and turn the job over to him," —- he glanced sideways at Hardy as he spoke, —- "or I'd hire some real mean, plug-ugly feller to wade in and clean 'em out. Failin' in that, I think I'd turn the whole outfit over to Rufe here and go away and fergit about it."

He added these last words with a frank directness which left no doubt as to his own convictions in the matter, and Lucy turned an inquiring eye upon Hardy. He was busily engaged in pounding a hole in the ground with a rock, and Lucy noted for the first time a trace of silver in his hair. The setting sun cast deep shadows in the set lines of his face and when he finally looked up his eyes were bloodshot and haggard.

"There's no use in talking to me about that job," he said morosely. "I've got tired of taking orders from a man that doesn't know what he's talking about, and I want to use my own judgment for a while. We won't let anything happen to your cattle, Miss Lucy, and I thank you very much, but I'm afraid I can't do it."

He stopped, and bowed his head, hammering moodily away at his hole in the rocky ground.

"Excuse me a minute, Miss Ware," said Creede, rising to his feet as the silence became oppressive. "Come over here, Rufe, I want to talk with you."

They stood with their heads together, Jeff tapping the little man on the chest with every word, and still there was the same dogged resistance. "Well, come on and let's find out," protested Creede at last, impatiently dragging him back.

"Miss Ware," he said politely, "what do you expect of this here supe? I might want that job myself, later on," he observed importantly.

Lucy smiled at the bare-faced fraud and hastened to abet it.

"I expect him to look after my cattle," she responded promptly, "and to protect my best interests according to his own judgment. The only thing I insist upon is that he leave his gun at home."

"I'm sorry," said Creede briefly. "And I needed the job, too," he added lugubriously. "How about your foreman?" he inquired, as if snatching at a straw. "Same thing, eh? Well, I'll go you —- next month."

He laughed, shrugged his shoulders, and crowded his big black sombrero down over his eyes until it gave him a comical air of despair.

"Luck's gone," he remarked, reaching parenthetically for a cigarette paper. "See you later." And, with a last roguish twinkle at Miss Lucy, he slouched off toward the fire.

His luck indeed had gone, but somewhere in that giant carcass which harbored the vindictive hate of an Apache, and the restless energy of a Texano, there still lingered the exuberant joyousness of a boy, the indomitable spirit of the pioneer, resigned to any fate so long as there is a laugh in it. As he drifted into the crowd Lucy's heart went out to him; he was so big and strong and manly in this, the final eclipse of his waning fortunes.

"Mr. Creede is a noble kind of a man, isn't he?" she said, turning to where Hardy was still standing. "Won't you sit down, Rufus, and let's talk this over for a minute. But before you decide anything, I want you to get a good night's sleep. You are a free man now, you know, and if there's any worrying to be done it's my funeral —- isn't it?"

If he heard her at all Hardy made no response to the jest. He stood before her, swaying dizzily as he groped about for his hat, which had fallen from his hand. Then at last a faint smile broke through the drawn lines in his face.

"That's right," he said, sinking down at her side, and as he settled back against the tree his eyes closed instantly, like a child whose bedtime has come. "I'm —- I'm so dead tired I can't talk straight, Lucy —- to say nothing of think. But —- I'll take care of you. We aren't sheeped out yet. Only —- only I can't —- I forget what I'm going to say." His head fell forward as he spoke, his hands hung heavy, and he slipped slowly to the ground, fast asleep.

After two days and nights of turmoil and passion his troubles were ended, suddenly; and as she raised him up Lucy Ware bent down quickly under cover of the dusk and kissed his rumpled hair.

CHAPTER XVI
THE DEPARTURE

The gentle hand of sleep, which held Hardy in a grip that was akin to death, blotting out the past and dispelling all remembrance of his sorrows, failed utterly to abate the fighting spirit of Jefferson Creede or sap the Spartan grimness of his purpose. Worn by the destroying anger of the previous day, thwarted and apparently defeated, he rose up at the first glow of dawn and set about his preparations with an unemotional directness which augured ill for Jasper Swope. Before the sun was an hour high he had the town herd on the trail for Bender, entrusted to the care of Bill Lightfoot and several others of whom he wanted to be rid. The camp was dismantled, the packs were loaded upon the spare horses, and the outfit was ready to start for Carrizo Creek before breakfast was more than finished in the ranch house. After a final survey to make sure that nothing had been overlooked in the scuffle, the *rodéo* boss waved his hand to the leaders; then, as the train strung out up the cañon, he rode over to the house to say good-bye. The last farewell is a formality often dispensed with in the Far West; but in this case the boss had business to attend to, and —- well, he had something to say to Kitty Bonnair, too.

Very quietly, in order not to awaken his partner —- whom he had picked up like a tired baby and stored away in the darkened bunk-room the evening before —- Creede opened the door of the living-room, greeted his lady-love with a cheerful grin, and beckoned Miss Lucy outside by a backward jerk of the head.

"Sorry to disturb you, Miss Ware," he said, "but we're movin' camp this mornin' and before I go I want to tell you about them cattle I'm just sendin' to town. If I didn't have other business on hand I'd go down with you gladly and sell 'em for you, but when you git to Bender you go to Chris Johansen, the cattle buyer, and give him this list. You won't savvy what it is but Chris will, and you tell him that if he don't give you the best market price for them cows he'll have to —- lick —- me! This is a dry year and feeders ain't much nohow, but I don't want to see no friend of mine robbed. Well, so-long, Miss Ware. Hope you have a good trip."

He gripped her hand awkwardly, picked up his bridle lash, and thrust one boot thoughtfully into the stirrup. Then, as if suddenly cognizant of a neglected duty, he snapped his foot out and threw the lash back on the ground.

"I'll say good-bye to the judge," he drawled, "so's to show they ain't no hard feelin'. Your old man don't exactly fit in these parts," he observed apologetically, "but he means well, I reckon. You can tell 'im some time that I was kind of excited when I quit."

His farewell was a sober and dignified affair, after the courtly school of the South —- no allusions to the past, no references to the future, merely a gentlemanly expression of regret that his guest's visit should have been so suddenly terminated. But when he turned to Miss Kitty his masterful eyes began to glow and waver and he shifted his feet uneasily.

"Kin I speak with you a minute outside?" he said at last; and Kitty, still eager to read the heart of Man, the Unfinished, followed after him, laughing as he stooped to pass his high hat through the door.

"Come on out by the corral," he urged, confidently leading the way. When they were concealed by the corner of the fence he stopped and dropped his bridle rein.

"Well, we've had a pretty good time together down here, hain't we?" he observed, twisting the fringe of his shaps and smiling at her from beneath his forelock. "I ain't got but a minute —- and there's some rough work ahead, I reckon —- but I jest wanted to —- well, I wanted to give you this." He dove down into his overalls' pocket and brought up a nugget, worn smooth by long milling around between his spare change and his jackknife.

"That's a chunk of gold I found over by Red Butte one time," he said, handing it over. "Thought you might want to keep it for me, you know. But say —- " He crowded his hands into his pockets and canted his head to one side, ogling her roguishly.

Kitty had never observed just such conduct before, and she was curious.

"Why —- what?" she inquired, tossing back her hair tantalizingly.

"Don't I git nothin' to remember you by, little girl?" he demanded, his voice vibrant with passion. "We've been pretty good friends, you know. In fact —- well, say, don't I git jest one kiss?"

He drew her gently into his arms as he spoke, waited a fraction of a second for her to resist, and then kissed her, suddenly and with masterful violence.

"One more," he pleaded insistently. "No? All right then," he said, swinging gracefully up on his horse as she pushed him away. "I'll always remember that one, anyhow!"

He leaned forward and Bat Wings shot away up the cañon like a charger that sniffs the combat, thundering out across the *parada* grounds, swinging beneath the giant mesquite, and plunging down the bank that led to the creek. And all the time his rider sat with one hand on the cantle, his white teeth flashing back a wistful smile.

Taken by surprise Kitty Bonnair stood staring blankly after him, rubbing her cheek which burned hot where he had kissed her. She would always remember that kiss too, and all too late she remembered to become indignant. But, no one being about, she laughed low to herself and hurried back to the house, her eyes downcast and pensive. She had known many men and lovers in her time, but never a one like Jeff Creede.

There was a sound of hasty packing in the Dos S ranch house that morning, and the wagon drove noisily up to the door. Rafael carried out the steamer trunks and luggage, the snake-skins, the smoky opals, the Indian baskets, the braided quirts, and all the scattered plunder that the cowboys had given Kitty and that she could not bear to leave behind. He saddled up their horses, clattering recklessly into the bunk-house where Hardy was sleeping in order to get his blankets, and still, unmindful of noise or preparation, or the friends who must say good-bye, he lay sprawled on the rough blankets, dead with sleep.

Rafael kicked off the brake and started on his weary journey around Red Butte to Moreno's, which would take him the rest of the day; Judge Ware, possessed to get out of the country before he became *particeps criminis* to some lawless outrage, paced restlessly up and down the *ramada*, waiting for the girls to get ready; and Kitty and Lucy, glancing guiltily at each other, fidgeted around in their rooms waiting for Rufus to wake up.

"I'm ready," said Lucy at last, putting the final touches to the room which he had given up to her. "Are you, Kitty?"

Their eyes met in an uneasy stare, each wishing the other would speak.

"Yes," said Kitty, "but —- shall we go without saying good-bye?"

"What in the world are you girls waiting for?" demanded the judge, thrusting his head impatiently in at the door. "I declare, I begin to think there is something in these jokes about Adam waiting for Eve to get her hat on straight. Now please come at once or we won't get to Moreno's in time for supper."

"But, father," protested Lucy, "Kitty and I do not wish to leave without saying good-bye to Rufus. Would you mind —- "

"No, no!" exclaimed Judge Ware irritably, "if he chooses to sleep all day —- "

"But, father!" burst out Lucy, almost tearfully, "he was so tired —- he fell asleep as soon as he sat down, and I never did get him to consent to be my superintendent! Don't you see —- "

"Well, write him a note then," directed the judge brusquely, "and leave it on his desk. Now, Lucy dear, really I'm getting so nervous I'm hardly accountable. *Please* hurry. And, Kitty, please hurry, too!"

Like two souls haled from the world without a word of explanation or confession, Kitty and Lucy both sat down under duress to pen a last appeal to the little man who, despite his stern disregard, somehow held a place in their hearts. Kitty could have wept with vexation at the thought of not seeing him again —- and after she had brought her mind to forgive him, too! She wrote blindly, she knew not what, whether it was accusation or entreaty, and sealed the envelope with a bang of her tiny fist —- and even then he did not awaken. Lucy wrote carefully, wrestling to turn the implacable one from his purpose and yet feeling that he would have his will. She sealed her note and put it upon his desk hesitatingly; then, as Kitty turned away, she dropped her handkerchief beside it. It was a time-worn strategy, such as only the innocent and guileless think of in their hour of adversity. When she ran back to recover it Lucy drew a dainty book from her bosom —- Mrs. Browning's "Sonnets from the Portuguese" —- and placed it across her note as if to save it from the wind, and between two leaves she slipped the forget-me-nots which he had given her at Hidden Water.

As the thud of horses' hoofs died away silence settled down upon the Dos S ranch house, the sombre silence of the desert, unbroken by the murmur of women's voices or the echo of merry laughter, and the sleeping man stirred uneasily on his bed. An hour passed, and then from the *ramada* there came a sound of wailing. Hardy rose up on his bed suddenly, startled. The memory of the past came to him vaguely, like fragments of an eerie dream; then the world came right and he found himself in the bunk-house, alone —- and Tommy outside, crying as if for the dead. Leaping up from his blankets Hardy opened the door and called him in —- hoarse, black, distorted, yet overflowing with love and affection. Poor little Tommy! He took him in his arms to comfort him, and bedded him down on the pillow. But when he stepped outside he found that his world too was vacant —- the house deserted, the corrals empty, the *rodéo* camp a smouldering fireplace, surrounded by a wilderness of tin cans.

As the slow grief of the forsaken came upon him he turned and went to his room, where the atmosphere of womankind still lingered to suggest the dear hands that were gone, and suddenly his eyes leaped to the letters left upon the table. It was Kitty's which he opened first, perhaps because it was nearest; but the torrent of inconsequential words confused him by their unreason and he turned to Lucy's, reading it over thoughtfully.

> "DEAR RUFUS:
>
> "We have waited a long time for you to wake up, and now father says we must go. You were so tired last night that I doubt if you heard a word I said, although I thought I was making a great impression in my new role as a business woman. I asked father to give me the ranch, not because I wanted to own it but to save you from your madness. The cattle are all mine now and I leave them in your care. Whatever you do I will consent to, if you will leave your guns at home. Is that too much for a friend to ask? I know that Mr. Creede is your friend too, and I admire your devotion to his cause, but I think you can do just as much for him and more by not risking your life in a battle against the sheep. They are so many, Rufus, and they have their rights, too. Father is confident that the Forest Reserve will be declared next Winter and then the sheep will be debarred forever. Can't you give over the fight for my sake? And I will pay you any price —- I will do anything you ask; but if you should be killed or kill some other man, I could never be happy again, though I gained the whole world. Dear Rufus, please —- but I leave it for you to decide —-
> "

The note ended abruptly, it was not even signed, and Hardy could imagine the agitation in which it was written. Dear little Lucy, always thinking of others, always considerate, always honest and reasonable. If only Kitty —- But no —- in her own right as Queen of Love and of his heart, she was above all criticism and blame. It was a madness, deeper than his anger against the sheep, mightier than his fiercest resentment —- he could not help it; he loved her. Changeable, capricious, untamed, she held him by her faults where virtues would hardly have sufficed in another. He had tried, and failed; so long as she was in the world he must love her. But what a life! He cast the letter from him and his heart turned to Jeff and the big fight, the battle that they had planned to wage together. In the rush and struggle of that combat he could forget the pangs which tortured him; he could have his revenge on life, which had treated him so shabbily! And yet —- and yet —- could he desert a friend like Lucy —- Lucy who would give her life to make him happier, who had always by every act tried to make him forget his sorrows?

For a long time he sat with his head bowed, thinking. Then he rose up and took down his long-barrelled Colt's, fingered it lovingly, and thrust it, scabbard and all, into the depths of his war bag.

As he rode down the hill into the camp that afternoon Creede came out to meet him, and when his eyes fell upon the empty belt, he smiled knowingly.

"Well, you woke up, did you?" he inquired, laying one hand carelessly on the bulge in Hardy's right shap, where modest cowboys sometimes secrete their guns. "Um-huh!" he grunted, slapping the left shap to make sure. "I suspected as much. Well, I congratulate you, supe —- if my girl had asked me I reckon I'd've give up my gun too. But she gimme a kiss, anyway," he added, tossing his head triumphantly.

"Who did?" demanded Hardy, coming suddenly out of his dream.

"Why, Kitty, sure," returned Creede artlessly; and then, noting the look of incredulity on his partner's face, he slapped him on the leg and laughed consumedly.

"Oh, you're not the only pebble on the beach," he cried. "Ump-um —- there are others! Say, it's hell to be in love, ain't it?"

He looked up at Hardy, the laughter still in his cheeks, but for once there was no answering smile. The large gray eyes were far away and distant, fixed vacantly upon the dust cloud where the sheep gathered in the east. Then, as if dismissing some haunting vision from his mind, the little man shook himself and drew away.

"That's right," he said solemnly, "it is."

Between the mouth of Hell's Hip Pocket and the cow camp at Carrizo Creek there lie three high ridges and three broad valleys, all running north and south from the Peaks to Bronco Mesa —- the heart of the upper range; and there in compact bands the invaders held their sheep. From the lower levels they strayed out gradually over the rocky mesa; above they clambered up toward the wooded peaks; but at night the sheepmen worked back to the three ridges and camped close together for defence. After many years of struggle they had at last obtained their legal rights —- their sheep were up to the ears in grama, eating out the heart of the cow country —- but Jeff Creede was just over the hill, and the Mexicans were afraid. For years now the huge form of "Grande" had loomed before them whenever they entered that forbidden range, and they had always given way before him. And now he had the little man Chico with him, the son of a soldier, so it was said, and a gentleman of *categoría*; he always carried a pistol and his eyes were stern and hard. What would not Chico and Grande do to them, now that they were like bees robbed of their long-hoarded honey, who have nothing left but their stings?

So the word passed around amongst the herders and camp rustlers, and Jim and Jasp rode from one camp to the other, cursing and exhorting and holding them to their work. The hour of victory had come, but their triumph was poisoned by a haunting fear for their sheep. One hundred thousand sheep —- five hundred thousand dollars' worth —- the accumulation of a lifetime —- and all in the hands of these cowardly Mexicans, not half of whom would fight! For the day or two that they held together they were safe, but when they spread out —- and spread they must, to reach the western pass —- then the cowmen could rush them at night like lions that raid a corral, scattering one band after the other, and the coyotes would do the rest! That was the joint in the armor of the sheepmen, and it robbed them of their sleep.

Evening came, and the fires of the camp rustlers on the ridges lit up the dust cloud that hung in the east. The hateful bray of the sheep was hushed, at last, and the shrill yell of the coyotes rose from every hilltop, bidding farewell to the sun; for as vultures and unnumbered birds of prey hovered in the wake of barbarian armies, casting their dread shadows upon the living and glutting upon the dead, so the coyotes follow tirelessly after the sheep, gorging upon chance carcasses and pulling down the strays. As the wild, gibbering chorus rose and quavered back from the cliffs the cowmen at Carrizo glanced up from their supper and swore, and in the general preoccupation Hardy put down his plate and slipped away to the corral. He was sitting on the fence listening to the mad yelping of the coyotes and watching the shadows gather among the peaks, when Creede strolled over and joined him. There were times when he could read Hardy like a book, but at others the little man's thoughts were hidden, and he brooded by himself. On such occasions, after a sufficient interval, Jeff esteemed it his duty to break in upon these unprofitable ruminations and bring him back to the light. So he clambered up on the top log and joined in the contemplation of nature.

"Hear them dam' coyotes," he observed sociably. "They'd cry that way if they'd had a chicken dinner, all around. I bet ye every one of 'em has got wool in his teeth, right now. Never you mind, birdie," he continued, apostrophizing a peculiarly shrill-voiced howler, "I'll give you a bellyful of mutton pretty soon, if it's the last act. What *you* going to do now, Rufe?"

"Well," answered Hardy, "I think I'll try and earn my salary by moving a few sheep. And of course we want to gather every beef critter we can now, while they're fat. The sheep seem to be hugging the mountain pretty close. What's the matter with working the Pocket Butte to-morrow and while the boys are riding we'll warn all the stragglers down there to keep up against the hills; then as soon as we get 'em located we'll jump in some day and move 'em!"

"Huh?" inquired Creede, shoving back his hat and staring. "Did I hear you say 'move 'em'? Well —- er —- I thought you left your gun at home," he suggested guardedly.

"That's right," admitted Hardy, "but don't you let that worry you any. I told you I'd help move those sheep, and I'll do it! We don't need guns, anyhow. Why, I'd just as soon tackle a rattlesnake bare-handed as go after Jasp Swope with my six-shooter. That's just what he's looking for, boy, with all those thirty-thirties behind him, and he'll have plenty of witnesses there to swear us into Yuma, too. I tell you, Jeff, I've been thinking this over, and I believe my boss is right."

"Sure," said Creede, showing his teeth in the twilight.

"Say, let up on that, will you?" exclaimed Hardy irritably. "I'm talking business. Now you let me tell you something." He paused, and fixed his eye on the dust cloud, intently. "I've moved that many sheep twice," he said, throwing out his hand, "and I left my gun at home."

"That's right," conceded Creede.

"Well now, I'll tell you what I'll do," continued Hardy. "If you'll leave your gun at home too and stay with me on this I'll undertake to shoot the last sheep out through West Pass inside of a week. And the only chance we take is of getting shot at or arrested for assault and battery. The Territorial Prison end of this gun business never did appeal me, anyway."

"No —- nor me either! But what's the scheme?"

The big cowboy leaned forward eagerly, his eyes flashing as he half guessed the plan.

"We ride out together," said Hardy, his voice far away, as if he saw it in his mind's eye, "unarmed —- and we notify every sheep-herder we see to move. If Jasp Swope or any of his men kill us while we're unarmed it'll be cold-blooded murder, and there'll be witnesses to prove it. And if the sheep don't move, *we'll move 'em*! What kind of a crime is that, anyway —- to drive sheep off the public range? There isn't an officer of the law within sixty miles, anyhow; and if anybody pulls a gun on us we can slug him in self-defence."

"Sure," agreed Creede, "but suppose one of them big-headed Chihuahua Mexicans should happen to shoot you?"

"Well then, I'd be dead," said Hardy soberly. "But wouldn't you rather be dead than shut up in that hell-hole down at Yuma?"

"Yes!" cried Creede, holding out his hands as if taking an oath. "I would, by God!"

"Well, come on then!" said Hardy, and they shook hands on it like brothers.

When the *rodéo* outfit was gathered together in the morning Jefferson Creede deliberately unstrapped his cartridge belt and threw his pistol back onto his bed. Then he winked at his partner as if, rightly understood, the action was in the nature of a joke, and led the way to Pocket Butte.

"You fellows rake the ridges to Bullpit Valley," he said, briefly assigning every man to his post. "Rufe 'n me'll hold 'em up for you about four o'clock, but don't rush the funeral —- we're goin' to move a few sheep first."

He smiled mysteriously as he spoke, staving off their pointed queries with equivocal answers.

"See you later," he observed, turning his horse into a sheep trail, and with that the outfit was forced to be content.

The offending sheep were found feeding along the eastern slope of a long ridge that led down from the upper ground, and the herders were camped on the summit. There were four men gathered about the fire and as the cowboys approached three of them picked up their carbines and sat off to one side, fingering the locks nervously. The appearance of Jeff Creede spelled trouble to all sheepmen and there were few camps on Bronco Mesa which did not contain a herder who had been unceremoniously moved by him. But this time the fire-eating cowman rode grandly into camp without any awe-inspiring demonstrations whatever.

"Are those your sheep?" he inquired, pointing to the grazing herd.

"*Sí señor*," responded the boss herder humbly.

"Very well," said Creede, "move 'em, and move 'em quick. I give you three days to get through that pass." He stretched a heavily muscled arm very straight toward the notch in the western hills and turned abruptly away. Hardy swung soberly in behind him and the frightened Chihuahuanos were beginning to breathe again after their excitement when suddenly Jeff stopped his horse.

"Say," he said, turning to the boss, "what you carryin' that cow's horn for?"

At this pointed inquiry the boss herder flinched and looked downcast, toying uneasily with the primitive instrument at his side.

"To blow," he answered evasively.

"Well, go ahead and blow it, then," suggested Creede amiably. "No —- go on! *I* don't care what happens. Aw here, let me have it a minute!"

He grabbed the horn away impatiently, wiped the mouthpiece with his sleeve, drew a long breath, and blew. A deep bass roar answered to his effort, a bellow such as the skin-clad hunters of antiquity sent forth when they wound the horn for their hounds, and the hills and valleys of Carrizo and the upper mesa echoed to the blast.

"Say, that's great!" exclaimed the big cowboy, good-naturedly resisting the appeals of the herder. "I used to have one like that when I was a boy. Oh, I'm a blower, all right —- listen to this, now!" He puffed out his chest, screwed his lips into the horn, and blew again, loud and long.

"How's that for high?" he inquired, glancing roguishly at his partner. "And I could keep it up all day," he added, handing the horn back, "only I've got business elsewhere."

"*Oyez, amigo,*" he said, bending his brow suddenly upon the Mexican herder, "remember, now —- in three days!" He continued the sentence by a comprehensive sweep of the hand from that spot out through the western pass, favored each of the three Chihuahuanos with an abhorrent scowl, and rode slowly away down the hogback.

"Notice anything funny over on that ridge?" he asked, jerking his head casually toward the east. "That's Swope and Co. —- the Sheepmen's Protective Association —- coming over to rescue *companero.*" A line of rapidly moving specks proved the truth of his observation, and Creede's shoulders shook with laughter as he noted their killing pace.

"I tumbled to the idee the minute I set eyes on that cow's horn," he said. "It's like this. Every boss herder has a horn; if he gits into trouble he blows it and all hands come a-runnin' to shoot holes in Mr. Cowman —- think I'll make one myself."

He halted behind a rock and scrutinized the approaching horsemen over the top.

"That's Jasp, in front," he observed impersonally. "I wouldn't mind ownin' that black mule of his'n, neither. We'll jest wait until they dip down into the cañon and then double in back of him, and scare up them *hombres* over at the mouth of Hell's Hip Pocket. We want to git 'em started out of that. I believe you're right, though, Rufe —- we can run this bunch out without firin' a shot."

That evening after the day's riding Creede sat down on his heels by the fire and heated the end of an iron rod. In his other hand he held a horn, knocked from the bleaching skeleton of a steer that had died by the water, and to its end where the tip had been sawed off he applied the red-hot iron, burning a hole through to the hollow centre.

"Jim," he said, turning to one of the Clark boys, "do you want a little excitement to-morrow? Well then, you take this old horn and go play hide 'n' seek with Jasp. Keep him chasin', and while the rest of the boys are gatherin' cattle Rufe and me will move a few sheep."

"Well, say," broke in Ben Reavis impatiently, "where do us fellers come in on this play? I thought there was goin' to be a few shap lessons and a little night work."

"Well," responded the *rodéo* boss philosophically, "any time you fellers want to go up against them thirty-thirties you can do so. It's your own funeral, and I'll promise to do the honors right. But I'm a law-abidin' cuss myself. I'm all the law now, ever since I talked with Jim Swope —- it's the greatest graft they is."

He paused, busily scraping his horn with a piece of glass.

"They's no doubt about it, fellers," he said at last, "we've been slow in the head. It's a wonder we ain't all of us makin' hat bands in Yuma, by this time. I used to think that if you didn't like a sheepman's looks the way to do was to wade in and work him over a little; but that's a misdemeanor, and it don't go now. It took as good a man as Rufe, here, to put me wise; but I leave my gun in camp after this. I've got them Greasers buffaloed, anyhow, and Jasp knows if he plugs me when I'm unarmed it'll be a sure shot for the pen. The time may come when guns is necessary, but I move that every man leave his six-shooter in his bed and we'll go after 'em with our bare hands. What d' ye say, Ben?"

Ben Reavis rose up on one elbow, rolled his eyes warily, and passed a jet of tobacco juice into the hissing fire.

"Not f'r me," he said, with profane emphasis.

"No, ner f'r me, either," chimed in Charley Clark. "A man stays dead a long time in this dry climate."

"Well, you fellers see how many of my steers you can ketch, then," said Creede, "and I'll move them sheep myself — leastways, me and Rufe."

"All right," assented Reavis resignedly, "but you want to hurry up. I saw a cloud o' dust halfway to Hidden Water this afternoon."

The next morning as the *rodéo* outfit hustled out to pick up what cattle they could before they were scattered by the sheep, Jim Clark, tall, solemn-faced, and angular, rode by devious ways toward the eastern shoulder of the Four Peaks, where a distant clamor told of the great herds which mowed the mountain slopes like a thousand sickles. Having seen him well on his way Creede and Hardy galloped down the cañon, switched off along the hillside and, leaving their horses among the rocks, climbed up on a rocky butte to spy out the land below. High ridges and deep cañons, running down from the flanks of the Four Peaks, lay to the east and north and west; and to the south they merged into the broad expanse of Bronco Mesa.

There it lay, a wilderness of little hills and valleys, flat-topped benches and sandy gulches threaded minutely with winding trails and cow paths, green with the illusion of drought-proof giant cactus and vivid desert bushes, one vast preserve of browse and grass from the Peaks to the gorge of the Salagua. Here was the last battle-ground, the last stand of the cowmen against the sheep, and then unless that formless myth, "The Government," which no man had ever seen or known, stepped in, there would be no more of the struggle; the green mesa would be stripped of its evanescent glory and the sheep would wander at will. But as long as there was still a chance and the cows had young calves that would die, there was nothing for it but to fight on, warily and desperately, to the end.

As Jefferson Creede looked out across that noble landscape which he had struggled so resolutely to save and saw the dust clouds of the sheep drifting across it, the tears came to his eyes and blinded his keen vision. Here at last was the end of all his struggles and all his dreams; another year, or two years, and the mesa would be devastated utterly; his cows would be hollow-flanked and gaunted; his calves would totter and die, their tender lips pierced with the spiny cactus upon which their hard-mouthed mothers starved; and all that fair land which he knew and loved so well would be lost to him forever. He raised his hand to his eyes as if shading them from the sun, and brushed the tears away.

"Well, look at those sons o' guns hike," he said, baring his teeth venomously, "and every band headed for Hidden Water! Go it, you tarriers — and if you can't stop to eat the grass, tromple on it! But wait, and if I don't push in some Greaser's face to-day it'll be because every one of them bands is headin' for the western pass."

He clambered slowly down from his perch and swung up into the saddle.

"Talkin' never did do much good with a sheep-herder," he observed wisely. "As the old judge used to say, 'you've got to appeal to his better nature' — with a club."

The most southerly of the seven bands was strung out in marching order, the goats in front, the hungriest sheep in the lead; and on both flanks and far behind, the groups and clusters of feeders, pushing out into the grassy flats and rearing up against the trees and bushes. Without a word to the herders Creede and Hardy took down their ropes and, swinging the *hondas* upon the goats, turned the advance guard northwest. The main herd and the drag followed, and then the herders, all in a bunch for courage.

"This is the last time I talk to you," said Creede, his voice stifled with anger. "Turn to the north, now, and keep a-goin'."

He put spurs to his horse and rode west to the second herd, and by noon they had turned all seven toward the western pass. Every herder had his cow's horn and some of them were blowing continually, but no one answered, and a messenger was sent east for aid. They camped for the heat of the day, making smoke upon the ridges, but no help came. As the sun sank low and the curly-necked Merinos rose up from their huddle and began to drift the Mexicans turned them perforce to the north, looking back sulkily toward the mouth of Hell's Hip Pocket where other smokes rose against the sky. Until the sun set they travelled, making their three miles and more, and not until they had corralled their flocks for the night did Chico and Grande, the little and big terrors of the sheep, give way from their strenuous labors.

It was two hours after dark when they rode wearily into the camp at Carrizo Creek. The fire was dying down to embers and the *rodéo* outfit, worn out, had turned in, some in the tin house, others outside, under the brush *ramada* to escape the dew. No one moved as they approached but Creede did not scruple to wake up Jim Clark in order to learn the news.

"How'd the old horn work?" he inquired cheerily.

"No good," grunted Clark, rolling over.

"Aw, go on, wouldn't they chase ye?"

"Nope. Nothin' doin'. Say, lemme sleep, will ye?"

"Sure," said Creede, "when I git through with you. Which way was them sheep travellin'?"

"Well, some was goin' straight up over the Four Peaks and the rest was p'intin' west. You and your old horn —- I nigh blowed my fool head off and never got a rise! They was all blowin' them horns over by the Pocket this aft."

"Um," said Creede, "they was *all* blowin', hey? And what else was they doin'?"

"Shootin', fer further orders, and driftin' their sheep. They's about a hundred thousand, right over the hill."

"Huh!" grunted Creede, turning to his belated dinner, "what d'ye make of that, Rufe?"

"Nothing," replied Hardy, "except more work."

It seemed as if he had hardly fallen asleep when Creede was up again, hurling the wood on the fire.

"Pile out, fellers!" he shouted. "You can sleep all day bimebye. Come on, Rufe —- d'ye want to find them sheep in the corral when you go back to Hidden Water?" And so with relentless energy he roused them up, divided out the work, and was off again for Bronco Mesa.

It was early when they arrived at the first deserted sheep camp, but search as they would they could see no signs of the sheep. The puny fire over which the herders had fried their bread and mutton was wind-blown and cold, the burros and camp rustlers were gone, and there was no guiding dust cloud against the sky. From the little butte where Creede and Hardy stood the lower mesa stretched away before them like a rocky, cactus-covered plain, the countless ravines and gulches hidden by the dead level of the benches, and all empty, lifeless, void. They rode for the second camp, farther to the west, and it too was deserted, the sheep tracks cunningly milled in order to hide the trail.

"They're gittin' foxy," commented Creede, circling wide to catch the trend of their departure, "but I bet you money no bunch of Chihuahua Greasers can hide twenty thousand sheep in my back yard and me not know it. And I'll bet you further that I can find every one of them sheep and have 'em movin' before twelve o'clock, noon."

Having crystallized his convictions into this sporting proposition the *rodéo* boss left the wilderness of tracks and headed due south, riding fast until he was clear of sheep signs.

"Now here's where I cut all seven trails," he remarked to his partner. "I happen to know where this sheep outfit is headin' for." With which enigmatic remark he jerked a thumb toward Hidden Water and circled to the west and north. Not half an hour later he picked up a fresh trail, a broad path stamped hard by thousands of feet, and spurring recklessly along it until he sighted the herd he plunged helter-skelter into their midst, where they were packed like sardines in the broad pocket of a dry wash.

"Hey there! *Whoopee —- hep —- hep!*" he yelled, ploughing his way into the pack; and Hardy swinging quickly around the flank, rushed the ruck of them forward in his wake. Upon the brow of the hill the boss herder and his helpers brandished their carbines and shouted, but their words were drowned in the blare and bray which rose from below. Shoot they dared not, for it meant the beginning of a bloody feud, and their warnings were unheeded in the *mêlée.* The herd was far up the wash and galloping wildly toward the north before the frantic Mexicans could catch up with it on foot, and even then they could do nothing but run along the wings to save themselves from a "cut." More than once, in the night-time, the outraged cowmen of the Four Peaks country had thus dashed through their bands, scattering them to the wolves and the coyotes, destroying a year's increase in a night, while the herders, with visions of shap lessons before them, fired perfunctory rifle shots at the moon. It was a form of reprisal that they liked least of all, for it meant a cut, and a cut meant sheep wandering aimlessly without a master until they became coyote bait —- at the rate of five dollars a head.

The *padron* was a kind man and called them *compadres*, when he was pleased, but if one of them suffered a cut he cursed, and fired him, and made him walk back to town. Hence when Chico and Grande suddenly gave over their drive and rode away to the northwest the Mexican herders devoted all their attention to keeping the herd together, without trying to make any gun plays. And when the stampede was abated and still no help came they drifted their sheep steadily to the north, leaving the camp rustlers to bring up the impedimenta as best they could. Jasper Swope had promised to protect them whenever they blew their horns, but it was two days since they had seen him, and the two *Americanos* had harried them like hawks.

Never had armed men so lacked a leader as on that day. Their orders were to shoot only in self-defence; for a war was the last thing which the Swope brothers wanted, with their entire fortunes at stake, and no show of weapons could daunt the ruthless Grande and Chico. All the morning the cow horns bellowed and blared as, sweating and swinging their *hondas,* the stern-eyed *Americanos* rushed band after band away. Not a word was passed —- no threats, no commands, no warnings for the future, but like avenging devils they galloped from one herd to the other and back again, shoving them forward relentlessly, even in the heat of noon. At evening the seven bands, hopelessly mixed and mingled in the panic, were halfway through the long pass, and the herders were white with dust and running. But not until dusk gathered in the valleys did Creede rein in his lathered horse and turn grimly back to camp.

His face was white and caked with dust, the dirt lay clotted in his beard, and only the whites of his eyes, rolling and sanguinary, gave evidence of his humanity; his shirt, half torn from his body by plunging through the cat-claws, hung limp and heavy with sweat; and the look of him was that of a madman, beside himself with rage. The dirt, the sweat, the grime, were as heavy on Hardy, and his eyes rolled like a negro's beneath the mask of dust, but weariness had overcome his madness and he leaned forward upon the horn. They glanced at each other indifferently and then slumped down to endure the long ten miles which lay between them and home. It had been a stern fight and the excitement had lulled their hunger, but now the old, slow pang gnawed at their vitals and they rolled like drunkards in the saddle.

It was a clear, velvety night, and still, after the wind of the day. Their horses jogged dumbly along, throwing up their heads at every step from weariness, and the noises of the night fell dully upon their jaded ears. But just as they turned into Carrizo Creek Cañon, Creede suddenly reined in old Bat Wings and held up his hand to Hardy.

"Did you hear that?" he asked, still listening. "There! Didn't you hear that gun go off? Well, I did —- and it was a thirty-thirty, too, over there toward the Pocket."

"Those herders are always shooting away their ammunition," said Hardy peevishly. "Come on, let's get back to camp."

"They don't shoot in the night-time, though," grumbled Creede, leading off again. "I'll bet ye some of them Greasers has seen a ghost. Say," he cried, "the boys may be out doin' some night ridin'!"

But when they rode into camp every man was in his blankets.

"Hey, what's all that shootin' goin' on over there?" he called, waking up the entire outfit in his excitement.

"Sheepmen," responded some sleeper briefly.

"Cleanin' their guns, mebbe," suggested another, yawning. "Did you move 'em, Jeff?"

"You betcher neck!" replied Creede promptly, "and I'm goin' back in the mornin', too."

The morning turned black, and flushed rosy, and fell black again, but for once the merciless driver of men slept on, for he was over-weary. It was a noise, far away, plaintive, insistent, which finally brought him to his feet —- the bleating of ewes to lambs, of lambs to mothers, of wethers to their fellows, beautiful in itself as the great elemental sounds of the earth, the abysmal roarings of winds and waves and waterfalls, but to the cowman hateful as the clamors of hell. As Creede stood in his blankets, the salt sweat of yesterday still in his eyes, and that accursed blat in his ears, his nerves gave way suddenly, and he began to rave. As the discordant babel drew nearer and nearer his passion rose up like a storm that has been long brewing, his eyes burned, his dirty face turned ghastly. Grabbing up his six-shooter he stood like a prophet of destruction calling down the wrath of God Himself, if there was a God, upon the head of every sheepman. But even as he cursed the first dirty brown wave spewed in over the ridge and swept down upon their valley. Then in a moment his madness overcame him and, raising his heavy pistol, he emptied it against them defiantly, while the resounding cliffs took up his wrath and hurled it back. A herder with his rifle leapt up on a distant rock and looked toward their camp, and at the sight the black anger of Jeff's father came upon him, filling him with the lust to kill.

He rushed into the house and came out with a high-power rifle. "You *will* stand up there and laugh at me, will you?" he said, deliberately raising the sights. "You —- "

He rested the rifle against one of the *ramada* posts, and caught his breath to aim, while the cowmen regarded him cynically, yet with a cold speculation in their eyes. Hardy alone sprang forward to spoil his aim, and for a minute they bandied words like pistol shots as they struggled for the gun. Then with a last wailing curse, the big cowboy snapped the cartridge out of his rifle and handed it over to his partner.

"You're right," he said, "let the dastard live. But if I ever git another chanst at Jasp Swope I'll kill him, if I swing for it! He's the boy I'm lookin' for, but you see how he dodges me? I've been movin' his sheep for two days! He's afraid of me —- he's afraid to come out and fight me like a man! But I'll git 'im —- I'll git 'im yet!"

"All right," said Hardy soothingly, "you can do it, for all of me. But don't go to shooting Mexicans off of rocks as if they were turkey buzzards —- that's what gets people into the pen. Now, you just take my advice for once and wash some of that dirt off your face. You're locoed, man —- you're not a human being —- and you won't be until you wash up and get your belly full."

Half an hour later they sat down to breakfast, the burly fighting animal and the man who had taught him reason; and as they ate the fierce anger of the cowboy passed away like mists before the morning sun. He heaped his plate up high and emptied it again, drinking coffee from his big cup, and as if ashamed of his brutishness he began forthwith to lay out a campaign of peace. With sheep scurrying in every direction across the range in the great drive that was now on it was no use to try to gather cows. What they had they could day-herd and the rest would have to wait. The thing to do now was to protect the feed around the water, so that the cattle would not have to travel so far in the heat of summer. No objection being offered he gave each man a watercourse to patrol, sending one over into the Pocket to see what had happened to Bill Johnson; and then, with his gun packed in his bed, he started back with Hardy to watch over Hidden Water.

The sun was well up as they topped the high ridge; and the mesa, though ploughed through and through by the trails of the hurrying sheep, still shimmered in its deceptive green. Not for a month had there been a cloud in the sky and the grass on the barren places was already withering in the heat, yet in the distance the greasewood and the *palo verdes* and giant cactus blended into one mighty sheet of verdure. Only on the ground where the feed should be were there signs of the imminent drought; and where the sheep had crossed the ground lay hard and baked or scuffled into dust. In the presence of those swift destroyers the dreaded *año seco* had crept in upon them unnoticed, but soon it would scourge the land with heat and dust and failing waters, and cattle lowing to be fed. And there before their eyes, clipping down the precious grass, tearing up the tender plants, shearing away the browse, moved the sheep; army after army, phalanx and cohort, drifting forward irresistibly, each in its cloud of dust. For a minute the two men sat gazing hopelessly; then Creede leaned forward in his saddle and sighed.

"Well," he observed philosophically, "they're movin', anyhow."

They rode down the long slope and, mounting a low roll, paused again apathetically to watch a band of sheep below.

"Say," exclaimed Creede, his eyes beginning to burn, "d'ye notice how them sheep are travellin'? And look at them other bands back yonder! By Joe!" he cried, rising in his stirrups, "we've got 'em goin'! Look at the dust out through the pass, and clean to Hell's Hip Pocket. They're hikin', boy, they're hittin' it up for The Rolls! But what in the world has struck 'em?"

He stood up straight in his saddle, swinging his head from east to west, but no band of horsemen met his eye. He looked again at the flock below him —- the goats, forever in the lead, heading straight for the western pass; the herders swinging their carbines upon the drag —- and seemed to study upon the miracle.

"Have you got any money to spare, Rufe?" he inquired quietly.

"Sure," responded Hardy.

"Well, then," said Creede deliberately, "I'd like to make you a sporting proposition. I'll bet you forty dollars to the price of a drink that old Bill Johnson has been shootin' up their camps. Will you go me? All right, and I'll make you a little side bet: I'll bet you any money that Jim Swope has lost some sheep!"

He spurred his horse recklessly down the hill, grinning, and at the clatter of rocks the fearful herders jumped forward and raised a great clamor behind their sheep, whistling and clubbing their guns, but the heart of the monster Grande was no longer turned to wrath. He laughed and called out to them, leaping his horse playfully over washouts and waving his black hat.

"*Cuidado, hombres,*" he shouted, "be careful —- do not hurry —- look at the nice grass!" But despite this friendly admonition the herders still yelled and whistled at their sheep, jabbing them spitefully with the sharp muzzles of their rifles until at last, all riot and confusion, they fled away bleating into the west.

CHAPTER XVIII
BAD BLOOD

The sheep were on the run, drifting across Bronco Mesa as if the devil was after them, and Creede could hardly stay on his horse from laughing —- but when he drew near to Hidden Water his face changed. There was a fresh sheep trail in the cañon and it led away from the ranch. He spurred forward like the wind, his eyes upon the tracks, and when he came in sight of the house he threw down his hat and swore. Of all the God-forsaken places in Arizona, the Dos S Ranch was the worst. The earth lay bare and desolate before it; the woodpile had disappeared; the bucket was thrown down the well. Never had the flat, mud buildings seemed so deserted or Tommy so tragic in his welcome. The pasture gate was down and even that holy of holies, the branding corral, stunk of sheep. Only the padlocked house had been respected, and that perforce, since nothing short of a sledgehammer could break its welded chain.

Unfastening the battered door they entered the living-room which once had been all light and laughter. There lay the dishes all clean and orderly on the table, the floors swept, the beds made, some withered flowers on Hardy's desk.

"Huh," grunted Creede, looking it over coldly, "we're on the bum, all right, all right, now. How long since they went away?"

"'Bout a year," replied Hardy, and his partner did not contradict him.

They cooked a hasty meal and ate it, putting the scraps in the frying-pan for Tommy.

"Go to it, Tom," said Creede, smiling wistfully as the cat lapped away at the grease. "He never could git used to them skirts rustlin' round here, could he?" And then there was a long silence.

Tommy sat up and washed his face contentedly, peering about with intent yellow eyes and sniffing at the countless odors with which his world was filled —- then suddenly with a low whining growl he lashed across the room like a tiger and leapt up into his cat hole. This was a narrow tunnel, punched through the adobe wall near the door and boxed in with a projecting cribbing to keep out the snakes and skunks. Through it when his protectors were away he could escape the rush of pursuing coyotes, or sally forth with equal ferocity when sheep dogs were about. He peered out of his porthole for a moment, warily, then his stump tail began to twitch, he worked his hind claws into the wood, and leapt. A yelp of terror from the *ramada* heralded his success and Creede ran like a boy to look.

"He's jumped one, by Joe!" he exclaimed. "What did I tell ye —- that cat is a holy terror on dogs!"

The dog in question —- a slinking, dispirited cur —- wagged its tail apologetically from a distance, shaking its bloody ears, while Tommy swelled and hissed viciously at him from his stronghold. It was a sheep dog, part collie, part shepherd, and the rest plain yellow —- a friendly little dog, too, and hungry. But the heart of Creede, ordinarily so tender, was hardened by his disasters.

"Git out of here!" he commanded roughly. "Git, you yap, or I'll burn you up with a bullet!"

"This is what comes of leavin' your gun off," he grumbled, as he unbound his bed and grabbed up his pistol. But as he stepped out into the open to shoot, his barbarity was checked by a clatter of hoofs and, looking up, he saw Jasper Swope on his big black mule, ambling truculently in across the open.

"Hyar!" he shouted, shaking his fist angrily, "don't you shoot my dog, you —- or I'll be the death of ye!"

"Oh, I don't know," responded Creede, bristling back at him. "Keep the blame pup away, then —- and keep that other dog away, too, or my cat'll eat 'im up! Well, I notice you took the occasion to come down and sheep me out," he observed, as Swope pulled up before the door.

"I *did* not," retorted the sheepman promptly, but grinning nevertheless at the damage, "but I see some other feller has though, and saved me the trouble." He ran his eye approvingly over the devastated homestead; and then, rising in his stirrups, he plunged suddenly into his set speech.

"I've took a lot off'n you, Jeff Creede," he shouted, swinging his arms wildly, "but I've got a bellyful of this night work! And I come down to tell you that next time you shoot up one of my camps there'll be trouble!"

"I never shot up your old camp," growled Creede, "nor any other camp. I'm dam' glad to hear that somebody else did though," he added vindictively, "and I hope to God he fixed you good and proper. Now what can I do for you, Mr. Swope?" he inquired, thrusting out his chin. "I suppose you must be hurryin' on, of course."

"No!" cried Swope, slapping his saddle horn vehemently. "I come down here to git some satisfaction out of you! My sheep has been killed and my men has been intimidated on this here public range, and I want to tell you right now, Mr. Creede, that this funny business has got to stop!"

"Well, don't choke!" said the cowman, fingering his gun coldly. "Go ahead and stop it, why don't you?"

He paused, a set smile on his lips, and for a moment their eyes met in the baleful glare which rival wolves, the leaders of their packs, confer upon each other. Then Hardy stepped out into the open, holding up his hand for peace.

"You are mistaken, Mr. Swope," he said quietly. "Jeff hasn't shot up any camps —- he hasn't even packed a gun for the last three days."

"Oh, he hain't, hey?" sneered the sheepman, showing his jagged teeth. "He seems to have one now."

"You betcher neck I have," cried Creede, flaring up at the implication, "and if you're lookin' for trouble, Jasp Swope, you can open up any time."

"W'y what's the matter with you?" protested Swope righteously. "You must have somethin' on your mind, the way you act."

Then without waiting for a reply to this innuendo he turned his attention to Hardy.

"He hain't shot up any camps," he repeated, "ner packed a gun for three days, hey? Now here's where I prove you a liar, Mr. Smarty. I seen him with my own eyes take six shots at one of my herders this very mornin' —- *and you was there!*"

He punctuated his speech by successive downward jabs of his grimy forefinger as if he were stabbing his adversary to the heart, and Hardy turned faint and sick with chagrin. Never had he hated a man as he hated this great, overbearing brute before him —- this man-beast, with his hairy chest and freckled hands that clutched at him like an ape's. Something hidden, a demon primordial and violent, rose up in him against this crude barbarian with his bristling beard and gloating pig eyes, and he forgot everything but his own rage at being trapped.

"You lie!" he cried passionately; and then in his anger he added a word which he had never used, a word which goes deep under the skin and makes men fight.

For a moment the sheepman sat staring, astounded by his vehemence; but before he could move the sudden silence was split by the yelp of a dog —- a wild, gibbering yelp that made them jump and bristle like hounds that are assailed from behind —- and, mingling stridently with it, was the harsh snarl of a cat. There was a swift scramble in the dust by the door, an oath from the sheepman, and the yellow dog dashed away again, with Tommy at his heels.

Creede was the first man to regain his nerve and, seeing his pet triumphant, he let out a whoop of derisive laughter.

"Ah-hah-hah!" he hollered, pointing with his pistol hand, "look at that, will ye —- *look* at 'im —- *yee-pah* —- go after 'im, Tommy —- we'll show the —- "

The fighting blood of the sheepman sided in as quickly with his dog.

"I'll kill that dam' cat!" he yelled, swinging down from his saddle, "if you don't let up! Hey, Nip! Sick 'im!" He turned and motioned to his other dog, which had been standing dumbly by, and instantly he joined in the chase. "Sick 'em, boy, *sick 'em!*" he bellowed, urging him on, and before Creede could get his face straight the long, rangy brindle had dashed up from behind and seized Tommy by the back.

"Git out o' that!" thundered the cowman; and then, without waiting on words, he threw his gun down on the dog and fired.

"Here —- none of that, now!" shouted Swope, whipping out his own pistol, and as he leapt forward he held it out before him like a sabre, pointed straight for the cowman's ribs. His intentions may have been of the best, but Hardy did not wait to see. The brindle dog let out a surprised yelp and dropped. Before Creede could turn to meet his enemy his partner leapt in between them and with a swift blow from the shoulder, struck the sheepman to the ground.

It was a fearful blow, such as men deal in anger without measuring their strength or the cost, and it landed on his jaw. Creede had seen men slugged before, in saloon rows and the rough fights that take place around a town, but never had he seen a single blow suffice —- the man's head go back, his knees weaken, and his whole body collapse as if he had been shot. If he had been felled like a bull in the shambles that goes down in spite of his great strength, Jasper Swope could not have been more completely stunned. He lay sprawling, his legs turned under him, and the hand that grasped the six-shooter relaxed slowly and tumbled it into the dust.

For a minute the two partners stood staring at each other, the one still planted firmly on his feet like a boxer, the other with his smoking pistol in his hand.

"By Joe, boy," said Creede slowly, "you was just in time that trip." He stepped forward and laid the fallen man out on his back, passing his gun up to Hardy as he did so.

"I wonder if you killed him," he muttered, feeling Jasp's bull neck; and then, as Hardy ran for some water, he remembered Tommy. But there was no Tommy —- only a little heap of fur lying very still out in the open.

"My God!" he cried, and leaving the man he ran out and knelt down beside it.

"Pussy!" he whispered, feeling hopelessly for his heart; and then, gathering the forlorn little wisp of fur in his arms, he hurried into the house without a word.

He was still in hiding when Jasper Swope came to and sat up, his hair drenched with water and matted with dirt. Staring doubtfully at the set face of Hardy he staggered to his feet; then the memory of the fight came back to him and he glared at him with a drunkard's insolence.

"Where's my gun?" he demanded, suddenly clapping his hand upon the empty holster.

"I'll take care of that for you," answered Hardy pointedly. "Now you pile onto that mule of yours and pull your freight, will you?" He led the black mule up close and boosted its master into the saddle, but Swope was not content.

"Where's that dastard, Jeff Creede?" he demanded. "Well, I wanter see him, that's all. And say, Mr. Smart Alec, I want that gun, too, see?"

"Well, you won't get it," said Hardy.

"I will that," declared Swope, "'nd I'll git you, too, Willie, before I git through with you. I've had enough of this monkey business. Now gimme that gun, I tell ye, or I'll come back with more of 'em and take it!"

He raised his voice to a roar, muffled to a beast-like hoarseness by his swollen jaws, and the *ramada* reverberated like a cavern as he bellowed out his challenge. Then the door was snatched violently open and Jefferson Creede stepped forth, looking black as hell itself. In one hand he held the sheepman's pistol and in the other his own.

"Here!" he said, and striding forward he thrust Swope's gun into his hand. "It's loaded, too," he added. "Now, you —- if you've got any shootin' to do, go to it!"

He stepped back quickly and stood ready, his masterful eyes bent upon his enemy in a scowl of unquenchable hate. Once before they had faced each other, waiting for that mysterious psychic prompting without which neither man nor beast can begin a fight, and Jim had stepped in between —- but Hardy stood aside without a word. It was a show-down and, bulldog fighter though he was, Jasper Swope weakened. The anger of his enemy overcame his hostile spirit without a blow, and he turned his pistol away.

"That's all I wanted," he said, shoving the gun sullenly into its holster. "They's two of you, and —- "

"And you're afraid," put in Creede promptly. He stood gazing at the downcast sheepman, his lip curling contemptuously.

"I've never seen a sheepman yet," he said, "that would fight. You've listened to that blat until it's a part of ye; you've run with them Mexicans until you're kin to 'em; you're a coward, Jasp Swope, and I always knowed it." He paused again, his eyes glowing with the hatred that had overmastered his being. "My God," he said, "if I could only git you to fight to-day I'd give everything I've got left!"

The sheepman's gaze was becoming furtive as he watched them. He glanced sidewise, edging away from the door; then, pricking his mule with his spurs, he galloped madly away, ducking his head at every jump as if he feared a shot.

"Look at the cowardly dastard!" sneered Creede bitterly. "D'ye know what he would do if that was me? He'd shoot me in the back. Ah, God A'mighty, and that dog of his got Tommy before I could pull a gun! Rufe, I could kill every sheepman in the Four Peaks for this —- every dam' one of 'em —- and the first dog that comes in sight of this ranch will stop a thirty-thirty." He stopped and turned away, cursing and muttering to himself.

"God A'mighty," he moaned, "I can't keep *nothin'*!" And stumbling back into the house he slammed the door behind him.

A gloom settled down over the place, a gloom that lasted for days. The cowboys came back from driving the town herd and, going up on the mesa, they gathered a few head more. Then the heat set in before its time and the work stopped short. For the steer that is roped and busted in the hot weather dies suddenly at the water; the flies buzz about the ears of the new-marked calves and poison them, and the mother cows grow gaunt and thin from overheating. Not until the long Summer had passed could the riding continue; the steers must be left to feed down the sheeped-out range; the little calves must run for sleepers until the fall *rodéo*. Sheep and the drought had come together, and the round-up was a failure. Likewise the cowmen were broke.

As they gathered about the fire on that last night it was a silent company —- the *rodéo* boss the gloomiest of them all. Not since the death of Tommy had his eyes twinkled with the old mischief; he had no bets to offer, no news to volunteer; a dull, sombre abstraction lay upon him like a pall. Only when Bill Lightfoot spoke did he look up, and then with a set sneer, growing daily more saturnine. The world was dark to Creede and Bill's fresh remarks jarred on him —- but Bill himself was happy. He was of the kind that runs by opposites, taking their troubles with hilarity under the impression that they are philosophers. His pretext for this present happiness was a professed interview with Kitty Bonnair on the evening that the town herd pulled into Moreno's. What had happened at this interview was a secret, of course, but it made Bill happy; and the more morose and ugly Jeff became about it the more it pleased Lightfoot to be gay. He sat on a box that night and sang *risqué* ditties, his enormous Colt's revolver dangling bravely at his hip; and at last, casting his weather eye upon Creede, he began a certain song.

> "Oh, my little girl, she lives in the town —- "

And then he stopped.

"Bill," said the *rodéo* boss feelingly, "you make me tired."

"Lay down an' you'll git rested, then," suggested Lightfoot.

> "*A toodle link, a toodle link, a too-oodle a day.*"

"I'll lay you down in a minute, if you don't shut up," remarked Creede, throwing away his cigarette.

"The hell you say," commented Lightfoot airily.

> "And last time I seen her she ast me to come down."

At this raw bit of improvisation the boss rose slowly to his feet and stalked away from temptation.

"And if anybody sees her you'll know her by this sign,"

chanted the cowboy, switching to an out-and-out bad one; and then, swaying his body on his cracker box, he plunged unctuously into the chorus.

"She's got a dark and rolling eye, boys;
She's got a dark and rolling eye."

He stopped there and leapt to his feet anxiously. The mighty bulk of the *rodéo* boss came plunging back at him through the darkness; his bruising fist shot out and the frontier troubadour went sprawling among the pack saddles.

It was the first time Creede had ever struck one of his own kind, —- men with guns were considered dangerous, —- but this time he laid on unmercifully.

"You've had that comin' to you for quite a while, Bill Lightfoot," he said, striking Bill's ineffectual gun aside, "and more too. Now maybe you'll keep shut about 'your girl'!"

He turned on his heel after administering this rebuke and went to the house, leaving his enemy prostrate in the dirt.

"The big, hulkin' brute," blubbered Lightfoot, sitting up and aggrievedly feeling of his front teeth, "jumpin' on a little feller like me —- an' he never give me no warnin', neither. You jest wait, I'll —- "

"Aw, shut up!" growled Old Man Reavis, whose soul had long been harrowed by Lightfoot's festive ways. "He give you plenty of warnin', if you'd only listen. Some people have to swallow a few front teeth before they kin learn anythin'."

"Well, what call did he have to jump on me like that?" protested Lightfoot. "I wasn't doin' nothin'."

"No, nothin' but singin' bawdy songs about his girl," sneered Reavis sarcastically.

"His girl, rats!" retorted the cowboy, vainglorious even in defeat, "she's my girl, if she's anybody's!"

"Well, about *your* girl then, you dirty brute!" snarled the old man, suddenly assuming a high moral plane for his utter annihilation. "You're a disgrace to the outfit, Bill Lightfoot," he added, with conviction. "I'm ashamed of ye."

"That's right," chimed in the Clark boys, whose sensibilities had likewise been harassed; and with all the world against him Bill Lightfoot retired in a huff to his blankets. So the *rodéo* ended as it had begun, in disaster, bickering, and bad blood, and no man rightly knew from whence their misfortune came. Perhaps the planets in their spheres had cast a malign influence upon them, or maybe the bell mare had cast a shoe. Anyhow they had started off the wrong foot and, whatever the cause, the times were certainly not auspicious for matters of importance, love-making, or the bringing together of the estranged. Let whatsoever high-priced astrologer cast his horoscope for good, Saturn was swinging low above the earth and dealing especial misery to the Four Peaks; and on top of it all the word came that old Bill Johnson, after shooting up the sheep camps, had gone crazy and taken to the hills.

For a week, Creede and Hardy dawdled about the place, patching up the gates and fences and cursing the very name of sheep. A spirit of unrest hovered over the place, a brooding silence which spoke only of Tommy and those who were gone, and the two partners eyed each other furtively, each deep in his own thoughts. At last when he could stand it no longer Creede went over to the corner, and dug up his money.

"I'm goin' to town," he said briefly.

"All right," responded Hardy; and then, after meditating a while, he added: "I'll send down some letters by you."

Late that evening, after he had written a long letter to Lucy and a short one to his father, he sat at the desk where he had found their letters, and his thoughts turned back to Kitty. There lay the little book which had held their letters, just as he had thrust it aside. He picked it up, idly, and glanced at the title-page: "Sonnets from the Portuguese." How dim and far away it all seemed now, this world of the poets in which he had once lived and dreamed, where sweetness and beauty were enshrined as twin goddesses of light, and gentleness brooded over all her children. What a world that had been, with its graceful, smiling women, its refinements of thought and speech, its aspirations and sympathies —- and Kitty! He opened the book slowly, wondering from whence it had come, and from the deckled leaves a pressed forget-me-not fell into his hand. That was all —- there was no mark, no word, no sign but this, and as he gazed his numbed mind groped through the past for a forget-me-not. Ah yes, he remembered! But how far away it seemed now, the bright morning when he had met his love on the mountain peak and the flowers had fallen from her hair —- and what an inferno of strife and turmoil had followed since! He opened to the place where the imprint of the dainty flower lay and read reverently:

> "If thou must love me, let it be for nought
> Except for love's sake only. Do not say
> 'I love her for her smile —- her look —- her way
> Of speaking gently —- for a trick of thought
> That falls in well with mine, and certes brought
> A sense of pleasant ease on such a day' —-
> For these things in themselves, Belovéd, may
> Be changed, or change for thee —- and love, so wrought,
> May be unwrought so. Neither love me for
> Thine own dear pity's wiping my cheek dry —-
> A creature might forget to weep, who bore
> Thy comfort long, and lose thy love thereby!
> But love me for love's sake, that evermore
> Thou mayst love on, through love's eternity."

The spell of the words laid hold upon as he read and he turned page after page, following the cycle of that other woman's love —- a love which waited for years to be claimed by the master hand, never faltering to the end. Then impulsively he reached for a fair sheet of paper to begin a letter to Kitty, a letter which should breathe the old gentleness and love, yet "for love's sake only." But while he sat dreaming, thinking with what words to begin, his partner lounged in, and Hardy put aside his pen and waited, while the big man hung around and fidgeted.

"Well, I'll be in town to-morrer," he said, drearily.

"Aha," assented Hardy.

"What ye got there?" inquired Creede, after a long silence. He picked up the book, griming the dainty pages as he turned them with his rough fingers, glancing at the headings.

"Um-huh," he grunted, "'Sonnets from the Portegees,' eh? I never thought them Dagos could write —- what I've seen of 'em was mostly drivin' fish-wagons or swampin' around some slaughterhouse. How does she go, now," he continued, as his schooling came back to him, "see if I can make sense out of it." He bent down and mumbled over the first sonnet, spelling out the long words doubtfully.

> "I thought once how The-o-crite-us had sung
> Of the sweet years, the dear and wished-for years,
> Who each one in a gracious hand appears
> To bear a gift for mortals, old or young:
> And as I mused it in his an —- "

"Well say, what's he drivin' at, anyway?" demanded the rugged cowboy. "Is that Dago talk, or is he jest mixed in his mind? Perfectly clear, eh? Well, maybe so, but I fail to see it. Wish I could git aholt of some *good* po'try." He paused, waiting for Hardy to respond.

"Say," he said, at last, "do me a favor, will ye, Rufe?"

The tone of his voice, now soft and diffident, startled Hardy out of his dream.

"Why sure, Jeff," he said, "if I can."

"No, no 'ifs' and 'ands' about it!" persisted Creede. "A lucky feller like you with everythin' comin' his way ought to be able to say 'Yes' once in a while without hangin' a pull-back on it."

"Huh," grunted Hardy suspiciously, "you better tell me first what you want."

"Well, I want you to write me a letter," blurted out Creede. "I can keep a tally book and order up the grub from Bender; but, durn the luck, when it comes to makin' love on paper I'd rather wrastle a bear. Course you know who it is, and you savvy how them things is done. Throw in a little po'try, will you, and —- and —- say, Rufe, for God's sake, help me out on this!"

He laid one hand appealingly upon his partner's shoulder, but the little man squirmed out from under it impatiently.

"Who is it?" he asked doggedly. "Sallie Winship?"

"Aw, say," protested Creede, "don't throw it into a feller like that —- Sal went back on me years ago. You know who I mean —- Kitty Bonnair."

"Kitty Bonnair!" Hardy had known it, but he had tried to keep her name unspoken. Battle as he would he could not endure to hear it, even from Jeff.

"What do you want to tell Miss Bonnair?" he inquired, schooling his voice to a cold quietness.

"Tell her?" echoed Creede ecstatically. "W'y, tell her I'm lonely as hell now she's gone —- tell her —- well, there's where I bog down, but I'd trade my best horse for another kiss like that one she give me, and throw in the saddle for *pelon*. Now, say, Rufe, don't leave me in a hole like this. You've made your winnin', and here's your nice long letter to Miss Lucy. My hands are as stiff as a burnt rawhide and I can't think out them nice things to say; but I love Kitty jest as much as you love Miss Lucy —- mebbe more —- and —- and I wanter tell her so!"

He ended abjectly, gazing with pleading eyes at the stubborn face of his partner whose lips were drawn tight.

"We —- every man has to —- no, I can't do it, Jeff," he stammered, choking. "I'd —- I'd help you if I could, Jeff —- but she'd know my style. Yes, that's it. If I'd write the letter she'd know it was from me —- women are quick that way. I'm sorry, but that's the way it is —- every man has to fight out his own battle, in love."

He paused and fumbled with his papers.

"Here's a good pen," he said, "and —- and here's the paper." He shoved out the fair sheet upon which he had intended to write and rose up dumbly from the table.

"I'm going to bed," he said, and slipped quietly out of the room. As he lay in his blankets he could see the gleam of light from the barred window and hear Jeff scraping his boots uneasily on the floor. True indeed, his hands were like burnt rawhide from gripping at ropes and irons, his clothes were greasy and his boots smelled of the corral, and yet —- she had given him a kiss! He tried to picture it in his mind: Kitty smiling —- or startled, perhaps —- Jeff masterful, triumphant, laughing. Ah God, it was the same kiss she had offered him, and he had run away!

In the morning, there was a division between them, a barrier which could not be overcome. Creede lingered by the door a minute, awkwardly, and then rode away. Hardy scraped up the greasy dishes and washed them moodily. Then the great silence settled down upon Hidden Water and he sat alone in the shadow of the *ramada*, gazing away at the barren hills.

CHAPTER XIX
THE BIG DRUNK

The sun rose clear for the hundredth time over the shoulder of the Four Peaks; it mounted higher, glowing with a great light, and the smooth round tops of the bowlders shone like half-buried skulls along the creek-bed; it swung gloriously up to its zenith and the earth palpitated with a panting heat. Summer had come, and the long days when the lizards crawl deep into their crevices and the cattle follow the scanty shade of the box cañons or gather in standing-places where the wind draws over the ridges and mitigates the flies. In the pasture at Hidden Water the horses stood head and tail together, side by side, each thrashing the flies from the other's face and dozing until hunger or thirst aroused them or perversity took them away. Against the cool face of the cliff the buzzards moped and stretched their dirty wings in squalid discomfort; the trim little sparrow-hawks gave over their hunting; and all the world lay tense and still. Only at the ranch house where Hardy kept a perfunctory watch was there any sign of motion or life.

For two weeks now he had been alone, ever since Jeff went down to Bender, and with the solitary's dread of surprise he stepped out into the *ramada* regularly, scanning the western trail with eyes grown weary of the earth's emptiness.

At last as the sun sank low, throwing its fiery glare in his eyes, he saw the familiar figure against the sky —- Creede, broad and bulky and topped by his enormous hat, and old Bat Wings, as raw-boned and ornery as ever. Never until that moment had Hardy realized how much his life was dependent upon this big, warm-hearted barbarian who clung to his native range as instinctively as a beef and yet possessed human attributes that would win him friends anywhere in the world. Often in that long two weeks he had reproached himself for abandoning Jeff in his love-making. What could be said for a love which made a man so pitiless? Was it worthy of any return? Was it, after all, a thing to be held so jealously to his heart, gnawing out his vitals and robbing him of his humanity? These and many other questions Hardy had had time to ask himself in his fortnight of introspection and as he stood by the doorway waiting he resolved to make amends. From a petty creature wrapped up in his own problems and prepossessions he would make himself over into a man worthy of the name of friend. Yet the consciousness of his fault lay heavy upon him and as Creede rode in he stood silent, waiting for him to speak. But Jeff for his part came on grimly, and there was a sombre glow in his eyes which told more than words.

"Hello, sport," he said, smiling wantonly, "could you take a pore feller in over night?"

"Sure thing, I can," responded Hardy gayly. "Where've you been all the time?"

And Creede chanted:

> "Down to Bender,
> On a bender,
> Oh, I'm a spender,
> You bet yer life!

"And I'm broke, too," he added, *sotto voce*, dropping off his horse and sinking into a chair.

"Well, you don't need to let that worry you," said Hardy. "I've got plenty. Here!" He went down into his pocket and tossed a gold piece to him, but Creede dodged it listlessly.

"Nope," he said, "money's nothin' to me."

"What's the matter?" asked Hardy anxiously. "Are you sick?"

"Yes," answered Creede, nodding his head wearily, "sick and tired of it all." He paused and regarded his partner solemnly. "I'm a miserable failure, Rufe," he said. "I ain't *got* nothin' and I ain't *worth* nothin'. I never *done* nothin' —- and I ain't got a friend in the world."

He stopped and gazed at the barren land despondently, waiting to see if his partner would offer any protests.

"Rufe," he said, at last, his voice tremulous with reproach, "if you'd only helped me out a little on that letter —- if you'd only told me a few things —- well, she might have let me down easy, and I could've took it. As it was, she soaked me."

Then it was that Hardy realized the burden under which his partner was laboring, the grief that clutched at his heart, the fire that burned in his brain, and he could have wept, now that it was too late.

"Jeff," he said honestly, "it don't do any good now, but I'm sorry. I'm more than sorry —- I'm ashamed. But *that* don't do you any good either, does it?"

He stepped over and laid his hand affectionately upon his partner's shoulder, but Creede hunched it off impatiently.

"No," he said, slowly and deliberately, "not a dam' bit." There was no bitterness in his words, only an acknowledgment of the truth. "They was only one thing for me to do after I received that letter," he continued, "and I done it. I went on a hell-roarin' drunk. That's right. I filled up on that forty-rod whiskey until I was crazy drunk, an' then I picked out the biggest man in town and fought him to a whisper."

He sighed and glanced at his swollen knuckles, which still showed the marks of combat.

"That feller was a jim-dandy scrapper," he said, smiling magnanimously, "but I downed 'im, all right. I couldn't quite lick the whole town, but I tried; and I certainly gave 'em a run for their money, while it lasted. If Bender don't date time from Jeff Creede's big drunk I miss my guess a mile. And you know, after I got over bein' fightin' drunk, I got cryin' drunk —- but I never did get drunk enough to tell my troubles, thank God! The fellers think I'm sore over bein' sheeped out. Well, after I'd punished enough booze to start an Injun uprisin', and played the faro bank for my wad, I went to sleep; and when I woke up it seemed a lo-ong time ago and I could look back and see jest how foolish I'd been. I could see how she'd jollied me up and got me comin', playin' me off against Bill Lightfoot; and then I could see how she'd tantalized me, like that mouse the cat had when you was down in Bender; and then I could see where I had got the big-head bad, thinkin' I was the only one —- and all the time she was *laughin'* at me! Oh, it's nothin' now —- I kin laugh at it myself in a month; but I'm so dam' *'shamed* I could cry." He lopped down in his chair, a great hulk of a man, and shook his head gloomily.

"They ain't but one girl I ever knowed," he said solemnly, "that wasn't stringin' me, and that was Sallie Winship. Sal liked me, dam'd if she didn't. She cried when she went away, but the old lady wouldn't stand for no bow-legged cowpuncher —- and so I git euchred, every time."

For lack of some higher consolation Hardy cooked up a big supper for his low-spirited partner, and after he had done the honors at the feast the irrepressible good health of the cowboy rose up and conquered his grief in spite of him. He began by telling the story of his orgy, which apparently had left Bender a wreck. The futile rage of Black Tex, the despair of the town marshal, the fight with the Big Man, the arrest by the entire *posse comitatus*, the good offices of Mr. Einstein in furnishing bail, the crying and sleeping jags —- all were set forth with a vividness which left nothing to the imagination, and at the end the big man was comforted. When it was all over and his memory came down to date he suddenly recalled a package of letters that were tied up in his coat, which was still on the back of his saddle. He produced them forthwith and, like a hungry boy who sees others eat, sat down to watch Rufe read. No letters ever came for him —- and when one did come it was bad. The first in the pack was from Lucy Ware and as Hardy read it his face softened, even while he knew that Creede was watching.

"Say, she's all right, ain't she?" observed Jeff, when his partner looked up.

"That's right," said Hardy, "and she says to take you on again as foreman and pay you for every day you didn't carry your gun."

"No!" cried Creede, and then he laughed quietly to himself. "Does that include them days I was prizin' up hell down in Bender? Oh, it does, eh? Well, you can tell your boss that I'll make that up to her before the Summer's over."

He leaned back and stretched his powerful arms as if preparing for some mighty labor. "We're goin' to have a drought this Summer," he said impressively, "that will have the fish packin' water in canteens. Yes, sir, the chaser is goin' to cost more than the whiskey before long; and they's goin' to be some dead cows along the river. Do you know what Pablo Moreno is doin'? He's cuttin' brush already to feed his cattle. That old man is a wise *hombre*, all right, when it comes to weather. He's been hollerin' '*Año seco, año seco,*' for the last year, and now, by Joe, we've got it! They ain't hardly enough water in the river to make a splash, and here it's the first of June. We've been kinder wropt up in fightin' sheep and sech and hain't noticed how dry it's gittin'; but that old feller has been sittin' on top of his hill watchin' the clouds, and smellin' of the wind, and measurin' the river, and countin' his cows until he's a weather sharp. I was a-ridin' up the river this afternoon when I see the old man cuttin' down a *palo verde* tree, and about forty head of cattle lingerin' around to eat the top off as soon as she hit the ground; and he says to me, kinder solemn and fatherly:

"'Jeff,' he says, 'cut trees for your cattle —- this is an *año seco.*"

" 'Yes, I've heard that before,' says I. 'But my cows is learnin' to climb.'"

"'*Stawano,*' he says, throwin' out his hands like I was a hopeless proposition. But all the same I think I'll go out to-morrow and cut down one of them *palo verdes* like he show'd me —- one of these kind with little leaves and short thorns —- jest for an expeeriment. If the cattle eat it, w'y maybe I'll cut another, but I don't want to be goin' round stuffin' my cows full of twigs for nothin'. Let 'em rustle for their feed, same as I do. But honest to God, Rufe, some of them little runty cows that hang around the river can't hardly cast a shadder, they're that ganted, and calves seems to be gittin' kinder scarce, too. But here —- git busy, now —- here's a letter you overlooked."

He pawed over the pile purposefully and thrust a pale blue envelope before Hardy —- a letter from Kitty Bonnair. And his eyes took on a cold, fighting glint as he observed the fatal handwriting.

"By God," he cried, "I hain't figured out yet what struck me! I never spoke a rough word to that girl in my life, and she certainly gimme a nice kiss when she went away. But jest as soon as I write her a love letter, w'y she —- she —- W'y hell, Rufe, I wouldn't talk that way to a sheep-herder if he didn't *know* no better. Now you jest read that" —- he fumbled in his pocket and slammed a crumpled letter down before his partner —- "and tell me if I'm wrong! No, I want you to do it. Well, I'll read it to you, then!"

He ripped open the worn envelope, squared his elbows across the table, and opened the scented inclosure defiantly, but before he could read it Hardy reached out suddenly and covered it with his hand.

"Please don't, Jeff," he said, his face pale and drawn. "It was all my fault —- I should have told you —- but please don't read it to me. I —- I can't stand it."

"Oh, I don't know," retorted Creede coldly. "I reckon you can stand it if I can. Now suppose you wrote a real nice letter —- the best you knowed how —- to your girl, and she handed you somethin' like this: 'My dear Mr. Creede, yore amazin' letter —- ' Here, what ye doin'?"

"I won't listen to it!" cried Hardy, snatching the letter away, "it's —- "

"Now lookee here, Rufe Hardy," began Creede, rising up angrily from his chair, "I want to tell you right now that you've got to read that letter or lick me —- and I doubt if you can do that, the way I happen to be feelin'. You got me into this in the first place and now, by God, you'll see it out! Now you *read* that letter and tell me if I'm wrong!"

He reared up his head as he spoke and Hardy saw the same fierce gleam in his eyes that came when he harried the sheep; but there was something beside that moved his heart to pity. It was the lurking sadness of a man deep hurt, who fights the whole world in his anguish; the protest of a soul in torment, demanding, like Job, that some one shall justify his torture.

"All right, Jeff," he said, "I will read it —- only —- only don't crowd me for an answer."

He spread the letter before him on the table and saw in a kind of haze the angry zigzag characters that galloped across the page, the words whose meaning he did not as yet catch, so swiftly did his thoughts rise up at sight of them. Years ago Kitty had written him a letter and he had read it at that same table. It had been a cruel letter, but unconsidered, like the tantrum of a child. Yes, he had almost forgotten it, but now like a sudden nightmare the old horror clutched at his heart. He steadied himself, and the words began to take form before him. Surely she would be gentle with Jeff, he was so big and kind. Then he read on, slowly, grasping at the meaning, and once more his eyes grew big with horror at her words. He finished, and bowed his head upon the table, while the barren room whirled before him.

From his place across the table the big cowboy looked down upon him, grim and masterful, yet wondering at his silence.

"Well, am I wrong?" he demanded, but the little man made no answer.

Upon the table before Hardy there lay another letter, written in that same woman's hand, a letter to him, and the writing was smooth and fair. Jeff had brought it to him, tied behind his saddle, and he stood before him now, waiting.

"Am I wrong?" he said again, but Hardy did not answer in words. Holding the crumpled letter behind him he took up his own fair missive —- such a one as he would have died for in years gone by —- and laid it on the fire, and when the tiny flame leaped up he dropped the other on it and watched them burn together.

"Well, how about it?" inquired Creede, awed by the long silence, but the little man only bowed his head.

"Who am I, to judge?" he said.

CHAPTER XX
THE DROUGHT

For a year the shadowy clouds had flitted past Hidden Water, drifting like flocks of snowy birds to their resting-place against the Peaks, and as the wind raged and the darkness gathered the cattle had raised their heads and bellowed, sniffing the wet air. In Summer the thunder-heads had mounted to high heaven and spread from east to west; the heat lightning had played along the horizon at night, restless and incessant; the sky had turned black and the south wind had rushed up, laden with the smell of distant showers. At last the rain had fallen, graciously, bringing up grass and browse, and flowers for those who sought them. But all the time the water lay in black pools along the shrunken river, trickling among the rocks and eddying around huge snags of driftwood, clear, limpid, sparkling, yet always less and less.

Where the winter floods had scoured the lowlands clear, a fuzz of baby trees sprang up, growing to a rank prosperity and dying suddenly beneath the sun. Along the river's edge little shreds of watercress took root and threw out sprouts and blossoms; the clean water brought forth snaky eel-grass and scum which fed a multitude of fishes; in the shadows of deep rocks the great bony-tails and Colorado River salmon lay in contented shoals, like hogs in wallows, but all the time the water grew less and less. At every shower the Indian wheat sprang up on the mesas, the myriad grass-seeds germinated and struggled forth, sucking the last moisture from the earth to endow it with more seeds. In springtime the deep-rooted mesquites and *palo verdes* threw out the golden halo of their flowers until the cañons were aflame; the soggy *sahuaros* drank a little at each sparse downpour and defied the drought; all the world of desert plants flaunted their pigmented green against the barren sky as if in grim contempt; but the little streams ran weaker and weaker, creeping along under the sand to escape the pitiless sun.

As Creede and Hardy rode out from Hidden Water, the earth lay dead beneath their horses' feet —- stark and naked, stripped to the rocks by the sheep. Even on Bronco Mesa the ground was shorn of its covering; the cloven hoofs of the sheep had passed over it like a scalping knife, tearing off the last sun-blasted fringe of grass. In open spaces where they had not found their way the gaunt cattle still curled their hungry tongues beneath the bushes and fetched out spears of grass, or licked the scanty Indian wheat from the earth itself.

With lips as tough and leathery as their indurated faces, the hardiest of them worked their way into bunches of stick-cactus and *chollas*, breaking down the guard of seemingly impenetrable spines and munching on the juicy stalks; while along the ridges long-necked cows bobbed for the high browse which the sheep had been unable to reach.

The famine was upon them; their hips stood out bony and unsightly above their swollen stomachs as they racked across the benches, and their eyes were wild and haggard. But to the eye of Creede, educated by long experience, they were still strong and whole. The weaklings were those that hung about the water, foot-sore from their long journeyings to the distant hills and too weary to return. At the spring-hole at Carrizo they found them gathered, the runts and roughs of the range; old cows with importunate calves bunting at their flaccid udders; young heifers, unused to rustling for two; *orehannas* with no mothers to guide them to the feed; rough steers that had been "busted" and half-crippled by some reckless cowboy —- all the unfortunate and incapable ones, standing dead-eyed and hopeless or limping stiffly about.

A buzzard rose lazily from a carcass as they approached, and they paused to note the brand. Then Creede shook his head bodingly and rode into the bunch by the spring. At a single glance the *rodéo* boss recognized each one of them and knew from whence he came. He jumped his horse at a wild steer and started him toward the ridges; the cows with calves he rounded up more gently, turning them into the upper trail; the *orehannas*, poor helpless orphans that they were, followed hopefully, leaving one haggard-eyed old stag behind.

Creede looked the retreating band over critically and shook his head again.

"Don't like it," he observed, briefly; and then, unlocking the ponderous padlock that protected their cabin from hungry sheepmen, he went in and fetched out the axe. "Guess I'll cut a tree for that old stiff," he said.

From his stand by the long troughs where all the mountain cattle watered in Summer, the disconsolate old stag watched the felling of the tree curiously; then after an interval of dreary contemplation, he racked his hide-bound skeleton over to the place and began to browse. Presently the rocks began to clatter on the upper trail, and an old cow that had been peering over the brow of the hill came back to get her share. Even her little calf, whose life had been cast in thorny ways, tried his new teeth on the tender ends and found them good. The *orehannas* drifted in one after the other, and other cows with calves, and soon there was a little circle about the tree-top, munching at the soft, brittle twigs.

"Well, that settles it," said Creede. "One of us stays here and cuts brush, and the other works around Hidden Water. This ain't the first drought I've been through, not by no means, and I've learned this much: the Alamo can be dry as a bone and Carrizo, too, but they's always water here and at the home ranch. Sooner or later every cow on the range will be goin' to one place or the other to drink, and if we give 'em a little bait of brush each time it keeps 'em from gittin' too weak. As long as a cow will rustle she's all right, but the minute she's too weak to travel she gits to be a water-bum —- hangs around the spring and drinks until she starves to death. But if you feed 'em a little every day they'll drift back to the ridges at night and pick up a little more. I'm sorry for them lily-white hands of yourn, pardner, but which place would you like to work at?"

"Hidden Water," replied Hardy, promptly, "and I bet I can cut as many trees as you can."

"I'll go you, for a fiver," exclaimed Creede, emulously. "Next time Rafael comes in tell him to bring me up some more grub and baled hay, and I'm fixed. And say, when you write to the boss you can tell her I've traded my gun for an axe!"

As Hardy turned back towards home he swung in a great circle and rode down the dry bed of the Alamo, where water-worn bowlders and ricks of mountain drift lay strewn for miles to mark the vanished stream. What a power it had been in its might, floating sycamores and ironwoods as if they were reeds, lapping high against the granite walls, moving the very rocks in its bed until they ground together! But now the sand lay dry and powdery, the willows and water-moodies were dead to the roots, and even the ancient cottonwoods from which it derived its name were dying inch by inch. A hundred years they had stood there, defying storm and cloudburst, but at last the drought was sucking away their life. On the mesa the waxy greasewood was still verdant, the gorged *sahuaros* stood like great tanks, skin-tight with bitter juice, and all the desert trees were tipped with green; but the children of the river were dying for a drink.

A string of cattle coming in from The Rolls stopped and stared at the solitary horseman, head up against the sky; then as he rode on they fell in behind him, travelling the deep-worn trail that led to Hidden Water. At the cleft-gate of the pass, still following the hard-stamped trail, Hardy turned aside from his course and entered, curious to see his garden again before it succumbed to the drought. There before him stood the sycamores, as green and flourishing as ever; the eagle soared out from his cliff; the bees zooned in their caves; and beyond the massive dyke that barred the way the tops of the elders waved the last of their creamy blossoms. In the deep pool the fish still darted about, and the waterfall that fed it was not diminished. The tinkle of its music seemed even louder, and as Hardy looked below he saw that a little stream led way from the pool, flowing in the trench where the cattle came to drink. It was a miracle, springing from the bosom of the earth from whence the waters come. When all the world outside lay dead and bare, Hidden Water flowed more freely, and its garden lived on untouched.

Never had Hardy seen it more peaceful, and as he climbed the Indian steps and stood beneath the elder, where *Chupa Rosa* had built her tiny nest his heart leapt suddenly as he remembered Lucy. Here they had sat together in the first gladness of her coming, reading his forgotten verse and watching the eagle's flight; only for that one time, and then the fight with the sheep had separated them. He reached up and plucked a spray of elder blossoms to send her for a keep-sake —- and then like a blow he remembered the forget-me-not! From that same garden he had fetched her a forget-me-not for repentance, and then forgotten her for Kitty. Who but Lucy could have left the little book of poems, or treasured a flower so long to give it back at parting? And yet in his madness he had forgotten her!

He searched wistfully among the rocks for another forget-me-not, but the hot breath of the drought had killed them. As he climbed slowly down the stone steps he mused upon some poem to take the place of the flowers that were dead, but the spirit of the drought was everywhere. The very rocks themselves, burnt black by centuries of sun, were painted with Indian prayers for rain. A thousand times he had seen the sign, hammered into the blasted rocks —- the helix, that mystic symbol of the ancients, a circle, ever widening, never ending, —- and wondered at the fate of the vanished people who had prayed to the Sun for rain.

The fragments of their sacrificial *ollas* lay strewn among the bowlders, but the worshippers were dead; and now a stranger prayed to his own God for rain. As he sat at his desk that night writing to Lucy about the drought, the memory of those Indian signs came upon him suddenly and, seizing a fresh sheet of paper, he began to write. At the second stanza he paused, planned out his rhymes and hurried on again, but just as his poem seemed finished, he halted at the last line. Wrestle as he would he could not finish it —- the rhymes were against him —- it would not come right. Ah, that is what sets the artist apart from all the under-world of dreamers —- his genius endures to the end; but the near-poet struggles like a bee limed in his own honey. What a confession of failure it was to send away —- a poem unfinished, or finished wrong! And yet —- the unfinished poem was like him. How often in the past had he left things unsaid, or said them wrong. Perhaps Lucy would understand the better and prize it for its faults. At last, just as it was, he sent it off, and so it came to her hand.

A PRAYER FOR RAIN

Upon this blasted rock, O Sun, behold
Our humble prayer for rain —- and here below
A tribute from the thirsty stream, that rolled
Bank-full in flood, but now is sunk so low
Our old men, tottering, yet may stride acrost
And babes run pattering where the wild waves tossed.
The grass is dead upon the stem, O Sun!

The lizards pant with heat —- they starve for flies —-
And they for grass —- and grass for rain! Yea, none
Of all that breathe may face these brazen skies
And live, O Sun, without the touch of rain.
Behold, thy children lift their hands —- in vain!
Drink up the water from this *olla's* brim

And take the precious corn here set beside —-
Then summon thy dark clouds, and from the rim
Of thy black shield strike him who hath defied
Thy power! Appease thy wrath, Great Sun —- but give
Ah, give the touch of rain to those that live!

As it had been a thousand years before, so it was that day at Hidden Water. The earth was dead, it gave forth nothing; the sky was clean and hard, without a cloud to soften its asperity. Another month and the cattle would die; two months and the water would fail; then in the last agonies of starvation and thirst the dissolution would come —- the Four Peaks would be a desert. Old Don Pablo was right, the world was drying up. Chihuahua and Sonora were parched; all Arizona lay stricken with the drought; in California the cattle were dying on the ranges, and in Texas and New Mexico the same. God, what a thing —- to see the great earth that had supported its children for ages slowly dying for water, its deserts first, and then its rivers, and then the pine-topped mountains that gave the rivers birth! Yet what was there for a man to do but take care of his own and wait? The rest was in the hands of God.

On the first morning that Hardy took his axe and went down to the river he found a single bunch of gaunted cattle standing in the shade of the big mesquites that grew against Lookout Point —- a runty cow with her two-year-old and yearling, and a wobbly calf with a cactus joint stuck across his nose. His mother's face showed that she, too, had been among the *chollas*; there was cactus in her knees and long spines bristling from her jaws, but she could stand it, while it was a matter of life and death to the calf. Every time he came near his mother she backed away, and whenever he began to nudge for milk she kicked out wildly. So Hardy roped him and twitched the joint away with a stick; then he pulled out the thorns one by one and went about his work.

Selecting a fine-leaved *palo verde* that grew against the point, he cleared a way into its trunk and felled it down the hill. He cut a second and a third, and when he looked back he saw that his labor was appreciated; the runty cow was biting eagerly at the first tree-top, and the wobbly calf was restored to his own. As the sound of the axe continued, a band of tame cattle came stringing down the sandy riverbed, and before the morning was over there were ten or twenty derelicts and water-bums feeding along the hillside. In the afternoon he cut more trees along the trail to Hidden Water, and the next day when he went to work he found a little band of weaklings there, lingering expectantly in the shadow of the cañon wall. As the days went by more and more of them gathered about the water, the lame, the sick, the crippled, the discouraged, waiting for more trees to be felled. Then as the feed on the distant ridges grew thinner and the number of cut trees increased, a great band of them hung about the vicinity of the ranch house constantly —- the herds from Hidden Water and the river, merged into one —- waiting to follow him to the hills.

For a mile up and down the cañon of the Alamo, the *palo verde* stumps dotted the hillside, each with its top below it, stripped to the bark and bared of every twig. As the breathless heat of July came on, Hardy was up before dawn, hewing and felling, and each day the long line of cattle grew. They trampled at his heels like an army, gaunt, emaciated; mothers mooing for their calves that lay dead along the gulches; mountain bulls and outlaws, tamed by gnawing hunger and weakness, and the awful stroke of the heat. And every day other bands of outlaws, driven at last from their native hills, drifted in to swell the herd. For a month Hardy had not seen a human face, nor had he spoken to any living creature except Chapuli or some poor cow that lay dying by the water. When he was not cutting trees on the farther ridges, he was riding along the river, helping up those that had fallen or dragging away the dead.

Worn and foot-sore, with their noses stuck full of cactus joints, their tongues swollen from the envenomed thorns, their stomachs afire from thirst and the burden of bitter stalks, the wild cattle from the ridges would stagger down to the river and drink until their flanks bulged out and their bellies hung heavy with water. Then, overcome with fatigue and heat, they would sink down in the shade and lie dreaming; their limbs would stiffen and cramp beneath them until they could not move; and there they would lie helpless, writhing their scrawny necks as they struggled to get their feet under them. To these every day came Hardy with his rawhide *reata*. Those that he could not scare up he pulled up; if any had died he dragged the bodies away from the water; and as soon as the recent arrivals had drunk he turned them away, starting them on their long journey to the high ridges where the sheep had not taken the browse.

Ah, those sheep! How many times in the fever of heat and work and weariness had Hardy cursed them, his tongue seeking unbidden the wickedest words of the range; how many times had he cursed Jim Swope, and Jasper Swope, the Mexicans, and all who had rushed in to help accomplish their ruin. And as the sun beat down and no clouds came into the sky he cursed himself, blindly, for all that had come to pass. One man —- only one —- at the mouth of

Hell's Hip Pocket, and the sheep might have been turned back; but he himself had seen the dust-cloud and let it pass —- and for that the cattle died. The sheep were far away, feeding peacefully in mountain valleys where the pines roared in the wind and the nights were cool and pleasant; but if the rain came and young grass sprang up on Bronco Mesa they would come again, and take it in spite of them. Yes, even if the drought was broken and the cattle won back their strength, that great army would come down from the north once more and sheep them down to the rocks! But one thing Hardy promised himself —- forgetting that it was the bootless oath of old Bill Johnson, who was crazy now and hiding in the hills —- he would kill the first sheep that set foot on Bronco Mesa, and the next, as long as he could shoot; and Jasp Swope might answer as he would.

Yet, why think of sheep and schemes of belated vengeance? —- the grass was gone; the browse was cleaned; even the *palo verde* trees were growing scarce. Day by day he must tramp farther and farther along the ridge, and all that patient, trusting army behind, waiting for him to find more trees! Already the weakest were left behind and stood along the trails, eying him mournfully; yet work as he would he could not feed the rest. There was no fine-drawn distinction now —- every *palo verde* on the hillside fell before his axe, whether it was fine-leaved and short-thorned, or rough and spiny; and the cattle ate them all. Mesquite and cat-claw and ironwood, tough as woven wire and barbed at every joint, these were all that were left except cactus and the armored *sahuaros*. In desperation he piled brush beneath clumps of fuzzy *chollas*, the thorniest cactus that grows, and burned off the resinous spines; but the silky bundles of stickers still lurked beneath the ashes, and the cattle that ate them died in agony.

Once more Hardy took his ax and went out in search of *palo verdes*, high or low, young or old. There was a gnarled trunk, curling up against a rocky butte and protected by two spiny *sahuaros* that stood before it like armed guards, and he climbed up the rock to reach it. Chopping away the first *sahuaro* he paused to watch it fall. As it broke open like a giant melon on the jagged rocks below, the cattle crowded about it eagerly, sniffing at the shattered parts —- and then the hardiest of them began suddenly to eat!

On the outside the wiry spines stood in rows like two-inch knife blades; but now the juicy heart, laid open by the fall, was exposed, and the cattle munched it greedily. A sudden hope came to Hardy as he watched them feed, and, climbing higher, he felled two more of the desert giants, dropping them from their foothold against the butte far down into the rocky cañon. As they struck and burst, and the sickly aroma filled the air, the starved cattle, bitten with a new appetite, rushed forward in hordes to eat out their bitter hearts. At last, when the battle had seemed all but over, he had found a new food, —- one that even Pablo Moreno had overlooked, —- each plant a ton of bitter pulp and juice. The coarse and wiry spines, whose edges would turn an axe, were conquered in a moment by the fall from the precipitous cliffs. And the mesa was covered with them, like a forest of towering pin-cushions, as far as the eye could see! A great gladness came over Hardy as he saw the starved cattle eat, and as soon as he had felled a score or more he galloped up to Carrizo to tell the news to Jeff.

The mesa was deserted of every living creature. There was not a snake track in the dust or a raven in the sky, but as he topped the brow of the hill and looked down into the cañon, Hardy saw a great herd of cattle, and Creede in the midst of them still hacking away at the thorny *palo verdes*. At the clatter of hoofs, the big man looked up from his work, wiping the sweat and grime from his brow, and his face was hard and drawn from working beyond his strength.

"Hello!" he called. "How's things down your way —- water holdin' out? Well, you're in luck, then; I've had to dig the spring out twice, and you can see how many cows I'm feedin'. But say," he continued, "d'ye think it's as hot as this down in hell? Well, if I thought for a minute it'd be as dry I'd take a big drink and join the church, you can bet money on that. What's the matter —- have you got enough?"

"I've got enough of cutting *palo verdes*," replied Hardy, "but you just lend me that axe for a minute and I'll show you something." He stepped to the nearest *sahuaro* and with a few strokes felled it down the hill, and when Creede saw how the cattle crowded around the broken trunk he threw down his hat and swore.

"Well —- damn —- me," he said, "for a pin-head! Here I've been cuttin' these ornery *palo verdes* until my hands are like a Gila monster's back, and now look at them cows eat giant cactus! There's no use talkin', Rufe, the feller that wears the number five hat and the number forty jumper ain't worth hell-room when you're around —- here, gimme that axe!" He seized it in his thorn-scarred hands and whirled into the surrounding giants like a fury; then when he had a dozen fat *sahuaros* laid open among the rocks he came back and sat down panting in the scanty shade of an ironwood.

"I'm sore on myself," he said. "But that's the way it is! If I'd had the brains of a rabbit I'd've stopped Jasp Swope last Spring —- then I wouldn't need to be cuttin' brush here all Summer like a Mexican wood-chopper. That's where we fell down —- lettin' them sheep in —- and now we've got to sweat for it. But lemme tell you, boy," he cried, raising a mighty fist, "if I can keep jest one cow alive until Fall I'm goin' to meet Mr. Swope on the edge of my range and shoot 'im full of holes! Nothin' else will do, somebody has got to be *killed* before this monkey business will stop! I've been makin' faces and skinnin' my teeth at that dastard long enough now, and I'm goin' to make him fight if I have to put high-life on 'im!"

He stopped and looked out over the hillside where the heat quivered in rainbows from the rocks, and the naked *palo verdes*, stripped of their bark, bleached like skeletons beside their jagged stumps.

"Say, Rufe," he began, abruptly, "I'm goin' crazy."

He shook his head slowly and sighed. "I always thought I was," he continued, "but old Bill Johnson blew in on me the other day —- he's crazy, you know —- and when I see him I knowed it! W'y, pardner, Bill is the most *reas-on-able* son-of-a-gun you can imagine. You can talk to him by the hour, and outside of bein' a little techy he's all right; but the minute you mention *sheep* to him his eye turns glassy and he's off. Well, that's me, too, and has been for years, only not quite so bad; but then, Bill is plumb sheeped out and I ain't —- quite!"

He laughed mirthlessly and filled a cigarette.

"You know," he said, squinting his eyes down shrewdly, "that old feller ain't so durned crazy yet. He wanted some ammunition to shoot up sheep-camps with, but bein' a little touched, as you might say, he thought I might hold out on 'im, so he goes at me like this: 'Jeff,' he says, 'I've took to huntin' lions for the bounty now —- me and the hounds —- and I want to git some thirty-thirtys.' But after I'd give him all I could spare he goes on to explain how the sheep, not satisfied with eatin' 'im out of house and home, had gone and tolled all the lions away after 'em —- so, of course, he'll have to foller along, too. You catch that, I reckon."

Creede drooped his eyes significantly and smoked.

"If it hadn't been for old Bill Johnson," he said, "we wouldn't have a live cow on our range to-day, we'd've been sheeped down that close. When he'd got his ammunition and all the bacon and coffee I could spare he sat down and told me how he worked it to move all them sheep last Spring. After he'd made his first big play and see he couldn't save the Pocket he went after them sheepmen systematically for his revenge. That thirty-thirty of his will shoot nigh onto two miles if you hold it right, and every time he sees a sheep-camp smoke he Injuned up onto some high peak and took pot-shots at it. At the distance he was you couldn't hear the report —- and, of course, you couldn't *see* smokeless powder. He says the way them Mexican herders took to the rocks was a caution; and when the fireworks was over they didn't wait for orders, jest rounded up their sheep and hiked!

"And I tell you, pardner," said the big cowman impressively, "after thinkin' this matter over in the hot sun I've jest about decided to go crazy myself. Yes, sir, the next time I hear a sheep-blat on Bronco Mesa I'm goin' to tear my shirt gittin' to the high ground with a thirty-thirty; and if any one should inquire you can tell 'em that your pore friend's mind was deranged by cuttin' too many *palo verdes*." He smiled, but there was a sinister glint in his eyes; and as he rode home that night Hardy saw in the half-jesting words a portent of the never-ending struggle that would spring up if God ever sent the rain.

On the day after the visit to Carrizo a change came over the sky; a haze that softened the edges of the hills rose up along the horizon, and the dry wind died away. As Hardy climbed along the rocky bluffs felling the giant *sahuaros* down into the ravines for his cattle, the sweat poured from his face in a stream. A sultry heaviness hung over the land, and at night as he lay beneath the *ramada* he saw the lightning, hundreds of miles away, twinkling and playing along the northern horizon. It was a sign —- the promise of summer rain!

In the morning a soft wind came stealing in from the west; a white cloud came up out of nothing and hovered against the breast of the Peaks; and the summer heat grew terrible. At noon the cloud turned black and mounted up, its fluffy summit gleaming in the light of the ardent sun; the wind whirled across the barren mesa, sweeping great clouds of dust before it, and the air grew damp and cool; then, as evening came on the clouds vanished suddenly and the wind died down to a calm. For a week the spectacle was repeated —- then, at last, as if weary, the storm-wind refused to blow; the thunder-caps no longer piled up against the Peaks; only the haze endured, and the silent, suffocating heat.

Day after day dragged by, and without thought or hope Hardy plodded on, felling *sahuaros* into the cañons, his brain whirling in the fever of the great heat. Then one day as the sun rose higher a gigantic mass of thunder-clouds leapt up in the north, covering half the sky. The next morning they rose again, brilliant, metallic, radiating heat like a cone of fire. The heavens were crowned with sudden splendor, the gorgeous pageantry of summer clouds that rise rank upon rank, basking like newborn cherubim in the glorious light of the sun, climbing higher and higher until they reached the zenith.

A moist breeze sprang up and rushed into the storm's black heart, feeding it with vapors from the Gulf; then in the south, the home of the rain, another great cloud arose, piling in fluffy billows against the grim cliffs of the Superstitions and riding against the flying cohorts that reared their snowy heads in the north. The wind fell and all nature lay hushed and expectant, waiting for the rain. The cattle would not feed; the bearded ravens sat voiceless against the cliffs; the gaunt trees and shrubs seemed to hold up their arms —- for the rain that did not come. For after all its pomp and mummery, its black mantle that covered all the sky and the bravery of its trailing skirts, the Storm, that rode in upon the wind like a king, slunk away at last like a beaten craven. Its black front melted suddenly, and its draggled banners, trailing across the western sky, vanished utterly in the kindling fires of sunset.

As he lay beneath the starlit sky that night, Hardy saw a vision of the end, as it would come. He saw the cañons stripped clean of their high-standing *sahuaros*, the spring at Carrizo dry, the river stinking with the bodies of the dead —- even Hidden Water quenched at last by the drought. Then a heavy sleep came upon him as he lay sprawling in the pitiless heat and he dreamed —- dreamed of gaunt steers and lowing cows, and skeletons, strewn along the washes; of labor, never ending, and sweat, dripping from his face. He woke suddenly with the horror still upon him and gazed up at the sky, searching vainly for the stars. The night was close and black, there was a stir among the dead leaves as if a snake writhed past, and the wind breathed mysteriously through the bare trees; then a confused drumming came to his ears, something warm and wet splashed against his face, and into his outstretched hand God sent a drop of rain.

CHAPTER XXI
THE FLOOD

The rain came to Hidden Water in great drops, warmed by the sultry air. At the first flurry the dust rose up like smoke, and the earth hissed; then as the storm burst in tropic fury the ground was struck flat, the dust-holes caught the rush of water and held it in sudden puddles that merged into pools and rivulets and glided swiftly away. Like a famine-stricken creature, the parched earth could not drink; its bone-dry dust set like cement beneath the too generous flood and refused to take it in —- and still the rain came down in sluicing torrents that never stayed or slackened. The cracked dirt of the *ramada* roof dissolved and fell away, and the stick frame leaked like a sieve. The rain wind, howling and rumbling through the framework, hurled the water to the very door where Hardy stood, and as it touched his face, a wild, animal exultation overcame him and he dashed out into the midst of it. God, it was good to feel the splash of rain again, to lean against the wind, and to smell the wet and mud! He wandered about through it recklessly, now bringing in his saddle and bedding, now going out to talk with his horse, at last simply standing with his hands outstretched while his whole being gloried in the storm.

As the night wore on and the swash of water became constant, Hardy lay in his blankets listening to the infinite harmonies that lurk in the echoes of rain, listening and laughing when, out of the rumble of the storm, there rose the deeper thunder of running waters. Already the rocky slides were shedding the downpour; the draws and gulches were leading it into the creek. But above their gurgling murmur there came a hoarser roar that shook the ground, reverberating through the damp air like the diapason of some mighty storm-piece. At daybreak he hurried up the cañon to find its source, plunging along through the rain until, on the edge of the bluff that looked out up the Alamo, he halted, astounded at the spectacle. From its cleft gate Hidden Water, once so quiet and peaceful, was now vomiting forth mud, rocks, and foaming waters in one mad torrent; it overleapt the creek, piling up its debris in a solid dam that stretched from bank to bank, while from its lower side a great sluiceway of yellow water spilled down into the broad bed of the Alamo.

Above the dam, where the cañon boxed in between perpendicular walls, there lay a great lagoon, a lake that rose minute by minute as if seeking to override its dam, yet held back by the torrent of sand and water that Hidden Water threw across its path. For an hour they fought each other, the Alamo striving vainly to claim its ancient bed, Hidden Water piling higher its hurtling barrier; then a louder roar reverberated through the valley and a great wall of dancing water swept down the cañon and surged into the placid lake. On its breast it bore brush and sticks, and trees that waved their trunks in the air like the arms of some devouring monster as they swooped down upon the dam. At last the belated waters from above had come, the outpourings of a hundred mountain creeks that had belched forth into the Alamo like summer cloudbursts. The forefront of the mighty storm-crest lapped over the presumptuous barrier in one hissing, high-flung waterfall; then with a final roar the dam went out and, as the bowlders groaned and rumbled beneath the flood, the Alamo overleapt them and thundered on.

A sudden sea of yellow water spread out over the lower valley, trees bent and crashed beneath the weight of drift, the pasture fence ducked under and was gone. Still irked by its narrow bed the Alamo swung away from the rock-bound bench where the ranch house stood and, uprooting everything before it, ploughed a new channel to the river. As it swirled past, Hardy beheld a tangled wreckage of cottonwoods and sycamores, their tops killed by the drought, hurried away on this overplus of waters; the bare limbs of *palo verdes*, felled by his own axe; and sun-dried skeletons of cattle, light as cork, dancing and bobbing as they drifted past the ranch.

The drought was broken, and as the rain poured down it washed away all token of the past. Henceforward there would be no sign to move the uneasy spirit; no ghastly relic, hinting that God had once forgotten them; only the water-scarred gulches and cañons, and the ricks of driftwood, piled high along the valleys in memory of the flood. All day the rain sluiced down, and the Alamo went wild in its might, throwing a huge dam across the broad bed of the river itself. But when at last in the dead of night the storm-crest of the Salagua burst forth, raging from its long jostling against chasm walls, a boom like a thunder of cannon echoed from all the high cliffs by Hidden Water; and the warring waters, bellowing and tumbling in their titanic fury, joined together in a long, mad race to the sea.

So ended the great flood; and in the morning the sun rose up clean and smiling, making a diamond of every dew-drop. Then once more the cattle gathered about the house, waiting to be fed, and Hardy went out as before to cut *sahuaros*. On the second day the creek went down and the cattle from the other bank came across, lowing for their share. But on the third day, when the sprouts began to show on the twining stick-cactus, the great herd that had dogged his steps for months left the bitter *sahuaros* and scattered across the mesa like children on a picnic, nipping eagerly at every shoot.

In a week the flowers were up and every bush was radiant with new growth. The grass crept out in level places, and the flats in the valley turned green, but the broad expanse of Bronco Mesa still lay half-barren from paucity of seeds. Where the earth had been torn up and trampled by the sheep the flood had seized upon both soil and seed and carried them away, leaving nothing but gravel and broken rocks; the sheep-trails had turned to trenches, the washes to gulches, the gulches to ravines; the whole mesa was criss-crossed with tiny gullies where the water had hurried away —- but every tree and bush was in its glory, clothed from top to bottom in flaunting green. Within a week the cattle were back on their old ranges, all that were left from famine and drought. Some there were that died in the midst of plenty, too weak to regain their strength; others fell sick from overeating and lost their hard-earned lives; mothers remembered calves that were lost and bellowed mournfully among the hills. But as rain followed rain and the grass matured a great peace settled down upon the land; the cows grew round-bellied and sleepy-eyed, the bulls began to roar along the ridges, and the Four Peaks cattlemen rode forth from their mountain valleys to see how their neighbors had fared.

They were a hard-looking bunch of men when they gathered at the Dos S Ranch to plan for the fall *rodéo*. Heat and the long drought had lined their faces deep, their hands were worn and crabbed from months of cutting brush, and upon them all was the sense of bitter defeat. There would be no branding in the pens that Fall —- the spring calves were all dead; nor was there any use in gathering beef steers that were sure to run short weight; there was nothing to do, in fact, but count up their losses and organize against the sheep. It had been a hard Summer, but it had taught them that they must stand together or they were lost. There was no one now who talked of waiting for Forest Reserves, or of diplomacy and peace —- every man was for war, and war from the jump —- and Jefferson Creede took the lead.

"Fellers," he said, after each man had had his say, "there's only one way to stop them sheep, and that is to stop the first band. Never mind the man —- dam' a herder, you can buy one for twenty dollars a month —- *git the sheep*! Now suppose we stompede the first bunch that comes on our range and scatter 'em to hell —- that's *fif-teen thousand dol-lars gone*! God A'mighty, boys, think of losin' that much real money when you're on the make like Jim Swope! W'y, Jim would go crazy, he'd throw a fit —- and, more than that, fellers," he added, sinking his voice to a confidential whisper, "he'd go round.

"Well, now, what ye goin' to do?" he continued, a crafty gleam coming into his eye. "Are we goin' to foller some cow's tail around until they jump us again? Are we goin' to leave Rufe here, to patrol a hundred miles of range lone-handed? Not on your life —- not me! We're goin' to ride this range by day's works, fellers, and the first bunch of sheep we find we're goin' to scatter 'em like shootin' stars —- and if any man sees Jasp Swope I'll jest ask him to let me know. Is it a go? All right —- and I'll tell you how we'll do.

"There's only three places that the sheep can get in on us: along the Alamo, over the Juate, or around between the Peaks. Well, the whole caboodle of us will camp up on the Alamo somewhere, and we'll jest naturally ride them three ridges night and day. I'm goin' to ask one of you fellers to ride away up north and foller them sheepmen down, so they can't come a circumbendibus on us again. I'm goin' to give 'em fair warnin' to keep off of our upper range, and then the first wool-pullin' sheep-herder that sneaks in on Bronco Mesa is goin' to git the scare of his life —- and the coyotes is goin' to git his sheep.

"That's the only way to stop 'em! W'y, Jim Swope would run sheep on his mother's grave if it wasn't for the five dollars fine. All right, then, we'll jest fine Mr. Swope fifteen thousand dollars for comin' in on our range, and see if he won't go around. There's only one thing that I ask of you fellers —- when the time comes, for God's sake *stick together!*"

The time came in late October, when the sheep were on The Rolls. In orderly battalions they drifted past, herd after herd, until there were ten in sight. If any sheepman resented the silent sentinels that rode along the rim he made no demonstration of the fact —- and yet, for some reason every herd sooner or later wandered around until it fetched up against the dead line. There were fuzzy *chollas* farther out that got caught in the long wool and hurt the shearers' hands; it was better to camp along the Alamo, where there was water for their stock —- so the simple-minded herders said, trying to carry off their bluff; but when Creede scowled upon them they looked away sheepishly. The *padron* had ordered it —- they could say no more.

"*Muy bien,*" said the overbearing Grande, "and where is your *padron?*"

"*Quien sabe!*" replied the herders, hiking up their shoulders and showing the palms of their hands, and "Who knows" it was to the end. There was wise counsel in the camp of the sheep-men; they never had trouble if they could avoid it, and then only to gain a point. But it was this same far-seeing policy which, even in a good year when there was feed everywhere, would not permit them to spare the upper range. For two seasons with great toil and danger they had fought their way up onto Bronco Mesa and established their right to graze there —- to go around now would be to lose all that had been gained.

But for once the cowmen of the Four Peaks were equal to the situation. There were no cattle to gather, no day herds to hold, no calves to brand in the pens —- every man was riding and riding hard. There was wood on every peak for signal fires and the main camp was established on the high ridge of the Juate, looking north and south and west. When that signal rose up against the sky —- whether it was a smoke by day or a fire by night —- every man was to quit his post and ride to harry the first herd. Wherever or however it came in, that herd was to be destroyed, not by violence nor by any overt act, but by the sheepmen's own methods —- strategy and stealth.

For once there was no loose joint in the cordon of the cowmen's defence. From the rim of the Mogollons to the borders of Bronco Mesa the broad trail of the sheep was marked and noted; their shiftings and doublings were followed and observed; the bitterness of Tonto cowmen, crazy over their wrongs, was poured into ears that had already listened to the woes of Pleasant Valley. When at last Jasper Swope's boss herder, Juan Alvarez, the same man-killing Mexican that Jeff Creede had fought two years before, turned suddenly aside and struck into the old Shep Thomas trail that comes out into the deep crotch between the Peaks, a horseman in *chaparejos* rode on before him, spurring madly to light the signal fires. That night a fire blazed up from the shoulder of the western mountain and was answered from the Juate. At dawn ten men were in the saddle, riding swiftly, with Jefferson Creede at their head.

It was like an open book to the cowmen now, that gathering of the sheep along the Alamo —- a ruse, a feint to draw them away from the Peaks while the blow was struck from behind. Only one man was left to guard that threatened border —- Rufus Hardy, the man of peace, who had turned over his pistol to the boss. It was a bitter moment for him when he saw the boys start out on this illicit adventure; but for once he restrained himself and let it pass. The war would not be settled at a blow.

At the shoulder of the Peak the posse of cowmen found Jim Clark, his shaps frayed and his hat slouched to a shapeless mass from long beating through the brush, and followed in his lead to a pocket valley, tucked away among the cedars, where they threw off their packs and camped while Jim and Creede went forward to investigate. It was a rough place, that crotch between the Peaks, and Shep Thomas had cut his way through chaparral that stood horse-high before he won the southern slope. To the north the brush covered all the ridges in a dense thicket, and it was there that the cow camp was hid; but on the southern slope, where the sun had baked out the soil, the mountain side stretched away bare and rocky, broken by innumerable ravines which came together in a *redondo* or rounded valley and then plunged abruptly into the narrow defile of a box cañon. This was the middle fork, down which Shep Thomas had made his triumphal march the year before, and down which Juan Alvarez would undoubtedly march again.

Never but once had the sheep been in that broad valley, and the heavy rains had brought out long tufts of grama grass from the bunchy roots along the hillsides. As Creede and Jim Clark crept up over the brow of the western ridge and looked down upon it they beheld a herd of forty or fifty wild horses, grazing contentedly along the opposite hillside; and far below, where the valley opened out into the *redondo*, they saw a band of their own tame horses feeding. Working in from either side —- the wild horses from the north, where they had retreated to escape the drought; the range animals from the south, where the sheep had fed off the best grass —- they had made the broad mountain valley a rendezvous, little suspecting the enemy that was creeping in upon their paradise. Already the distant bleating of the sheep was in the air; a sheepman rode up to the summit, looked over at the promised land and darted back, and as the first struggling mass of leaders poured out from the cut trail and drifted down into the valley the wild stallions shook out their manes in alarm and trotted farther away.

A second band of outlaws, unseen before, came galloping along the western mountain side, snorting at the clangor and the rank smell of the sheep, and Creede eyed them with professional interest as the leaders trotted past. Many times in the old days he had followed along those same ridges, rounding up the wild horses and sending them dashing down the cañon, so that Hardy could rush out from his hiding place and make his throw. It was a natural hold-up ground, that *redondo*, and they had often talked of building a horse trap there; but so far they had done no more than rope a chance horse and let the rest go charging down the box cañon and out the other end onto Bronco Mesa.

It was still early in the morning when Juan Alvarez rode down the pass and invaded the forbidden land. He had the name of a bad *hombre*, this boss herder of Jasper Swope, the kind that cuts notches on his rifle stock. Only one man had ever made Juan eat dirt, and that man now watched him from the high rocks with eyes that followed every move with the unblinking intentness of a mountain lion.

"Uhr-r! Laugh, you son of a goat," growled Creede, as the big Mexican pulled up his horse and placed one hand complacently on his hip. "Sure, make yourself at home," he muttered, smiling as his enemy drifted his sheep confidently down into the *redondo*, "you're goin' jest where I want ye. Come sundown and we'll go through you like a house afire. If he beds in the *redondo* let's shoot 'em into that box cañon, Jim," proposed the big cowman, turning to his partner, "and when they come out the other end all hell wouldn't stop 'em —- they'll go forty ways for Sunday."

"Suits me," replied Jim, "but say, what's the matter with roundin' up some of them horses and sendin' 'em in ahead? That boss Mexican is goin' to take a shot at some of us fellers if we do the work ourselves."

"That's right, Jim," said Creede, squinting shrewdly at the three armed herders. "*I'll* tell ye, let's send them wild horses through 'em! Holy smoke! jest think of a hundred head of them outlaws comin' down the cañon at sundown and hammerin' through that bunch of sheep! And we don't need to git within gunshot!"

"Fine and dandy," commented Jim, "but how're you goin' to hold your horses to it? Them herders will shoot off their guns and turn 'em back."

"Well, what's the matter with usin' our tame horses for a hold-up herd and then sendin' the whole bunch through together? They'll strike for the box cañon, you can bank on that, and if Mr. Juan will *only* —- " But Mr. Juan was not so accommodating. Instead of holding his sheep in the *redondo* he drifted them up on the mountain side, where he could overlook the country.

"Well, I'll fix you yet," observed Creede, and leaving Jim to watch he scuttled down to his horse and rode madly back to camp.

That afternoon as Juan Alvarez stood guard upon a hill he saw, far off to the west, four horsemen, riding slowly across the mesa. Instantly he whistled to his herders, waving his arms and pointing, and in a panic of apprehension they circled around their sheep, crouching low and punching them along until the herd was out of sight. And still the four horsemen rode on, drawing nearer, but passing to the south. But the sheep, disturbed and separated by the change, now set up a plaintive bleating, and the boss herder, never suspecting the trap that was being laid for him, scrambled quickly down from his lookout and drove them into the only available hiding-place —- the box cañon. Many years in the sheep business had taught him into what small compass a band of sheep can be pressed, and he knew that, once thrown together in the dark cañon, they would stop their telltale blatting and go to sleep. Leaving his herders to hold them there he climbed back up to his peak and beheld the cowboys in the near distance, but still riding east.

An hour passed and the sheep had bedded together in silence, each standing with his head under another's belly, as is their wont, when the four horsemen, headed by Jeff Creede himself, appeared suddenly on the distant mountain side, riding hard along the slope. Galloping ahead of them in an avalanche of rocks was the band of loose horses that Alvarez had seen in the *redondo* that morning, and with the instinct of their kind they were making for their old stamping ground.

Once more the sheepman leaped up from his place and scampered down the hill to his herd, rounding up his pack animals as he ran. With mad haste he shooed them into the dark mouth of the cañon, and then hurried in after them like a badger that, hearing the sound of pursuers, backs into some neighboring hole until nothing is visible but teeth and claws. So far the boss herder had reasoned well. His sheep were safe behind him and his back was against a rock; a hundred men could not dislodge him from his position if it ever came to a fight; but he had not reckoned upon the devilish cunning of horse-taming Jeff Creede. Many a time in driving outlaws to the river he had employed that same ruse —- showing himself casually in the distance and working closer as they edged away until he had gained his end.

The sun was setting when Creede and his cowboys came clattering down the mountain from the east and spurred across the *redondo*, whooping and yelling as they rounded up their stock. For half an hour they rode and hollered and swore, apparently oblivious of the filigree of sheep tracks with which the ground was stamped; then as the *remuda* quieted down they circled slowly around their captives, swinging their wide-looped ropes and waiting for the grand stampede.

The dusk was beginning to gather in the low valley and the weird evensong of the coyotes was at its height when suddenly from the north there came a rumble, as if a storm gathered above the mountain; then with a roar and the thunder of distant hoofs, the crashing of brush and the nearer click of feet against the rocks a torrent of wild horses poured over the summit of the pass and swept down into the upper valley like an avalanche. Instantly Creede and his cowboys scattered, spurring out on either wing to turn them fair for the box cañon, and the tame horses, left suddenly to their own devices, stood huddled together in the middle of the *redondo*, fascinated by the swift approach of the outlaws. Down the middle of the broad valley they came, flying like the wind before their pursuers; at sight of Creede and his cowboys and the familiar hold-up herd they swerved and slackened their pace; then as the half-circle of yelling cowmen closed in from behind they turned and rushed straight for the box cañon, their flint-like feet striking like whetted knives as they poured into the rocky pass. Catching the contagion of the flight the tame horses joined in of their own accord, and a howl of exultation went up from the Four Peaks cowmen as they rushed in to complete the overthrow. In one mad whirl they mingled —- wild horses and tame, and wilder riders behind; and before that irresistible onslaught Juan Alvarez and his herders could only leap up and cling to the rocky cliffs like bats. And the sheep! A minute after, there were no sheep. Those that were not down were gone —- scattered to the winds, lost, annihilated!

Seized by the mad contagion, the cowboys themselves joined in the awful rout, spurring through the dark cañon like devils let loose from hell. There was only one who kept his head and waited, and that was Jefferson Creede. Just as the last wild rider flashed around the corner he jumped his horse into the cañon and, looking around, caught sight of Juan Alvarez, half-distraught, crouching like a monkey upon a narrow ledge.

"Well, what —- the —- hell!" he cried, with well-feigned amazement. "*I* didn't know you was here!"

The sheepman swallowed and blinked his eyes, that stood out big and round like an owl's.

"Oh, that's all right," he said.

"But it wouldn't 'a' made a dam' bit of difference if I had!" added Creede, and then, flashing his teeth in a hectoring laugh, he put spurs to his horse and went thundering after his fellows.

Not till that moment did the evil-eyed Juan Alvarez sense the trick that had been played upon him.

"*Cabrone!*" he screamed, and whipping out his pistol he emptied it after Creede, but the bullets spattered harmlessly against the rocks.

Early the next morning Jefferson Creede rode soberly along the western rim of Bronco Mesa, his huge form silhouetted against the sky, gazing down upon the sheep camps that lay along the Alamo; and the simple-minded Mexicans looked up at him in awe. But when the recreant herders of Juan Alvarez came skulking across the mesa and told the story of the stampede, a sudden panic broke out that spread like wildfire from camp to camp. Orders or no orders, the timid Mexicans threw the sawhorses onto their burros, packed up their blankets and moved, driving their bawling sheep far out over The Rolls, where before the *chollas* had seemed so bad. It was as if they had passed every day beneath some rock lying above the trail, until, looking up, they saw that it was a lion, crouching to make his spring. For years they had gazed in wonder at the rage and violence of Grande Creede, marvelling that the *padron* could stand against it; but now suddenly the big man had struck, and *bravo* Juan Alvarez had lost his sheep. Hunt as long as he would he could not bring in a tenth of them. *Ay, que malo!* The boss would fire Juan and make him walk to town; but they who by some miracle had escaped, would flee while there was yet time.

For two days Creede rode along the rim of Bronco Mesa —- that dead line which at last the sheepmen had come to respect, —- and when at last he sighted Jim Swope coming up from Hidden Water with two men who might be officers of the law he laughed and went to meet them. Year in and year out Jim Swope had been talking law —- law; now at last they would see this law, and find out what it could do. One of the men with Swope was a deputy sheriff, Creede could tell that by his star; but the other man might be almost anything —- a little fat man with a pointed beard and congress shoes; a lawyer, perhaps, or maybe some town detective.

"Is this Mr. Creede?" inquired the deputy, casually flashing his star as they met beside the trail.

"That's my name," replied Creede. "What can I do for you?"

"Well, Mr. Creede," responded the officer, eying his man carefully, "I come up here to look into the killing of Juan Alvarez, a Mexican sheep-herder."

"The killin'?" echoed Creede, astounded.

"That's right," snapped the deputy sheriff, trying to get the jump on him. "What do you know about it?"

"Who —- me?" answered the cowman, his eyes growing big and earnest as he grasped the news. "Not a thing. The last time I saw Juan Alvarez he was standin' on a ledge of rocks way over yonder in the middle fork —- and he certainly was all right then."

"Yes? And when was this, Mr. Creede?"

"Day before yesterday, about sundown."

"Day before yesterday, eh? And just what was you doin' over there at the time?"

"Well, I'll tell ye," began Creede circumstantially. "Me and Ben Reavis and a couple of the boys had gone over toward the Pocket to catch up our horses. They turned back on us and finally we run 'em into that big *redondo* up in the middle fork. I reckon we was ridin' back and forth half an hour out there gittin' 'em stopped, and we never heard a peep out of this Mexican, but jest as we got our *remuda* quieted down and was edgin' in to rope out the ones we wanted, here comes a big band of wild horses that the other boys had scared up over behind the Peaks, roaring down the cañon and into us. Of course, there was nothin' for it then but to git out of the way and let 'em pass, and we did it, dam' quick. Well, sir, that bunch of wild horses went by us like the mill tails of hell, and of course our *remuda* stompeded after 'em and the whole outfit went bilin' through the box cañon, where it turned out Juan Alvarez had been hidin' his sheep. That's all I know about it."

"Well, did you have any trouble of any kind with this deceased Mexican, Mr. Creede? Of course you don't need to answer that if it will incriminate you, but I just wanted to know, you understand."

"Oh, that's all right," responded the cowman, waving the suggestion aside with airy unconcern. "This is the first I've heard of any killin', but bein' as you're an officer I might as well come through with what I know. I don't deny for a minute that I've had trouble with Juan. I had a fist fight with him a couple of years ago, and I licked him, too —- but seein' him up on that ledge of rocks when I rode through after my horses was certainly one of the big surprises of my life."

"Uh, you was surprised, was ye?" snarled Swope, who had been glowering at him malignantly through his long recital. "Mebbe —- "

"Yes, I was surprised!" retorted Creede angrily. "And I was like the man that received the gold-headed cane —- I was *pleased*, too, if that's what you're drivin' at. I don't doubt you and Jasp sent that dam' Greaser in there to sheep us out, and if he got killed you've got yourself to thank for it. He had no business in there, in the first place, and in the second place, I gave you fair warnin' to keep 'im out."

"You hear that, Mr. Officer?" cried the sheepman. "He admits making threats against the deceased; he —- "

"Just a moment, just a moment, Mr. Swope," interposed the deputy sheriff pacifically. "Did you have any words with this Juan Alvarez, Mr. Creede, when you saw him in the cañon? Any trouble of any kind?"

"No, we didn't have what you might call trouble —- that is, nothin' serious."

"Well, just what words passed between you? This gentleman here is the coroner; we've got the body down at the ranch house, and we may want to suppeenie you for the inquest."

"Glad to meet you, sir," said Creede politely. "Well, all they was to it was this: when I rode in there and see that dam' Mexican standin' up on a ledge with his eyes bulgin' out, I says, 'What in hell —- *I* didn't know you was here!' And he says, 'Oh, that's all right.'"

"Jest listen to the son-of-a-gun lie!" yelled Jim Swope, beside himself with rage. "*Listen* to him! He said that was all right, did he? Three thousand head of sheep stompeded —- "

"Yes," roared Creede, "he said: 'That's all right.' And what's more, there was another Mexican there that heard him! Now how about it, officer; how much have I got to take off this dam' sheep puller before I git the right to talk back? Is he the judge and jury in this matter, or is he just a plain buttinsky?"

"I'll have to ask you gentlemen to key down a little," replied the deputy noncommittally, "and let's get through with this as soon as possible. Now, Mr. Creede, you seem to be willing to talk about this matter. I understand that there was some shots fired at the time you speak of."

"Sure thing," replied Creede. "Juan took a couple of shots at me as I was goin' down the cañon. He looked so dam' funny, sittin' up on that ledge like a monkey-faced owl, that I couldn't help laughin', and of course it riled him some. But that's all right —- I wouldn't hold it up against a dead man."

The deputy sheriff laughed in spite of himself, and the coroner chuckled, too. The death of a Mexican sheep-herder was not a very sombre matter to gentlemen of their profession.

"I suppose you were armed?" inquired the coroner casually.

"I had my six-shooter in my shaps, all right."

"Ah, is that the gun? What calibre is it?"

"A forty-five."

The officers of the law glanced at each other knowingly, and the deputy turned back toward the ranch.

"The deceased was shot with a thirty-thirty," observed the coroner briefly, and there the matter was dropped.

"Umm, a thirty-thirty," muttered Creede, "now who in ——- " He paused and nodded his head, and a look of infinite cunning came into his face as he glanced over his shoulder at the retreating posse.

"Bill Johnson!" he said, and then he laughed ——- but it was not a pleasant laugh.

There were signs of impending war on Bronco Mesa. As God sent the rain and the flowers and grass sprang up they grappled with each other like murderers, twining root about root for the water, fighting upward for the light —- and when it was over the strongest had won. Every tree and plant on that broad range was barbed and fanged against assault; every creature that could not flee was armed for its own defence; it was a land of war, where the strongest always won. What need was there for words? Juan Alvarez was dead, shot from some distant peak while rounding up his sheep —- and his sheep, too, were dead.

They buried the boss herder under a pile of rocks on Lookout Point and planted a cross above him, not for its Christian significance, nor yet because Juan was a good Catholic, but for the Mexicans to look at in the Spring, when the sheep should come to cross. Jim Swope attended to this himself, after the coroner had given over the body, and for a parting word he cursed Jeff Creede.

Then for a day the world took notice of their struggle —- the great outside world that had left them to fight it out. Three thousand head of sheep had been killed; mutton enough to feed a great city for a day had been destroyed —- and all in a quarrel over public land. The word crept back to Washington, stripped to the bare facts —- three thousand sheep and their herder killed by cattlemen on the proposed Salagua Reserve —- and once more the question rose, Why was not that Salagua Reserve proclaimed? No one answered. There was another sheep and cattle war going on up in Wyoming, and the same question was being asked about other proposed reserves. But when Congress convened in December the facts began to sift out: there was a combination of railroad and lumber interests, big cattlemen, sheepmen, and "land-grabbers" that was "against any interference on the part of the Federal Government," and "opposed to any change of existing laws and customs as to the grazing of live stock upon the public domain." This anomalous organization was fighting, and for years had been fighting, the policy of the administration to create forest reserves and protect the public land; and, by alliances with other anti-administration forces in the East, had the President and his forester at their mercy. There would be no forestry legislation that Winter —- so the newspapers said. But that made no difference to the Four Peaks country.

Only faint echoes of the battle at Washington reached the cowmen's ears, and they no longer gave them any heed. For years they had been tolled along by false hopes; they had talked eagerly of Forest Rangers to draw two-mile circles around their poor ranches and protect them from the sheep; they had longed to lease the range, to pay grazing fees, anything for protection. But now they had struck the first blow for themselves, and behold, on the instant the sheep went round, the grass crept back onto the scarred mesa, the cattle grew fat on the range! Juan Alvarez, to be sure, was dead; but their hands were clean, let the sheepmen say what they would. What were a few sheep carcasses up on the high mesa? They only matched the cattle that had died off during the drought. When they met a sheep-herder now he gave them the trail.

Tucked away in a far corner of the Territory, without money, friends, or influence, there was nothing for it but to fight. All nature seemed conspiring to encourage them in their adventure —- the Winter came on early, with heavy rains; the grass took root again among the barren rocks and when, in a belated *rodéo*, they gathered their beef steers, they received the highest selling price in years. All over Arizona, and in California, New Mexico, and Texas, the great drought had depleted the ranges; the world's supply of beef had been cut down; feeders were scarce in the alfalfa fields of Moroni; fat cattle were called for from Kansas City to Los Angeles; and suddenly the despised cowmen of the Four Peaks saw before them the great vision which always hangs at the end of the rainbow in Arizona —- a pot of gold, *if the sheep went around*. And what would make the sheep go around? Nothing but a thirty-thirty.

The price of mutton had gone up too, adding a third to the fortune of every sheepman; the ewes were lambing on the desert, bringing forth a hundred per cent or better, with twins —-

and every lamb must eat! To the hundred thousand sheep that had invaded Bronco Mesa there was added fifty thousand more, and they must all eat. It was this that the sheepmen had foreseen when they sent Juan Alvarez around to raid the upper range —- not that they needed the feed then, but they would need it in the Spring, and need it bad. So they had tried to break the way and, failing, had sworn to come in arms. It was a fight for the grass, nothing less, and there was no law to stop it.

As the news of the trouble filtered out and crept into obscure corners of the daily press, Hardy received a long hortatory letter from Judge Ware; and, before he could answer it, another. To these he answered briefly that the situation could only be relieved by some form of Federal control; that, personally, his sympathies were with the cattlemen, but, in case the judge was dissatisfied with his services —- But Judge Ware had learned wisdom from a past experience and at this point he turned the correspondence over to Lucy. Then in a sudden fit of exasperation he packed his grip and hastened across the continent to Washington, to ascertain for himself why the Salagua Forest Reserve was not proclaimed. As for Lucy, her letters were as carefully considered as ever —- she wrote of everything except the sheep and Kitty Bonnair. Not since she went away had she mentioned Kitty, nor had Hardy ever inquired about her. In idle moments he sometimes wondered what had been in that unread letter which he had burned with Creede's, but he never wrote in answer, and his heart seemed still and dead. For years the thought of Kitty Bonnair had haunted him, rising up in the long silence of the desert; in the rush and hurry of the round-up the vision of her supple form, the laughter of her eyes, the succession of her moods, had danced before his eyes in changing pictures, summoned up from the cherished past; but now his mind was filled with other things. Somewhere in the struggle against sheep and the drought he had lost her, as a man loses a keep-sake which he has carried so long against his heart that its absence is as unnoticed as its presence, and he never knows himself the poorer. After the drought had come the sheep, the stampede, fierce quarrels with the Swopes, threats and counter-threats —- and then the preparations for war. The memory of the past faded away and another thought now haunted his mind, though he never spoke it —- when the time came, would he fight, or would he stay with Lucy and let Jeff go out alone? It was a question never answered, but every day he rode out without his gun, and Creede took that for a sign.

As the Rio Salagua, swollen with winter rains, rose up like a writhing yellow serpent and cast itself athwart the land, it drew a line from east to west which neither sheep nor cattle could cross, and the cowmen who had lingered about Hidden Water rode gayly back to their distant ranches, leaving the peaceful Dos S where Sallie Winship had hung her cherished lace curtains and Kitty Bonnair and Lucy Ware had made a home, almost a total wreck. Sheep, drought, and flood had passed over it in six months' time; the pasture fence was down, the corrals were half dismantled, and the bunk-room looked like a deserted grading camp. For a week Creede and Hardy cleaned up and rebuilt, but every day, in spite of his partner's efforts to divert his mind, Jeff grew more restless and uneasy. Then one lonely evening he went over to the corner where his money was buried and began to dig.

"What —- the —- hell —- is the matter with this place?" he exclaimed, looking up from his work as if he expected the roof to drop. "Ever since Tommy died it gits on my nerves, bad." He rooted out his tomato can and stuffed a roll of bills carelessly into his overalls pocket. "Got any mail to go out?" he inquired, coming back to the fire, and Hardy understood without more words that Jeff was going on another drunk.

"Why, yes," he said, "I might write a letter to the boss. But how're you going to get across the river —- she's running high now."

"Oh, I'll git across the river, all right," grumbled Creede. "Born to be hung and ye can't git drowned, as they say. Well, give the boss my best." He paused, frowning gloomily into the fire. "Say," he said, his voice breaking a little, "d'ye ever hear anything from Miss Bonnair?"

For a moment Hardy was silent. Then, reading what was in his partner's heart, he answered gently:

"Not a word, Jeff."

The big cowboy sighed and grinned cynically.

"That was a mighty bad case I had," he observed philosophically. "But d'ye know what was the matter with me? Well, I never tumbled to it till afterward, but it was jest because she was like Sallie —- talked like her and rode like her, straddle, that way. But I wanter tell you, boy," he added mournfully, "*Sal* had a heart."

He sank once more into sombre contemplation, grumbling as he nursed his wounds, and at last Hardy asked him a leading question about Sallie Winship.

"Did I ever hear from 'er?" repeated Creede, rousing up from his reverie. "No, and it ain't no use to try. I wrote to her three times, but I never got no answer —- I reckon the old lady held 'em out on her. She wouldn't stand for no bow-legged cowpuncher —- and ye can't blame her none, the way old man Winship used to make her cook for them *rodéo* hands —- but Sallie would've answered them letters if she'd got 'em."

"But where were they living in St. Louis?" persisted Hardy. "Maybe you got the wrong address."

"Nope, I got it straight —- Saint Louie, Mo., jest the way you see it in these money-order catalogues."

"But didn't you give any street and number?" cried Hardy, aghast. "Why, for Heaven's sake, Jeff, there are half a million people in St. Louis —- she'd never get it in the world."

"No?" inquired Creede apathetically. "Well, it don't make no difference, then. I don't amount to a dam', anyhow —- and this is no place for a woman —- but, by God, Rufe, I do git awful lonely when I see you writin' them letters to the boss. If I only had somebody that cared for me I'd prize up hell to make good. I'd do anything in God's world —- turn back them sheep or give up my six-shooter, jest as she said; but, nope, they's no such luck for Jeff Creede —- he couldn't make a-winnin' with a squaw."

"Jeff," said Hardy quietly, "how much would you give to get a letter from Sallie?"

"What d'ye mean?" demanded Creede, looking up quickly. Then, seeing the twinkle in his partner's eye, he made a grab for his money. "My whole wad," he cried, throwing down the roll. "What's the deal?"

"All right," answered Hardy, deliberately counting out the bills, "there's the ante —- a hundred dollars. The rest I hold back for that trip to St. Louis. This hundred goes to the Rinkerton Detective Agency, St. Louis, Missouri, along with a real nice letter that I'll help you write; and the minute they deliver that letter into the hands of Miss Sallie Winship, formerly of Hidden Water, Arizona, and return an answer, there's another hundred coming to 'em. Is it a go?"

"Pardner," said Creede, rising up solemnly from his place, "I want to shake with you on that."

The next morning, with a package of letters in the crown of his black hat, Jefferson Creede swam Bat Wings across the swift current of the Salagua, hanging onto his tail from behind, and without even stopping to pour the water out of his boots struck into the long trail for Bender.

One week passed, and then another, and at last he came back, wet and dripping from his tussle with the river, and cursing the very name of detectives.

"W'y, shucks!" he grumbled. "I bummed around in town there for two weeks, hatin' myself and makin' faces at a passel of ornery sheepmen, and what do I git for my trouble? 'Dear Mister Creede, your letter of umpty-ump received. We have detailed Detective Moriarty on this case and will report later. Yours truly!' That's all —- keep the change —- we make a livin' off of suckers —- and they's one born every minute. To hell with these detectives! Well, I never received nothin' more and finally I jumped at a poor little bandy-legged sheep-herder, a cross between a gorilla and a Digger Injun —- scared him to death. But I pulled my freight quick before we had any international complications. Don't mention Mr. Allan Q. Rinkerton to me, boy, or I'll throw a fit. Say," he said, changing the subject abruptly, "how many hundred thousand sheep d'ye think I saw, comin' up from Bender? Well, sir, they was sheep as far as the eye could see —- millions of 'em —- and they've got that plain et down to the original sand and cactus, already. W'y, boy, if we let them sheepmen in on us this Spring we'll look like a watermelon patch after a nigger picnic; we'll be cleaned like Pablo Moreno; they won't be pickin's for a billy goat! And Jim 'n' Jasp have been ribbin' their herders on scandalous. This little bandy-legged son-of-a-goat that I jumped at down in Bender actually had the nerve to say that I killed Juan Alvarez myself. Think of that, will ye, and me twenty miles away at the time! But I reckon if you took Jasp to pieces you'd find out he was mad over them three thousand wethers —- value six dollars per —- that I stompeded. The dastard! D'ye see how he keeps away from me? Well, I'm goin' to call the *rodéo* right away and work that whole upper range, and when the river goes down you'll find Jeff Creede right there with the goods if Jasp is lookin' for trouble. Read them letters, boy, and tell me if I'm goin' to have the old judge on my hands, too."

According to the letters, he was; and the boss was also looking forward with pleasure to her visit in the Spring.

"Well, wouldn't that jar you," commented Creede, and then he laughed slyly. "Cheer up," he said, "it might be worse —- they's nothin' said about Kitty Bonnair."

Sure enough —- not a word about Kitty, and the year before Lucy had spoken about her in every letter! There was something mysterious about it, and sinister; they both felt it.

And when at last the wagon came in, bearing only Judge Ware and Lucy, somehow even Jeff's sore heart was touched by a sense of loss. But while others might dissemble, Bill Lightfoot's impulsive nature made no concealment of its chiefest thought.

"Where's Miss Bunnair?" he demanded, as soon as Lucy Ware was free, and there was a sudden lull in the conversation roundabout as the cowboys listened for the answer.

"I'm sorry," said Miss Ware, politely evasive, "but she wasn't able to come with me."

"She'll be down bimeby, though, won't she?" persisted Lightfoot; and when Lucy finally answered with a vague "Perhaps" he turned to the assembled cowboys with a triumphant grin. "Um, now, what'd I tell you!" he said; and one and all they scowled and stabbed him with their eyes.

The *rodéo* camp was already established beneath the big mesquite, and while three or four careless cowmen held the day herd over against the mesa the rest of the outfit was busy raking The Rolls. It was all very different from what Judge Ware and Lucy had anticipated. There was no sign of excitement in their midst, no ostentatious display of arms or posting of patrols, and what surprised the judge most of all was that in their friendly gatherings around the fire there was no one, save Hardy, who would argue against the sheep.

The judge had been on to Washington and was possessed of all the material facts, but nobody was interested any more in the Salagua Forest Reserve; he had consulted with the Chief Forester and even with the President himself, laying before them the imminence of the danger, and they had assured him that everything possible would be done to relieve the situation. Did it not, then, he demanded, behoove the law-abiding residents of prospective forest reserves to coöperate with such an enlightened administration, even at the risk of some temporary personal loss? And with one voice the Four Peaks cowmen agreed that it did. There was something eerie about it —- the old judge was dazed by their acquiescence.

Of all the cowmen at Hidden Water, Rufus Hardy was the only man who would discuss the matter at length. A change had come over him now; he was very thin and quiet, with set lines along his jaw, but instead of riding nervously up and down the river as he had the year before he lingered idly about the ranch, keeping tally at the branding and entertaining his guests. No matter how pedantic or polemical the old judge became, Hardy was willing to listen to him; and Lucy, hovering in the background, would often smile to hear them argue, the judge laying down the law and equity of the matter and Rufus meeting him like an expert swordsman with parry and thrust. Day by day, his prejudice wearing away from lack of any real opposition, Judge Ware became more and more pleased with his daughter's superintendent; but Lucy herself was troubled. There was a look in his eyes that she had never seen before, a set and haggard stare that came when he sat alone, and his head was always turned aside, as if he were listening. The sheep came trooping in from the south, marching in long lines to the river's edge, and still he sat quiet, just inside the door, listening.

"Tell me, Rufus," she said, one day when her father was inspecting the upper range with Creede, "what is it that made you so sad? Is it —- Kitty?"

For a minute he gazed at her, a faint smile on his lips.

"No," he said, at last, "it is not Kitty." And then he lapsed back into silence, his head turned as before.

The wind breathed through the *corredor*, bringing with it a distant, plaintive bleating —- the sheep, waiting beyond the turbid river to cross.

"I have forgotten about Kitty," he said absently. "For me there is nothing in the world but sheep. Can't you hear them bleating down there?" he cried, throwing out his hands. "Can't you smell them? Ah, Lucy, if you knew sheep as I do! I never hear a sheep now that I don't think of that day last year when they came pouring out of Hell's Hip Pocket with a noise like the end of the world. If I had been there to stop them they might never have taken the range —- but after that, all through the hot summer when the cattle were dying for feed, every time the wind came up and roared in my ears I would hear sheep —- *baaa, baaa* —- and now I hear them again."

He paused and looked up at her intently.

"Do you know what that noise means to me?" he demanded, almost roughly. "It means little calves dying around the water hole; mothers lowing for their little ones that they have left to starve; it means long lines of cows following me out over the mesa for brush, and all the trees cut down. Ah, Lucy, how can your father talk of waiting when it means as much as that?"

"But last year was a drought," protested Lucy pitifully. "Will it be as bad this year?"

"Every bit! Did you notice that plain between Bender and the river? It will be like that in a week if we let them cross the river."

"Oh," cried Lucy, "then you —- do you mean to turn them back?"

"The river is very high," answered Hardy sombrely. "They cannot cross." And then as a quail strikes up leaves and dust to hide her nest, he launched forth quickly upon a story of the flood.

The Salagua was long in flood that Spring. Day after day, while the sheep wandered uneasily along its banks rearing up to strip the last remnants of browse from the tips of willows and burro bushes, it rolled ponderously forth from its black-walled gorge and flowed past the crossing, deep and strong, sucking evenly into the turbid whirlpool that waited for its prey. At the first approach of the invaders the unconsidered zeal of Judge Ware overcame him; he was for peace, reason, the saner judgment that comes from wider views and a riper mind, and, fired by the hope of peaceful truce, he rode furtively along the river waving a white handkerchief whenever he saw a sheep-herder, and motioning him to cross. But however anxious he was for an interview the desires of the sheepmen did not lean in that direction, and they only stared at him stolidly or pretended not to see.

Thwarted in his efforts for peace the judge returned to camp deep in thought. The sheep were at his very door and nothing had been done to stay them; a deadly apathy seemed to have settled down upon the cowmen; after all their threats there were no preparations for defence; the river was not even patrolled; and yet if quick action was not taken the upper range might be irreparably ruined before the reserve was proclaimed. Not that he would countenance violence, but a judicious show of resistance, for instance, might easily delay the crossing until the President could act, or even so daunt the invaders that they would go around. It was not strictly legal, of course, but the judge could see no harm in suggesting it, and as soon as the cowmen were gathered about their fire that evening he went out and sat down by Creede, who lay sprawled on his back, his head pillowed on his hands, smoking.

"Well, Jefferson," he began, feeling his way cautiously, "I see that the sheep have come down to the river —- they will be making a crossing soon, I suppose?"

Creede sucked studiously upon his cigarette, and shifted it to a corner of his mouth.

"W'y yes, Judge," he said, "I reckon they will."

"Well —- er —- do you think they intend to invade our upper range this year?"

"Sure thing," responded Creede, resuming his smoke, "that's what they come up here for. You want to take a last long look at this grass."

"Yes, but, Jefferson," protested the judge, opening up his eyes, "what will our cattle feed upon then?"

"Same old thing," answered Creede, "*palo verde* and giant cactus. I've got most of mine in the town herd."

"What!" exclaimed Judge Ware, astounded at the suggestion, "you don't mean to say that you are preparing to go out of business? Why, my dear Jefferson, this country may be set aside as a forest reserve at any minute —- and think of the privileges you will be giving up! As an owner of cattle already grazing upon the range you will be entitled to the first consideration of the Government; you will be granted the first grazing permit; there will be forest rangers to protect you; the sheep, being transient stock and known to be very destructive to forest growth, will undoubtedly be confined to a narrow trail far below us; by the payment of a nominal grazing fee you will be absolutely guaranteed in all your rights and watched over by the Federal Government!"

"Oh, hell!" exclaimed the big cowboy, rising up suddenly from his place, "don't talk Government to me, whatever you do! W'y, Judge," he cried, throwing out his hands, "they ain't no Government here. They ain't no law. I could go over and kill one of them sheep-herders and you wouldn't see an officer in two days. I've lived here for nigh onto twenty-six years and the nearest I ever come to seein' the Government was a mule branded 'U. S.'"

He stopped abruptly and, striding out into the darkness, picked up a log of wood and laid it carefully upon the fire.

"Judge," he said, turning suddenly and wagging an accusing finger at his former employer, "I've heard a lot from you about this reserve, how the President was goin' to telegraph you the news the minute he signed the proclamation, and send a ranger in to protect the range, and all that, but I ain't seen you *do* nothin'! Now if you're goin' to make good you've got jest about three days to do it in —- after that the sheep will have us dished. Maybe you could use your pull to kinder hurry things up a little —- do a little telegraphin', or somethin' like that."

"I'll do it!" cried the judge, taking the bait like a fish, "I'll do it at once! I want your best horse, Jeff, and a guide. I'll wire the chief forester from Bender!"

"Keno!" said Creede sententiously, "and give my regards to Teddy."

As the old judge disappeared over the western rim the next morning the *rodéo* boss smiled grimly behind his hand, and glanced significantly at Hardy. Then, with the outfit behind him, he rode slowly up the cañon, leaving his partner to his steady job as "family man" —- entertaining the boss.

For two days the sheepmen watched the river eagerly, waiting for a drop; then suddenly, as the snow water ran by and a cool day checked the distant streams, it fell, and the swift pageant of the crossing began. At sun-up a boss herder rode boldly out into the current and swam it with his horse; brawny Mexicans leapt into the thicket of *palo verdes* that grew against the cliff and cut branches to build a chute; Jasper Swope in his high sombrero and mounted on his black mule galloped down from the hidden camp and urged his men along. Still the same ominous silence hung about the shore where Juan Alvarez lay buried beneath the cross. There was no watcher on Lookout Point, no horsemen lurking in the distance; only the lowing of the day herd, far up the cañon, and the lapping of muddy waters. Across the river the low *malpai* cliffs rose up like ramparts against them and Black Butte frowned down upon them like a watch tower, but of the men who might be there watching there was no sign.

The sheepman studied upon the situation for a while; then he sent a messenger flying back to camp and soon a hardy band of wethers came down, led by an advance guard of goats, and their plaintive bleating echoed in a confused chorus from the high cliffs as they entered the wings of the chute. Already the camp rustlers had driven them out on the slanting rock and encircled the first cut with their canvas wagon cover, when Jasper Swope held up his hand for them to stop. At the last moment and for no cause he hesitated, touched by some premonition, or suspicious of the silent shore. One after another the herders clambered back and squatted idly against the cool cliff, smoking and dangling their polished carbines; the sheep, left standing upon the rock, huddled together and stood motionless; the goats leapt nimbly up on adjacent bowlders and gazed across the river intently; then, throwing up his hand again, the sheepman spurred his black mule recklessly into the water, waving his big hat as he motioned for the sheep to cross.

As the long hours of that portentous morning wore on, palpitating to the clamor of the sheep, a great quiet settled upon Hidden Water. Sitting just within the door Hardy watched Lucy as she went about her work, but his eyes were wandering and haggard and he glanced from time to time at the Black Butte that stood like a sentinel against the crossing. In the intervals of conversation the bleating of the sheep rose suddenly from down by the river, and ceased; he talked on, feverishly, never stopping for an answer, and Lucy looked at him strangely, as if wondering at his preoccupation. Again the deep tremolo rose up, echoing from the cliffs, and Hardy paused in the midst of a story to listen. He was still staring out the doorway when Lucy Ware came over and laid her hand on his shoulder.

"Rufus," she said, "what is it you are always listening for? Day after day I see you watching here by the door, and when I talk you listen for something else. Tell me —- is it —- are you watching for Kitty?"

"Kitty?" repeated Hardy, his eyes still intent. "Why no; why should I be watching for her?"

At his answer, spoken so impassively, she drew away quickly, but he caught her hand and stopped her.

"Ah no," he said, "if I could only listen for something else it would be better —- but all I hear is sheep. I'm like old Bill Johnson; I can still shoot straight and find my way in the mountains, but every time I hear a sheep blat I change. Poor old Bill, he's over across the river there now; the boys have heard his hounds baying up in the high cliffs for a week. I've seen him a time or two since he took to the hills and he's just as quiet and gentle with me as if he were my father, but if anybody mentions sheep he goes raving crazy in a minute. Jeff says he's been that way himself for years, and now it's got me, too. If I get much worse," he ended, suddenly glancing up at her with a wistful smile, "you'll have to take me away."

"Away!" cried Lucy eagerly, "would you go? You know father and I have talked of it time and again, but you just stick and stick, and nothing will make you leave. But listen —- what was that?"

A succession of rifle shots, like the popping of wet logs over a fire, came dully to their ears, muffled by the bleating of sheep and the echoing of the cliffs. Hardy leapt to his feet and listened intently, his eyes burning with suppressed excitement; then he stepped reluctantly back into the house and resumed his seat.

"I guess it's only those Mexican herders," he said. "They shoot that way to drive their sheep."

"But look!" cried Lucy, pointing out the door, "the Black Butte is afire! Just see that great smoke!"

Hardy sprang up again and dashed out into the open. The popping of thirty-thirtys had ceased, but from the summit of the square-topped butte a signal fire rose up to heaven, tall and straight and black.

"Aha!" he muttered, and without looking at her he ran out to the corral to saddle Chapuli. But when he came back he rode slowly, checking the impatience of his horse, until at last he dismounted beside her. For days his eyes had been furtive and evasive, but now at last they were steady.

"Lucy," he said, "I haven't been very honest with you, but I guess you know what this means —- the boys are turning back the sheep." His voice was low and gentle, and he stood very straight before her, like a soldier. Yet, even though she sensed what was in his mind, Lucy smiled. For a month he had been to her like another man, a man without emotion or human thought, and now in a moment he had come back, the old Rufus that she had known in her heart so long.

"Yes," she said, holding out her hand to him, "I knew it. But you are working for me, you know, and I cannot let you go. Listen, Rufus," she pleaded, as he drew away, "have I ever refused you anything? Tell me what you want to do."

"I want to go down there and help turn back those sheep," he said, bluntly. "You know me, Lucy —- my heart is in this fight —- my friends are in it —- and I must go."

He waited for some answer, but Lucy only turned away. There were tears in her eyes when she looked back at him and her lips trembled, but she passed into the house without a word. Hardy gazed wonderingly after her and his heart smote him; she was like some sensitive little child to whom every rough word was a blow, and he had hurt her. He glanced at the signal fire that rolled up black and sombre as the watcher piled green brush upon it, then he dropped his bridle rein and stepped quickly into the house.

"You must forgive me, Lucy," he said, standing humbly at the door. "I —- I am changed. But do not think that I will come to any harm —- this is not a battle against men, but sheep. No one will be killed. And now may I go?" Once more his voice became low and gentle and he stood before her like some questing knight before his queen, but she only sat gazing at him with eyes that he could not understand.

"Listen, Lucy," he cried, "I will not go unless you tell me —- and now may I go?"

A smile came over Lucy's face but she did not speak her thoughts.

"If you will stay for my sake," she said, "I shall be very happy, but I will not hold you against your will. Oh, Rufus, Rufus!" she cried, suddenly holding out her hands, "can't you understand? I can't set myself against you, and yet —- think what it is to be a woman!" She rose up and stood before him, the soft light glowing in her eyes, and Hardy stepped forward to meet her; but in that moment a drumming of hoofs echoed through the doorway, there was a rush of horsemen leaning forward as they rode, and then Jefferson Creede thundered by, glancing back as he spurred down the cañon to meet the sheep.

"My God!" whispered Hardy, following his flight with startled eyes, and as the rout of cowboys flashed up over the top of Lookout Point and were gone he bowed his head in silence.

"Lucy," he said, at last, "my mind has been far away. I —- I have not seen what was before me, and I shall always be the loser. But look —- I have two friends in all the world, you and Jeff, and you are the dearer by far. But you could see as Jeff went by that he was mad. What he will do at the river I can only guess; he is crazy, and a crazy man will do anything. But if I am with him I can hold him back —- will you let me go?" He held out his hands and as Lucy took them she saw for the first time in his shy eyes —- love. For a moment she gazed at him wistfully, but her heart never faltered. Whatever his will might be she would never oppose it, now that she had his love.

"Yes, Rufus," she said, "you may go, but remember —- me."

CHAPTER XXIII
THE LAST CROSSING

The rush and thunder of cow ponies as they hammered over the trail and plunged down through the rocks and trees had hardly lost its echoes in the cliffs when, with a flash of color and a dainty pattering of hoofs, Chapuli came flying over the top of Lookout Point and dashed up the river after them. The cowmen had left their horses in the deep ravine at the end of the *malpai* bluffs and were already crouched behind the rampart of the rim rocks as close as Indian fighters, each by some loophole in the blackened *malpai*, with a rifle in his hand. As Hardy crept in from behind, Jeff Creede motioned him to a place at his side greeting him at the same time with a broad grin.

"Hello, sport," he said, "couldn't keep out of it, eh? Well, we need ye, all right. Here, you can hold straighter than I can; take my gun and shoot rainbows around the leaders when they start to come across."

"Not much," answered Hardy, waving the gun away, "I just came down to keep you out of trouble."

"Ye-es!" jeered Creede, "first thing I know you'll be down there fightin' 'em back with rocks. But say," he continued, "d'ye notice anything funny up on that cliff? Listen, now!"

Hardy turned his head, and soon above the clamor of the sheep he made out the faint "*Owwp! Owwwp!*" of hounds.

"It's Bill Johnson, isn't it?" he said, and Creede nodded significantly.

"God help them pore sheepmen," he observed, "if Bill has got his thirty-thirty. Listen to 'em sing, will ye! Ain't they happy, though? And they don't give a dam' for us —- ump-um —- they're comin' across anyway. Well, that's what keeps hell crowded —- let 'er go!"

There was a glitter of carbines against the opposite cliffs where the spare herders had taken to cover, but out on the rocky point where the chute led into the river a gang of Mexicans and two Americans were leading their wagon cover around a fresh cut of goats and sheep. On the sand bar far below the stragglers from the first cut, turned back in the initial rush, were wandering aimlessly about or plodding back to the herd, but the sheepmen with bullheaded persistence were preparing to try again. Chief among them towered the boss, Jasper Swope, wet to the waist from swimming across the river; and as he motioned to the herders to go ahead he ran back and mounted his mule again. With a barbaric shout the Mexicans surged forward on the tarpaulin, sweeping their cut to the very edge; then, as the goats set their feet and held back, a swarthy herder leapt into the midst and tumbled them, sheep and goats alike, into the water. Like plummets they went down into the slow-moving depths, some headfirst, some falling awkwardly on their backs or slipping like beavers on a slide; there was a prolonged and mighty splash and then, one by one the heads bobbed up and floated away until, led by the high-horned goats, they struck out for the opposite shore. Below, yelling and throwing stones to frighten them, a line of Mexicans danced up and down along the rocky shore, and to keep them from drifting into the whirlpool Jasper Swope plunged boldly into the water on his mule.

Sink or swim, the sheep were in the water, and for a minute there was a tense silence along the river; then, as the goats lined out, a rifle shot echoed from the cliffs and a white column of water rose up before the leader. He shook his head, hesitated and looked back, and once more the water splashed in his face, while the deep *ploomp* of the bullet answered to the shot. Fighting away from the sudden stroke the goat lost his headway and, drifting, fouled those below him; a sudden confusion fell upon the orderly ranks of the invaders and, like a flock of geese whose leader is killed, they jostled against one another, some intent on the farther shore and some struggling to turn back. Instantly a chorus of savage shouts rose up from along the river, the shrill yells of the cowboys mingling with the whooping and whistling of the sheepmen, until at last, overcome by the hostile clamor, the timid sheep turned back toward the main herd, drawing with them the goats. For a minute Jasper Swope fought against them, waving his hat and shouting; then, rather than see them drift too far and be drawn into the clutch of the whirlpool, he whipped his mule about and led them back to the shore.

A second time, calling out all his men to help, the boss sheepman tried to cross the goats alone, intending to hold them on the shore for a lure; but just as they were well lined out the same careful marksman behind the *malpai* threw water in their faces and turned them back. But this time Jasper Swope did not lead the retreat. Slapping his black mule over the ears with his hat he held straight for the opposite shore, cursing and brandishing his gun.

"You dam', cowardly passel of tail-twisters!" he cried, shaking his fist at the bluffs, "why don't you come out into the open like men?"

But a grim silence was his only answer.

"Hey, you bold bad man from Bitter Creek, Texas!" he shouted, riding closer to the beach. "Why don't you come down and fight me like a man?" His big voice was trembling with excitement and he held his pistol balanced in the air as if awaiting an attack, but Jefferson Creede did not answer him.

"I'll fight you, man to man, you big blowhard!" thundered Swope, "and there goes my pistol to prove it!" He rose in his stirrups as he spoke and hurled it away from him, throwing his cartridge belt after it. "*Now*," he yelled, "you've been sayin' what you'd do; come out of your hole, Jeff Creede, I want ye!"

"Well, you won't git me, then," answered Creede, his voice coming cold and impassive from over the rim. "I'll fight you some other time."

"Ahrr!" taunted Swope, "hear the coward talk! Here I stand, unarmed, and he's afraid to come out! But if there's a man amongst you, send him down, and if he licks me I'll go around."

"You'll go around anyhow, you Mormon-faced wool-puller!" replied the cowman promptly, "and we're here to see to it, so you might as well chase yourself."

"No, I like this side," said the sheepman, pretending to admire the scenery. "I'll jest stay here a while, and then I'll cross in spite of ye. If I can't cross here," he continued, "I'll wait for the river to fall and cross down below —- and then I'll sheep you to the rocks, you low-lived, skulkin' murderers! It's a wonder some of you don't shoot *me* the way you did Juan Alvarez, down there." He waved his hand toward the point where the wooden cross rose against the sky, but no one answered the taunt.

"*Murderers*, I said!" he shouted, rising up in his saddle. "I call you murderers before God A'mighty and there ain't a man denies it! Oh, my Mexicans can see that cross —- they're lookin' at it now —- and when the river goes down they'll come in on you, if it's only to break even for Juan."

He settled back in his saddle and gazed doubtfully at the bluff, and then at the opposite shore. Nature had placed him at a disadvantage, for the river was wide and deep and his sheep were easy to turn, yet there was still a chance.

"Say," he began, moderating his voice to a more conciliatory key, "I'll tell you what I'll do. There's no use shooting each other over this. Send down your best man —- if he licks me I go around; if I lick him I come across. Is it a go?"

There was a short silence and then an argument broke out along the bluff, a rapid fire of exhortation and protest, some urging Creede to take him up, others clamoring for peace.

"No!" shouted Jefferson Creede, raising his voice angrily above the uproar. "I won't do it! I wouldn't trust a sheepman as far as I could throw a bull by the tail! You'd sell your black soul for two bits, Jasp Swope," he observed, peering warily over the top of the rock, "and you'd shoot a man in the back, too!"

"But look at me!" cried Swope, dropping off his mule, "I'm stripped to my shirt; there goes my gun into the water —- and I'm on your side of the river! You're a coward, Jeff Creede, and I always knowed it!"

"But my head ain't touched," commented Creede dryly. "I've got you stopped anyhow. What kind of a dam' fool would I be to fight over it?"

"I'll fight ye for nothin', then!" bellowed the sheepman. "I'll ——" He stopped abruptly and a great quiet fell upon both shores. From the mouth of the hidden ravine a man had suddenly stepped into the open, unarmed, and now he was coming out across the sands to meet him. It was Rufus Hardy, dwarfed like David before Goliath in the presence of the burly sheepman, but striding over the hard-packed sand with the lithe swiftness of a panther.

"*I'll* fight you," he said, raising his hand in challenge, but Swope's answer was drowned in a wild yell from Creede.

"Come back here, Rufe, you durn' fool!" he called. "Come back, I tell ye! Don't you know better than to trust a sheepman?"

"Never mind, now," answered Hardy, turning austerely to the bluff. "I guess I can take care of myself."

He swung about and advanced to the stretch of level sand where Swope was standing. "What guarantee do I get," he demanded sharply, "that if I lick you in a fair fight the sheep will go around?"

"You ——- lick ——- me!" repeated the sheepman, showing his jagged teeth in a sardonic grin. "Well, I'll tell ye, Willie; if you hit me with that lily-white hand of yourn, and I find it out the same day, I'll promise to stay off'n your range for a year."

"All right," replied Hardy, suddenly throwing away his hat. "You noticed it when I hit you before, didn't you?" he inquired, edging quickly in on his opponent and beginning an amazing bout of shadow boxing. "Well, *come on, then!*" He laughed as Swope struck out at him, and continued his hectoring banter. "As I remember it your head hit the ground before your heels!"

Then in a whirlwind of blows and feints they came together. It was the old story of science against brute strength. Jasper Swope was a rough-and-tumble fighter of note; he was quick, too, in spite of his weight, and his blows were like the strokes of a sledge; but Hardy did not attempt to stand up against him. For the first few minutes it was more of a chase than a fight, and in that the sheepman was at his worst, cumbered by his wet clothes and the water in his shoes. Time and again he rushed in upon his crouching opponent, who always seemed in the act of delivering a blow and yet at the moment only sidestepped and danced away. The hard wet sand was ploughed and trampled with their tracks, the records of a dozen useless plunges, when suddenly instead of dodging Hardy stepped quickly forward, his "lily-white hand" shot out, and Jasper Swope's head went back with a jerk.

"You son-of-a-goat!" he yelled, as the blood ran down his face, and lowering his head he bored in upon Hardy furiously. Once more Hardy sidestepped, but the moment his enemy turned he flew at him like a tiger, raining blows upon his bloody face in lightning succession.

"*Huh!*" grunted the sheepman, coughing like a wood-chopper as he struck back through the storm, and the chance blow found its mark. For a moment Hardy staggered, clutching at his chest; but as Swope sprang forward to finish his work he ducked and slipped aside, stumbling like a man about to drop.

A shrill yell went up from the farther shore as Hardy stood swaying in his tracks, and a fierce shout of warning from the bluff; but Jasper Swope was implacable. Brushing the blood from his eyes he stepped deliberately forward and aimed a blow that would have felled an ox, straight at his enemy's head. It missed; the drooping head snapped down like Judy before Punch and rose up again, truculently; then before the sheepman could regain his balance Hardy threw his whole strength into a fierce uppercut that laid Swope sprawling on his back.

A howl of triumph and derision rose up from the rim of the bluff as the burly sheepman went down, but it changed to a sudden shout of warning as he scrambled back to his feet again. There was something indescribably vengeful about him as he whirled upon his enemy, and his hand went inside his torn shirt in a gesture not to be mistaken.

"Look out there, Rufe!" yelled Creede, leaping up from behind his rock pile. "Run! *Jump into the river!*" But instead Hardy grabbed up a handful of sand and ran in upon his adversary. The pistol stuck for a moment in its hidden sling and as Swope wrenched it loose and turned to shoot, Hardy made as if to close with him and then threw the sand full in his face. It was only an instant's respite but as the sheepman blinked and struck the dirt from his eyes the little cowman wheeled and made a dash for the river. "*Look out!*" screamed Creede, as the gun flashed out and came to a point, and like a bullfrog Hardy hurled himself far out into the eddying water. Then like the sudden voice of Nemesis, protesting against such treachery, a rifle shot rang out from the towering crags that overshadowed the river and Jasper Swope fell forward, dead. His pistol smashed against a rock and exploded, but the man he had set himself to kill was already buried beneath the turbid waters. So swiftly did it all happen that no two men saw the same —- some were still gazing at the body of Jasper Swope; others were staring up at the high cliff whence the shot had come; but Jeff Creede had eyes only for the river and when he saw Hardy's head bob up, halfway to the whirlpool, and duck again to escape the bullets, he leapt up and ran for his horse. Then Bill Johnson's rifle rang out again from the summit of his high cliff, and every man scrambled for cover.

A Mexican herder dropped his gun suddenly and slipped down behind a rock; and his *compadres*, not knowing from whence the hostile fire came, pushed out their carbines and began to shoot wildly; the deep cañon reverberated to the rattle of thirty-thirtys and the steady *crack, crack* of the rifle above threw the sheep camp into confusion. There was a shout as Creede dashed recklessly out into the open and the sand leapt up in showers behind him, but Bat Wings was running like the wind and the bullets went wide of their mark.

Swinging beneath the mesquite trees and scrambling madly over stones and bushes he hammered up the slope of Lookout Point and disappeared in a cloud of dirt, but as Hardy drifted around the bend and floated toward the whirlpool there was a crash of brush from down the river and Creede came battering through the trees to the shore. Taking down his *reata* as he rode he leapt quickly off his horse and ran out on the big flat rock from which they had often fished together. At his feet the turbid current rolled ponderously against the solid wall of rock and, turning back upon itself, swung round in an ever-lessening circle until it sucked down suddenly into a spiral vortex that spewed up all it caught in the boiling channel below. There in years past the lambs and weaklings from the herds above had drifted to their death, but never before had the maelstrom claimed a man.

Swimming weakly with the current Hardy made a last ineffectual effort to gain the bank; then fixing his eyes upon his partner he resigned himself to the drag of the whirlpool, staking his life on a single throw of the rope. Once the plaited rawhide was wetted it would twist and bind in the *honda* and before Creede could beat it straight and coil it his partner would be far out in the centre of the vortex. Planting his feet firmly on the rock the big cowboy lashed the kinks out of his *reata* and coiled it carefully; then as the first broad swirl seized its plaything and swung him slowly around Creede let out a big loop and began to swing it about his head, his teeth showing in a tense grin as he fixed his eyes upon the mark. At each turn his wrist flexed and his back swayed with a willowy suppleness but except for that he was like a herculean statue planted upon the point.

The maelstrom heaved and rocked as it swung its victim nearer and like a thing with life seemed suddenly to hurry him past; then as Hardy cried out and held up a hand for help the rope cut through the air like a knife and the loop shot far out across the boiling water. It was a long throw, fifty feet from the rock, and the last coil had left his tense fingers before the noose fell, but it splashed a circle clean and true about the uplifted hand. For a moment the cowboy waited, watching; then as the heavy rope sank behind his partner's shoulders he took in his slack with a jerk. The noose tightened beneath Hardy's arms and held him against the insistent tug of the river; and while the whirlpool roared and foamed against his body Creede hauled him forth roughly, until, stooping down, he gathered him into his arms like a child.

"My God, boy," he said, "you're takin' big chances, for a family man —- but say, what did I tell you about sheepmen?"

The Mexicans were still firing random shots along the river when Creede lifted his partner up on Bat Wings and carried him back to Hidden Water. Long before they reached the house they could see Lucy standing in the doorway, and Hardy held himself painfully erect in the saddle, with Creede steadying him from behind; but when Bat Wings halted before the *ramada* Jeff broke rudely in on the play acting by taking the little man in his arms and depositing him on a bed.

"Fell into the river," he said, turning with a reassuring smile to Lucy, "but he ain't hurt none —- only kinder weak, you know. I reckon a little hot tea would help some, bein' as we're out of whiskey, and while you're brewin' it I'll git these wet clothes off. Yes'm, we're havin' a little trouble, but that's only them locoed Mexicans shootin' off their spare ammunition." He dragged up a cot as he spoke and was hurriedly arranging a bed when Lucy interposed.

"Oh, but don't leave him out here!" she protested, "put him back in his own room, where I can take care of him."

"All right," said Creede, and picking him up from his bare cot beneath the *ramada* he carried Hardy into the little room where he had lived before Lucy Ware came. "I guess your troubles are over for a while, pardner," he remarked, as he tucked him into the clean white bed, and then with a wise look at Lucy he slipped discreetly out the door.

As she entered with the tea Hardy was lying very limp and white against the pillow, but after the hot drink he opened his big gray eyes and looked up at her sombrely.

"Sit down," he said, speaking with elaborate exactness, "I want to tell you something." He reached out and took her hand, and as he talked he clung to it appealingly. "Lucy," he began, "I didn't forget about you when I went down there, but —- well, when Jasper Swope came out and challenged us my hair began to bristle like a dog's —- and the next thing I knew I was fighting. He said if I licked him he'd go round —- but you can't trust these sheepmen. When he saw he was whipped he tried to shoot me, and I had to jump into the river. Oh, I'm all right now, but —- listen, Lucy!" He drew her down to him, insistently. "Can't you forgive me, this time?" he whispered, and when she nodded he closed his heavy eyes and fell asleep.

When he awoke in the morning there was nothing to show for his fierce fight with Swope or his battle with the river —- nothing but a great weariness and a wistful look in his eyes. But all day while the boys rode back and forth from the river he lay in bed, looking dreamily out through the barred window or following Lucy with furtive glances as she flitted in and out. Whenever she came near he smiled, and often the soft light crept into his eyes, but when by chance he touched her hand or she brushed back his hair a great quiet settled upon him and he turned his face away.

It was Creede who first took notice of his preoccupation and after a series of unsatisfactory visits he beckoned Lucy outside the door with a solemn jerk of the head.

"Say," he said, "that boy's got something on his mind —- I can tell by them big eyes of his. Any idee what it is?"

"Why, no," answered Lucy, blushing before his searching gaze, "unless it's the sheep."

"Nope," said Creede, "it ain't that. I tried to talk sheep and he wouldn't listen to me. This here looks kinder bad," he observed, shaking his head ominously. "I don't like it —- layin' in bed all day and thinkin' that way. W'y, that'd make *me* sick!"

He edged awkwardly over to where she was standing and lowered his voice confidentially.

"I'll tell you, Miss Lucy," he said, "I've known Rufe a long time now, and he's awful close-mouthed. He's always thinkin' about something away off yonder, too —- but this is different. Now of course I don't know nothin' about it, but I think all that boy needs is a little babyin', to make him fergit his troubles. Yes'm, that boy's lonely. Bein' sick this way has took the heart out of 'im and made 'im sorry for himself, like a kid that wants his mother. And so —- well," he said, turning abruptly away, "that's all, jest thought I'd tell you." He pulled down his hat, swung dexterously up on Bat Wings and galloped away down the valley, waving his hand at the barred window as he passed.

Long after the clatter of hoofs had ceased Lucy stood in the shade of the *ramada*, gazing pensively at the fire-blasted buttes and the tender blue mountains beyond. How could such rugged hillsides produce men who were always gentle, men whose first thought was always of those who loved them and never of fighting and blood? It was a land of hardships and strife and it left its mark on them all. The Rufus that she had known before had seemed different from all other men, and she had loved him for it, even when all his thought was for Kitty; but now in two short years he had become stern and headstrong in his ways; his eyes that had smiled up at her so wistfully when he had first come back from the river were set and steady again like a soldier's, and he lay brooding upon some hidden thing that his lips would never speak. Her mutinous heart went out to him at every breath, now that he lay there so still; at a word she could kneel at his side and own that she had always loved him; but his mind was far away and he took no thought of her weakness. He was silent —- and she must be a woman to the end, a voiceless suppliant, a slave that waits, unbidden, a chip on the tide that carries it to some safe haven or hurries it out to sea.

With downcast eyes she turned back into the house, going about her work with the quiet of a lover who listens for some call, and as she passed to and fro she felt his gaze upon her. At last she looked up and when she met his glance she went in and stood beside his bed.

"What is it you want, Rufus?" she asked, and his face lit up suddenly as he answered with his eloquent eyes, but he could not speak the word.

"Who am I?" he murmured, musingly, "to ask for all the world?" But he held close to the little hands and as he felt their yielding his breath came hard and he gazed up at her with infinite tenderness.

"Dear Lucy," he said, "you do not know me. I am a coward —- it was born in me —- I cannot help it. Not with men!" he cried, his eyes lighting up. "Ah, no; my father was a soldier, and I can fight —- but —- "

He paused and his vehemence died away suddenly. "Lucy," he began again, still clinging to her hands for courage, "you have never laughed at me —- you have always been gentle and patient —- I will tell you something. You know how I ran away from Kitty, and how when she came down here I avoided her. I was afraid, Lucy, and yet —- well, it is all over now." He sighed and turned restlessly on his pillow. "One day I met her up the river and she —- she called me a coward. Not by the word —- but I knew. That was the day before the sheep came in through Hell's Hip Pocket, and even Jeff doesn't know of the fights I had that night. I went out yesterday and fought Jasper Swope with my bare hands to wipe the shame away —- but it's no use, I'm a coward yet." He groaned and turned his face to the wall but Lucy only sighed and brushed back his hair. For a minute he lay there, tense and still; then as her hand soothed him he turned and his voice became suddenly soft and caressing, as she had always liked it best.

"Don't laugh at me for it, Lucy," he said, "I love you —- but I'm afraid." He caught her hands again, gazing up wistfully into her eyes, and when she smiled through her tears he drew her nearer.

"Lucy," he whispered, "you will understand me. I have never kissed any one since my mother died —- could —- could you kiss me first?"

"Ah, yes, Rufus," she answered, and as their lips met he held her gently in his arms.

CHAPTER XXIV
THE END OF IT ALL

There is a mocking-bird at Hidden Water that sings the songs of all the birds and whistles for the dog. His nest is in a great cluster of mistletoe in the mesquite tree behind the house and every morning he polishes his long curved bill against the *ramada* roof, preens out his glossy feathers, and does honor to the sun. For two years, off and on, Hardy had heard him, mimicking orioles and larks and sparrows and whistling shrilly for the dog, but now for the first time his heart answered to the wild joy of the bird lover. The world had taken on light and color over night, and the breeze, sifting in through the barred window, was sweet with the fragrance of untrampled flowers.

April had come, and the grass; the air was untainted; there was no braying by the river —- the sheep had gone. It had been bought at the price of blood, but at last there was peace. The dreamy *quah*, *quah* of the quail was no longer a mockery of love; their eggs would not be broken in the nest but the mothers would lead forth their little ones; even the ground-doves and the poor-wills, nesting in last year's sheep tracks, would escape the myriad feet —- and all because a crazy man, hiding among the cliffs, had shot down Jasper Swope. Without hate or pity Hardy thought of that great hairy fighting-man; the God that let him live would judge him dead —- and Bill Johnson too, when he should die. The sheep were gone and Lucy had kissed him —- these were the great facts in the world.

They were sitting close together beneath the *ramada*, looking out upon the sunlit valley and talking dreamily of the old days, when suddenly Hardy edged away and pointed apologetically to the western trail. There in single file came Judge Ware in his linen duster, a stranger in khaki, and a woman, riding astride.

"There comes father!" cried Lucy, springing up eagerly and waving her hand.

"And Kitty," added Hardy, in a hushed voice. Not since they had come had he spoken of her, and Lucy had respected his silence. Except for the vague "Perhaps" with which she had answered Bill Lightfoot's persistent inquiries he had had no hint that Kitty might come, and yet a vague uneasiness had held his eyes to the trail.

"Tell me, Lucy," he said, drawing her back to his side as the party dipped out of sight in the interminable thicket of mesquites, "why have you never spoken of Kitty? Has anything dreadful happened? Please tell me quick, before she comes. I —- I won't know what to say." He twisted about and fixed an eye on the doorway, but Lucy held out a restraining hand.

"It has been a great secret," she said, "and you must promise not to tell, but Kitty has been writing a play."

"A play!" exclaimed Hardy, astounded, "why —- what in the world is it about?"

"About Arizona, of course," cried Lucy. "Don't you remember how eager she was to hear you men talk? And she collected all those spurs and quirts for stage properties! Why, she wrote books and books full of notes and cowboy words while she was down here and she's been buried in manuscript for months. When she heard that you were having the round-up early this year she was perfectly frantic to come, but they were right in the midst of writing it and she just couldn't get away."

"They?" repeated Hardy, mystified. "Why who —- "

"Oh, I forgot," said Lucy, biting her lip. Then in a lower voice she added: "She has been collaborating with Tupper Browne."

"Tupper Browne! Why, what does he know about Arizona?" cried Hardy indignantly, and then, as Lucy looked away, he stopped short.

"Oh!" he said, and then there was a long silence. "Well, Tupper's a good fellow," he remarked philosophically. "But Lucy," he said, starting up nervously as the sound of horses' feet came up from the creek bed, "you'll —- you'll do all the talking, won't you?"

"Talking!" repeated Lucy, pausing in her flight. "Why, yes," she called back, laughing. "Isn't that always the woman's part?" And then she fell upon Kitty's neck and kissed her. Hardy came forward with less assurance, but his embarrassment was reduced to a minimum by Judge Ware who, as soon as the first greetings were over, brought forward the mild-mannered gentleman in khaki and introduced him.

"Mr. Shafer," he said, "this is my superintendent, Mr. Hardy. Mr. Shafer represents the United States Forestry Service," he added significantly.

"Ah, then you must bring us good news!" cried Hardy, holding out his hand eagerly.

"Yes," answered the official modestly, but his speech ended with that word.

"I am convinced," began Judge Ware, suddenly quelling all conversation by the earnestness of his demeanor. "I am convinced that in setting aside the Salagua watershed as a National Forest Reserve, our President has added to the record of his good deeds an act of such consummate statesmanship that it will be remembered long after his detractors are forgotten. But for him, millions of acres of public land now set aside as reserves would still be open to the devastation of unrestricted grazing, or have passed irrevocably into the power of this infamous land ring which has been fighting on the floor of Congress to deprive the American people of their rights. But after both houses had passed a bill depriving the executive of his power to proclaim Forest Reserves —- holding back the appropriations for the Forestry Service as a threat —- he baffled them by a feigned acquiescence. In exchange for the appropriations, he agreed to sign the act —- and then, after securing the appropriations, he availed himself of the power still vested in him to set aside this reserve and many other reserves for our children and our children's children —- and then, gentlemen, true to his word, he signed the bill!"

Judge Ware shook hands warmly with Mr. Shafer at the end of this speech and wished him all success in protecting the people's domain. It was a great day for the judge, and as soon as Creede and the other cowmen came in with the day's gather of cattle he hastened out to tell them the news.

"And now, gentlemen," he said, holding up his hand to stop the joyous yelling, "I wish to thank you one and all for your confidence in me and in the good faith of our Government. It called for a high order of manhood, I am sure; but in not offering any armed resistance to the incoming of the sheep your loyalty has withstood its supreme test."

"How's that?" inquired Creede, scratching his head doubtfully. Then, divining the abysmal ignorance from which the judge was speaking, he answered, with an honest twinkle in his eye: "Oh, that's all right, Judge. We always try to do what's right —- and we're strong for the law, when they is any."

"I'm afraid there hasn't been much law up here in the past, has there?" inquired Mr. Shafer tactfully.

"Well, not so's you'd notice it," replied the big cowboy enigmatically. "But say, Judge," he continued, making a point at the old gentleman's linen duster, "excuse *me*, but that yaller letter stickin' out of your pocket looks kinder familiar. It's for me, ain't it? Um, thanks; this detective outfit back in St. Louie is tryin' to make me out a millionaire, or somethin' like that, and I'm naturally interested." He tore the letter open, extracted a second epistle from its depths and read it over gravely. "Well, boys," he observed, grinning cheerfully as he tucked it away in his shaps, "my luck always did run in bunches —- *I'm rich!*"

He strode briskly over to the corral, caught up a fresh horse and, riding back to the camp, began to go through his war bag hurriedly. He was in the midst of a feverish packing, throwing away socks and grabbing up shirts, when a gay laugh from the house attracted his attention. He listened for a moment abstractedly; then he flew at his work once more, dumping everything he had out on his bed and stuffing what he needed back into his war bag; but when there came a second peal of laughter, he stopped and craned his neck.

"Well —- I'll —- be —- dam'd!" he muttered, as he recognized the voice, and then he flew at his work again, manhandling everything in sight. He was just roping his enormous bed, preparatory to depositing it in the bunk-house, when Kitty Bonnair stepped out of the house and came toward him, walking like a boy in her dainty riding suit. There was a great noise from the branding pen and as she approached he seemed very intent upon his work, wrestling with his bundle as if he were hog-tying a bull and using language none too choice the while, but Kitty waited patiently until he looked up.

"Why, howdy do, Mr. Creede," she cried, smiling radiantly. "I got a new idea for my play just from seeing you do that work."

The cowboy regarded her sombrely, took a nip or two with his rope's end, jerked the cords tight, and sat down deliberately on the bundle.

"That's good," he said, wiping the sweat from his eyes. "How's tricks?" There was a shadow of irony in his voice but Kitty passed it by.

"Fine and dandy," she answered. "How are you coming?"

"Oh, pretty good," he conceded, rising up and surveying the battlefield, "and I reckon I ain't forgot nothin'," he added meaningly. He kicked his blanket roll, tied his war bag behind the saddle, and hitched up his overalls regally. "Sorry I ain't goin' to see more of you," he observed, slipping his six-shooter into his shaps, "but —- "

"What, you aren't *going*?" cried Kitty, aghast. "Why, I came all the way down here to see you —- I'm writing a play, and you're the hero!"

"Ye-es!" jeered Creede, laughing crudely. "I'm Mary's little lamb that got snatched bald-headed to make the baby laugh."

"You're nothing of the kind," retorted Kitty stoutly. "You're the hero in my play that's going to be *acted* some day on the stage. You kill a Mexican, and win a beautiful girl in the last act!"

"That's good," commented Creede, smiling grimly, "but say, that Mex. will keep, won't he —- because I'm due back in St. Louie."

"Oh!" cried Kitty, clasping her hands in despair. "St. Louis! And won't I *ever* see you any more?"

"Well, you might," conceded the cowboy magnanimously, "if you wait around long enough."

"But I *can't* wait! I've got to finish my last act, and I came clear down here, just to hear you talk. You can't imagine how interesting you are, after living up there in the city," she added naively.

"No," grumbled Creede, picking up his bridle lash, "but say, I've got to be goin'!" He hooked a boot negligently into the stirrup and looked back over his shoulder. "Anything else I can do for you?" he inquired politely.

"Oh, you dear Jeff!" cried Kitty ecstatically, "yes! Do come back here and let me tell you!" He kicked his foot reluctantly out of the stirrup and stalked back, huge and commanding as ever, but with a puzzled look in his eye.

"Bend your head down, so I can whisper it," she coaxed, and brute-like he bowed at her bidding. She whispered a moment eagerly, added a word, and pushed his head away. For a minute he stood there, thinking ponderously; then very deliberately he pulled his six-shooter out of his shaps and handed it over to her.

"All right," he said, "but say" —- he beckoned her with an inexorable jerk of the head —- "what do *I* git, now?" He looked down upon her as he had on the morning they had parted, out behind the corral, and the hot blood leaped into Kitty Bonnair's cheeks at the memory of that kiss. For a moment she hesitated, twisting her trim boot into the ground, then she drew the coveted pistol from her belt and handed it back.

"Well, since you insist," he said, and very sternly he thrust the redeemed weapon back into his shaps. A change came over him as he regarded her; there was an austere tightening of his lips and his eyes glowed with a light that Kitty had never seen before.

"That was a rough deal you gave me, girl," he said, his voice vibrant with anger, "and I ain't forgotten it. You dropped your rope over my horns and gave me a little run and then you took your turns and *busted* me like a wild steer! And then maybe you laughed a little," he suggested, with a searching glance. "No? Well, it's all right, as far as I'm concerned —- my hide's whole, and I'm rope-wise —- but I'll tell you, Miss Kitty, if you'd jest keep this gun of mine and shoot some feller once in a while we'd all enjoy it more." He paused, and as Kitty stood downcast before this sudden censure he smiled to himself, and a twinkle of mischief crept into his masterful eyes.

"But don't mind a little thing like that, girl," he said, throwing out his hands largely. "*You* don't lose no friends by tryin' to educate us a little —- ump-umm! Of course I'm kinder sore over that letter, but you look good to me yet, Kitty!"

"Why —- Mr. Creede!" faltered Kitty, looking up.

"That's right," asserted Creede, lowering his voice confidentially, "they was something about you that caught my eye the first time I saw you." He laughed, showing all his white teeth, and at the same time his eyes were very grave.

"Come over here," he said, "and I'll tell you what it was. No —- I won't kiss you —- come on up close." Wondering at her own acquiescence, Kitty Bonnair obeyed, and with a mysterious smile he stooped down until his lips were close to her ear.

"You remind me of my girl," he whispered, "back in St. Louie!" And then with a great laugh he broke away and leapt triumphantly into the saddle.

"*Whoop-eee!*" he yelled. "*Watch me fly!*" And spreading his arms like a bird he thundered away down the western trail.

There was a strange stillness about the old ranch house when Kitty came back to it and she wondered vaguely where Lucy and Rufus were, but as she stepped inside the dirt *ramada* the quiet seemed to lay its spell upon her and she halted by the doorway, waiting for a last glimpse of Jeff as he went up over the western rim. The bawling of cattle and the shrill yells of the cowboys no longer tempted her to the *parada* ground —- she was lonely, and there was no one who cared for her. Yet, somewhere within, she could hear the murmur of voices, and at last when she could endure it no longer she turned and entered quickly. The big living-room where they had so often sat together was vacant now, but Hardy's door was open, and as she looked in she saw them standing together —- Lucy with downcast eyes, and Rufus, holding both her hands. It was all very innocent and lover-like, but when their lips met she turned and fled to her room.

Half an hour later Kitty emerged from her hiding, robed like a woman; there was a new grace about her as she stood before them, a new dignity, and she wore fresh flowers in her hair, forget-me-nots, picked from among the rocks as she rode toward Hidden Water.

"Bless you, my children," she said, smiling and holding out her hands, "I shall die an old maid." And then she kissed them both.